PORTLANDTOWN

Also by Rob DeBorde

Fish on a First-Name Basis

PORTLANDTOWN

A Tale of the Oregon Wyldes

Rob DeBorde

St. Martin's Griffin
New York

This is a work of fiction. All of the characters, organizations, and events portrayed in this novel are either products of the author's imagination or are used fictitiously.

www.stmartins.com

ISBN 978-1-250-00664-6 (paperback)
ISBN 978-1-250-01860-1 (e-book)

First Edition: October 2012

10 9 8 7 6 5 4 3 2 1

For Sue

PORTLANDTOWN

PROLOGUE

—◆—

"Yer ma ain't gonna like this one bit."

Walter Peterson was not in the habit of talking to corpses, certainly not those recently removed from the ground after seventeen months of peaceful slumber. He might speak a word of kindness to the deceased before laying them to rest, presuming he had known their bodies in life. That included most of Astoria's longtime residents, among them Abigail Ellison, whose withered body now lay before him, facedown in the mud, one arm dangling into an open grave. Her mother, Margret, whose early-morning constitutionals often brought her to the top of the hill to visit her daughter, would be horrified to find the girl in such a state. Walter knew this, which is how he came to be standing in the pouring rain at four o'clock in the morning, a shovel in one hand, Winchester rifle in the other.

"I ain't happy 'bout it, neither," he said to the woman. Abigail did not respond. The dead rarely did.

Walter had already buried the Ellison girl once. As Astoria's only undertaker he'd moved earth for more than seventy of his neighbors since taking the job a decade earlier. It was good, meaningful work, and relatively uneventful compared to his previous employment as a rubbish collector in Portland. The only disturbances under Walter's watch had been a botched grave robbing and an unsupervised burial. The former had been drunkards seeking treasure within the crypt of Astoria's second wealthiest man, Captain Caleb Jennings. The thieves were no doubt disappointed to discover the captain's relatives had beaten them to it.

More curious was the unmarked grave that had appeared two months into the caretaker's tenure. Despite questioning nearly everyone in town, Walter was unable to learn the identity of the cemetery's mysterious new occupant. Since none of the locals had gone missing, he'd dug no deeper, figuring it wise to leave the dead undisturbed, lest they become restless.

Walter knelt beside the corpse, the third such desecration he'd discovered that night. First had been Tim Johnson, a local fisherman, who'd drowned in a horse trough seven years prior. Walter had found the man's skull in the grass next to an uneven hole dug down to his coffin, the top portion of which had been roughly chopped away. A little farther up the hill, Vernon Schilling sat upright within his grave, body intact but fully extracted from the pine box he'd been buried in the summer before. A tree root had hooked the dead man's jacket, keeping him from toppling over.

Two rows and six stones to the west, Walter had found Abigail.

"Best get inside 'fore you wash away with the weather."

A flicker of light caught Walter's eye.

"Who's there?" he said, barely loud enough for his own ears to hear. A quick scan of the cemetery revealed nothing but trees and tombstones through the rain.

Walter tightened his grip on the rifle. He almost hadn't brought it, figuring the light he'd seen from his window to be nothing more than a lonely mourner unable to pass the night without visiting a loved one. It had happened, more than once during a downpour. The rain made people do strange things.

Somewhere a pane of glass shattered.

Walter froze. A flash of light drew his eyes to the back of the cemetery where it glowed brightly for a moment and then was swallowed by the ground. Someone was digging another hole. And he was standing in it.

A fresh pile of earth lay beside the grave of Abraham Alcott, dead since March 1874, one of the few locals buried before Walter had assumed caretaker duties. The lack of a personal connection didn't make Walter any less uneasy about what was being done to the man's remains, and as he approached the faintly glowing hole in the ground, he considered shooting the villain on sight.

A familiar voice rising from the grave gave him pause.

"Are you him?"

Walter cautiously peered over the mound of dirt to see the body of a man slumped at the bottom of the grave, a broken lantern between his feet. He was older, sixty at least, but still carried the musculature of a younger man. A waterlogged nightshirt clung to his body, the weight of it seeming to press him deeper into the muck. Cuts on his hands and feet continued to seep, though the blood was quickly washed away by the rain. His face was pale, but familiar. And he was breathing.

"Marshal Kleberg?"

Marshal James Kleberg, retired, looked up at the caretaker and blinked. He'd never felt so tired in his life.

"Him?" he whispered.

Walter knelt beside the hole. "Marshal, what happened?"

Abruptly, the old man thrust a skull before Walter's face.

"Is it him?"

"What? Marshal, I don't—"

"Holes, man! In his head! Do you see them?"

Walter stared at the muddy skull floating before him. A mat of black hair attached to a thin layer of skin slipped away, completing thirteen years of decomposition. Numerous teeth were missing, as was the jawbone, but the skull appeared otherwise intact.

Walter reached out but did not touch the wet bone. "Do you mean from a bullet? I don't see any holes, 'cept for the eyes and nose."

The marshal drew the skull back, holding it before his face until the dead man came into focus.

"Damn," he said, dropping the skull into the mud. Slowly, he became aware of the stone cross looming overhead. It was worn, but the name was clear enough.

ABRAHAM THOMAS ALCOTT
APRIL 21 1837–
MARCH 7 1874

"Alcott. That's not him." The marshal tried to remember what he was he looking for—was it a grave?

"I don't understand, Marshal. Who did this to you?"

The marshal sighed. He felt his chest go up and down, a sign he took to mean he wasn't on the verge of dying despite the pain that seemed to crawl over every inch of his being. He looked at the caretaker—Peterson, that was his name. Did he know?

"I can't . . ." the marshal began, before trailing off.

"Can't what, Marshal?"

"Find," he managed. "Can't find . . ."

Walter leaned back, wondering if an old man could dig up four graves in the dark all by himself.

"Who, Marshal? Who can't you find?"

The marshal repeated the question in his head, for that was what had brought him to this place on such a miserable night. He was looking for someone, someone buried in the cemetery, someone he wasn't supposed to forget.

The marshal felt a sharp prick in his hand and opened it to see faint words scraped into the palm as if by a dry quill.

WAT IS NAME?

The marshal stared at the words for a moment and then looked up at the caretaker, his tears masked by the raindrops rolling off his cheek.

"I don't remember."

1

In his dream, *Joseph Wylde wakes to the sound of a baby crying—his baby, his daughter. It's steady, in distress, and not alone. Also crying, softer, but in sync with his sister, is a baby boy. Joseph has a son and a daughter. Twins.*

Before Joseph can rise from his bed, pain screams from behind his eyes. His hands instinctively reach for his face, but stop short. He knows what to expect but is still surprised to find a cloth about his head, laid over his eyes. Someone has seen fit to bandage him, or perhaps to cover that which should not be seen. Joseph is blind, has been for five days, thanks to—

Your children are crying, Joseph.

Joseph stands, steadying himself against a wall he knows he can't see—but he can. This is his room, the small corner bedroom on the second floor of the marshal's home. He can feel the loose floorboard just beyond the edge of the bed, hear the wood groan as he steps off—was it ever so loud? To his left there's a small nightstand, and then, three paces, a door. He searches for the handle, but finds none. It's open. He knows he can't see this—but he can.

In the hallway, the crying is louder and there's something else: creak-

ing, back and forth. Someone is sitting in his father-in-law's old rocking chair, the one Joseph repaired after Kate cracked one of the legs. She was going to give birth to a giant, he'd teased her, a bear of a child. Kate said there would be two. She had known, even then.

The crying keeps time with the old wood, as if in motion, closer and then farther away. Joseph is halfway down the stairs before realizing he's begun the descent. He opens his mouth, not entirely sure what will come out.

"Kate?"

Joseph hears the shallow gasp as it catches in his wife's throat. The creaking doesn't stop. He reaches the landing.

The stench of the man hits Joseph's nostrils, a mixture of sweat, worn leather, and gun oil. Stronger still is the scent of blood—not of the man, but other men . . . dead men.

In his dream, *Joseph hears the sound of metal slide across leather as the Hanged Man draws the red-handled gun from its holster. His eyes don't see the bastard set the barrel of the pistol across his daughter's skin—* but he can see it.

The smell of salt brought Joseph back to the present. It was faint, just a hint in the air, but getting stronger. They were almost there.

Joseph stood at the port rail of the steamer *Alberta*, having left Portland at eleven minutes past eight that morning en route to Astoria. By his estimation, it was now midafternoon. They'd made good time. Not a surprise considering the boat was traveling with the current, but whether that would remain an advantage was yet to be seen. Thanks to the nearly twenty pounds of refined Oregon firestone allotted for the burn upriver, the captain had promised Joseph would see some real speed on the voyage home.

Joseph smiled at the thought.

He couldn't see, of course, in any traditional sense. That didn't stop him from keeping one eye open—the right—to maintain appearances. It gathered no information, but since the scarring was less obvious, he'd trained the otherwise useless organ to deliver the proper cultural signals—blink, squint, stare, etc. It was Joseph's experience that people were more comfortable when they could look a man in the eye and receive the same in return.

His left eye was covered by a worn leather patch that hid what most found difficult to look at. Kate claimed the milky-white iris added another layer of complexity to her husband's handsome face. Joseph thought he was complicated enough. Despite the damage, the eye still picked up faint, undefined light and shadow, which Joseph found mostly a distraction. He was blind by any modern medical standard, and had been for more than a decade.

In that time, Joseph had discovered those same standards suggested that other senses could be developed to make up for the loss of his sight. He'd found numerous cases where the blind were able to use sounds, vibrations, even smells, to create a picture of the world around them. Such studies were generally considered scientifically dubious, but Joseph didn't doubt them. After all, he was blind and had read the documents himself.

Joseph closed his eye.

He could *see* the river rushing by below, waves peeling away from the hull toward a shore that was closer on the port side of the ship than the starboard.

He could *see* the chubby man standing twenty feet to his right, puffing on a cigar and tugging his three-sizes-too-small coat tighter around his belly.

He could *see* the blue sky, puffy clouds, and, most important, the sun. Such a treat was not to be missed, even in May, which was why Joseph had spent so much of the journey standing at the rail, letting the light warm his face.

And now he could see his son, Samuel, staring up at him, wondering if his father was still lost in the dark memory that had invaded his waking thoughts so often in recent weeks. Joseph knew the boy had been standing at the rail for only a moment, but his approach had been nearly silent. He was becoming every bit as stealthy as his mother, which was a source of both pride and concern for Joseph.

"Hello, Kick," he said, using the nickname Kate had given her son while he was still inside her.

"Hello," the boy replied. Kick, who'd turned eleven the week before, watched his father's face for a sign. Joseph had never actually seen him through his own eyes, but he knew his son had wavy auburn hair, a slightly square jaw, and bright green eyes, just like his mother. The oversize ears and nose had been gifts from his father, which Kick had yet to grow into.

Joseph tilted his head to his son, giving him what he wanted.

"I'm fine," he said.

"Okay. Maddie said I should check."

"Your sister worries too much. I'm fine."

"Okay."

Kick turned his attention to the river. He couldn't smell the salt in the air, but knew they were close because the river was wider. He leaned over the rail, letting the spray cool his face.

"Careful," said Joseph. "You'll have to swim the rest of the way if you fall in."

"I won't fall. Plus I'm a good swimmer."

"I'm better," said Maddie, already leaning over the rail on Joseph's right. He hadn't noticed her approach at all. He'd thought only Kate could do that, and now both his children had effectively snuck up on him in broad daylight—not that the day or light made a difference. They'd been practicing.

"Hello, Madeline. I didn't see you there."

Maddie beamed, unable to help herself. The hair and freckles she shared with her brother, but the smile was all her own.

"Did I scare you?"

"No, but I am surprised you were able to hang over the edge with what must be a very full tummy. Did you leave any of the sugar rolls for your brother?"

Maddie dropped back onto the deck. She licked her lips, tasting both cinnamon and sugar. Joseph could have told her it was on her fingers as well.

"Kick ate some, too."

"Only one! I only had one."

"That's fine, Kick. But was that before or after the engineer chased you out of the steam room?"

Kick blinked, and then eyed his sister. She shook her head—she hadn't told. Kick raised his right hand, flicked his wrist twice, and made a looping motion with his first two fingers. Maddie returned the gesture, adding a jab and several more loops to the message, none of which was particularly friendly.

Joseph smiled. The hand signals had replaced a form of gibberish the twins used to communicate when they didn't want their parents to know what they were saying. Between them, Joseph and his wife had picked up enough of the language to listen in, which was when the kids switched to the hand signals. They generally tried to hide them from Kate, but assumed their father wasn't going to decipher the visual language anytime soon. Joseph did sometimes have trouble following the speedy hand motions, which is why he'd long since given up trying. There was no point, as both kids wore so many of their emotions on their faces.

"We'll be in port soon," Joseph said, letting the kids off the hook. "Go grab your things, and meet me up above."

Kick hopped onto the lower rail and off again before following his sister into the main compartment of the steamer.

Joseph closed his senses, letting some of the emotion he'd felt earlier creep back into his waking mind. Kick and Maddie were born the day he'd lost his sight. He was more than a hundred miles away at the time, and it had taken him four days to stumble home in the endless dark. After sleeping most of the fifth, he'd awakened to an uninvited guest and the first inkling that a new light might be available to him. That had been exactly eleven years ago to the day.

Joseph felt the boat rumble beneath his feet as it turned slightly to the south. Astoria would appear shortly on the Oregon side of the river, with its fishing boats, ore merchants, and colorful houses on the hill. With only a little effort, Joseph pushed the past away and opened his senses to what lay ahead.

"I see Mr. Hendricks!" Maddie said, pointing to a short man waving from the dock.

He was not alone. At least a dozen locals stood waiting for passengers, many of whom were waving alongside Joseph and the twins. The Port of Astoria was bustling with activity. In addition to the *Alberta*, a second, much larger steamer was docked alongside, having arrived from San Francisco a few hours earlier. The passengers had departed, but the holds of the ship continued to be unloaded by an ore-powered mechanical arm. Two smaller barges were also docked nearby, both weighted down to the waterline by mounds of what appeared to be gray slate. Neither was in the process of being loaded or unloaded, but a dozen men with guns stood along the docks on either side of the boats.

After disembarking, the Wyldes were met by Charlie Hendricks, owner and operator of Astoria's oldest store, Hendricks' Dry Goods. Charlie was short, round, and bald, but had a generous personality that he claimed made up for the physical "gifts" God had seen fit to give him. He knew everyone in town and had made it his business to meet their extended families. As a result, he was always up on the latest gossip, local and otherwise.

Joseph offered his hand. "Hello, Mr. Hendricks. Thanks for coming."

"Well met, as always," Charlie said, glancing past Joseph to the boat. "Where's Katherine? Don't tell me she didn't make the trip."

"She and her father disagree on the specifics of the relocation," Joseph said, hoping his tone and arching eyebrow were enough for Charlie to move on to another subject.

"Oh," Charlie said, glancing at the twins. "Well, I'm sure he'll be happy to see you. Afraid I'm not much in the way of company. And my cooking is even worse."

"I'm sure it's fine," Joseph said, following Charlie up the pier. "Lot of activity about."

"It's the ore. They found another vein above Paulsen Creek. Big one, I'm told. The barges come in almost daily, now."

Kick climbed onto a pile of ropes to get a better look at the nearest barge.

"Is that it? I thought it was orange," he said, mildly disappointed.

"It is, once it's been refined," said Charlie. "That's mostly shale. The good stuff is locked inside in little-bitty pieces. They're actually building a refinery across the river so they don't have to transport so much unusable material."

"Across the river?"

Charlie frowned. "They say it's because the north side gets more sun—more sun! You believe that? Politics is what it is."

"I'm sure," Joseph said. He slowed his pace, adding space between them and the twins. "I appreciate you looking out for the marshal."

"Happy to do it."

"How's his mood?"

"Lousy."

Joseph nodded. "He can be a hard man to like."

"He's always been friendly to me, but he is on his own. Has been for . . . eight years?"

"Nearly ten."

"I know you and Kate have been to visit—more than some families, to be sure—and he has friends here, acquaintances and such, but a man of his experiences, of his fame . . ." Charlie hesitated, and then added, "Frankly, I'm not surprised he got a little confused. It happens at his age."

Joseph nodded, but the truth was that it did surprise him. He'd heard the details of his father-in-law's "confusion" from the Astoria constable, who'd held him for a day before releasing him to Charlie. It just didn't feel right. The man had slowed down in recent years, perhaps become more forgetful, but a sudden breakdown seemed unlikely. Jim Kleberg was a hard man, but he was still his own man. Joseph would not believe otherwise until he spoke to the marshal.

He owed him that much.

"Oh, it's you," said the marshal, frowning over a smile before it could begin. He'd come quickly to the top of the stairs but now descended without enthusiasm.

"Hello, Marshal," said Joseph.

He was sixty-four years old, ten of them retired, but Jim Kleberg still appreciated being addressed as "Marshal." The job was who he was and always would be. The man standing at the bottom of the stairs was smart enough to know that.

"Where's the clan?" he asked, offering a hand to Joseph, who shook it.

"I sent Kick and Maddie up to the house to get started. Kate didn't come."

The marshal looked Joseph up and down, lingering over the man's right eye.

"Okay."

Charlie came through the door behind Joseph. "Hello, Marshal. All's well I assume. Did you find the sandwiches I left?"

The marshal nodded. "Wasn't hungry, but thanks."

"Oh, all right," Charlie said. He stood for a moment, waiting for one of the other two men to say something. Finally, he did. "Well, perhaps I should check in on my roses, let you two catch up."

Charlie walked though the kitchen to the back door. The marshal waited to hear the latch before turning to Joseph.

"Your idea to set me up here?"

"Charlie volunteered."

"Figured as much," the marshal said, rubbing his hands together. "Treats me like a damn baby, always following me around, watching, asking questions."

"He's just worried. We all were."

"I ain't no invalid. Offered to do some gardening, but Charlie hid all the shovels. Afraid I'd dig up his prize roses or somethin'. Damn things looked dead anyway."

Joseph waited for the man to say more, but instead the marshal walked into the living room and sat down in an oversize chair facing a large picture window. Joseph followed, stepping around the chair to stand next to the fireplace, where a mound of embers still radiated warmth.

"Well, it's good to see ya, I guess. How long you stayin'?"

"The steamer's running back tomorrow afternoon," Joseph said. "Should be enough time to get things in order, I think."

"Not much of a visit."

Joseph looked at the marshal.

"Marshal, you know why we're here. You're coming to live with us in Portland. I'm sure you remember—"

"You think I don't remember?"

"I didn't say that."

The marshal leveled a long, bony finger at the younger man. "But that's what you *think*."

Joseph wasn't ready for this conversation—had, in fact, little desire to have it at all. It dawned on him that his wife had not come for this very reason.

"I know this isn't what you wanted, Marshal."

"Damn right it isn't!" the marshal said, and was up from his chair and out the front door before Joseph could stop him.

Joseph found the marshal on the porch, leaning against a weathered railing. Astoria spilled out below the house, the glow of a few street lamps already visible in the predusk light.

"I'm sorry, Marshal. I know this isn't easy, but it's for the best."

"You sure?"

"I am."

The marshal took a deep breath and let it out.

"What if I ain't?"

"Well, I'm sure once you're in Portland this will make more sense. You always said you wanted to be closer to your grandkids."

"That's not what I mean." The marshal rubbed his forehead, trying to dislodge the thought that had been there since he'd agreed to the move four days earlier. "What if I'm not supposed to leave?"

Joseph shook his head. "The house will be fine. And we're not going to sell it, if that's what you're worried about."

"No, I . . . I don't know."

Joseph measured his words carefully. "It's all right, Marshal. It happens to everybody as they get older."

"You really want to have this conversation?"

Joseph closed his eye. The world didn't look any different, but the gesture wasn't for him.

"Maybe we should head up to the house," he said. "We've got a lot to do."

"What? You think I won't be a son of a bitch around the gran'childs?"

"No, but I thought you'd want to supervise while a pair of eleven-year-olds packed all your worldly possessions."

The marshal was unable to suppress a grin this time. A small laugh escaped, as well.

"Eleven?" The marshal turned the number over in his head. "Eleven years ago last week, right? Wednesday?"

"That's right."

"See? I ain't lost all my faculties yet." The marshal took another long look at the hill that rose up behind Astoria. He could see his house and the cemetery beyond, its fence reflecting the last rays of sunlight. "Startin' to forget the rest, though."

"Come to Portland," Joseph said, and put on a hand on the man's shoulder. "In a week's time, this will feel right, you'll see."

"I'll see, huh?" The marshal returned his gaze to the town. "Says the man with one good eye."

"I see well enough. I see a man who helped me once—saved me."

"I don't need saving, Joseph."

"I know." Joseph could feel the anger slip from the marshal as he gently applied pressure to the older man's shoulder.

"I forgot some things, is all." The marshal smiled again. "Course, last time I remembered anything I wound up covered in mud and splinters."

"Don't worry. I told Maddie to hide all the shovels."

Maddie pushed open the curtains on the front window, letting in what little daylight remained, before turning back to the room. To say that the marshal's home was sparsely decorated would be generous. The only furniture on the first floor consisted of a well-traveled trunk, three mismatched chairs, a small square table, and an old rocker pushed into the corner next to a fireplace that otherwise dominated the space.

"Not much to pack," Kick said.

"I think there's more upstairs," Maddie said, not really sure if it was true. They'd stayed at the house at least a dozen times, but she couldn't recall it ever being so empty. Maybe it would seem different with more people inside.

Kick took a seat in the rocking chair. "I always liked this chair," he said, pushing hard off the floor. Soon he was trying to see how far he could rock without tipping over, each swing squealing a little louder on the bare wood floor.

"Kick, stop it. Mother said no furniture."

"Too bad," Kick said, gracefully hopping out of the chair. "I'm going upstairs. You coming?"

"I'll be up in a minute."

Kick stared at his sister for a beat and then jogged up the stairs.

Maddie glanced about the room, her eyes lingering on the rocking chair. She was glad they weren't taking the furniture.

A few minutes later, Maddie found her brother lying on the marshal's bed, staring at the ceiling.

"Done packing already?"

"Look," Kick said, pointing straight up. Maddie followed the direction of his finger to the uneven brown mark on the ceiling.

"What is it?"

"A leak. I mean, it was a leak—it's dried up, now. But it must have been a good one to leave that big of a stain."

"We should tell Gran'pa, make sure he knows."

"He knows," Kick said, smiling. "It's right above his head. I bet it dripped on him while he was sleeping." Kick tapped his forehead several times with a finger. He then stood up on the bed, never taking his eyes off the watermark on the ceiling, and spun to look at it from different angles.

"Looks like a witch from this side. Or maybe a cat."

Maddie frowned. "You're not supposed to stand on the bed."

"I took off my shoes."

Maddie stared at her brother, trying to mimic the glare she'd seen her mother use on more than one occasion.

"You ain't Ma," he said and dropped into a sitting position on the edge of the mattress, which instantly propelled him into the air again and onto his feet directly in front of his sister. "Ma's got crazy eyes."

Maddie tilted her head down slightly. She was taller than Kick, just barely, but enough that when they met eye-to-eye he had to look up slightly.

"You're supposed to do what I say," she said.

"Says who?"

"It's implied. I'm the oldest."

"By three minutes."

Maddie turned and walked away. "Not my fault you were born lazy."

Kick stared after his sister. He could chase after her, try to come up with a witty retort, which Maddie would no doubt knock back at him, smarter and sharper . . . or he could see what else was hidden in the watermark above the marshal's bed. Kick went limp and fell backward onto the bed.

"Hey, from this angle, it looks like a wolf."

Joseph and the marshal arrived at the house to find few things packed. Kick had thoughtfully cataloged all the leaks, which he described for his grandfather in great detail. Maddie had managed to organize the kitchen, although she was quick to point out there was little in the way of edible food. Joseph had expected this, which was why he'd brought a few provisions from home. To the marshal, who had subsisted on Charlie's cooking for half a week, day-old stew had never tasted so good.

The next morning, all were up with the sun to organize and pack the marshal's belongings. He'd decided to bring only a few boxes of clothes, books, papers, and other artifacts of his years as a United States marshal. The rest would be stored in the attic. Anything too big to fit up the narrow staircase would stay where it was.

It was while his grandfather picked through an upstairs closet that Kick decided to ask the question that had been buzzing around his brain all morning.

"Did you really dig up a grave?"

The marshal popped his head out of the closet and stared at Kick, wondering if he'd heard the question right. The wide-eyed look on Maddie's face suggested he had.

"Well, yes, I suppose I did."

"Really?"

The marshal wondered who had told the kids, before deciding no one had. It was more likely one of them had overheard a conversation not intended for his or her ears, probably hers. Maddie would have told her brother, of course, and Kick simply wanted to know more. Who wouldn't?

"Yup," he said. "Several, in fact. Cracked open the coffins with an ax. Wasn't hard; most of 'em were rotted through."

Maddie was just as shocked as her brother, which was how the question escaped her mouth before she could stop it: "Why?"

The marshal hesitated. "I don't know. Seemed like a good idea at the time."

The marshal turned back to his search, leaving Maddie and Kick to work out a follow-up. Kick made a gesture with his hand, suggesting they should press a little more. Maddie shook her head.

"Of course," said the marshal, poking his head out of the closet. "Probably best not to talk about it, least not around your folks. It makes your pa uncomfortable—ghosts and such."

Both kids nodded.

"How about you get up to the attic, see if there's anything worth rescuing 'fore we fill it up with the rest of this junk."

"Sure," said Kick, bolting up the narrow staircase on the right side of the closet. Maddie lingered for a moment and then followed her brother up.

The marshal waited until he could hear both kids moving around above before allowing a wave of anxiety to wash over him. He was forgetting something again, something important. It was closer this time. He thought the answer was in the house. He'd find it.

Someone would.

Joseph twisted the rocking chair around the turn at the top of the stairs and placed it in the corner where it fit snuggly against the sloping roof. With barely five feet of clearance at its highest point, the attic was also a tight fit for Joseph. Despite his superior senses, he'd already banged his head twice on the same overhead beam. If Kate found out—and she would—he'd never hear the end of it. Joseph started back down the stairs, but stopped on the second step, where his six-foot frame could stand without hunching over. He rubbed the back of his head.

"Still hurt?" asked Maddie.

"A little. How goes the search? Find anything interesting?"

"There's a very nice saddle, but I assume that's going to stay."

"It is."

"Everything else is old, broken, or both," Maddie said, flipping open a large chest. "It's too bad these dresses weren't stored better, because some of them are very pretty." Maddie held up a long yellow dress. The color was still vibrant, but the edges were frayed and the fringe had been eaten away.

"Those must have belonged to Martha," Joseph said.

"I thought so."

The twins had never met their grandmother. Joseph had known the marshal's wife only briefly before she died, and at the time he was not the kind of man most mothers sought for their daughters. Still, she'd treated him fairly, some might say generously. Joseph hoped he'd paid her back in kind.

"How about you," Joseph said, turning to look directly at a stack of boxes. Kick popped up from his hiding spot, a mischievous grin on his face.

"I found some more leaks. Oh, and this . . ." Kick picked up a small wooden box about eighteen inches wide and twelve inches deep. The top had decorative vines carved around the edges with a rose in the center.

"What is it?" Joseph asked.

"It's a box."

"Yes, I mean what's inside it?"

"Oh," Kick said. He flipped open the lid, revealing a cloth-covered interior but nothing else. "It's empty."

"Bring it here."

Kick stepped over the clutter and passed the box to his father. It was heavy, probably too heavy for an empty box. Joseph ran his fingers across the lid, letting the carvings tell their story. He'd never encountered the box before, but knew right away that the marshal had made it. He recognized the cuts in the wood as coming from the same hand as had made the mirror frame hanging above Kate's dresser. Joseph raised the lid. Most of the aromatic information stored within had been released the first time Kick opened the box, but Joseph could still pick out a single, earthy scent beneath the musty wood, and maybe one more—the ocean.

"See? Empty," said Kick. "If the marshal doesn't want it, can I have it?"

Joseph closed the lid and handed the box back to his son.

"Ask him."

The marshal stared at the box in his lap. He didn't have to open it to know what was inside.

"I'm sorry, Kick, but I can't let you have this. Belonged to your grandmother, and I think your ma might want it."

"Oh."

"She used to keep seashells in it. I don't know what happened to them."

Kick's eyes lit up. "I do! There's a pile of shells up in the attic."

"Well, why don't you go collect 'em. If you see one you like, keep it. Maddie, too."

"Thanks, Gran'pa," Kick said, and darted back up the stairs.

The marshal turned his attention back to the box. He opened the lid and ran a hand along the cloth until he felt it give a little. There he pushed down, releasing the hidden latch that held the false bottom in place. The second lid lifted slightly, revealing a dark compartment. The marshal knew what lay inside. He hadn't forgotten.

The marshal pressed the bottom back into place and closed the lid. He then unspooled the belt from his waist and wrapped it around the box, securing it tightly. It would come with him to Portland and he would never open it again.

Charlie arrived just before one o'clock with a horse-drawn cart and a basket of biscuits from which everyone sampled, but no one returned for seconds. They loaded up a half-dozen boxes and the saddle the marshal had refused to leave behind despite Joseph's protests. The Wyldes didn't have a horse, but the marshal felt that was a poor argument against owning a quality saddle.

A few neighbors stopped by to wish the marshal well, none of whom mentioned the business in the graveyard. Walter Peterson even returned the shovel and ax, which Joseph placed in the shed without comment.

An hour later, the marshal stood at the rail of the *Alberta*, watching Astoria fade in the distance. As the last hillside home vanished from sight, he felt a weight lift from his heart. It was as if the top button of his shirt had loosened, his belt unbuckled, and his boots kicked off—all at the same time. He felt good, relaxed, happy.

Joseph leaned on the rail next to his father-in-law.

"You'll be back."

The marshal shook his head. "No, I don't think I will. But it's all right. I should have done this a long time ago."

Joseph smiled. "I'm glad to hear you say that."

"So am I."

The two men stood silently at the rail for a time, enjoying the sun on their faces, the brisk air, and the sound of the river churning in the wake of the boat.

Were you to ask any resident of Astoria about May 17, 1887, he or she would have told you it was lovely. The sun shone brightly, hinting at the drier-than-usual summer to come. The fishing was excellent, the best it'd been in weeks. The Second Bank of Astoria opened for business, founded largely on "amber" gold. In short, it was a good day to be in Astoria.

It was a good day for all but one longtime resident who suddenly felt a huge weight fall upon him without warning. This man, a fellow of barely seventeen years, had never known such a feeling, had never felt such anxiety. With it came a memory of a day long since buried in the deep recesses of his mind.

And he remembered everything.

2

The Port of Portland was the busiest in the Pacific Northwest, second only to San Francisco in overall West Coast water traffic. For a time, it seemed Seattle with its expansive sound and natural shipping lanes would become the region's capital of commerce, but the discovery of vast firestone deposits in western and central Oregon had changed everything. The city's inland location and ready access to the deep waters of the Columbia River assured the amber rush would run through Portland.

Most of Portland's waterfront property was not on the great river proper but rather on the banks of a prime tributary, the Willamette. A tri-city vote in 1861 had folded East Portland and Albina into the city, stretching it across the Willamette and south to the Tualatin River. The friendly annexation, coupled with the surge of immigrants and fortune seekers, helped Portland quadruple its population in less than twenty years. By 1887, nearly sixty thousand souls claimed the title "Portlandian," many of whom saw their new home for the first time from the water.

In the 1870s, the arrival of a large steamship would have been an event most residents turned out to see, but by the end of the next decade, dozens of the big steamers were arriving every week.

Smaller, passenger stern- and paddlewheel steamers coming from all points on the Columbia docked at the waterfront by the hour. The metropolitan harbor could accommodate a dozen riverboats and on many days its berths were filled to capacity with eager souls searching for a new life in the Northwest.

The irony was that passengers usually found it drier while on the water. The downtown streets regularly flooded during the spring thaw and when not swamped offered only muddy passage around the larger puddles. The steam-powered streetcars that were supposed to alleviate the public's transportation woes ground to a halt when the water reached its normal April levels and sometimes stayed stuck in the mud until June. Newer construction—of which there was plenty—required raised sidewalks by city ordinance, although whether a few feet of dry would be helpful was hotly debated among longtime residents. In truth, the locals liked it wet. Most owned small dories or canoes for the wettest days and had little trouble navigating the raised scaffolding and planks that stretched across the streets like so many makeshift bridges. It was said that all one needed to survive the spring in Portland was a raincoat and a good sense of balance.

Kate Wylde was more than capable of traversing the slender downtown walkways, though on this morning her feet had actually touched ground on more than one occasion. Three days of sunshine and moderate temperatures had forced the floodwaters to recede slightly, which was not welcome news to those counting on the rain to keep the city floating through the annual Portland Rain Festival. Muddy roads and sunny skies were not welcome on a schedule of events that included cloud spotting and canoe races. For her part, Kate was not displeased by the appearance of the sun, but a strong sense of civic pride meant she hoped to see the rain return, perhaps tomorrow or the day after that.

The ten years that Kate had lived in Portland had been the happiest of her life. She'd raised her family here, and thus the twins had never known life outside the city. That was fine with Kate. She'd lived through the harsh winters of the back country and seen her mother make do without so much as a whisper of complaint, but it was not for her. Kate was a city girl, had been since the moment she and Joseph had arrived in Portland and discovered its public schools, electrified streetlights, and local sewer lines.

Kate had watched the city grow right along with her family, its buildings multiplying each year, always getting bigger and taller. Eighteen eighty-seven had seen the opening of the Morrison Bridge, the first to cross the Willamette River, and work had already begun on a second crossing, this one made of steel. The medical college had opened the preceding fall, and that summer a public zoo would open in Washington Park, just up the hill from the house the Wyldes called home. At last count, the city had fifteen theaters, two opera houses, three department stores, a dozen hotels, and a baseball team.

Kate paused at the corner of Alder Street and Third Avenue. This close to the river, the road remained completely under water, but the expansion of the docks had brought one of the wooden piers two blocks into downtown, where it split and connected with two larger raised walkways that ran the length of Second Avenue. More than a dozen small skiffs were tied to the posts nearest the ramp, as was a single horse who seemed none too happy to be standing in three feet of water. Kate made her way across the last plank and onto the extended pier.

The waterfront was crowded with travelers, merchants, locals collecting visitors, and a few of the yellow-eyed men who hung around the docks day and night. They were prospectors, or had been before they'd become too sick to dig. It wasn't the ore but the black dust that collected around it that made the men cough and their whites turn the color of yolks. Most hung around the water, hoping to catch on with a boat heading south to warmer, drier climes, but few crews would have them. Kate had never heard of the condition spreading, but few people were willing to chance sharing close quarters with the diseased.

Kate drifted among the people, letting the ebb and flow of the foot traffic give her direction. She'd made the forty-five-minute walk and wade from the house without testing herself, but now she was ready. It took only a moment and then she was gone, hidden from view, not a face in the crowd but lost in it.

Kate had vanished.

She was there, of course, invisible not to the eye but rather to the mind. Kate thought of it as stepping into a communal blind spot. The harder someone searched, the easier it was for her to stay out of sight.

Kate had developed this trick after years of teasing the one man whose eyes didn't get in the way of his vision. Joseph had always been able to find her, no matter where or how she hid, until she'd discovered that sight wasn't the only way of seeing. Just as Joseph had honed his other senses to replace his eyes, Kate had learned to minimize the nonvisual clues that gave her away.

The result was that Joseph had a hard time finding his wife when she didn't want to be found. Any observer who happened to catch the show would think Kate had simply disappeared. The city, of course, offered the best of backdrops, but Kate had practiced in the wild as well. She was every bit as good hiding among the trees as she was the telegraph poles. The crowded pier made it easy.

A group of twenty people had gathered on the dock allotted to the *Alberta*, which was due to arrive at the top of the hour. Standing among the family and friends was Jim Gates, mayor of Portland, and a pair of advisers, one of whom Kate recognized as the deputy mayor. She liked the mayor, had supported him, but was less than eager to make herself available to his approach.

That didn't stop her from being curious.

"You're sure it's this boat?" the mayor said, not bothering to look at either of the men standing next to him.

"Yes, sir," said Avery Harris, the younger man to his left. "It's this one, the *Alberta*."

"Good, good. And both men are onboard?"

Avery hesitated, glancing at the man standing on the mayor's right. Deputy Mayor Bart Hildebrandt frowned at his colleague.

"Yes, Mr. Mayor," said Bart. "I personally confirmed that both Mr. Wylde and his father-in-law are onboard."

The mayor nodded. "Excellent."

Jim Gates considered himself a good businessman and an even better politician, but he was not a patient man. He'd won his first election by running a campaign that never slowed down long enough to give the press (or the opposition) time to find fault with his politics. He talked fast and promised a lot, which made it very hard for most listeners to recall anything but the last words out of his mouth. That's why he always ended speeches with a joke.

Upriver, the *Alberta* came into view as it made the turn just north of downtown.

"Here it comes, sir."

"Right on schedule," said the mayor, loudly enough for the people around him to hear. He then leaned to his right and spoke so that no one but the deputy could hear. "We'll make a show of it with the old man, but I'll be speaking to Mr. Wylde alone."

"Actually, Mr. Mayor," said a woman's voice, "I'd like to say hello to my husband first—if that's all right with you."

The mayor blinked twice before realizing the disembodied voice was coming from a slender red-haired woman standing directly in front of him.

"Mrs. Wylde!" he said, effortlessly slipping into his public persona. "A pleasure to see you again. Here to greet the family, I assume."

"As are you, it appears."

"Er, yes," said the mayor, only slightly disarmed. "I've got a bit of business to discuss with Joseph. I hope that's all right."

Kate smiled. "Of course," she said, failing to add that she knew all about the mayor's business and had spent nearly as much time as her husband coming up with a solution to the politician's problem.

"My father made the trip, as well," she added. "He's going to be living with us here in Portland."

"That's wonderful. A man of his stature will no doubt become a respected resident of the city. I'll make it my mission to get his endorsement."

"I'm sure he'll look forward to that."

The mayor's smile faltered slightly.

"You should ask him to take part in the festival," Kate said, offering an olive branch.

"Oh? You think he'd be interested?"

"I'm sure he would. He's a show-off," she lied. "And he's got plenty of stories to tell. He might even offer a demonstration of some of those old marshaling skills of his. He does like to shoot things."

The mayor beamed. "Mrs. Wylde, you've made my day."

The *Alberta* began the wide turn into port at that moment, announcing its arrival with the clanging of a bell and great release of steam.

"Welcome!" exclaimed the mayor, making a broad swipe of the air with his left arm. "Welcome to Portlandtown!"

Avery waved enthusiastically at no one in particular. The deputy mayor offered a weak salute, and then remembered Mrs. Wylde. He turned, ready to explain away his halfhearted gesture, only to find the woman gone. He scanned the crowd but could not see her, even though she'd been standing at his side only a moment before.

Maddie leaned forward, squinting at the crowded pier below. Kick climbed onto the rail next to her and stretched even farther out.

"Do you see her?" he asked.

"Not yet."

They'd played this game with their mother on numerous occasions, usually downtown, where the crowds made for more of a challenge. They were good at finding her, or thought they were. Kate would never admit that most of the twins' successes were the result of her deliberate mistakes, but when she'd wanted to win, she had. Joseph was the only person who could find her at the top of her game, and even then he wasn't always on target.

Joseph stepped up to the rail next to the twins.

"See her yet?"

"No," said Kick. "She's dug in good."

Maddie nodded.

Joseph turned to the city and opened his senses. Portland poured over him, offering a wave of sensory input. Joseph filtered out the noise—the voices, the laughter, the working city, and water flowing in a hundred different directions in and around the flooded streets. Gradually, he focused on the people closest to the *Alberta*. There were nineteen, maybe twenty souls waiting to greet family, friends, and neighbors. Joseph recognized a few of those present and noted that Kate wasn't the only person waiting for him. The mayor was among the crowd, no doubt looking for an update on the matter he'd asked Joseph to look into a week earlier. He had an assistant with him and the deputy mayor.

That was interesting.

Joseph delved further, letting the sounds of downtown drop away. The air, usually a fragrant mixture of rain, mud, and beer, was surprisingly dry. A few days of sun had given the floodwaters a funk that would turn rancid if they didn't recede soon.

It was there among the local fragrances that Joseph found her— *lilac.*

Kate was very fond of lilacs and kept a box of dried flowers in the bedroom. To maintain the natural perfume, she opened it only when in a certain mood. Joseph was quite fond of these moods and as such had developed a hair-trigger sensory response to lilac. He could smell flowers in bloom more than a mile away.

Kate must have been crushing a few petals in her hand, letting the flower's scent mingle with the local aroma. She was teasing Joseph and he loved it.

"Come on," he said, turning away from the rail. "Let's go find your grandfather."

"You found her?" Kick said, closing his eyes and sniffing the air, trying desperately to follow his father's lead.

"You're not going to find her, Kick," said Joseph. "Not today."

Kick jumped off the rail and made for the stairwell ahead of Joseph. Maddie followed, lingering for a moment at the top of the steps.

"Lilacs," she said and bounced down the stairs after her brother.

The marshal was already jawing at a porter by the time the kids and Joseph caught up to him on the pier.

"Son, I don't want to have to tell you twice. The goods with the saddle, there's a small box . . ."

"Don't worry, Marshal," Joseph said, releasing the porter with a nod. "I've taken care of everything."

The marshal frowned. After a pleasant start to the voyage, the marshal's mood had soured, and he'd spent most of the journey upriver sitting alone. Twice he'd demanded to inspect his things, and was talked out of a third only after Joseph told him to leave it be. Joseph wanted very much to avoid further confrontation and was glad to feel Kate's presence behind her father.

"Hello, Dad."

The marshal turned to his daughter, who gave him a hug before he could say a word.

"How was the journey?"

"Too sunny," the marshal said. "Spent most of the trip looking for shade."

"I'm sure it'll start raining again soon. It always does."

Kate slipped around the marshal to her husband. "And how was your trip?" Before Joseph could answer, Kate kissed him on the cheek, her lips lingering next to his before she pulled away. The scent of lilacs was overpowering.

"Fine," Joseph said.

Kate knew every practiced expression at Joseph's disposal and was pleased to see a look of genuine befuddlement on his face. She'd managed to greet her father without starting an argument and to remind her husband of exactly how much he loved her. That left only the twins.

"Hello, Kick," she said, as the boy materialized by her side.

"I almost found you."

"Really?"

"I was very close," Kick said, grasping his mother's left hand. "I think the sun got in my eyes."

"The sun set ten minutes ago," said Maddie, taking her mother's other hand.

"That's true," said Kate. "But I believe it was still visible above the hill when the boat came in."

"It was!" said Kick. "Ha!"

Kate gave Maddie a smile, which she returned.

Joseph would have liked to let the moment linger, but the mayor was practically coughing up a lung, trying to make his presence known.

"Mayor Gates?"

"Ah, Joseph! I was hoping to run into you today. Back from the coast, are you?"

"Yes, that's right. Good to see you. And may I introduce my father-in-law, James Kleberg."

"Jim Gates," the mayor said, vigorously shaking the marshal's hand. "Marshal Kleberg, it is an honor to be in your presence. Welcome to Portlandtown."

"Portland*town*?"

"So says the city charter. Fallen out of fashion, I'm afraid. Apparently, local sign makers can't be bothered with so many letters!"

"Oh."

"I do hope you'll find our fair city to your liking. It's not as rough and tumble as you're used to, but we do have our fair share of skullduggery now and again."

"I'm retired. Don't see too many skulls these days."

Joseph felt Kate's grip tighten slightly on his hand.

"Of course not!" said the mayor. "But certainly you saw your share of action as a United States marshal, am I right?"

"I suppose."

"Come now, Marshal Kleberg, there's no need to be modest. You're a hero of the West. Without men like yourself—and Joseph, of course—we'd never have had the will to build this beautiful city."

The marshal didn't blush, but Joseph sensed his discomfort.

"I appreciate the kind words, but that was a long time ago," said the marshal. "Don't think this city needs my help, 'cept maybe to lay a few sandbags."

"Yes, you've caught us with our boots wet," said the mayor. "But things are drying out—too soon, if you ask me."

"How's that?"

"Well, it's all this sun! I'm afraid it's going to upend our plans for the festival next week."

"It's the Rain Festival," said Kate. "I told you about that, re-member?"

The marshal nodded a little too quickly.

"Oh, it's great fun," said the mayor. "Folks come from miles around just to stand out in the Oregon rain."

"Waist-deep by the looks of it," said the marshal. Kick laughed, earning a smile from his grandfather.

"One can only hope," said the mayor, not at all sarcastically. "Of course, we also like to showcase other things that elevate our state, including our citizens. I daresay a notable figure such as you would make a fine addition to the celebration. Folks always enjoy meet-ing their historical heroes."

The marshal shot a look at Joseph. "Do they, now?"

"Absolutely! Your mere presence would be enough to draw a crowd, but perhaps you could also offer a demonstration of that legendary marksmanship."

A gunshot rang out in the marshal's memory, the last he'd ever taken. It was gone by the time he found his voice again.

"It's been a long time," he said. "Doubt I could hit the river from the backside of that boat."

"Then share a few tales of adventure. I know of at least one story that would keep any audience riveted, especially a firsthand account."

Kate took her father's arm. "It might be fun, Dad."

Joseph felt the marshal look to him for help, and for a moment he wasn't sure what to offer. He could have found an excuse, something to keep the marshal occupied through the festival, but in the end he didn't have to.

"All right, I'll do it."

"Excellent!" said the mayor, once again shaking the marshal's hand. "Avery will fill you in on the details." The mayor deftly passed off the marshal to his assistant and turned his attention to Joseph. "A moment, Joseph, if I might."

The mayor walked Joseph down the pier, his deputy trailing at a discreet distance.

"I'm surprised you found the time to retrieve your father-in-law. I can only assume that means our business is well undertaken."

"Nearly completed, sir. I only have to confirm my suspicions, which shouldn't take more than a day."

"You found the culprit so quickly?"

Joseph nodded. "Send a man around to the bookstore on Thursday and I'll have your answer. Send someone you trust."

"I'll send Bart," said the mayor, motioning to his deputy.

Joseph knew the deputy was listening and was impressed that the man didn't flinch at the mention of his name.

"You've really got this figured out in a week's time?"

"I'm afraid you're not as popular as you think. It was a close election."

"And the next one is going to be even closer, which is why I need this resolved. Perhaps you should just give me a name right now."

"Thursday. And, now, if you'll excuse me, I have to attend to my newly extended family."

Joseph strode up the pier, leaving the mayor and his deputy to wonder how much he'd actually discovered.

———

Twenty minutes later, Joseph found himself floating up Yamhill Street on a small flat-bottomed skiff loaded with the marshal's belongings. The waters had receded slightly since he'd left on his errand, although not enough to make the business district passable to anything with wheels. The boat would carry them as far as Sixth Street, where a cart would be waiting to take them the rest of the way home.

A young Chinese man deftly maneuvered the vessel through the waterlogged streets using a long wooden pole. There were dozens of similar craft spread about the city, each under the command of a similarly skilled Celestial boatman. The local Chinese population kept mostly to itself, rarely venturing out of the Second Avenue neighborhood that had become the nation's second-largest Chinatown. But when the streets filled with water each spring, it was Chinese boats that offered the fastest (and cheapest) transport across the city. Not surprisingly, the Rain Festival's annual regatta had been won by a Chinese national four years running.

The young man directed the craft around another water taxi heading in the opposite direction and then steered back into the center of the canal. Joseph scanned ahead and caught a glimpse of Kick darting across a raised scaffold stretched over the next intersection. He stopped in the center of the slender plank and waved at his father. Joseph waved back. Kick raced on, followed closely by Kate and Maddie.

"I thought you were a bookseller," said the marshal.

Joseph turned to the marshal, who sat leaning against the saddle he'd refused to leave in Astoria. He hadn't said a word since leaving the pier.

"I am. Store's just around the corner, in fact." Joseph craned his neck. "I think you can see it if you look, just past the smoke shop. There's the sign, see? 'Booksellers and Navigation.'"

"Navigation?"

"Maps and such."

"Oh," said the marshal. "That what the mayor was after? He lost or something?"

Joseph smiled. "Not exactly."

The marshal stared at Joseph, waiting for more. Joseph considered the boatman's presence before continuing, ultimately deeming the man an unlikely spy.

"The mayor has a problem and I agreed to help."

"What kind of problem?"

"The kind that doesn't want to be addressed in public."

The marshal's brow furrowed. "He a crook?"

"No," Joseph said, suppressing a grin. "I wouldn't work for the man if I thought he was flaunting the law. It's simply a delicate situation, something that requires a certain amount of flexibility that local law enforcement can't provide."

"What?" said the marshal, leaning a little farther back against his saddle. "Like the Pinkertons?"

"Definitely not. Those men are too up front with their tactics. We offer a more discreet investigation."

The marshal's attention refocused on Joseph. "'We'?"

Joseph smiled. "You know as well as I that Kate is more than capable of handling herself."

"Do I?"

"Yes, Marshal, I believe you do. Besides, we're not exactly going after hardened criminals. Most of what we do is simply to help folks uncover the truth."

It was the marshal's turn to smile. "It's been my experience that gettin' the truth outta someone is a lot harder than chasin' some half-wit road agent."

Joseph laughed. "Can't say as I disagree, but that's what makes a service like ours particularly valuable."

The marshal nodded. "I'm guessing you don't advertise in the local paper."

"Word of mouth, mostly."

"So, how do you spread the word if all your clients want to keep their secrets?"

Joseph considered this. In the past five years he and Kate had done perhaps three dozen jobs for various residents of the city, most connected by family, friends, or local politics. A few clients had arrived without a reference, but Joseph assumed they were simply being discreet.

"We rely on a certain amount of shared information among our clients," he offered. "We're not trying to hide. The folks we help are free to discuss what we've done."

"You trust 'em?"

"I think you've dealt with too many criminals in your time, Marshal." Joseph braced himself as the boat came to a stop in the shallows of the Sixth Avenue intersection. "Most people are trustworthy. The ones that aren't are easy to spot."

The marshal got to his feet and stepped out of the boat into six inches of water. Kate and the twins were already there, sitting on the edge of the buckboard cart. The marshal turned back to Joseph.

"You might think you can see 'em, the bad ones, but they're not always so obvious. Sometimes they look pretty good."

Joseph remembered a much younger man, a man with no scars about his eyes, no family, and no fears save for those that came with running from the law every day and night. What did he look like? Did he look like a bad man or just a man?

It was a question Joseph had long since answered, but one that someone, somewhere, asked every day.

3

Henry Macke was having a bad day.

He was tired and his head hurt. Bad dreams had once again forced him to rise before the sun rather than suffer another minute lying in bed afraid to close his eyes. The nightmares didn't make a lick of sense, but Henry was certain he knew what they meant.

The dead man was his responsibility.

The reason why he'd suddenly recalled every detail of the Hanged Man's demise bothered Henry more than the memory itself. Everyone knew the story—half the town of Astoria had witnessed the bloody shootout on Second Street, if local accounts were to be trusted—but Henry knew more. He knew what had happened after the smoke cleared. He'd seen the confrontation and the last shot fired. He knew the body was buried on the hill without a marker, and he knew exactly where to find it.

Five times he'd caught himself climbing the hill with no recollection of starting the journey. On two of those trips he'd been carrying a shovel. Was he supposed to watch over the body? Bury it deeper? Move it? None of these seemed like good options to Henry, who in his seventeen years of living in the same small town had visited the cemetery only once that he could recall. He doubted that paying his respects with a shovel would go over well with the caretaker, especially given recent events.

If Henry had been less preoccupied, he might have found it intriguing that a major player in the Hanged Man's death had been caught digging in the very ground that now demanded so much of his attention. The old marshal's nocturnal adventures were still a subject of local interest, but Henry heard little of it. He was concerned only with the dead man buried on the hill. The body was his responsibility and he would take care of it.

Plus, his head hurt, he was tired, and a man with a gun was threatening to shoot him. Henry was definitely having a bad day.

"Give me the cash, friend, or we'll be repainting the walls bloodred," said the tall man with uneven sideburns.

Henry suspected that the man, whom he recognized as a semilocal scofflaw named Bill Mason, meant every word, except perhaps for the part about being a friend. It was Henry's dumb luck he'd come to work early. He wasn't supposed to be at the store before noon, but here he was, having barely finished his breakfast, held at gunpoint. There were actually three men with guns, but only Mason's was pointed at Henry. One was enough.

"That's all right, Henry," said Asa Langdon, trying his darnedest to sound calm. "Give him what he wants."

Henry glanced at his boss. Asa owned three of the storefronts along Main Street—Asa's Fine Tailoring, Asa's Hardware, and Asa's General Mercantile. The later was where he spent a good portion of the day, greeting neighbors, gossiping, and touting the merits of his latest merchandise. It was Asa who three years earlier had given Henry a job after his father died, leaving little behind but debt. Henry had always been grateful and, until three days ago, would have called the man a friend, possibly even a father of sorts.

Today, he didn't want to hear from Asa Langdon.

Henry looked in the till. It didn't take long to add up the contents.

"Three dollars and thirty-seven cents," he said, scooping the cash out of the drawer and handing it to the man with the gun. "That's all we've got."

Mason looked at the meager offering in Henry's hand and then slapped it away, scattering the coins across the store's wooden floor.

"Where's the rest of it!" he barked, aiming his gun at Henry's face to underscore his displeasure.

Henry backed up slightly, not out of fear but concern that the agitated outlaw might accidently fire his weapon, thus making it impossible for him to take care of the body on the hill. Henry found this line of thinking odd.

"That's all there is," said Asa, taking a step toward Mason.

Mason swung his gun toward the owner. "Don't lie to me, old man. I know there's a safe—there's always a safe."

"No, there isn't," said Henry. "At the end of the day he takes the cash down the street to the bank—'cept on Fridays. That's when he heads down to Dillard's lookin' to get drunk and buy a couple whores." Henry saw the surprise on Asa's face, and discovered he didn't care.

"I didn't ask for no damn biography," said Mason. "I want the money."

"Try the bank," said Henry.

"Bank is closed," said Hugh Dryer, the shorter of the two other robbers. "Both of 'em."

Henry didn't even try to hide the smile.

"That's it then, there's no money," said Asa. "Why don't you take some merchandise and be on your way. Those silver buckles are worth twenty bucks each. Have 'em all."

The third man, Hugh's younger brother Charlie, stuffed his gun into its holster and leaned over the glass case to examine the contents. "Hey, these look pretty nice. Got to be ten, twelve here. At twenty apiece that ain't bad."

"You think?" said Mason. "I bet he marks them up to twenty, but buys them for . . . what?" Mason looked from Asa to Henry. "Three dollars each?"

"Two," said Henry.

"Dammit, Henry, shut up!"

Mason laughed. "No, friend, keep talkin'. There must be something in this store worth stealing."

Henry scanned the room. Two freestanding shelves took up the center of the store, stocked on both sides with merchandise, mostly housewares. The walls on three sides held floor-to-ceiling shelves that contained dry goods, assorted liquids, and other daily necessities. A display case running the length of the store on one side was filled with the more valuable merchandise, but Henry doubted that much under the glass was worth more than ten dollars.

"That pocket watch is worth maybe fifteen. I wouldn't give a spit for the rest of the crap on hand," Henry said, looking directly at Asa. Nothing in his gaze suggested he was sorry for his assessment.

Mason laughed louder. "I like you," he said, letting the gun dip momentarily before bringing it back up to Henry's face. "Unless you're lying to me. You sure there ain't one piece of merchandise in this whole damn store worth a spit? Not one thing of value?"

Henry hesitated. A thought occurred to him—not just a thought but an idea, perhaps even an answer to the problem he wasn't sure he had. Before he could think better of it, he opened his mouth.

"Not in this store."

Mason cocked his head. He lowered the gun all the way this time and circled the counter to stand next to Henry.

"But you know where there is something of value."

Henry nodded.

"Well, friend," Mason said, sounding a little more like he meant it. "Do tell."

Henry looked at Mason. Without the gun between them, the man seemed much less threatening.

"I know where the body is buried."

These were not the words Mason had expected to hear. "What body?"

"His," Henry said, pointing to a framed newspaper clipping on the wall. The headline at the top of the *Astoria Telegram* from May 17, 1876, read: MASSACRE ON SECOND STREET: HANGED MAN SHOT DEAD! Beneath the headline was a photo of a broad-shouldered man slumped against a wall, his head tilted to one side. The image was dark, but good enough to make out the scar around the dead man's neck.

"I know where the Hanged Man is buried," Henry said.

Mason looked at Henry, but said nothing. He stepped around the counter, once more lining up in front of the younger man, but still he said nothing. It was Charlie who finally broke the silence.

"Who did they hang?"

"They didn't hang nobody," Mason said. "He's talking about *the* Hanged Man, the vilest, meanest, blackest heart ever to beat on God's great land . . . or so they say."

"That's right," said Henry. "And he was killed right here in Astoria, laid to rest by a single man."

"I heard it was a hundred," said Mason.

"You heard wrong."

Mason watched Henry closely, looking for a sign he was lying. Henry didn't give away a thing.

"Henry, I don't know what you think you're doing, but you're wrong," Asa said. "They burned the body. Burned it rather than let that evil take root."

"They didn't burn the body," said Henry. "I was there, I saw what happened. The Hanged Man was buried on top of the hill beneath six feet of Oregon mud and he's still there today."

Mason, having decided against shooting anyone, holstered his gun. He kept all other options on the table. "What do I want with a dead man?"

"The last shot, the shot that finally killed him, was fired from his own gun," Henry said. "They buried him with it."

"I find that hard to believe."

"It's true. I saw Marshal Kleberg fire it a dozen times into the corpse and then throw it into the box."

"You saw him fire it?"

Henry nodded. "A dozen times."

Mason let his hand fall on the butt of his gun as he turned the story over in his head.

"Mason, we best get movin' on," Hugh said. "I don't like standing around with my gun drawn any longer than I have to."

"Tie him up," Mason said, pointing to Asa. He turned to Henry. "We'll be needing directions."

"No," Henry said. "I'm coming with you."

"I don't think so."

"You want the location, you gotta take me with you. I'm sick of this place, this life. I want to dig that bastard up and let whatever evil is left on him seep back into this town until it rots."

Mason looked at Henry, wondering if he might be seeing him for the first time. As it turned out, Mason was a very good judge of character, and as such pegged Henry as an angry young man in need of direction, purpose, and possibly a surrogate father. Mason wouldn't offer any of those things, but he liked the idea of having another member of the gang to boss around.

"This store sell shovels?"

"It never misses," said Hugh, raising his pistol and mock firing at nothing in particular. "That's what Pa told us. You point and it don't never miss the target."

"That's not right," said Charlie. "Pa said it just killed folks— that every bullet went straight into your heart."

"Which means it never misses, ya idiot."

Charlie considered this. "What if you point it at the ground?"

"Then you'd hit the ground."

"But what if you was wantin' to kill a man and you fired in the opposite direction?"

Hugh sighed. "I guess the bullet would bounce off a tree or something."

Charlie was not convinced. He again raised his gun, this time lining up a nearby fir tree in his sights. He hesitated, then pulled back the hammer.

"Fire that and you won't need a ricochet to do the job," said Mason. "I'll put a bullet in you myself."

Charlie holstered the pistol. "I wasn't going to shoot."

Henry watched the exchange from the bottom of a hole he'd already spent more than an hour digging. The grave was not in the cemetery proper but well outside its border on the south side of the hill. Despite the lack of a headstone or any other marker, he knew this was the right spot. His memory of the day was clear and, per- haps more telling, he could feel the dead man beneath his feet.

Henry tossed a shovelful of dirt over the side of the excavation and paused to check his progress. His efforts had thus far produced a five-foot-deep hole, several piles of wet earth, and three bodies— two women and a man whose funeral Henry had attended the preceding summer. The man's gravestone remained unmolested and visible at the edge of the cemetery twenty yards to the north. Henry told Mason he couldn't imagine why someone would have moved the body. He told himself the shallow depression in the ground connecting the two graves could not be what it looked like.

"It never needs reloading," Henry said, adding a shovelful of dirt to the nearest pile. "Doesn't matter how many times you fire, the Hanged Man's gun never runs out of bullets. Ever."

Charlie and Hugh looked at Henry. "You seen this?"

"I saw the Hanged Man shoot seventeen men on Second Street. I never saw him reload."

"Coulda had more than one gun," said Charlie.

"When the marshal went to bury the bastard, he wasn't dead. Had thirty bullets in him, at least, but he was still twitchin'. Marshal pried the gun out of his hand and shot him in the heart. That stopped the twitchin', but just to be sure he shot him eleven more times, the last one square in the forehead. Didn't reload."

Hugh and Charlie shared a look. Charlie opened his mouth to ask another question, but Mason beat him to it.

"Why didn't you dig it up?"

"What?"

Mason approached the edge of the hole. "You knew it was here all this time. Why didn't you come get it for yourself?"

Henry stopped digging. He knew the answer, of course. Henry hadn't gone after the gun because he'd forgotten it existed until a few days ago. Even then, it hadn't occurred to him the gun might be worth something until another pistol was shoved in his face.

"The old marshal," he said. "The man that killed the Hanged Man, he lives in the last house we passed on the way up. I couldn't get to it with him watchin' all the time."

Mason looked over his shoulder at the cemetery. The marshal's excavations had been repaired, but the fresh graves were obvious.

"And he's the one that tore up them other graves?"

"Yep."

"Suppose he was looking for something?"

"Might've been. Didn't find it."

Mason again found himself taking a closer look at the young store clerk. For no reason he could surmise, he believed Henry. This was not like him. Bill Mason had managed a career in general mayhem specifically by not putting faith in others. It hadn't been a spectacularly successful campaign, but he was still a free man despite the tidy sum put on his head by the Oregon Mining Company.

"Charlie, grab a shovel," he said. "Give our new friend some help."

Charlie felt like protesting, but didn't. Henry had taken his position on the bottom rung of the gang and even if it was only temporary, he wanted to enjoy it as long as possible. Charlie picked up a shovel and began swiping at the nearest pile in an attempt to move some of the dirt out of the way.

"Hey!" Henry yelped, dodging a small avalanche of soil.

Charlie quickly changed tactics to stem the flow. "Sorry."

Henry took a deep breath before removing the dirt Charlie had returned. He wasn't tired, which was surprising given his time in the hole. He would have at least expected his shoulders to ache, but each dig and lift seemed to energize him. The soft loam removed, Henry reversed the shovel and brought it down hard on the leading edge of his excavation, striking something solid.

"I'm there."

Henry scraped at the soil until the top of the coffin became visible. It was nothing special, just a pine box, but the wood was in remarkably good shape given the amount of time it'd been in the ground. Henry punched the top of the box several times with the sharp edge of the shovel.

"It's pretty solid. Give me the pry bar."

Hugh passed Henry a long iron pry bar. All three outlaws clustered around the edge of the hole, causing another avalanche of dirt. Henry hardly noticed. He jammed the slender end of the bar under the crosspiece of the lid and forced it upward. The nails squeaked in defiance but came undone easily.

It occurred to Henry that he didn't know which end of the coffin he was opening. His hole was offset from the true grave and thus only about a third of the box was exposed. If he broke through to find feet, what would he do then? Grab the dead man around the ankles and pull? Henry drove the crowbar between the slats and mentally crossed his fingers.

The center slat snapped and Henry pulled it back, revealing two rows of yellow teeth.

"Jesus," whispered Hugh.

Henry broke off the remainder of the slat and, for the first time since finding the coffin, stopped trying to get into it.

The Hanged Man's lips had curled back to a lifeless grin, but he was otherwise more alive than any dead man ought to be. Thick strands of straw-colored hair fell across an unusually long face, partially obscuring eyes that might open at any moment. Cheeks, while pale and weathered, were not the brittle mask of a decade-old corpse. There was meat between skin and bone, and it was just as fresh as the day he died.

Mason unfolded the newspaper clipping he'd brought from the store. The resemblance was striking.

"Looks like our man."

Henry didn't need to see the picture. He reached out to touch the face he'd seen in his dreams.

"Still soft."

Hugh leaned into the hole to take a closer look. "When did you say this fella died?"

"Eleven years ago last Tuesday."

"How come he ain't a pile of bones?" asked Charlie.

Henry shook his head. "I don't know," he said, unsure if that was the truth.

"Cursed," said Mason. "Like his gun."

"You sure it's him?" Hugh said. "Not just a body like them others we found?"

Henry pushed aside a matted shock of hair to reveal a small black hole in the dead man's forehead.

"Show me his neck," said Mason.

Henry used the crowbar to loosen more of the boards, breaking them off where the box disappeared into the earth. The Hanged Man's head and upper body were now in full view. A tattered leather coat stretched across broad shoulders that filled the coffin side to side. Henry pulled open the collar and undid the top button of an undershirt that had once been white but was now bloodstained for eternity. He spread the fabric wide to reveal a deep rope burn cut into a neck still defined by muscle and tendon.

"It's him," Mason said. "Or another man made his name cheating death."

For a moment, no one said a word. Henry felt an inexplicable urge to leap from the hole and run as fast as he could down the hill. He would run to the river and then jump in and swim until he made it to the other side or his lungs gave out and he drowned. For a moment, this seemed like a very good idea. Charlie reminded him of why it wasn't.

"Where's the gun?"

Henry blinked and then reached inside the dead man's coat. The body was warm. Henry nearly pulled back his hand, but forced himself to feel around before abandoning the search after only a few seconds.

"I can't reach in far enough," he offered as an excuse.

"Pull him out," said Mason.

Henry looked at Mason. "Um, how exactly should I . . ."

Before Henry could finish, Mason jumped into the hole and grabbed the dead man under the armpits. He must have felt the heat coming from the body, because, for just a moment, Henry thought he would let go. Instead, Mason dug deeper and lifted the dead man to a sitting position. He ripped open the jacket to reveal an undershirt marked by numerous bloodstained holes and an empty holster riding high on the waist. Mason reached behind the body, feeling around for an unseen weapon. He came back empty-handed.

"Grab his right arm."

Together they lifted the body from the box and into the hands of Charlie and Hugh. The brothers barely got the dead man out of the hole before dropping him to the ground.

"Jesus, he weighs a ton," Charlie moaned. "Them others weren't so heavy."

Mason brushed the dirt off his clothes and climbed out of the hole. He then turned to offer Henry a hand up—except he didn't.

"Stay there," Mason said. Not taking his eyes off Henry, he said, "Find anything?"

Hugh looked up from the corpse. "Nice pair of boots, but no gun."

Mason smiled at Henry. "Check the box."

Henry got to his knees and reached into the box. There was more dirt, a handful of rocks, and nothing else. Henry ducked his head down, but there wasn't enough light to see anything beyond the opening.

"I can't see all the way in. Guess we dig out some more."

"No need," Mason said. "You climb in, feel around."

Henry thought briefly of protesting, but didn't. It was only an empty box. It wasn't until Henry had twisted his body around the broken lid and was halfway into the darkness on his back that he realized what might happen to him if there was no gun.

"You stuck?" Mason asked.

"No," Henry said. The gun was here, he told himself. It had to be. He'd seen it eleven years ago and he'd seen it in his head the past three days. Henry twisted a little more and slid his slender frame all the way into the coffin. It was tight, but he was shorter than the Hanged Man and so had some room to maneuver.

Henry felt around the space at his sides, finding more dirt and what felt like a piece of torn cloth. He reached forward and found the end of the box was close. His head was less than a foot from the wood, perhaps only six inches. The coffin seemed smaller than it had only moments before, and familiar, as if from a dream.

Henry felt something hit his feet. He raised his head as far as it would go and could just make out his boots in the light. A few clods of dirt fell into the coffin. They were already starting to bury him.

"Mason?"

"Did you find it?"

"No—wait, just wait!"

Henry jabbed his hands above his head—nothing. He felt along the edge to the right corner (empty) and then to the left, where he touched something cold and metal. His fingers closed around the barrel of a pistol and Henry allowed himself to breathe again.

"I found it! Pull me out!"

Henry felt hands grab his ankles and he was yanked backward. When his waist reached the opening, a hand appeared into which Henry shoved the gun. A few more clumps of dirt fell into the box and then the avalanche stopped. Henry pushed forward, awkwardly twisting his body in order to fold himself back around and out of the opening. As he scraped along the bottom of the box he felt something else slide past his arm. Once free of the coffin, he got to his feet and peered over the top of the hole. He could just see Mason and Hugh examining the pistol. They appeared to be having trouble deciding on a target.

Henry ducked back down and reached into the darkness, finding what he was looking for on the first try. It was a small, leatherbound book about six inches tall. It had a strap tied around it and a worn symbol scratched into the front that appeared to be a bird. To Henry it looked like one of the crows that lived in Astoria yearround, although the neck seemed proportionally too long. Henry untied the strap and opened the book to the first page.

Everything changed.

Henry felt safe. He was suddenly free of the fear and worry that had plagued him, from both his reclaimed memories and the uncertainty of the present situation. Warmth flowed through him, filling him with a vitality that was both new and familiar at the same time. This was the feeling that had sustained him throughout the dig, perhaps even pushed him into action.

Henry focused on the page. It was blank. He flipped to the next and found a rough circle drawn around a smaller circle filled in with black ink. Henry touched the small black spot and felt a tingle in his finger.

"Mine."

Henry flipped another page and found handwritten words filling every inch of space on both sides of the spread. He held the book aloft to catch more of the lantern light but found he didn't recognize the words—not all of them. There were English words, and some he thought were French and possibly Spanish, as well as a few he didn't recognize at all. There were more on the next spread and, of course, the next. Henry let the pages flip freely, finding the same dense collection of handwriting on every one.

It was magic.

Henry knew it, as sure as he knew he would read and reread every word in the book until he understood them all.

Henry flipped again, more slowly this time. There were notes, randomly scattered among the pages, scribbled between lines, and in the margins, in a hand different from the rest. Someone else had tried to decipher the language but had not gotten very far.

Henry would do better.

He turned back to the beginning of the book, but the loud crack of a gunshot caused him to clamp the cover shut.

Henry peered out of the hole to see Mason taking aim at a grave marker about thirty feet away. He fired, putting a second chip in the stone. He glanced at Henry, then quickly fired four more shots at his target.

Henry scrambled out of the hole, only to find that Mason had turned the pistol on him.

"What are you doing?"

"What do you think?" Mason said, thumbing back the hammer.

"Wait, don't—"

The hammer snapped into place, but the weapon didn't fire. Startled, Henry took a step back, lost his footing in the loose soil, and slid back into the hole. He landed on his feet and then fell into a sitting position. Mason appeared above him, holding the pistol.

"Wrong color," he said, holding the weapon so Henry could clearly see the dark brown handle.

"That's not his gun," Henry said. "That's not what was buried with him."

"I gathered, which is both good and bad for you. Good in that you didn't just get shot, but bad because as soon as I reload, I'm going to be needing a reason not to try again without the target practice."

"I saw the old man throw the gun into the grave, the red gun!"

Mason looked to his partners. Hugh shrugged. Charlie shook his head.

"I found this in the coffin," Henry said, holding up the book. He hated the idea of giving Mason the book—of the man even *touching* it—but it was his only play.

"What is it?"

"It's a book full of spells, I think, and other things."

Mason finished reloading the pistol, held it for a moment, then shoved it behind his belt.

"Toss it here."

Henry started to throw the book, hesitated, then set it on the edge of the hole at Mason's feet. Mason kept an eye on Henry as he bent to pick it up. He flipped through the pages, stopping every so often to stare at the text.

"What language is this?"

"English. French and Spanish, too, and maybe some others."

Mason looked at Henry and then back at the book. Hugh peered over his shoulder.

"What's with the book?"

"Henry says it's a magic book."

"With curses and such?" Charlie asked.

"Spells," said Henry. "Maybe curses, too." Henry honestly didn't know the difference, but he understood that the book held both. He didn't know why.

Mason tried to read a passage but quickly gave up. He closed the book.

"You can read this?" he said, holding it up.

"Yes," Henry said. "Enough of it."

"Enough for what?"

"Enough to know that book is what made the Hanged Man the most dangerous son of a bitch to ever draw breath."

Mason stared at Henry. From inside the hole, Henry's eyes barely made it to boot level, but Mason was impressed by their intensity. The life he'd seen in the store was even more eager to live now that it had tasted the fear of death. Mason felt proud for giving the young man such an important life experience. Perhaps he would offer him more.

Mason held out a hand, which Henry grasped after a barely noticeable hesitation. Back on equal footing, Henry reached for the book before it was offered. This Mason noticed, but he still gave the man what he wanted.

"Still want to ride with us?"

"Yes," Henry said, clutching the book tightly to his chest.

Mason grinned, put an arm around Henry, and then turned to Charlie and Hugh. "Boys, what do you say? We got room for one more?"

"You got a horse?" asked Hugh.

"I can get one."

Hugh shrugged. "Fine by me."

Charlie didn't care for Mason's sudden show of affection but doubted his opinion would matter one way or another. He smiled, more genuinely than he'd intended.

"Can you cook?"

"No."

"Then you'll fit right in."

"It's settled then." Mason gave Henry a hard slap on the back, then turned his attention to the dead man lying on the ground at their feet.

"Sorry about the gun," Henry said.

"Don't be," Mason said, pulling the pistol from his belt. "It's a nice gun. Worth more than anything back in that shop of yours."

Henry nodded.

"Besides, we got another prize, too."

Henry tightened his grip on the book. "Oh?"

Mason motioned to the Hanged Man.

"Got us a famous dead man," Mason said. "That's worth something, wouldn't you say?"

"I don't know, maybe," said Henry. "But who would you sell it to?"

"The *who* I already know," Mason said. "It's the *how much* I'm interested in."

4

The taste of blood lingered in the creature's mouth, metallic and bitter. This was not the sweet nectar that had sustained it so many nights past. This claret flowed from within, bringing pain and the cold realization that death would come soon.

Beneath the city, away from the men and the stinging light they worshipped, the creature should have been safe. It knew this place, every twist and turn, every sunken alcove and watery passage. From here the creature could stalk its prey, strike quickly, and retreat to feed at its leisure. Any man who dared follow would never see his precious sunshine again.

"William Jacoby!"

The creature hissed as the words bounced off brick and stone, crowding the dark. The name was a lie, a thief of the mind, feeble and small, but always gnawing, biting. Many times the creature had feasted on the weak, but this one—*this name*—would not succumb. A dozen times devoured, but still it persisted.

And now it was given voice.

"Lieutenant Jacoby, I know you are hurt."

The African was strong. Alone in the dark sanctuary of the underground, the man was nearly the creature's equal. But he was not alone. A demon served at his side, quick and vicious. Twice it had bitten and both times the creature could not fight back—could not even see the demon. Hurt and afraid, it had fled.

No more.

The creature longed to feed, to taste fear that was not its own and swallow it like the rest. This man must fear. All men do.

"Please, William, I only wish to help."

Lies! Devious, delicious lies . . .

"Jacoby is gone!"

The voice was wet and ragged. Andre Labeau tilted his head, listening for more. He didn't wait long.

"I swallowed him whole!"

The creature cackled, no doubt hoping to cover the pain in its voice.

Andre dimmed the lantern in his hand and whispered to the darkness beside him, "Tunnel on the left. Hurt, but still dangerous."

A shadow passed through a sliver of light and vanished into the black. Andre followed, moving as silently through the muck as his oversize frame would allow.

It'd been an hour since they followed Lieutenant Jacoby into the foul-smelling labyrinth beneath San Francisco, ten minutes since Andre had tussled with the creature the officer had become. He'd gotten the better of the beast, a murderous fiend responsible for the deaths of five men and seven women. Andre also knew the lieutenant to be a kind and generous man, one who was horrified by the monster he had become. This was why his onetime instructor had asked Andre to do what the man could not.

William Jacoby wanted to die.

Andre had resisted, arguing against such a cure until he could witness the transformation with his own eyes. Two nights ago he had and as a result a child nearly died. Tonight he would fulfill his old friend's wishes.

Heavy, labored breathing came to Andre from the darkness ahead. A chest full of broken ribs might be enough to end the creature, but he would not allow the man trapped inside to suffer such an agonizing death. Andre believed Lieutenant Jacoby to be still alive, buried beneath the rage of his darker half. Each time he succumbed, his mind grew weaker. The physical transformation was traumatic, but it was madness that finally doomed the man.

"I can smell you, dark man."

Andre stopped. The voice was close, barely ten feet ahead of him. There would be no retreat this time.

Andre brought the lantern to life, revealing the creature before him. It was shirtless, pale, and thin, its skin drawn tightly over sinewy muscle and bone. William Jacoby was not a small man, but, transformed, his features were unnaturally long, adding height and length, though not mass. Were it not for the low ceiling, the creature would have stood eight feet at least, its hands dragging on the ground.

The eyes, yellowed from the poison injected into them, protested the light, but soon found Andre. The creature smiled, revealing two rows of tall, bloodied teeth.

"Your friend is dead, voodoo man."

Andre's heart sank. If the creature could call upon the lieutenant's knowledge, it had broken the man. Jacoby was gone.

"Goodbye, William," he said, pushing his words through the mortal veil as he had been taught many years ago. The echo of his voice floated briefly in the air before abruptly vanishing with a *pop*. Andre brought his will to the creature.

"Prepare yourself, demon."

The creature flinched back, its eyes darting about, searching for something in the black.

"You will not see her," Andre said, moving forward. "She is too fast for you."

"Lies!"

Andre lunged at the creature, driving his shoulder into a chest full of broken bones. The beast gasped in pain, but slipped free before being overcome. Andre struck again, this time with fists against the monster's lower back, forcing it upright until its head struck the bricks embedded in the ceiling.

A wild swing knocked Andre back, giving the creature time to find its fighting stance. Rivulets of blood rolled down its cheeks as the beast turned to face the man who would surely kill it.

"All men are afraid," it hissed.

Andre slid sideways, stalking the edge of the light.

"As are you."

The creature lunged, but Andre was ready. He spun to his left, grabbing an outstretched arm and twisting until the creature's shoulder dislocated. The beast howled and lashed out with its good arm, raking its claws across Andre's neck, finally drawing the blood that propelled so much of its desire.

Overwhelmed by the scent, it couldn't resist sliding a finger into its mouth.

"So sweet, so—"

Pain abruptly exploded across the back of the creature's skull. It blinked back the light, trying to stay conscious, knowing the demon would come again. When it did, the creature's right knee gave way, crippled by a foe it could not see or hear. The beast lashed out, flailing at the darkness in all directions.

"Show yourself!"

"I am here."

The creature spun to see a young woman standing before it, a tiny thing, no larger than a child. She stood perfectly still and yet it could not see her clearly. Only her eyes revealed themselves, glowing brightly in the dark, beckoning the beast forward. They would keep it safe.

The creature reached out a bony hand, only to find the vision gone, evaporated, as if it had never been there.

"Don't leave me!" it cried before a pair of massive hands cut off what little air still flowed to the creature's crippled lungs.

Andre drove the beast into the shallow water, pressing both knees into its back. The creature struggled violently, but Andre held fast, letting his weight drown the abomination. In thirty seconds it was over. The creature was dead.

Andre stood over the body, waiting to see if Lieutenant Jacoby would reappear. He was glad when his friend did not.

Andre emerged from the sewer to see the sun setting and a young Indian woman with long black hair waiting for him. Naira offered a hand, which completely disappeared into her partner's when taken.

"You're going to be late," she said.

"Perhaps, but I would rather not arrive at the gala stinking of a bog."

Andre peered into the darkness at his feet. He could just make out a trickle of water running at the base of the tunnel.

"You will see to William?"

Naira nodded.

"Thank you."

Andre stood for a moment, listing to the city exhale after what must have been a very long, deep breath. It was a sound he'd become familiar with over the years, one he never tired of hearing. The healing would begin soon.

In the calm, Andre became aware of something else: a distant pounding, steady, and coming closer. It, too, was familiar, but from where Andre could not recall.

"What is it?" Naira asked.

"I am not sure. Do you not hear that?"

"Hear what?"

Andre raised a hand as the drum beat thrice more—and then it was gone. He waited, but it did not return.

"Well?"

Andre shrugged.

"Echoes, nothing more."

Andre splashed water onto his cheeks and opened his eyes to the mirror. Nothing had changed. He still saw the same fear staring back at him, the same truth.

The damned thing was in this world again.

Andre knew it was true. He should have suspected as much after the first wave struck him in the street, but the thought had never occurred to him. After a third pounding brought him to his knees while speaking to a group of civic leaders in the Palace Hotel's Grand Ballroom, he had been able to think of nothing else. He must have looked a sight, because their initial reaction had been to hail one of the many doctors in attendance, thinking Andre had taken ill. He'd played along for a time, hoping a fever would rise to lay claim to his affliction, but it never came. He would not escape so easily.

Andre used a hotel washcloth to dry his face and then carefully folded and placed it on the small dressing table next to the sink. Once more he took stock of the man hunched over in the mirror. The patches of gray above his ears were nothing new, but he was sure they'd been smaller when last he checked. He tilted his head forward and was pleased to discover no discernible change in the thickness or color of the hair on top of his head. It was a small victory, but he would take it.

Standing up straight, Andre felt each vertebra snap into place as his spine realigned itself. At six feet eight inches tall, he often had to bend at the waist to clear a doorway, duck into a carriage, or descend into the flooded underground. Such height, along with a startlingly muscular frame, had proven useful in certain situations, particularly those involving conflict. After forty-eight years, forty of them above six feet, Andre had participated in few physical altercations, despite his penchant for "rilin' up the locals," as his mother was fond of saying. He'd walked away victorious from every one.

Andre preferred to match his less obvious but perhaps more impressive wits against anyone foolish enough to challenge him intellectually. Though he'd had no formal education—not a surprise given the color of his skin—Andre had learned to read at the age of five, a talent he used to devour every book, paper, and periodical that crossed his path. This included all subjects scientific, mathematical, historical, cultural, and mythological. That there was so much conflict to be found in the interpretation of the written word came as no surprise to Andre. Still, after four decades of bending, Andre was regularly thankful for high ceilings and low expectations.

It was his intellectual pursuits that had initially brought him to San Francisco, specifically his time spent studying and living with the Indian tribes of California, Oregon, and the Washington Territory. Andre was fascinated by the myriad of cultures and customs and had made it his mission to share his findings with a populace largely ignorant of the people he considered the original Americans. Accepting Lieutenant Jacoby's invitation to speak on the effects of Western expansion before the U.S. Pacific Railway Commission had provided just such an opportunity. The lieutenant's true motivations had not become clear until after Andre arrived.

The novelty of a Negro man speaking on behalf of the American Indian was not lost on Andre. He had encountered more than a few freemen living in the West who found it odd that his considerable gifts of persuasion were being put to use for a people who were not his own. Andre rejected such arguments. His cause was to educate, enlighten, and hopefully pass on something about the nature of mankind. That he chose to stand up for another race of people reinforced the fact that a dark-skinned man could be on equal footing with other scholars.

Andre's prior pursuits, those that had dominated three-quarters of his life, rarely came up now in casual conversation.

Andre exited the washroom, ignoring the unpacked trunk beside the door. The preceding day's edition of the *San Francisco Examiner* lay on the bed, the front page dominated by the latest "sewer beast" sightings. A few pages in was an article about the expansion hearings that described a "giant redwood of a man with bark as black as night." The story also made reference to Andre's "eloquent and educated articulation," as well as the nickname first bestowed upon him by Chief Joseph of the Nez Percé Indians, the Voodoo Cowboy. It was silly, but Andre rather liked it, even if it wasn't particularly accurate.

Was it ever? Andre thought not. There wasn't an ounce of voodoo in him and there never had been—he believed that. Unfortunately, a few more of his mother's words chose that moment to refresh his memory:

"Go on an' tell yo'self whatever you needs," she'd said. "Gawd, he know inna end."

Andre had his suspicions about God, but his mother was rarely off target. What did his intentions matter if the end result was the unleashing of so much evil? He'd wrestled with this line of thinking before and, as a result, had sacrificed much of who he'd been to make amends. On his darkest days, he knew his best efforts would never be enough. How could they?

Andre slapped his hands to his face sharply, breaking the spell before it could steal another moment. He was shocked by the strength of it, the bleakness, and how quickly it had filled him with despair. It wasn't a true spell, not by half, but rather the memory of the thing calling to him from across a great distance. It had been so long and yet it felt as if it was in the room with him.

That would at least make the damned thing easier to find.

Andre decided to pack, regardless of how he felt. He'd barely unlatched the trunk when the door to the suite opened. Naira strode into the room and stopped in front of him. Both her wide-brimmed hat and worn leather coat were damp, though not overly so. At first glance, she looked more like a teenage boy than the twenty-one-year-old woman Andre knew her to be. He thought it might be the pants.

"Did you find passage?"

Naira nodded. "Seven A.M., pier seventeen."

"Good."

Andre turned back to his trunk. Naira stood her ground, never taking her eyes off the much larger man.

"No trouble with the arrangements, I assume."

"None."

Andre smiled. There wouldn't have been any trouble, of course. In their seven years together, Naira had never failed a task he'd given her, regardless of the situation. She had a way about her that simply put folks at ease. It was her eyes. They were larger than any Andre had ever seen, and when a man looked into them, he couldn't help but feel comfortable, trusting. It wasn't magic but rather a kind of ocular hypnosis that Naira claimed was a common trait among her people.

Andre had long ago learned there was more to see in Naira than what her eyes revealed, but to him she'd offered the information freely. He had been decidedly slower in sharing his secrets in return.

"I am fine," he said, folding a shirt and placing it in his trunk.

Naira sat on the edge of the bed, hands clasped in her lap. She said nothing.

"You can sit there and stare at me as long as you want, but there is nothing wrong with me."

"Can you still feel it?"

Andre didn't answer right away. He slid open the bottom drawer of the armoire to retrieve a pair of neatly folded shirts. When he turned back to the trunk, Naira leaned in, making her stare even more obvious.

"Yes, I can still feel it. It will not go away, not by itself."

Naira leaned back on the bed and pulled off her hat. A wave of long, black hair rolled down her back, making it much harder to mistake her for a boy.

"I don't like it," she said.

"Neither do I, but would you have me ignore it?"

"I didn't say that."

"Nor should you think it," Andre said, flipping the trunk lid closed. "I know you were not with me then—I am thankful for that—but this is not a trivial matter."

"I know."

Andre sat on the bed next to Naira. She was beautiful, a fact he'd been keenly aware of since the day he'd found her lying unconscious in a creek bed on the north side of Mount Rainier. Now, as then, his first instinct was to take care of her, to protect her. There was love between them, but it was that of a father and daughter and nothing more.

Naira felt the same, although she might have disagreed as to who was head of the family.

"I do not know why it has resurfaced," Andre said. "I do not know how. I was very careful to bury it deep, not only in the earth, but the mind as well. If that mind is lost, then so too should the book be."

"But it's not."

Andre nodded. "Of that I am certain."

"Has it been read?"

"I think not," Andre said, hoping this was true. "But it will be soon enough. This is a book that wants to be read, after all. Whether or not it is understood—this is where our good fortune will live or die."

"You speak of it as if it were alive."

Andre lifted the trunk onto the bed. It was heavy, though not for him.

"Not alive," he said. "But it does derive its power from the living. Without a soul to turn the page, it is but ink on paper."

Andre could tell that Naira had more questions, but he wasn't ready to answer them. He barely had time to process the memories that resurfaced along with feelings about the book. Trying to explain his actions, even to his friend, would be difficult. Fortunately, Naira knew enough of the story not to press Andre for more when he wasn't ready to tell it.

Andre peered out the window.

"Is it still raining?"

"Waning," Naira said, twisting her hair into a bun. She tucked it beneath her hat and got to her feet. "The sun will be shining by the time we leave port."

"Then there is no reason to wait. I would prefer to be onboard before any other passengers arrive."

Andre retrieved a worn duster from a coat rack by the door. Despite the custom cut, the jacket barely reached his knees. He snatched up his trunk and a wide-brimmed Stetson from the rack and turned to Naira.

"Shall we?"

Naira looked Andre up and down.

"You wear your fear well," she said.

"Always have."

The fast steamer *Año Nuevo* left San Francisco en route to Portland at 7:17 A.M. on Thursday, May 19, 1887. According to the Oregon Steamship Company, which owned and operated the line out of San Francisco, the journey would take between forty-eight and fifty-six hours, depending on sailing conditions. The trip was intended to be nonstop to Portland, but soon after leaving port the captain announced the ship would make an unscheduled stop in Astoria. No reason was given.

5

The marshal sat on the edge of his new bed, fully dressed but not yet ready to join the family for breakfast. In his lap was the empty but suspiciously heavy, wooden box with a rose carved into the lid. The belt he'd used to secure it for the journey to Portland was once again around the old man's waist. It was the only belt he'd brought and the marshal needed it to keep his pants from falling down. He had reminded himself of this twice already.

In the morning light, the marshal could pick out the faint orange and yellow coloring of the rose. The paint was mostly gone now, but the artistry in the carving was still apparent. The strokes were smooth and well defined, cut into the wood by hands that knew how to use a knife. Once upon a time, he'd been good at something besides chasing outlaws.

"Don't open it," he said, just to hear the words aloud.

The marshal hesitated, then opened the lid anyway. The box was still empty. He felt around for the sweet spot and then released the hidden pressure latch with a single deft touch. Carefully, he lifted the false lid out of the box to reveal an additional three inches of space. The compartment was separated into five sections, the largest of which took up the top half and bottom right third of the box.

Four of the cells held individual items: a small, oblong flask, a U-shaped wrench, a press mold, and a two-inch bar of solid lead. Tucked tightly into the largest subdivision was an object wrapped in cloth. The shape was unmistakable.

The marshal lifted the Hanged Man's pistol from the box and unfolded the cloth, letting it fall around his hand so as not to touch the object within. This he hadn't forgotten.

In his thirty-plus years as a lawman, Jim Kleberg had encountered more ways to kill a man than he cared to remember, but few things did the job more definitively than a Colt Walker pistol. Designed for the Texas Rangers in 1847, the Walker was powerful enough to bring down a horse from a hundred yards. No revolver before—or since—had been forged to deliver such firepower, a fact the marshal took some comfort in. Only God should be allowed to carry so much deadly force in one hand.

The marshal tested the gun's weight. He guessed five pounds, more than double that of a typical revolver. The length was equally absurd, with the barrel, a gleaming black tube of hardened steel, accounting for two-thirds of the almost foot-and-a-half total. The cylinder, hammer, and loading lever were scorched, rendering them nearly as black as the barrel, and even the trigger guard held little of its original brass luster.

Only the plow-shaped handle displayed any color, though undoubtedly it was not the original factory finish. According to numerous stories, the handle's red hue was painted with the blood of the Hanged Man's victims. The marshal thought the crimson grip was more likely the result of a few coats of cherrywood stain. Dried blood would have produced a much darker, almost brown tone.

In addition to the color, there were other modifications not mentioned in any of the legends. Some changes were practical, such as the small latch attached to the underside of the barrel's muzzle to hold the loading lever in place. Others, like the strange symbols etched into the cylinder, served no obvious purpose, at least none the marshal could see.

"This ain't no Colt," he whispered, hoping the sound of his own voice would dispel the unease in his chest. "Not anymore."

The Walker itself was a rarity. Samuel Colt had made only a few thousand, before moving on to more successful designs. The hidden compartment in the rose box had originally been built to hold the marshal's Colt Navy, a smaller but much more practical weapon than the Walker. The marshal had used the gun for nearly twenty years, even after the cartridge revolution made cap-and-ball revolvers relics of the past. As far as the marshal was concerned, modern six-shooters, with their swing-out cylinders, speed loaders, and double-action triggers, were the chief reason why unnecessary gunplay had become so prevalent in the West. Any idiot could shoot a so-called Peacemaker, but it took a professional to properly prime, load, and fire a percussion revolver.

Despite a few newspaper reports that suggested otherwise, the marshal had only once needed to reload his weapon immediately after emptying all six chambers. That was during the altercation in Astoria, and even then he'd been supported by three dozen men. He'd had plenty of time to reload.

There had already been so much shooting that day. By the time the marshal found himself on the hill, alone (was he?) it was after midnight. He would bury the dead man—

"He wasn't dead," said the marshal. "Not yet. Not until . . ."

He shot the bastard with his gun—*this* gun. That was how the weapon ended up in the marshal's hand, how it came to be in his possession. He needed it to finish the job. There wouldn't be time to reload, and this weapon—

"Never needs reloading."

The marshal blinked and was shocked to find the Hanged Man's pistol sitting comfortably in his right hand. When had he taken it from the left? Why was his finger on the trigger? The gun felt heavy, but without the cloth barrier between the weapon and his skin, it somehow felt better, right.

"Safe."

That was why he'd kept the gun eleven years ago. It was the right thing to do—*the safe thing*. It would have been too dangerous to leave such a weapon out in the open, so he had taken it, and replaced it with his own.

Why had he buried his own gun?

Before the marshal could come up with a suitable answer, he noticed that the empty cloth in his left hand wasn't actually empty. A tiny, conical object lay in the middle of the wrap—a bullet. That made sense; there'd been only one round left in the gun after he'd fired it eleven years ago. One round was all it took.

The marshal examined the bullet more closely. There were flecks of orange crystal in the lead, most likely the result of mixing black powder with firestone, a tactic some shootists claimed produced a bigger bang. It was the marshal's experience that mixing orange and black usually resulted in a ruptured cylinder and the loss of several fingers.

Despite the scorching on the body of the gun, there was no evidence the Hanged Man's revolver had ever disobeyed its master.

The marshal dropped the bullet into the small compartment with the lead already in it, and then laid the cloth in the larger space. He considered setting the pistol back in the box, then decided to hold on to the Hanged Man's weapon awhile longer.

"Mine, now."

Kate's hand froze an inch from the bedroom door. Had she just heard a voice? She allowed herself a moment of worry before deciding that talking to himself probably wasn't the worst thing her father could be doing. She knocked.

"Breakfast is on."

Kate heard a few muffled noises followed by the sound of something solid hitting the floor.

"Dad!"

Kate opened the door to see the marshal on his knees in front of his bed, holding a wooden box.

"Are you all right?"

"Yes, yes. I'm fine."

Kate went to her father to help him up. She reached for his hand but got only an elbow. The marshal kept both hands on the box.

"I just dropped this. Clumsy is all."

Kate looked at the box. She recognized it immediately.

"I didn't know you still had that."

Kate ran a hand across the surface of the box, suddenly recalling a time when she was eight years old and wanted nothing more than to play in her mother's room.

"I was going to surprise you," the marshal said.

Kate let her hand linger a little too long near the lip of the box. She was about to open it when the marshal took a step back.

"I thought I'd give it a new coat of paint."

"Oh. All right."

Kate considered asking why the marshal wanted to keep the contents of the box to himself, but bit her tongue. She'd promised not to pry any more than was necessary, and since Joseph had already gotten much more out of him than they'd expected, this was not necessary. When her father was ready to share more, he would. If he needed to keep some secrets, that was fine with Kate. For now.

Kate walked to the window and pushed the curtains open. Downtown Portland spread out below the house, its waterlogged streets gleaming in the early-morning sun.

"How do you like the view?"

"Too many buildings."

"Well, it looks like another beautiful day. Not a cloud in the sky."

"Your mayor will be disappointed."

Kate laughed. "Yes, I suppose he will."

"Odd bird, is he?"

"He's a politician."

Satisfied that the box was buried deep enough in the closet, the marshal turned back to his daughter.

"I've known my fair share of politicians. They weren't all cheats and liars—most were, of course—but not all of 'em."

"Jim Gates isn't a bad man."

"Doesn't have to be. Might be the guy standing next to him is dirty, or the fella behind him. Don't usually have to dig too far to find someone wants that kind of power for the wrong reasons."

Joseph had mentioned the marshal's interest in their investigations, but until now her father hadn't broached the subject with Kate. She'd spent so much time worrying about what kind of a burden he was going to be, it had never occurred to her that her father might be an asset when it came to the family business.

"If you want to know more about the investigation, just ask."

"I'm not lookin' to stick my nose in where it's not welcome. I'm just saying be careful, is all."

"I'm not stepping in front of the trolley, Dad. It's only an investigation. And it's done, or nearly so. Joseph's going to finish things up this morning. You don't need to worry about it."

"I'm your father. The hell else am I supposed to do?"

"How about eat some breakfast?"

"I could do that."

Breakfast was buttermilk biscuits, sausage, coffee, and a bowl of blackberries picked from a bush growing outside the kitchen window. The coffee was lukewarm but otherwise it was the best meal the marshal had eaten in months. Having slept through the morning's offerings the day before, the marshal made a promise to himself never to do that again.

"Blackberries are sure good."

"They grow like weeds around here," said Kate. "And these are early this year. You'll be sick of them in another month."

"I doubt that."

The marshal popped another berry into his mouth as Kate cleared his plate from the table. His was the only setting left, as the rest of the family had already eaten and gone about readying themselves for the day.

Kate finished rinsing the plate in the sink and put it on the drying rack on the counter. In addition to running water, the kitchen had a gas stove and an electric icebox, one of the first of its kind in Portland. Joseph found the technology fascinating, but had suggested such a device might not be a worthwhile investment given the temperate climate. Kate was confident that come summer, the first glass of iced lemonade that found its way into her husband's hand would help him see the light.

Kate offered the last of the berries to the marshal, which he snatched from the bowl with violet-stained fingertips.

"Don't worry," she said. "There'll be more tomorrow."

The marshal tossed the last berry into his mouth just as Joseph came into the kitchen. He was wearing a loose-fitting brown coat with short lapels and rounded hems over a vest and trousers. All three garments were made of the same dark, checked material, which made for a clean but casual look.

The marshal stared at Joseph.

"Think your tailor forgot to cut the arms off your waistcoat, son."

Joseph fastened the top button of the coat, leaving the others undone.

"You don't like the style?"

"Busy, don't you think?"

Kate grabbed her father's berry-stained hand before it could feel the hem of Joseph's coat. She passed him the damp cloth in her hand and then turned to admire Joseph.

"It's a sack suit," she said. "And it's supposed to be more casual. Men living in Portland don't feel the need to take themselves so seriously, thus they're allowed to dress more comfortably."

The marshal nodded. "It does look like a couple of burlap sacks sewn together. How much you pay for wares like that?"

"Thirty-eight dollars," said Joseph.

The marshal coughed loudly, but Kate shot her father a look before he could say a word.

For Joseph, the silence was proof that the family dynamic was not going to change as much as they had feared.

Ten minutes later, Joseph walked out the front door of the house his neighbors had affectionately nicknamed the Pumpkin Palace. It was by no means a palace, certainly not when compared to some of the Gothic behemoths in the Portland Heights, but its steeply pitched gabled roof, decorative spindlework, and solitary location atop the southwestern slope gave it an attractive profile. The fact that it was predominantly orange with green and black trim also made it look somewhat like a giant, Victorian pumpkin.

The view from almost any spot on the property was spectacular. A covered porch ran the length of the house on two sides, framing a panorama of the entire Willamette Valley. Joseph's "view" was just as spectacular due to the countless hours he'd spent absorbing every detail Portland and the surrounding valley had to offer. When he turned to face the city, every building, block, and back alley was at his disposal, stored as part of a mental map that constantly updated as Joseph's senses collected new information.

Joseph breathed deeply. The air was dry and unseasonably warm. The smell of fetid water drifted on the breeze, threatening to overcome the pleasant combination of barley and hops that greeted him on most mornings, courtesy of City Brewery. If the temperature reached eighty degrees, as Joseph thought it might, downtown would become unbearable for those with an average sense of smell.

Joseph turned back to the house.

"Kick, Maddie, let's go!"

A moment later, Kick burst through the front door and slid to a stop before his father.

"Are we taking the trolley?"

"I thought we'd rough it today," Joseph said, motioning to a winding wooden staircase that descended 211 steps from beside their home to Montgomery Street at the bottom of the hill.

A cable railway had recently been built one ridge over in an attempt to attract more home builders to the Portland Heights. At little more than a quarter mile, the line didn't cover much distance, but the altitude adjustment made it a worthwhile ride for those on their way up the slope.

"Can we ride it later, on the way home?"

"Maybe."

Kick smiled and sailed down the path toward the staircase.

"Wait up," Maddie yelled, rushing past her father.

"Thought you might want this," Kate said, placing a black bowler hat on her husband's head.

"Thank you."

"Are you sure you don't want me there?"

"It'll be fine, Kate."

"Another set of eyes might not hurt. No one will even know I'm about, unless there's trouble."

"I don't expect any trouble."

"And when has that ever made a difference? Remember Oregon City? If I hadn't been with you, the situation would *not* have turned out fine."

"This isn't Oregon City. This is downtown in the middle of the day."

"Morning," Kate corrected.

"Even better," Joseph said. "And this is the mayor's office, not a gang of road agents. I think I can handle a rogue civil servant, should one decide to show up."

Kate nodded but said nothing.

"I'll be fine," Joseph said, and kissed his wife softly on the forehead. "Trust me."

Kate stared at Joseph. She knew he could read the emotions on her face without seeing them, so she didn't bother to vocalize her displeasure.

"I'll come by later this morning," she said finally. "To make sure you were right."

"Bring the marshal," Joseph said, starting down the porch steps. "I'm sure he'd like to see the store."

Joseph hurried across the yard. He stopped to wave at the top of the staircase, then took off after the kids, who were already near the bottom.

The marshal watched Joseph descend the staircase from the second-floor window of his bedroom. He didn't like the look of the stairs, but guessed he would be following in his son-in-law's footsteps soon enough. Kate had mentioned something about showing him around the city, which the marshal took to mean walking. He suspected there might be some wading involved, as well. He hoped there would be no shopping for new suits.

When Joseph was out of sight, the marshal had an idea to check his wardrobe for suitable attire—something to placate his daughter's need to play "dress up Dad." He had brought most of his clothes from Astoria and thought there must be something that would look good to her eyes.

The marshal opened the closet and was shocked to see the wooden box open, its hidden compartment exposed. The main space was empty.

The marshal was not surprised to see the Hanged Man's gun already in his hand.

6

The first thing Henry saw was the dead man's journal in his hand. It was open to a slightly torn page covered with dense scribbling. He tried to read the words, but few made sense in the morning light.

Henry raised his face to the sun, trying to remember how he'd come to be standing alone in the middle of a small forest clearing. He shouldn't be. He'd ridden out of Astoria with three men . . . and something else.

Had the dead man led him here?

Henry scanned the page again, sensing that the words had made sense at another time, perhaps to another person. Could that have been him? He searched for meaning in the black swirls and found nothing.

"Chicken scratches," he said to no one.

Henry surveyed his surroundings. He was on a long, sloping hill covered by white and yellow wildflowers. He heard waves crashing behind him, suggesting the ocean was near enough that he should see it through the trees. He couldn't, but closer inspection revealed a path worn through the flowers that ended at his feet.

Henry snapped the book closed and walked into the forest, fol-lowing the trail he must have made in the night. That he couldn't remember such misadventure suggested he'd been asleep at the time, which was troubling, but an improvement over the nightmares of earlier in the week.

The path was clear enough, though the forest itself was denser than any Henry had previously encountered. The trees grew unnaturally close, blocking more and more of the light the farther he progressed. He still heard the ocean, though it grew fainter with each step.

Shouldn't he be moving toward it?

When the woods abruptly ended, Henry was shocked to find himself standing on the beach, ten feet from the crashing surf. He spun to see the forest's edge a hundred feet behind him. The book was again open in his hand.

Henry stared at the page, at words just out of focus, which was how he saw footprints in the sand—his and another's, side by side, walking from the woods to the water's edge.

He was not alone.

Henry felt the dead man beside him but refused to turn. To look upon the man would make him real, something Henry desperately did not want to be true. A hand fell on his shoulder, and a cold whisper brought a single word:

"Read."

Henry ran.

Halfway to the trees, he saw a thin line of gray smoke rising behind a pile of driftwood. Henry stumbled into the campsite to find his companions dead, their corpses piled on top of one another beside a smoldering fire. Gnawing at the remains were three monsters Henry recognized immediately. Buried with the Hanged Man, they were now damned to follow him, feeding on the unlucky souls that crossed his path.

Only that wasn't true. They hadn't been buried with the man but had clawed their way to him through mud and death—had been commanded to do so. When they raised their heads in unison, the gore in their mouths hanging slack, Henry knew they would follow him, too.

He was their master, now.

"Where you been?"

Henry blinked and Mason materialized before him, looking much more alive than he had moments before.

Henry blinked once more and saw the burlap-wrapped body propped up against a log, a poorly tied noose fastened around the neck.

"Couldn't sleep," Henry said, tucking the book into his coat pocket. He recognized the nightmare for what it was, but saw no reason to share.

"Miss your bed, do yeh?"

"Been a while since I slept out of doors is all."

Mason grinned. "Wait 'til it rains," he said, and walked away, carefully stepping over the Hanged Man's body.

Henry glanced at the dead man but refused to linger, forcing himself to look elsewhere. Just offshore, a huge, haystack-shaped rock sprouted from the Pacific, a monument he knew to be less than thirty miles south of Astoria. Henry had assumed they'd ridden a hundred miles the night before, but they weren't even out of the county.

Was that far enough?

Henry considered his crimes: assisting in a holdup, horse thievery, grave robbing. Technically, he hadn't participated in the holdup. If anything, he'd minimized Asa's losses to a few shovels and one employee. The owner of the horses he'd liberated from the livery might have a legitimate complaint, but Henry thought they'd done the deed without witnesses. He'd even protested stealing the second horse until Mason made clear who would be riding in the extra saddle.

As for the body, Henry didn't think it was a crime to dig it up if no one knew it was there.

Henry finally allowed his gaze to fall on the Hanged Man's corpse. Twenty feet of rope kept the burlap in place, which to Henry look like a caterpillar's cocoon. Hugh had fashioned the noose, which his brother found quite amusing. Henry had not.

Henry took a step toward the body, intending to remove the false collar, but the pain between his legs stopped him cold.

"Not used to the saddle, huh?" said Charlie.

Henry staggered to a nearby log but found little comfort in sitting.

"Just wait. Another day and you'll be slung over the horn like your buddy there."

"I'll be fine," Henry said.

Charlie frowned. "Can't figure why he brought you along. Don't see the worth in it."

Henry looked at Charlie. He couldn't remember anything he'd said or done to earn the animosity in the man's tone.

"I'll try to prove my worth."

"You do that."

Henry stared for a moment longer, then put a hand in his pocket and immediately felt the hair on the back of his neck go down. Soon the throb in his groin subsided as well.

Henry gathered his bedroll and tied it to the back of a saddle they'd stolen along with the horses. Besides the clothes he wore, Henry hadn't brought much from Astoria. Mason had allowed him to retrieve his hat, coat, and anything else that would fit in a saddle bag, which was very little. Henry didn't care. Standing in his room in

Asa's house, he couldn't find a single item worth taking. The only thing that seemed important was that which he'd dug out of the ground earlier in the day. It was only on his way out of the house that he thought to pilfer one of the fat man's rifles. The gun, which Henry had never fired and didn't even know how to load, was now secured to the saddle beneath his bedroll.

"You know how to use that?" Mason asked, eyeing the rifle.

"Yes."

Mason tugged on the stock, pulling the Winchester partly from its slot.

"Hardly been used."

"Asa wasn't much of a shootist."

Mason slid the rifle back into place and motioned for Henry to follow him.

"Grab a shoulder," he said, leaning over the Hanged Man's cocoon.

Henry grabbed a handful of burlap and together they dragged the corpse to the extra gelding. Mason then took the loose rope attached to the body's center mass and threw it over the saddle.

"After he's up, go around and pull him over."

Henry hadn't been involved in mounting the Hanged Man's body the night before and was shocked by the weight of it. Lifting the corpse to a standing position was difficult, even for the two of them, and had it been Henry left to hold it up right he'd have crumpled to the ground. He raced around the horse, grabbed the rope, and pulled as Mason lifted. Slowly, the body rolled over the saddle until it hung freely, more or less balanced. The horse shuffled its feet, obviously not pleased at the rider forced upon him.

"Doesn't seem too happy, does he?" Mason said, as he secured the ropes underneath the saddle. "Can't hardly blame him. Son of a bitch is heavy for a dead man."

"Yes," Henry said, though he was doubtful weight had anything to do with the animal's discomfort. "How far do we have to ride today?"

"Far enough. Why? You tired from all that late-night reading?"

Henry blinked.

"What?"

"I saw you. Had your nose in that book all night. You must have some mighty good vision to see so well in the dark. You part Indian, or something?"

Henry searched his memory but found nothing to support Mason's claim outside of his early-morning jaunt. He'd been dead tired when they'd stopped the night before, and after forcing a hunk of jerky down his throat he had gone to sleep.

"I don't know what you're talking about."

"He's right," Charlie said. "I saw you when I got up to take a leak. Heard you, too, mumbling a bunch of nonsense words."

"Find me a curse in there that keeps my gun loaded, and you can mutter all you want," Mason said, as he pulled himself onto his horse.

Henry forced a smile and then climbed onto his own mount.

"You didn't answer my question," he said. "How far are we riding?"

"Well, that all depends on how popular the circus is in Tillamook," Mason said, urging his horse forward.

"The circus?"

"Garibaldi's Traveling Wild Western Caravan, Museum and Menagerie," said Hugh, as he directed his horse around Henry's. "We passed 'em a week ago headin' the other way. Said they was going to set up in Tillamook for a time."

Henry's horse stepped sideways as the horse trailing Hugh's moved past, giving it as wide a birth as possible. Henry, not being the most accomplished rider, did his best to turn the animal around.

"Why do we care about some traveling circus?"

"They got a tent full of human curiosities," Charlie said. "Freaks and such."

Henry turned the information over in his head, finally coming to the only conclusion that made any sense. He urged his horse forward until he was alongside Mason's.

"We're selling him to a freak show?"

"'Weird Wild West Prodigies and Oddities' is what they call it," Mason said. "Got a Fiji mermaid, couple of Borneo midgets, Siamese twins, pig with one eye—that sort of thing. Seems to me they ain't got enough West in their Wild, so maybe the remains of a famous outlaw might fill out the quota."

"But he's dead."

"Don't matter. They got shrunken heads and Indian scalps, too. If they don't want to display the whole body they can put the head on a pedestal and be done with it. Of course, they gotta buy the whole man. I ain't sellin' him by the pound."

At the top of the hill, Mason turned his mount south, sticking to a ridge that ran along the coastline. Henry tried to keep pace.

"I would think there'd be laws against displaying the dead in such a manner."

Mason sniffed. "Where you been livin', kid?"

"Astoria. All my life."

"It shows. Ever seen a hanging?"

"No."

"I seen a couple. Saw one last year, in Butte."

"Dawson brothers," offered Hugh.

"That's right," Mason said. "Got themselves caught trying to ambush a stage. Killed a little girl in the process. Gut shot. Took her three days to die. Time they got around to the hanging, they're must have been a thousand folks showed up looking for a piece.

After the hanging, the townsfolk pulled down the bodies, lit a fire, and watched the pair burn to bone. They left the blackened bodies to rot in the street for a month before someone cleaned 'em up.

"Now, this Hanged Dude here, he's a piece of history. He's famous, like Jesse James or old Wild Bill, maybe more so. But unlike them, this one's an evil bastard. Nobody shed a tear over his passing or made up adventures he never had just to sell penny stories. He's just like them fools in Butte. Folks hated him. I don't imagine anyone will mind his remains up on display."

"But they'll actually want to see him? They'll pay?"

"Hell yes. A famous name, outlaw or otherwise, still draws a crowd. Always has, always will."

Henry tried to imagine such a display but found the idea of a public viewing repulsive.

"He doesn't have one," he said.

Mason eyed Henry. "Doesn't have what?"

"A name. Not a Christian one, at least."

Charlie frowned. "A man with no name? That's bull. Every man has a name."

"Apparently not," Hugh said.

"Well, how'd he get the one he got?"

"What do you think that scar on his neck come from?" Mason said. "Figure he did that himself?"

"Pa told us he was hung twice," Hugh said. "And he come back from the gallows both times."

"Pa said he was rescued," Charlie added.

"No, Charlie, what he said was 'resurrected,' but I wouldn't put much stock in that, 'less you think the dead can rise from the grave."

"I don't, which is why I said 'rescued.'"

Hugh gave his brother a stern look, but Charlie didn't notice. He was waiting for Henry to jump back into the conversation. He planned to trip him up when he did.

"It was supposed to scare folks," Henry said. "He invented it himself to make people believe he could cheat death."

The sureness in his voice gave Charlie pause. Mason noticed it, as well.

"You don't think the scar on his neck is proof enough he fell off the hanging tree?" Mason asked.

A memory that was not his own opened into Henry's mind, that of a man—the Hanged Man—strung up and swaying from a gallows pole in the center of an unknown mountain town. A dozen men stood by, some holding torches that threw just enough light to illuminate the scene. A stiff wind cut through the gathering, scattering the light momentarily. When it returned, the noose was empty.

And then he was on them.

Henry removed his hand from his pocket and the sharpness of the memory faded.

"It's proof of something," he said. "Maybe that some folks don't know a noose from a necktie."

Mason laughed. Charlie saw Hugh crack a smile and felt his place in the gang slip a little further beyond his grip.

7

———◆———

Joseph's daily journey from the heights to the family bookstore on Alder Street included walking and streetcar riding, the amount of each dependent on the route and how well he timed his hop-ons. On a good day, the trip might take twenty minutes. Because the floods had grounded so many of the streetcars, today's excursion would require walking, wading, jumping, precarious sidewalk balancing, and, if he was lucky, a ride up Third Avenue on the fire brigade's floating water-cannon apparatus. His best time since the big melt: forty-eight minutes. Since he had the twins with him, Joseph figured it would take an hour to navigate Portland's downtown waterworks.

Thus far, they'd made good time. Montgomery was clear all the way to Fifth Avenue, and the sidewalks were mostly dry from there to Third. The fire barge had already passed, however, which meant a twelve-block hike up Third Avenue, navigating two to three feet of water, semisubmerged sidewalks, and increased local congestion.

Thanks to Joseph's unique sense of place, he was better able to navigate unpredictable downtown conditions than most locals were. In ten years of living in the city, he'd walked every street, avenue, and road on both sides of the river and knew which had the best drainage and the highest sidewalks. Half the foot traffic in his store at this time of year consisted of people looking for directions, which Joseph gave away for free.

Half a block from Third, the trio came upon an alley where the scaffolding bridging the gap between sidewalks had collapsed. Rather than search for a way around, Joseph grabbed Maddie and ferried her across the knee-deep water. Kick didn't wait for a ride.

"I would have carried you," Joseph said, lifting his son onto the sidewalk.

"I got my waders on," Kick said, and proceeded to dump the liquid contents of each boot back into the flooded street. He then slipped the not-quite-knee-high waders back on without further explanation.

The twins were due to spend the day organizing a shipment of new books that had arrived earlier in the week. They'd helped more and more each year, and this summer Joseph was planning to put them to work full-time cataloging the many books, periodicals, maps, and navigation charts that had yet to be properly sorted. Joseph would have done the job himself, but even his remarkable sight had its limitations. Years of practice had trained the touch receptors on the tips of his fingers to pick up most of the subtle raised shapes created when ink was applied to paper, but the kids' eyes could simply process the information faster.

That a store selling books would need more than a single employee to ring up the occasional sale might have come as a surprise to those in other parts of the country, but not here. Portland was a town in love with the written word. There were seven booksellers within the city limits and all of them did a brisk business. Joseph's shop had been successful, practically from day one, and as such had always carried additional inventory to feed the voracious reading habits of the locals. Even when shipments were late, Wylde's had new titles available, thanks to Kate's insistence that they accept the customer's own books in trade, rather than require currency for every purchase. The general rule was two for one, depending on the condition of the used volumes and the cost of the new text. The result was shelves overflowing with books, many of which were out of print or otherwise unavailable locally.

It was ten past nine by the time the trio reached Alder Street, just under an hour since leaving the house. Joseph was pleased.

"Lot of folks out this morning," Maddie said.

Alder crossed Third Avenue in the heart of the downtown business district and only a few blocks from the waterfront. On every day but Sunday it was crowded with tradesmen, merchants, shoppers, and travelers. The seasonal widening of the Willamette may have slowed the pace, but with local floodwaters at an average depth of only two and a half feet, the deluge was manageable. Much of the business to be done on First and Front Streets had simply relocated a few blocks west, to where horse-drawn carts could still gain passage. Some of the storefronts on Third had actually seen an increase in sales, while others found new opportunities setting up floating markets and other waterproof enterprises.

Wylde's, Booksellers and Navigation was two doors off the main thoroughfare, but a well-placed sign made it easily visible to anyone walking (or wading) past.

Joseph put a hand on his son's shoulder, redirecting him away from open water.

"Kick, I want you to make it across to the store without filling up your boots, okay?"

"I wasn't gonna dive in. There's a boat coming."

Joseph caught the unmistakable odor of cigars and sweat just before the small canoe bumped into the plank sidewalk.

"Good morning, Ted."

"And to you, my young friend," said the owner of the T. Williamson Tobacco Company. Joseph doubted Ted Williamson was more than five years older than himself, but something had aged the man beyond the forty winters he'd counted. He coughed as frequently as some of the yellow-eyed miners and smelled almost as bad, although Joseph wondered if his own heightened sense of smell was exaggerating the man's offenses. He was certainly pleasant enough.

"Care for a lift?"

Joseph and the kids climbed into the boat for the short journey across Alder Street. Ted handed an oar each to Kick and Maddie.

"She wobbles a bit, so try to keep her on an even keel."

The kids put both oars in the water and were in sync immediately. Ted had a moment to be impressed before a coughing jag overtook him.

"All right there, Ted?" Joseph asked.

Ted waved off the concern but continued coughing. Upon reaching the other side, he stumbled out of the boat, barely keeping himself upright. He turned to offer a hand to the kids, but both hopped onto the boardwalk before Ted had raised himself upright. Joseph exited last, tying off the boat at a lamppost between the bookstore and Ted's tobacco shop.

"Come on," Joseph said, resting a hand on Ted's shoulder. "Let's get you a glass of water."

Ted nodded and followed Joseph into his store.

Gaining entrance to most businesses in the flooded areas required a step down from the raised sidewalk, usually over some kind of sandbag barricade. Wylde's required a step up to the front door due to an architect who had designed the building immediately following an inundation, a fact Joseph was thankful for every spring.

Inside the shop, sixteen-foot shelves lined both sides of the main room, the highest books on each accessible only by a rolling ladder attached to a railing near the top. The main floor featured nine double-sided bookshelves spread out around three sides of a curved central counter that faced the main entrance. The floor itself was long, not wide, with the back third closed off for storage on the first floor. A wrought-iron staircase wound its way to a second-floor loft, where more books filled even more shelves.

Ted was only a few feet inside the door when Maddie approached him with a glass of water.

"Here you are, Mr. Williamson."

Ted drank deeply, regaining a little color as he drained the glass.

"Thank you, dear. All this moisture about, but Doc Barnes says it's the rain that keeps me right. Clears the sinuses, he says. Apparently, this dry air does nothing to assuage the phlegm in my lungs."

"I'd wager the precipitation will return soon enough," Joseph said.

"Oh?"

"Plenty of snow left to melt on the mountain. If it stays warm another day or two, we'll be freshly flooded by Monday. I might actually have to sandbag the front door."

Ted nodded. "I already got my finer wares on high ground. Wet smokes is bad for business. Speaking of which, I best be getting open myself. Thanks for the refreshment."

Ted turned to leave, but stopped before reaching the exit.

"Almost forgot," he said, reaching into the leather pouch slung over his shoulder. "I have something for you."

Ted pulled out a thick, clothbound book and passed it to Joseph.

"From my sister in Michigan. She swears it will change my life, but I've hardly the time for it."

Joseph ran his fingers across the cover. The letters were cut so deeply into the binding they practically screamed at his touch.

"'Dr. Chase's Information for Everybody: An Invaluable Collection of Practical Recipes for Merchants, Grocers, Saloon-Keepers, Druggists, Tanners, Jewelers, Gunsmiths, Barbers, Bakers, Farmers, and Families Generally, New and Improved by the Publisher,'" Joseph read. "That's a mouthful."

"And that's only the title. I tried perusing the chapter on bee-keeping, but the letters were so small I could barely see past the paper after ten minutes."

Joseph flipped the book open. A few pages in he found the index with such entries as: "Amusements for the Young"; "Gangrene, Treatment of"; "Oyster Pie"; "Rats, to Destroy"; and "Sinking at Pit of Stomach."

"Seems a wealth of information."

"Yours to plumb, my friend. Read it, sell it—use it as kindling, if you like. I have no use for it."

Joseph set the book on the counter next to a short stack of other titles yet to be shelved. "Thank you, Ted."

Ted raised his arm to wave as he exited the store.

Kick hopped onto the stool next to his father.

"Is Mr. Williamson sick?"

"I don't know," Joseph said. "He doesn't seem well."

"Might be the croup," Maddie said from above them both. She was speaking from six rungs up the ladder on the left side of the store. "Bobby Henderson's little sister got the croup and all she did was cough and make this funny wheezing noise."

"I doubt Mr. Williamson has the croup."

"'Attending symptoms of the croup include inflammation of the windpipe, spasms of the muscles of the throat, cough, and difficult respiration,'" Kick said, reading from the latest addition to the Wylde library. "Sounds like the croup."

"It's not," Joseph said. "But just in case, is there a cure I should be aware of?"

Kick studied the entry. "This says a tonic of equal parts goose oil and urine, one tablespoon every fifteen minutes."

"That's disgusting," Maddie said. "I think I'd probably throw up."

"You're supposed to," Kick said. "That's how you know it's workin'."

Joseph closed the book in Kick's hands. "Let's file this one under Home Remedies and Natural Wisdom."

Kick hopped off the stool and then passed the book to his sister. "Ready?" he asked.

"Ready," Maddie said, locking her arms around the closest rung.

Kick got on one side of the ladder and pushed. Even with his sister's weight, it slid easily along the wall, rolling past most of the shelves before coming to a stop near the back of the store. Maddie climbed two more rungs and then slid the volume into place between *Baldwin's Best Cures* and a book on tongue ailments.

The twins spent the better part of the next hour taking turns on the ladder, trying to roll to a stop nearest the shelf position of each new book their father gave them. It was a game they were very good at, and one Kate would have frowned upon had she been familiar with it. Joseph referred to it as "restocking the shelves," so as not to alert the boss.

At a few minutes to ten, Joseph directed the kids to the storage area beneath the loft. A single lamp illuminated the windowless room jam-packed with shelves and the store's inventory overflow. Each aisle had just enough room to stand, although some had stacks of books that blocked further progress. The storeroom was colder than the main floor, musty, and a little spooky.

"I know this isn't as much fun as riding the ladder, but I need you to go through these boxes, pull out the new titles, and file the rest."

"Does this mean we don't get to hear about the mayor's job?" Maddie asked.

They knew. Of course they knew.

Joseph shook his head. "It would be best for you to stay in here, just while I speak to the mayor's man."

"Because some things are private," Kick said.

"Yes," Joseph said, knowing the less he offered on the subject, the better.

The twins took to the boxes without complaint, leaving Joseph to return to the store. It was only after their father had closed the door that they began formulating a plan to listen in on his meeting.

Joseph had barely returned to the counter when the mayor strolled through the front door, followed by his deputy.

"Good morning, Joseph!"

"Mayor Gates, I wasn't expecting you this morning," Joseph said, offering his hand.

"Given the nature of this business, I felt it best to make a personal appearance, hear the news firsthand."

"That really wasn't necessary," Joseph said, eyeing the deputy. "I've no doubt Mr. Hildebrandt would have made a full report of my findings."

"Oh, I trust Bart implicitly. He's been with me for nearly six years, now."

"Nine," said the deputy.

"That's right. Nine years by my side. We've been through more elections, campaigns, and other political shenanigans than I've time to recount—and we've been through a few of those, too," the mayor said, delighted by his own wordplay. He placed a hand on the deputy's shoulder. "Still, I can't have him taking on all my burdens, not alone."

"No, I suppose not," Joseph said.

"Now, Mr. Hildebrandt, if you wouldn't mind."

The deputy locked the front door and flipped the sign hanging in the window from Open to Closed.

Satisfied, the mayor turned to Joseph.

"All right, my friend, show me what you've got."

Kick shifted his footing atop the makeshift stack of boxes he and Maddie had thrown together so they could see through a tiny crack near the ceiling.

"It's the mayor and that other guy," he said.

"The deputy?"

"I think so. The guy with the bushy eyebrows."

"What are they saying?"

"I don't know, I can't . . . wait, Father just retrieved something from behind the counter. It's an envelope. He's opening it."

"What's inside?"

Kick strained to see through the slender opening.

"Papers, I think," he said, and then tilting his head sideways added, "and some pictures, too."

"Pictures of what?"

Joseph handed the three wrinkled daguerreotypes to the mayor.

"Here are the three images you gave me."

The mayor stared at the pictures. He'd seen them before, and found the emotions that had accompanied his initial viewing renewed. All three images showed the same thing: the mayor, attired in a dark frock, tie, and top hat, standing with his hands at his chest and a broad smile on his face. Aside from the overly sunny expression, it was his standard pose for any formal portrait. It wasn't the smile, however, that had caused the mayor so much consternation, but rather the company. Young women stood on either side of the mayor, one on each arm, both sporting equally happy grins but decidedly fewer clothes. In fact, they were completely nude.

"I am still at odds with this portrait, my friend. I did not pose for it, nor would I have," he said forcibly. "This cannot be me. It *is* not!"

"I know," said Joseph, as he passed the mayor another photo. "Here's a fourth image, recovered during my investigations."

The fourth picture, crisp and clear, having never been crushed out of frustration, was identical to the others except the man in this image had no face. A white mask, possibly made of cloth, covered all of the man's head and neck below his hat.

"What is this?"

"That's the original."

"I don't understand. This is not me."

"No, but this is," Joseph said, handing the mayor a two-month-old clipping from the *Portlandian*. It was a picture made at the ceremony celebrating the opening of the Morrison Street Bridge, and featured the mayor, front and center, grinning alongside the bridge's architect. A closer examination of the image, specifically of the mayor's face, revealed an exact match for the expression found in the boudoir portrait.

Joseph pointed to one of the crumpled photos in the mayor's hand.

"The only part of this image that's real—that's you—is the face, and it was borrowed from this image captured months ago."

The mayor's eyes flitted from one image to next.

"Yes, yes, I see it. I've the same glint in my eye. Look here, Bart, they're the same."

"It's appears so," said the deputy mayor, peering over his boss's shoulder.

"But how is this possible, Joseph?" asked the mayor. "What do you see that I do not?"

Joseph smiled. He had, of course, never seen the pictures in question. There was nothing for him to interpret by touch in any of the daguerreotypes. He could smell the chemicals on the paper, even the sweat left over from the mayor's furious handlings, but it wasn't until Kate described the images to him in great detail (minus the giggles) that he understood what he was and was not seeing.

"It's a forgery, Mayor; a composite that combines elements from two separate pictures into one. It's seamless, but it's a lie."

"Remarkable," the mayor said, genuinely impressed.

"And effective," said Joseph. "I gather you've yet to convince the governor or Secretary Milson of your innocence."

"As I'm sure was the intent. In truth, I doubt either man took offense, but both seem convinced my reelection efforts would be damaged if such an image were to become public. They suggested I pay off the blackmailer, but if it could be proven to be fraudulent I might be able to sway their opinions."

"It's a complicated process, one that requires a delicate manipulation of light and shadow, but one that I could demonstrate if called upon," Joseph said, knowing it would never come to that.

"Excellent!"

The deputy mayor laid a hand on the mayor's shoulder.

"That may be good enough for the intellectuals, Mr. Mayor, but explaining such a distinction to the general public, especially after such a sensational image has been printed in the newspaper, is another matter altogether. There's bound to be some confusion amongst the lesser minds."

"Do they get a vote?"

"I'm afraid so," said Bart.

"Yes, you're right, of course," said the mayor, a little defeated. "Then we nip it in the bud before it comes to that, which leaves us with the man. You said you had a name."

"I do," said Joseph. "Seamus Greeley."

The mayor glanced at Bart, who shook his head.

"Never heard of him," said the mayor.

Joseph nodded. "Mr. Greeley has a small apartment on Ash Street. It was there that I found this print, along with a store of photographic chemicals and papers, but no equipment."

"In other words, he saw you coming," said the deputy mayor. "He's gone?"

"In a manner of speaking."

For the first time, Joseph gave his full attention to the deputy mayor, who was not glad to have it. Even with only one eye, Joseph's stare could penetrate deeply into the intentions of a man, regardless of whether he was an intellectual or in possession of a lesser mind. It was meant to unnerve. At that moment, Deputy Mayor Bart Hildebrandt could attest to its success.

"I still don't know the man," said the mayor. "I'd hope that my blackmailer at least has a rooting interest in whether I win or lose."

"I believe he does, Mr. Mayor," said Joseph, "and has for at least nine years."

Kick blinked and then looked through the slit in the wall again. Something was off in the room. The emotion of the scene he'd been watching had changed. He didn't have the words or understanding to explain it, but he knew something was going to happen—something bad.

"Maddie, I think something is—"

"Wrong," finished Maddie. "I feel it, too."

Kick looked at his sister. It wasn't the first time they'd shared each other's intuition, but it'd never been so strong.

"What do we do?"

"I don't—"

And that's when the first shot rang out.

8

A few minutes before the mayor and his deputy walked through the front door of Wylde's, Booksellers and Navigation, Kate stepped off the Jefferson Street trolley and onto a muddy platform just above Fifth Avenue. This was as far as the streetcar could go without risking becoming fouled in the floodwaters. A series of sodden planks half submerged in the soggy street provided passage to the sidewalk, which Kate made without a misstep.

"We're on foot the rest of the way."

"Good," the marshal said, hopping from the last plank to the sidewalk.

"You're not tired?"

"Heck no. Used to it. Astoria ain't but one big hill."

Kate smiled. She hoped that meant the marshal had spent some time beyond the walls of his own house. Her vision of him alone, slowing going stir crazy, had grown over the past year, culminating in its near certainty after the incident in the graveyard. *"At least he got outside,"* Joseph had commented. Kate was not amused.

Still, if he could keep up with her now, perhaps he'd done better on his own than she'd thought.

A few blocks on, Kate stopped at a corner behind a line of

pedestrians waiting to cross a narrow, elevated walkway. A small skiff floated beneath the bridge, pushed along by a lone Chinese man. Several tightly wrapped packages were stacked in the well of the boat, guarded by a small, flat-faced dog with big eyes, straw-colored fur, and a curly tail.

"What is that?" said the marshal, eyeing the animal directly as it drifted past. The dog appraised the marshal briefly, then seemed to lose interest and turned its attention elsewhere.

"Laundry service," Kate said.

"No, no, in the boat. That some kind of Siamese cat?"

"It's a dog. A pug. Chinese are fond of them, although there's a family a few blocks above us that has one, too."

"That's a dog?"

"Be sure to tell Maddie you saw one. She's quite fond of them—pugs, I mean. She says their eyes are big and round, just like a person's."

The marshal watched the laundry boat cross the flooded street to a storefront on the other side. The dog remained seated while its master clambered over the side to deliver his packages.

"You're sure that's a dog."

"Yes. Now, come on. We've a ways to go yet."

Five blocks from the family store, Kate finally got up the nerve to ask the question that had been on her mind since they'd left the house.

"Would you like to help out? With the business, I mean."

The marshal considered the offer. "I don't know much about bookselling."

"No, I mean with our other work, our investigations."

The marshal said nothing. When Kate had asked the question, his mind had been elsewhere, back at the house, perhaps, in his room. It took him a moment to shake loose what he'd left behind.

"Help out with the investigations," he repeated, more for himself than his daughter. "You want me to dig out my badge? It ain't legal. I'm not affiliated with the U.S. Marshals, or even Clatsop County, for what it's worth."

"No, I don't mean like that," Kate said, deciding not to add that Joseph already had a badge that he'd flashed on several occasions despite its dubious legality. "It's just you've got a lot of experience dealing with certain low-level elements of society. And it seems our investigations occasionally take us into situations where practical experience in this area might be a useful tool to lean on."

The marshal took his daughter's arm, stopping her in the middle of the sidewalk.

"Are you in trouble, Katie?"

"Absolutely not!"

"Sounds to me like you are," the marshal said. "Sounds to me like you're wantin' someone to look over your shoulder, someone knows how to handle a weapon."

"That's not it at all," Kate said, wondering if her words sounded as false to her father as they did to her own ears. "I'm just saying," she began, but got no further.

The marshal relaxed his grip but didn't let go of Kate's arm.

"What?"

"Most of what we do is fairly benign, boring even. But there are times, rare occasions, when I think it would be wise to have an experienced lawman on our side to help negotiate certain situations."

"Negotiate, huh?" the marshal said, letting go of his daughter's arm. "Sounds like a fancy way of sayin' 'shoot somebody.'"

"I doubt it'll ever come to that."

The marshal recalled the conversation with Joseph and his insistence that Kate knew how to handle herself . . . *in certain situations.*

"What's your husband think of this idea?"

"It was his," Kate said, which was a lie. It wasn't Joseph's idea—not yet, anyway.

The marshal considered the offer. There was no doubt he would take it, would run whatever kind of *negotiations* his daughter had in mind, but he was pleased to find himself more than a little excited about the idea. It felt good. It felt right.

He would need to wear a gun.

"Course I'll help you, Katie. Whatever you need. Just tell me when and where and I'll back your man with whatever set of skills you fancy are best suited for the, ah, negotiations."

"Thanks, Dad," Kate said as she curled an arm around her father's and pulled him back into the flow of the morning's foot traffic.

"So, does this mean you're expectin' a specific conversation to commence this morning?"

Kate laughed.

"Not at all. I would say this morning's business will be as boring as usual."

Joseph heard the deputy mayor pull the small, two-shot pocket revolver from his coat, cock the hammer, and place the muzzle at the back of the mayor's head, but he didn't react, initially. He knew about the gun, of course, had since the man walked through the door, but he was still surprised the deputy had chosen to act so rashly. He wouldn't make that mistake again.

"Bart, what is the meaning of this?" demanded the mayor.

"I'd think it obvious, Jim."

"What? Are you in league with this Greeley?"

The deputy mayor's eyes went wide.

"You are such a stupid man," he said and depressed the trigger, deciding only the instant before the hammer fell to raise the angle of the weapon.

The bullet passed close enough to part the hairs on top of the mayor's head. Joseph heard it ricochet off the spiral staircase and lodge in a book on the second-floor loft. He thought momentarily of the kids in the storeroom and then returned his attention to the mayor and his deputy. The kids were smart. They would stay out of sight.

Bart brought the handle of the pistol sharply down on the back of the mayor's head, then repositioned it at the base of the man's skull.

"I'm Greeley, you moron!"

The mayor cringed, stung by his deputy's words as much as by the butt of his gun. He looked to Joseph for help, although whether more for safety or satisfaction, Joseph wasn't sure.

"There is no Seamus Greeley," Joseph said. "There never was. Your deputy forged him from the ether to keep me off his scent."

Bart leaned in close to the mayor's ear. "He's a clever one, isn't he? You should have put him on the payroll years ago."

"It was a good plan, but the trail left for me to find Seamus was clumsy and more revealing than I believe he intended."

Bart put a hand on the mayor's shoulder and slid the gun around to his temple. He eyed Joseph.

"You're a prideful man, aren't you, Joseph? You couldn't simply accuse me out in the open. It had to be face-to-face. That was foolish."

"To each his own," said Joseph.

The deputy mayor grinned. "And now I'm a fool."

The gun turned from the mayor's temple, requiring only a slight readjustment to find its new target. Joseph would have missed the motion completely had it not been for the faintest of gasps he heard coming behind him.

"Do you suppose a hole in the head would throw you off the trail?"

Joseph knew he could move out of the way of any shot fired by the deputy, but would leave the mayor vulnerable in doing so. He remained still.

"Foolish pride notwithstanding, I'm still at a loss, gentlemen," said the mayor. "Why exactly is there a gun at my head?"

Bart stepped back, resetting the weapon low on the mayor's skull.

"My reasons are simple enough. I don't like you. I never have, although what man is really worthy company in an arrangement such as ours? Better to find enjoyment in the work, but I'm afraid even that has lost its appeal. Mostly, however . . ." The deputy mayor flinched several times and then seemed to shake it off. "Mostly I just hate the goddamn rain. I hate it. Everything's wet here, every day, all the time. Whole wretched town is nothing but a giant mud hole ten months out of the year."

"That's not true," said the mayor. "Look at today! It's lovely, sunny, must be eighty degrees."

"And yet we're under three feet of water and will be for weeks! And you can't wait for it to start raining again."

"Well, of course, for the festival—"

"Damn the festival! Who wants to tromp around in the muck and mire, in the damp, dark cold? Nobody! Just you and your soggy followers."

The mayor sighed. "I didn't know you felt that way, Bart."

Bart turned his gaze from the back of the mayor's head. The gun remained on target.

"Maybe you should listen more carefully when you're not the one doing the talking."

"Fine," said the mayor. "What do you have to say?"

Kick pushed his sister's feet above his head and through the trap-door that led to the loft above the storeroom. Maddie reappeared an instant later.

"Gimme your hands," she whispered, reaching back through the small opening.

Kick stretched as far as he could, which was just enough. Maddie pulled him over the edge and soon both were beneath a table at the back of the space. The twins crept forward slowly, keeping on their hands and knees, until they reached the railing at the front edge of the loft.

The view from above didn't change the situation—their father and the mayor were still held at gunpoint by the deputy mayor.

"What do we do?" Maddie asked.

"I don't know."

"Because you don't know, or because you don't know what's going to happen? You can't tell yet, right?"

Kick looked at his sister. They rarely spoke about it, but the twins' ability to predict how a situation would unfold had become increasingly accurate. For years they'd been able to act as one, knowing instinctively what the other would do or say in almost any situation. Recently, they'd found their instincts leading them beyond their own to the actions of others. They could guess how a person might react, what he might say, even when exactly he was going to do it. They couldn't predict the future exactly, but they could follow its path and intercept it down the line.

They rarely spoke about it, because they didn't have to. They understood what they could do and that was enough.

"Something still seems wrong," Kick said. "Like I can't see everything."

"Maybe we can't. We're not close enough, or something's out of sight, or—"

"Hidden."

Maddie nodded.

Both watched the scene below, waiting for something to reveal itself, something they couldn't see but knew was there.

". . . Two days I spent, sitting on my hands, waiting for you to finish your damn meeting. Not once did you consult my opinion of the situation. Not once! And I had an opinion, of that you can be most certain."

"Bart, I'm going cut you off there, because I've made an executive decision. This ends now."

"Excuse me?"

"I believe I'm in the right, here," the mayor said, and then, in what was likely the bravest (and stupidest) thing he would ever do in his life, he turned to face his colleague directly.

Joseph was just as surprised as the deputy.

"Bart, you need to put that weapon away and see reason. This is not the way men—professional men—behave. I'll have none of it in my administration."

Bart stared at the man whose life he'd nearly ended minutes before. "You think you can talk your way out of this? That you can just open the great maw and spew forth a proclamation to end hostilities, is that it?"

Joseph knew the deputy had decided to pull the trigger a full minute before the shot was fired. He heard it in the man's voice. Resentment and anger had been joined by futility, which in Joseph's experience were never a good combination.

"I fail to see how violence will serve our current situation in any meaningful manner," said the mayor. "You're not thinking this through, Bart."

Joseph retreated to the counter behind him, moving slowly so as not to attract attention. Without raising his shoulders, he found two books within reach: a first edition of Herman Melville's *Moby Dick* and the latest edition of the *Chicago Journal of Tanning & Blackening*. Melville's was by far the thicker tome (and the more valuable), but as Joseph slid the book off the counter he wondered if it might be too heavy for the maneuver he intended to employ. It was too late to test it now.

"This is foolishness, Bart. I'll see you removed by morning. You'll never get a dime. I don't care who you try to peddle this false smut to, I'll not have it!"

"Who's the fool now, Jim?"

Joseph bent slightly at the knees and then popped up quickly, flipping his wrist so as to launch the novel over the back of his head in a long, arcing rotation. The motion was silent and practically invisible save for the book now flipping end over end above the men's heads. As it was, neither the mayor nor his deputy saw the book even as it fell between them at the exact moment Bart fired his weapon.

The bullet struck the book squarely, sending it slamming into the mayor, who toppled backward in front of Joseph.

A path now clear to his target, Joseph let fly with the journal, striking the deputy squarely in the face with the leading edge.

The deputy howled in pain and dropped to one knee, clutching his face. Blood began to pour from between his fingers.

Joseph grabbed the mayor's hand and led him around the counter, between several shelves, all the way to the back of the store, where they found cover beneath a four-foot shelf filled with oversize research volumes on topics of a botanical nature.

"Are you hurt?"

"I don't . . . I don't think so," the mayor said, only just starting to catch his breath. He still clutched the book that had saved his life tightly to his chest. Closer inspection revealed a hole in the front cover and a small raised bump in the back. The mayor flipped through the pages and was nearly to the end before a small, flattened slug slipped harmlessly into Joseph's outstretched hand. The bullet, which had no problem cutting through most of Melville's epic, had stopped thirteen pages shy of the end.

"Lucky I used the first edition," Joseph said. "Thicker paper."

The mayor nodded silently.

Joseph raised his head and listened. The mayor's breathing was by far the loudest thing in the room, but not the only thing. The deputy remained at the front of the store, his breathing wet, but in control. Joseph's attack would do little permanent damage, though blood continued to flow from the deputy's nose and scalp, making it hard for him to see as he reloaded his weapon.

Not reloading, Joseph thought, *checking the chambers*. The deputy had another gun.

"How many weapons does he carry?"

"I assume it was the Remington that was put to my skull. He also has a small five-shot revolver, and a six-inch blade that he carries inside the left breast pocket."

Joseph wasn't surprised he'd missed the knife, but the second pistol bothered him. He should have caught that, but hadn't. He'd been sloppy. Kate was going to be mad.

Maddie handed Kick a small but solid book about the rearing and harvesting of the eastern oyster. Kick tested its weight, nodded, and then turned his attention back to the scene below.

The deputy mayor stood at the counter, stooped slightly but still high enough to see the tops of most of the shelves. He held a revolver in his right hand, a bloodied handkerchief in his left. He scanned the room, looking left and right repeatedly, but never up.

Their father and the mayor were not visible directly, but a line of polished metal panels near the ceiling gave away their position at the back of the store to anyone who knew how to read the amorphous reflections.

Kick held the book up before his face, waiting. He and Maddie watched the deputy move forward around the counter, past the center table, look left and then right, and move forward again. He was halfway to the back of the store.

When he looked to his right again, Kick lofted the book into the air.

Bart was three rows from Joseph and the mayor when the book hit the ground near the front of the store. The deputy turned and fired twice, losing one bullet in the wall, the other in an explosion of pages that had been an architectural history of Florence.

Joseph clamped a hand on the mayor to keep him from crying out. He knew immediately what had happened, but found the advantage he now had—three shots, down from five—was not worth the exchange—four targets, up from two.

Kate was definitely going to be mad.

"Stay here," Joseph whispered. "And stay silent."

The mayor nodded.

At the front of the store, Bart checked the door once more, scanning the boardwalk as he did. A handful of pedestrians could be seen on the other side of the flooded street, but no one seemed to be paying the bookshop any extra attention. The deputy turned back to the store.

"Here I was beginning to think you'd lighted out a back exit, leaving me to stumble around until reinforcements arrived."

Joseph slipped around a shelf on the west side of the store and listened. The deputy was against the wall on the opposite side, moving toward the back but no longer bothering to stay low. The twins were in the loft, beneath the table along the railing. Nothing gave them away, but it made sense this was where they'd be. He turned his face upward and shook his head slowly, knowing they could see him, hoping they would do as they were told.

Kick frowned.

Maddie slipped back from the edge. When her brother did not, she grabbed him by the belt and pulled.

Kick's face slipped into the shadow just before the deputy turned his gaze upward. Bart scanned the room, taking in the entire space. There was no movement in the loft and nothing on the ground floor. Sunlight bouncing off the water outside sparkled in a series of panels that ran along the ceiling, otherwise the space was still.

That was when the deputy noticed the ladder at his side.

Joseph heard the creak of the ladder as Bart took his first tentative step and knew immediately it would take only a half-dozen more before the mayor, and possibly himself, would be visible to the deputy.

Moving quickly and staying low, Joseph slipped around the shelf and stopped behind the counter, which would provide cover from all but the top of the ladder. He would have to make sure the deputy never got that high.

Bart reached the sixth of ten steps with his back to the ladder, one hand holding firm, the other gripping his pistol. After ascending each rung, he stopped to scan the store. So far, nothing had revealed itself.

Movement caught his eye near the door. A book slid to a stop, which the deputy quickly had in his sights, but managed not to fire on.

"I'll not be wasting any more ammunition on your inventory, Mr. Wylde."

Bart waited, but received no reply. The deputy climbed two more rungs, steadied himself, and scanned the room. He found what he was looking for near the back of the store.

"Point of order, Mr. Wylde," he said, using his heel to push the ladder slightly to the right. "Can you speak to terms?"

"What terms would that be, Mr. Hildebrandt?" Joseph asked, bouncing his voice off the shelf in front of him so that it echoed about the room.

"Surrender, of course. I've no need to sacrifice you for the sins of our common employer. In fact, I'd be perfectly happy to let you go right on living, assuming we can find a solution that leaves us both comfortably situated."

That the deputy was lying Joseph had no doubt. What concerned him, however, was the angle he was encroaching upon, which would give him a clear shot of the mayor. The ladder had stopped moving, which suggested he'd already found it. Joseph's options ran out. He heard the hammer draw back on the deputy's gun and decided to give the man another target.

Joseph leaped from behind the counter and ran directly at the wall on the other side of the store.

The deputy swung his gun around, but wobbled on the ladder, forcing himself to get his footing before finding his aim.

Joseph leaped at an angle he hoped was accurate and landed squarely on the ladder opposite the one the deputy now occupied. His momentum got the ladder rolling, but a swift kick off the second shelf pushed him along faster. A gunshot tore into the row of books he'd just passed by.

The deputy panned with his target and fired again, taking a chunk out of the rung directly above Joseph's head.

Joseph felt a dozen tiny splinters bounce off his face, a few of which stuck. Sensing his luck (and shelf space) was about to run out, he dropped off the ladder and rolled smoothly onto one knee next to the crouching mayor. Without hesitating, he grabbed the mayor and yanked him backward, once again saving the man's life as the deputy's bullet whizzed past his head and into the floor.

"You lucky bastard!"

The deputy drew back the hammer and fired again, knowing full well the futility of pulling the trigger on an empty chamber. A moment later he leaped from his perch onto the nearest shelf, which toppled over, sending a flood of books and the deputy sliding across the floor. He tried to stand, but found the footing untenable among the shifting materials. When his feet finally did find purchase he had just enough time to draw his knife before a book struck the side of his head. He wobbled, but didn't go down. A second book glanced off the bridge of his nose and soon the blood was flowing again. He had enough of his wits to know the second book had come from above, but when he looked to the loft there was no one there.

"I'm right here, Mr. Hildebrandt."

The deputy never saw the last book to hit him that day, which turned out to be an oversize collection of Canadian maps swung by Joseph at very close range. Joseph delivered the blow with such force that a section of the title remained embossed on the deputy's forehead for some hours afterward. The more immediate result was that Deputy Mayor Bart Hildebrandt was unconscious even before he fell backward into the books.

Joseph had just enough time to let out the breath he'd been holding when he heard the front lock unlatch and the door swing open.

"Don't know why it's locked, it shouldn't be unless—" was all Kate managed to say to her father before she spied the blood on the floor. A moment of panic flared and then she spied her husband standing over the unconscious man atop a pile of books in the middle of the store. Then she saw her kids.

"Hey, Mom!" Kick called from the loft railing. "Look what we did."

Kate looked from her son to her husband.

"It's not as bad as it looks," Joseph said, knowing the opposite was about to be true for himself.

Kate said nothing.

The marshal, sensing his place in the family business was secure, picked up the deputy's knife.

"Must have been quite a conversation," he said.

An hour later, Bart Hildebrandt left the bookstore still woozy, but on his feet. His hands were locked in large black shackles, a request of the mayor so as to make it obvious to the crowd gathered outside exactly who the villain was in this situation.

Joseph thought the police escorting the soon-to-be former deputy was enough, but he chose not to say anything. He was keeping his mouth shut for the time being.

"I'm very sorry for the inconvenience, Mr. Mayor," Kate said. "Sometimes private investigations have a way of becoming public."

"True, but I believe I can spin an assassination attempt. All good politicians have at least one on their résumé. The trick is to make sure it's not the *last* thing."

Kate smiled. "I understand."

"And don't be too hard on your man, here," the mayor said, laying a hand on Joseph's shoulder. "His command of the situation was top notch. Fearless. I don't think any one of us was in mortal danger for more than ten minutes. Fifteen tops."

Kate's smile faltered. "Mortal danger?"

The mayor held up the book that would be featured in numerous newspapers nationwide over the coming weeks.

"My new *holey* Bible," he said, poking a finger through the cover.

Kate eyed the book and then her husband. Joseph pretended not to notice.

"Now, I'm afraid it's going to be a busy day for me, so we'll leave the, um, settlement of our business arrangement on the table for the moment, if that's all right."

"At your convenience, Mr. Mayor."

"Wonderful! Make it Saturday afternoon. I'm having a garden party for some of the early-arriving festival guests. The whole family is welcome, of course. And I might even have another job for you."

Kate raised an eyebrow.

"Something much less dangerous, I assure you."

Joseph nodded. "We'll be happy to discuss it Saturday."

"Excellent. Two sharp. Garden attire, if you please."

The mayor left the store to the cheers of several dozen well-wishers. It was the kindest reception he'd received since taking office.

Kate watched the politician disappear into the crowd. A single tear slipped down her cheek as Joseph put an arm around her.

"It's all right."

"No, I'm going to kill you," she said.

"I know," Joseph said, pulling his wife into both arms. "But it's all right."

9

———◆———

Henry bit through the nail of his left thumb, spit it to the ground, and read the same mixed-up sentence for the third time.

Into the black, dense and back, a capite
ad calcem, ab aeterno, and nothing less,
huis-clos of six pieds de profond, a
muana tucka of twelve, no more, truky,
tamby, maso.

"They're directions," he whispered aloud to no one. Directions for what, he wasn't sure. Henry thought it might refer to a familiar space six feet underground, but what went in the space?

"A muana tucka of twelve, no more."

The deeper he read—nearly forty pages so far—the denser the language became, more complicated and confusing. Henry could read the English well enough, and some of the French, but the words he took to be Spanish (which were actually Latin) were a struggle, and the gibberish—in fact, phonetically spelled African words of more than a dozen tribes—was impenetrable.

Except when it wasn't.

"*Muana tucka* means 'young boy,'" Henry said, knowing it was true, but not how he knew it. This had happened more than once.

Henry scanned the campsite. Mason, Hugh, and Charlie were asleep in their bedrolls, having drifted off hours ago. The Hanged Man's canvas-wrapped body was propped up against a tree stump to Henry's right. Charlie thought it a fine joke that Henry should once again sleep next to his friend. They had, after all, both spent time in the same underground accommodations, even if Henry's stay had been much shorter.

Henry didn't care where the dead man lay. He was too engrossed in his reading to mind the stink of death. He'd waited until all three men were past waking before cracking open the notebook. The light from the fire had faded, but the soft glow of the remaining embers coupled with the moonlight was enough for Henry to read by. On subsequent late-night readings, Henry would find the words always became clearer as the light waned.

Despite his spotty progress, Henry had never felt more satisfied. The more he read, the more the words took hold in his mind, even if he didn't grasp all of their meanings. And that's not to say he didn't understand much of it. This was a collection of spells, pure and simple. There didn't seem to be any rhyme or reason to the order, although the complexity of the procedures seemed to increase with each turn of the page. Earlier entries had rarely been more than half a page in length and some were only a sentence or two. The phrase that currently bounced around in Henry's head was part of a three-page entry, the overall intent of which Henry had yet to grasp.

There were also spells that featured notes written in a hand different from that of the original author, offering translations and in some cases alterations to the main text. The annotations were, thankfully, written in English, which helped Henry unlock the meaning of a few words repeated in other spells.

One such spell described how to control the actions of a silent man, a simpleton according to the notes, by speaking a series of phrases into the ear. Listening to his new partners' breath in the night air, Henry wondered if "silent" meant "sleeping." He flipped back a dozen pages to the text that suddenly seemed very clear twenty minutes after he'd read it. He scanned the words again. There were three lines, a succession of calls to the mind of a *silent man lacking intellect and purpose*," according to the note scribbled underneath.

Henry found he was looking at Charlie, repeating the words in his head to see how they felt. They felt good.

Henry slipped from beneath his blanket and strode quietly around the outside of the circle to where Charlie lay on his side, his hat crushed beneath his shoulder. Charlie's hand was at his face, his thumb having yet to find its way home. Henry leaned close to the man and whispered in his ear.

"Hear me le silence et observez mes mots bien, ut ego iacio upon thee, is meus unus verus meledictio. Mes mots sont words, mes souhaits your own, my command vestri votum, mes per factum vestri own."

A breath caught in Charlie's throat and then slowly escaped through his nose. When he was breathing normally again, Henry continued.

"Rise at my voix et la suivent bien, hear this meus unus verus meledictio."

Charlie's breathing paused again, but this time his eyes popped wide open as well.

Henry stumbled backward but managed to right himself before hitting the ground. He dropped the book in the process and was searching for it when he realized Charlie had stood and was now watching him intently.

"I'm sorry," Henry said, loud enough to be heard by all. Thankfully, neither of the sleeping men stirred.

Charlie said nothing.

Henry found the book and pulled it to his breast. Charlie continued to hover over him, staring, even as Henry got his feet. Charlie's gaze followed his progress, never breaking away or blinking.

"Charlie?" Henry said, a little softer.

Charlie said nothing.

Henry checked the other men. Hugh's snoring seemed louder but otherwise there was no change.

Henry looked directly at Charlie. The man's eyes were locked on Henry's, but on closer inspection they appeared not to see him, not in a way that a conscious man would. Henry waved his hand before Charlie's face.

Nothing.

Before he could think better of it, Henry poked the man in the forehead with a finger.

Nothing.

Henry stole a glance at the book in his hand, licked his lips, and then spoke the first words that popped into his head.

"Walk into the woods."

Without hesitation, Charlie stepped forward and would have walked through Henry had he not jumped out of the way. Twenty feet from the campsite, Charlie came to a tree that he carefully circled before returning to his original course. He stumbled a few strides later but did not fall. It barely slowed him down.

Henry stared for a moment longer, before giving chase.

"Stop," Henry said as he caught up to Charlie.

Charlie stopped.

Henry stepped in front of the man. Charlie stared straight ahead, but as Henry moved into his line of vision, his eyes seemed to find Henry's and lock on. Henry swayed from side to side. Charlie's glare followed the movements precisely.

"Weird," Henry said.

Charlie blinked once.

"Can you understand what I'm saying?"

Charlie nodded.

"Can you speak?"

"Yes," Charlie said without any emotion.

Henry smiled. The momentary fear he'd felt was gone, replaced by an exhilaration he'd never known. The spell worked. He had control of Charlie. *How much?*

"Slap yourself in the face."

Charlie slapped his face hard enough to make Henry flinch. Charlie blinked several times and for a moment his eyes lost their focus. Henry snapped his fingers before the man's face.

"Right here, friend."

Charlie's gaze returned front and center.

"That's better. We're not done experimenting yet."

Henry looked Charlie up and down. A moment of calm passed over him. It would be the last he would feel for a very long time.

"Drop your trousers," he said, letting his amusement take charge.

Charlie undid his belt buckle and wiggled his hips until his pants fell around his boots, exposing a dingy pair of long underwear spotted with holes. Henry grinned at what he had wrought and found he wanted more of the same.

"Walk."

Charlie tried to stride forward but quickly became entangled in his pants and fell face-first into a large fern.

Henry laughed loudly, unable to repress his delight.

On the ground, Charlie fought with the fern, appearing to be trying both to stand and to walk at the same time. This made Henry laugh harder.

"Get up, fool!"

Charlie ceased kicking the ground and started to get to his knees. In doing so, he put a hand directly into the base of a thistle bush.

"Ow!"

Charlie blinked and this time he recognized the scene before his eyes. He was on the ground, pants were around his ankles, and Henry was there, laughing at him.

"Son of a whore!"

Charlie leaped to his feet before Henry could react and hit him with a wild roundhouse right, driving him to the ground. Henry never let go of the book.

"To hell with you!" Charlie barked, as he pulled up his trousers. "Next time I catch you sneakin' a peek, I'll cut your throat. Go on and laugh, see if I don't!"

Charlie strode off, leaving Henry to reflect on his success. He rolled his jaw, shocked by how much it hurt. His father had hit him, of course, but never like that and never in the face. It was a disturbing feeling, but it didn't erase what he'd done: he'd taken control of the man with just a few words, some of which he didn't even fully understand.

And this was one of the simpler spells in the book—imagine what he could do once he'd read them all!

A sharp pain cut through Henry's skull from his forehead to the base of his spine. It was followed by a wave of nausea, which passed only after he vomited most of the beans he'd consumed earlier in the evening onto the forest floor. Henry waited, but a second wave never came. Instead, a headache quickly took hold that would last the rest of the night. Worse still was the pain in Henry's already swelling jaw. He wouldn't be whispering again for some time, but Henry didn't care.

There was so much to read.

10

Andre Labeau is seven years old when he learns the brightest light often casts the darkest shadow.

He's a smart boy, and smart boys often do dumb things, which is how Andre ends up with chicken scratches across his chest and up and down both arms. The cuts aren't deep and on a boy Andre's size they hardly seem cause for alarm, but that doesn't stop him from shedding a tear as his mama sets him right.

"Whatchoo thinkin goin in there? Chicken coop ain't no place fo a boy afta dark."

"I'm sorry, Mama."

"Course you is," Andre's mama says. "Stealin eggs is fo foxes and fools, neither of which is you."

"I wasn't stealin no eggs."

"Oh? You afta a chicken?"

"No, Mama. I'm a kill it."

Andre's mama slaps her son without hesitation. The sting is more painful than any of the cuts on his arm, but the surprise holds back any further tears.

"You do and don't see if you get worse from Mistah Bouvant."

"But I goin set us free!"

Andre's mama raises her hand again but delivers no blow. Andre never flinches.

"How you goin do that?"

The smile that forms on Andre's face is as big as his secret.

"Magic!"

Andre's mama smiles, too, and then laughs, full and hearty. She wraps her arms around him—as far as they'll go—and holds him tightly.

"Boy, you is beautiful. Big and beautiful."

"It was Miss Haddie told me what to do."

Andre's mama loosens her embrace.

"Haddie? Whatchoo talkin to her fo? That woman bring us mo trouble."

"But she show me how to cast a charm and told me about the hoodoo—"

"Hoodoo? Voodoo more like. She got a dark shadow hangin o'er her shoulders, Andre. Best stay away from her."

Andre's mama returns her attention to her son's wounds, but he pulls away.

"I ain't afraid, Mama."

"No, I don't imagine," she says. "But I am. And I ain't brought you this far to have some voodoo witch scrape yo soul with her black secrets. Yo mama have a time cleanin you up afta that."

"I don't needa be clean, Mama. I know right an wrong. I can tella difference."

"And whatchoo goin do with the darkness comes yo way? Close yo eyes? Fo'get you ever known it?"

"No, Mama, I won't fo'get. I'll remember. Won't be a black word can touch me when I know em all."

Andre's mama hears the truth in her son's voice, even if the words bring dark thoughts to mind.

"Why you wanna know so much?" she asks. "Always with questions.

Ain't you got enough keep yo head full you gotta fill it up with blackness, too?"

Andre says nothing as he pulls his shirt over his head.

Andre's mama sees in her son the man he will become. Like his body, his mind is maturing quickly, she hopes not too quickly.

"Keep it secret," she says.

"I will."

"I mean it, Andre. Don't ever let on you know."

"I won't."

Andre is a good boy, his mama knows that. He'll do what he's told. She prays to God so he will.

"Andre," his mama says, "words have power. In yo head, yo tongue, and onna paper. Don't keep em in mori'n one spot. Don't speak em and don't write em down."

"Yes, Mama."

But he does write the words down, because even though he is a smart boy, smart boys sometimes do dumb things. He writes them all down and tells himself he's being careful by using the words and phrases of his Master and his People as well as his own to disguise their meaning.

And when he's older and wiser, he continues to write because knowledge is power and the book is a very powerful thing, indeed. It's not until the book slips from his possession that Andre understands exactly how dangerous that power can be.

Andre was lying on his cot, wide awake despite the late hour and relatively calm seas, when the first explosion rocked the ship. He leaped to his feet and had just managed to pull his jacket over his shoulders when a second rumble shook the vessel from bow to stern.

"Too soon," Andre murmured, as he pulled on his boots and headed for the door. Naira was waiting when he opened it.

"Engine room," she said.

Andre was not surprised.

The ship's engineer gave his captain the news twenty minutes later: two of the main pressure valves had failed to release, causing the primary steam chamber to explode. The second combustion was the result of an extreme loss of pressure created by the first.

The captain, a seventeen-year veteran of West Coast water routes, had experienced his share of at-sea mishaps, but this was his first aboard the *Año Nuevo,* a ship considered one of the most dependable vessels currently in service.

"Must have been a hell of a pressure spike," said the captain. "No one in the steam room caught that?"

"It happened so fast. Every needle was steady one minute and in the red the next. I couldn't shut it down fast enough."

The captain seemed unconvinced. Andre was not.

Moments before the engineer delivered his assessment, the wheelhouse had been crowded with people, many of whom had no business being there. The first mate chased most back to their quarters. Andre made it clear his presence would be tolerated.

Andre asked the engineer directly, "How long to repair the damage?"

"I can get us limping in an hour, but we'll need to dock to make thorough repairs."

The captain grumbled something under his breath. "Do it," was all Andre managed to discern.

The captain turned away from his engineer to study a set of coastal charts laid out on a table in the center of the room.

"I'm sorry," he said to Andre, "but it doesn't look like we'll be reaching Astoria by Saturday."

"No, I do not believe you will, captain. In fact, I think your immediate journey may be at an end. You need to take us to port."

The captain glanced at the man who had already dictated more changes to his itinerary than any passenger he'd previously had aboard his ship. He was a giant, sure, but it wasn't simply his size that had convinced the captain to modify his schedule. It was his demeanor. The man was too damn polite. There was something else, too, something he couldn't quite explain, but he was certain his agreement with the giant African and his native companion was required. For what he couldn't say.

Andre smiled. "Any port will do, of course."

"Sure," the captain, returning his gaze to the chart. "We can reach Newport by Saturday morn, barring further misadventure, but you don't need to leave the ship. Yaquina Bay is fairly well protected, so she'll be plenty comfortable."

"I thank you, but we will take our leave at that time."

"If that's what you wish."

Andre nodded to the captain and then ducked out of the room, followed by the young native woman.

The captain hadn't even realized she was in the room.

"Is it the book?" Naira asked.

She and Andre stood near the bow of the steamer, taking in the cool evening air with a dozen other very disappointed passengers. Word had spread quickly that the ship would be making for Newport, but no farther.

"The wake of it," Andre said. "Like the ripples that roll across the surface after a stone hits water. I can feel them when they pass, a pulse amplified for my presence, possibly because of it. The ship can feel them, too, and if we stay aboard I fear a disabled engine will be the least of her worries."

"What of the book's new owner?"

"I doubt he has anything to do with it. Though I suspect he feels the wake just as strong, maybe more so."

Naira looked into the night sky, her eyes appearing to reflect the moonlight more brightly than the source.

"You're sure it's not a *her*?"

Andre let the question hang in the air for a moment before answering. He knew Naira was not making a general inquiry—that she had a specific *her* in mind—but he chose to ignore the implication, at least for now.

"I am," he said eventually. "I think it would feel different in the presence of a woman. A man holds it now, a young man, I believe. I can scarcely think of anything worse."

"It was written by a young man, was it not?"

Andre nodded. "Much of it was. It was only by dumb luck and the will of the gods that the thing did not twist his intentions into something uncontrollable. I still know that young man, Naira, I feel him in my heart, but I can never forgive him."

"That debt has been paid, Andre."

"Perhaps. But what of the older man? I may not be forgiving, but I do not fault the young man for his intentions, misguided though they were. But much of the book was compiled by a man of many summers, a man who should have known the folly of such a collection, the danger of it—a man who should have known better. I fear that debt remains unpaid and overdue."

Naira looked at Andre with the eyes that had spoken truth to him for nearly a decade. He saw in them the same as ever and it made him remember exactly who and where he was—and where he was going.

"I apologize," he said, shaking his head, but smiling. "The ease with which my thoughts are corrupted is disturbing. You must watch me, my friend. Until I am able to reconcile its presence I may be prone to more negativity than either of us is accustomed to."

Naira nodded.

Andre stared across the water. The dark outline of the southern Oregon coast was barely visible, a slender swatch of nothingness between the water and the night sky. A single light blinked on and off in the distance.

"It calls to me, Naira. It taunts me from both my past and present. I should never have let it be."

"You didn't have a choice."

"Oh?"

"I believe you didn't. There was only truth in the story you told me. I would know if there wasn't."

She would know, of that Andre was certain. He couldn't lie to her, even if he believed the lie himself.

But the story wasn't a lie and it wasn't false. His actions in Astoria eleven years earlier had been carefully arranged to ensure there would be no mistakes. Andre couldn't destroy the book then, but it should have been safe buried beneath soil and so many secrets. Was its resurrection the result of accident or expedition? There was, of course, a more likely target for those seeking treasure, but that did nothing to ease Andre's mind. A man who would seek out the dead—especially this particular corpse—was already on the path of darkness.

Andre took a deep breath and slowly let it go. "Regardless of how it has come to be in this world again, it is my responsibility to see the book removed. I will not allow it to be used as it once was."

"Could it be? As I recall, you said you took some care in its compilation. A kind of cipher, wasn't it?"

Andre chuckled. "Enough of a nuisance to slow down a simple man, perhaps even a man with some education. But I discovered after repeated readings the disguised words begin take on meaning, even as they appear to have none. They reveal themselves. It was my mistake to think that shifting tongues would rob the words of their power to those who could not read them. I was a fool to write them down in the first place."

"You were eight."

"And then I was nine, then ten, then twenty, but I still continued to fill the pages."

Naira raised an eyebrow.

"No, I am still here," Andre said, pulling his coat tighter against a growing wind. "It will not have its way with me that easily. But what I did was still foolish."

"And what of this young man who carries the book now? Is he a fool or merely foolish?"

"Either would be preferable to a man who sees the thing for what it is, but continues to turn the page."

11

———•———

The air inside the tent was cold and damp and not at all to Henry's liking. Since leaving Astoria he'd grown unusually comfortable in his own skin, a condition he attributed to recent reading materials. Even now, he could feel the book pulsing against his chest, the warmth radiating through his body, but without the words to focus on, Henry was forced to attend a reality that offered little in the way of comfort.

Presently, a tiny woman with one arm and no legs sat on a stool near the opening of the tent, offering a toothy grin to all who entered. Recent arrivals included a tall, slender man in a loose-fitting suit whose skin hung from his bones like a damp rag, a short, apish man covered from head to toe with thick, matted hair, and a balding, middle-aged man who was unremarkable in all regards save for the fact that it was his name painted atop every banner in the camp.

Mason, whose body language suggested he was equally uncomfortable in the presence of the carnival people, stood beside Henry, with Hugh and Charlie close behind. The Hanged Man's body lay at their feet, unwrapped from head to chest. To Henry it appeared the deceased had lost some of his resilience, but was otherwise in excellent condition for a decade-old corpse. This, as it turned out, was not a selling point.

"I don't see it, boys," said John Garibaldi, rubbing the salt-and-pepper stubble beneath his chin. "I just don't see it."

Mason answered quickly, "What's not to see? He's got the scar, you got the story. It's the Hanged Man."

Garibaldi looked from Mason to Henry. "Yes, a very compelling tale, possibly even true."

"Every word," said Henry.

"Possibly, but even I can see this fellow is, to put it politely, a might fresh for a man dispatched eleven years ago."

Henry and his new friends had arrived in Tillamook just before noon to find the carnival doing a brisk business on a hill overlooking the small coastal community. Mason fumed when told their transaction would have to wait until the midday break, but Hugh and Charlie were content to explore the many tents and sideshows of the so-called Wild Western Caravan. Henry had stayed with the horses, tasked with watching over the corpse until it was time to make the sale. He didn't mind.

It gave him the chance to read.

One passage in particular stood out, a section that spoke of the dead, the surprising flexibility of their condition, and their potential service to the living. Henry had never thought of the dead as being particularly useful, but the book spoke of this as something very real and very powerful. Perhaps it was a coincidence that the passage had been written primarily in English and French, making its translation easier. The corpse at Henry's feet suggested otherwise.

Garibaldi turned to the man on his right. "Carl, what do you think?"

The skinny man knelt next to the body. He had long, gray hair and a thin mustache, neither of which did much to distract from his bony frame. Had he been lying next to the corpse rather than examining it, Henry would have said two bodies were for sale.

"Well, sir, he's been dead awhile, but a decade seems doubtful. Decomposition is only just beginning to set in. And the flesh seems almost tender to the touch, still got a bit of bounce to it. Wish I could say the same."

"Check his eyes," said Garibaldi.

The skinny man spread his bony fingers across the dead man's face and forehead and pulled back the eyelids, revealing two giant black pupils surrounded by a ring of gray and slightly yellowed whites.

Henry tried to look away, but the eyes followed him, kept his gaze even when they were all but closed. Henry had little doubt the Hanged Man was watching him, waiting.

"*Dios mío,*" said the apeman, quickly crossing his chest.

"Yes," said the skinny man. "I daresay that is unusual. Eyes are one of the first things to go as moisture exits a body."

"That's 'cause it rains all the time in Astoria," said Mason. "All that mud must have kept him from drying out."

"As I recall, it was sunny when we were there last," offered the one-armed woman.

Mason sneered at the little woman, who only smiled in return.

Garibaldi put a hand on the skinny man's shoulder. "What's your assessment then?"

"It could be him—I won't say it's not. I saw a 'Gyptian in New York City looked to be a few months out of the ground, but was said to be a thousand years, at least. Someone were to bury a body up north where the ground stays frozen year-round, they might could've kept it whole for a time, preserved like what we got here." The skinny man looked over the Hanged Man once more. "Still, based on the eyes alone, I doubt he could be more than a month gone, probably less."

"A month!" barked Mason. "Son of a . . . did you smell him?"

"I did," said the skinny man. "And I daresay that's another give-away. Only the freshly dead stink of it. A dusty old corpse would smell of earth and little more."

"It's the curse," said Henry. "That's what kept him whole."

The others in the group, most of whom had barely noticed Henry even when he was telling his story, stared at him now.

"He was a devil in life, kept alive by dark secrets that few men know. He survived the noose, he survived the gun. It wasn't until a hundred men descended on him with the Lord's righteous doom that he fell. Check the body. You'll find at least a dozen holes in addition to the one in his forehead."

"He was used for target practice," said the apeman. "Could have been one of you, all we know."

"Look at the hands," Henry said. "Tell me, what do you see?"

The skinny man glanced at Garibaldi, who nodded. He then unwrapped the Hanged Man's right hand, revealing a wrinkled but plump appendage that did little to challenge the skinny man's assessment of the body's age. The fingernails, however, told a different story.

"My, my," said the skinny man. "That is interesting."

"What?"

The skinny man grasped the Hanged Man's wrist and raised it for all to see. The nails at the end of the thumb and first finger were black and broken shortly past the tips, but the other three remained intact and curled beyond the digits in uneven corkscrews.

"Take a man quite a few years to grow nails like that," he said. "A very patient and very careful man."

"Or a very dead man," said Henry.

The skinny man hesitated before finally shaking his head. "No, not dead," he said. "But not living either."

"What's that's supposed to mean?" Mason said.

The skinny man lowered the Hanged Man's wrist and stood up. He looked at Henry, then at his boss.

"There are methods of preservation that could account for the condition, methods that are not practiced in this part of the world. Not that I've seen, anyway."

Garibaldi frowned. "So, now you're saying it could be him?"

"I am saying it is possible the body could be a decade old. As to the identity, I have no conclusion." The skinny man took another look at the corpse. "But if it is him, I would strongly advise against purchase. It's not worth the trouble."

The skinny man left the tent without another word. Mason grinned, unable to help himself.

"There you go. It's him."

Garibaldi raised an eyebrow. "Not what he said, friend."

"Oh, then you've run across other cursed dead men with scars like this one here?"

The apeman leaned close to his boss and whispered something in his ear.

"Get him," said Garibaldi.

The apeman exited the tent, leaving Garibaldi and the small woman alone with Mason and his gang. If he was concerned about this situation, he didn't show it.

"Where's the gun?"

"What gun?"

Garibaldi smiled. "That I have yet to pass on this obviously unique opportunity should not be taken lightly, Mr. Mason. Do not insult my intelligence. Where is it?"

Mason looked at the weapon on his hip. He pushed back the instinct to draw and instead pulled the gun from its holster and handed it butt-first to the carnival boss.

Garibaldi studied the pistol, turning it over in his hands.

"This was buried with the man?"

"Yup."

Garibaldi nodded. "A little paint on the handle would help sell it, son."

"You think I'm lyin'?"

"Are you?"

Mason held his tongue for a moment, then said, "I ain't afraid to admit it. We dug the son of a bitch up for the pistol."

"Something beat you to it."

Mason shrugged. "That was all he had."

Garibaldi stepped around the corpse. "Body's worth more with the real weapon. Hell, the gun's probably worth more than flesh and bone all by itself."

Henry felt Mason's stare fall on the side of his head, but didn't turn. He wasn't afraid of the man, not anymore, but Mason was still dangerous.

"We've got his book," said Charlie.

Before Henry could stop him, Charlie had reached inside Henry's coat and snatched the book from his pocket.

"Here," he said, handing the book to Garibaldi. "It's got all his black magic in it, and such."

"No, that's not part of the deal."

Henry lunged at the book, but Mason caught him by the collar and held him at arm's length.

Garibaldi waited for the scrum to end before opening the book. Satisfied, he flipped through the pages, stopping occasionally to study a passage. His eyes drifted across the words, following their meaning for a time before losing interest. He closed the book and flipped it back to Henry.

"Two bits for the book."

"It's not for sale," Henry said, ignoring the hand on his neck that suggested otherwise.

Garibaldi looked at the corpse, then at Mason. "I'll give you ten dollars for it."

"Ten? I could get ten from a saloon down in Tillamook."

"Try your luck then. I got a fellow works for me says he met the man 'fore he was put down. He's going to take a look at what you're offering here and if he doesn't call him risen from the grave, you'll walk away with nothing, save for your friend, here."

Mason stared at the carnival master.

"Twenty-five."

Garibaldi smiled. "Twenty. And for that I'll keep the weapon, as well."

Hugh leaned in to Mason. "Take it and let's be rid of the thing."

Mason glanced at Henry, eyeing the book in his hand. Henry clutched it even tighter.

"Twenty, then," he said, and held his hand out across the Hanged Man's body. Garibaldi took it, shook once, and let go.

"Mary?"

The one-armed girl drew a small purse from her blouse and passed it to her boss. He drew forth a handful of coins and passed them to Mason.

"Some fine shows on tap tonight. Stick around, if you like. No charge."

"Thanks," said Charlie.

Mason finished counting the coins and then nodded. "We could take in a show."

Garibaldi gave another half smile and then turned toward the exit just as the apeman returned with another man covered in mud up to his chest.

The circus boss stopped the new arrivals and turned them around, but not before the muddy man got a look at the corpse on the ground. His eyes went wide and his mouth slipped open.

Henry thought the words on his lip might've been *it's him*, but he was shuffled out of the tent before they could be heard.

Mason, Hugh, and Charlie celebrated their successful sale by spending most of the profits at a drinking establishment in Tillamook. Henry joined in the first round, but soon retreated to a corner of the saloon that offered just enough light to read. Hugh and Charlie were content to let him be, but Mason eventually sought Henry out, a half-empty bottle in his hand.

"You owe me two bits."

Henry looked up from the book. He'd just finished rereading the passage containing the spell he'd used on Charlie the night before. The words were still clear in his mind. Given the man's inebriated state, it would be very easy to talk Mason into smashing the bottle over his head and then using the broken shards to slit his own throat. Henry could almost see it. Instead, he reached into his pocket and pulled out a single coin.

"Here's a dollar. Keep the change."

Mason snatched up the coin, grunting under his breath. He started to turn, but hesitated.

"I can read, too."

"Can you?" Henry said, gripping the book a little tighter.

"My mama taught me. Maybe I take me a read from that book, see if I can't find out what's got you so interested." Mason leaned over the table. "What say you to that?"

Henry tilted forward in his chair. Mason's eyes were barely able to keep focus, but as the young man drew close, they seemed to still.

"It's like nothing you've ever known," he said, his voice smooth and inviting. "It's alive and speaks in the language of your soul. It speaks only the truth. Do you want to know the truth? Are you ready to hear it?"

Henry set the book on the table.

"Shall I read to you?"

Mason felt the hair on the back of his neck stand on end. What senses weren't buried beneath half a bottle of whiskey suggested he step back from the table immediately, but his legs refused to do their part.

Henry cracked open the book. "I know just the passage."

Mason blinked and, for just a moment, saw clearly that Henry was dangerous, very dangerous. He would have to go, the sooner the better.

Mason shook his head and used the bottle to push himself upright. "You're not through with us, you know. You ain't proved nothin' yet."

Henry smiled and closed the book. "I wasn't out to prove anything, Bill. I'm just along for the ride."

Mason took another long drink from the bottle and stumbled back from the table, catching himself before he fell.

"Friends," he said, addressing no one particular. "The circus is in town. Got a hell of a freak show, I hear."

"Seen it," said a man at the bar.

"Did you, now? Good for you!" Mason swallowed another tilt of the bottle. "But they got a new freak, just today. Might be worth a look."

Henry watched Mason stumble down to the other end of the bar, where a pair of young women lingered. He held up the coin Henry had just given him. Neither woman seemed particularly impressed, but one of them took the dollar and led Mason down a hall and out of sight.

The saloon was quiet for a time, more suitable for reading.

A thick fog bank had rolled over the coast by the time Henry and the others returned to the carnival. Despite the gloom, the midway was crowded with townsfolk eager to explore the many games of chance, live performances, and other oddities on display. Lit by torchlight, the colorful tents and attractions took on an otherworldly glow in the mist.

On one stage, a man in a top hat introduced Mandu and Wattu, the Wild Men of Borneo. A diminutive, dark-skinned man in a tight-fitting suit scrabbled onstage to stand next to the barker. This was Mandu, the gentle savage, refined in the ways of Western man. His less-refined twin, Wattu, soon appeared through a trapdoor in the stage, shrieking and wagging his tongue (and other appendages) at the crowd.

Across the midway, a broad-shouldered man with an even broader mustache balanced a long iron bar on his head weighed down on either side by squirming children. He shared his stage with an equally bulky woman who had snatched up two men from the crowd and now held them aloft with a single hand. The men squirmed more than the children.

Content simply to sit and watch the faces of the locals react was Fanny Brown, the Big Foot Girl of Oregon. She reclined in a rocking chair, an afghan draped over her legs. When a patron drew near she pulled back the blanket to reveal a pair of puffed and disfigured size-36 feet. The more revulsion she engendered, the more her delight.

A half-dozen similar performers and prodigies lined the path to the big top. There were other tents and trailers, some with small lines of people waiting to see the likes of Madame Morgana or the Human Flame. Henry was content to stroll the midway, but Hugh and Charlie soon went in search of a performer they'd encountered earlier, explaining that the "lady in knots" required their company. Mason, too drunk to keep up, lingered at Henry's side.

"Where's the dead man?" he said, scanning the crowd. "There he is!"

Mason staggered toward a small stage at the end of the midway, knocking a pair of children over in the process. Henry followed, though not so close as to be an obvious friend of the drunkard.

Onstage, the skinny man stood beneath a sign proclaiming him to be the "Living Dead Dude." He wore a long, hooded robe that covered everything but his sunken face. There were gasps of horror when the robe slipped to the stage, revealing not so much a man but a skeleton clad only in a short loincloth. He strode to the edge of the dais and spread his arms wide.

"I am the living dead," he said in a voice much deeper than what Henry remembered from their earlier meeting. "Do not fear me."

"You're not the dead man," Mason mumbled and then staggered off through the crowd.

The skinny man eyed Mason, then slowly turned his gaze to Henry. "Do you fear the dead that walk upright, young man?"

"No."

"A brave soul." The skinny man cast his gaze upon a couple standing to Henry's side, who quickly shrunk back. "Braver than most."

"He's right, though," Henry said. "You're no dead man."

The skinny man's eyed darted back to Henry. "Do not speak ill of the deceased, my friend." He then dropped from the stage and was upon Henry in one swift, fluid motion. There were more gasps from the audience, many of whom backed away.

Henry didn't flinch.

The skinny man leaned in, his cheekbone nearly touching Henry's. When he spoke, his voice was a whisper that only Henry could hear. "Hold your tongue so far from home, Henry Macke. The dead hear more than you think."

Before Henry could respond, the skinny man slipped back onto the platform and climbed beneath his robe. He cast a sweeping gaze across the crowd and then disappeared into a small tent behind the stage.

Henry stood for a moment as the crowd dispersed before going in search of Mason.

Henry found the man in front of a tent second only to the big top in overall size. A long line of people filed through the front entrance, a line that snaked its way halfway around the tent and then back onto the midway. A hastily made sign declared that for only a dime a person could view the corpse of the Hanged Man. John Garibaldi himself stood outside the tent, declaring that this attraction was required viewing for any man, woman, or child who wanted to see the *real* West.

"It's true!" he said, projecting his voice well beyond the multitude already in line for the viewing. "After a decade frozen in the hardened permafrost of the great northern wilds, the vilest villain ever to terrorize the West has returned to pay for his sins. See with your own eyes the scar upon his neck left by the rope that could not hang him! Be amazed at the number of shots it took to finally fell the man. Was it one? Five? A dozen? Look and see!"

Garibaldi laid eyes on Mason and Henry. A sly smile crossed his lips.

"And don't miss the cursed weapon of the killer, the red-handled pistol, its wood stained with the blood of a hundred victims, maybe more."

Henry was impressed. Garibaldi had turned on his investment quickly and would probably make it back (and then some) in one night. It occurred to him that he hadn't thought of the Hanged Man once since they'd left the circus, since the body had ceased to be in their possession. He saw no reason to join the line to remind him of what he was missing.

Mason had other ideas.

"You son of a bitch," he said, his anger helping to smooth over the alcohol. "You're gonna get rich off my dead man?"

Garibaldi eyed Mason coldly. "Just business, son. Go on and have a look, see how the professionals do it."

Garibaldi lifted the front flap of the tent a bit wider and beckoned Mason to enter. Mason didn't hesitate.

Henry did. He could feel the Hanged Man once more, a weight laid on his shoulders he no longer wanted to carry. Henry could see him dangling by a rope, his eyes wide open, laughing at God for thinking his death would bring peace.

"You coming?" Garibaldi asked. "It's only free as long as I hold her open."

Henry meant to say no, had every intention of turning on the spot and walking away, but instead he found himself moving forward into the darkness.

"He'll haunt your dreams!" Garibaldi said as he let the flap fall back. "Who among you fears not the Angel of Death!"

Inside the tent, the line of people followed a roped path that circled past a collection of smaller displays showcasing various Western artifacts. Among them were numerous Indian weapons and tribal garb, a selection of unusual animal skeletons, and a large red-and-black striped lizard, very much alive, hissing at the onlookers from inside a slatted wooden cage. In the center of the enclosure, a round glass case displayed two shriveled fingers, which according to a carefully lettered sign were all that remained of famed lawman Charlie Lancaster. The case next to it featured a fist-size chunk of solid firestone crystal half buried in the sand and an open invitation to reach through the small hole in the top of the display to claim the stone. A pair of rattlesnakes curled up on either side of the stone ensured there would be no takers.

Henry cut across the queue, skipping the minor artifacts until he came upon the main attraction. Mason was already there, leaning over the ropes intended to restrain him. Henry reached out to pull Mason back, but never laid a hand on him. His eyes fell upon the Hanged Man and it was all he knew.

The body was not strung up but rather laid in a coffin stood on end. Torches on either side flickered in the dead man's eyes, both wide open and uncomfortably alive. The body was naked from the waist up, revealing a lanky, unevenly muscular torso riddled with bullet holes. A noose tied loosely around the Hanged Man's neck hung to his waist, where it frayed, as if cut in midexecution. Tucked into the front of his trousers was a pistol, its butt painted bright red. Even from ten feet away Henry could see that some of the pigment had rubbed off on the dead man's stomach, looking very much like dried blood.

"Sons of bitches," Mason said softly.

Henry blinked and was surprised to find his arm still outstretched, hand hovering over Mason's shoulder. He pulled it back, managing to look away just that long before the dead man's gaze commanded his attention once more. Nearly everyone who passed through the tent that night would claim the Hanged Man's eyes followed them.

Only one would be right.

Mason leaned close to Henry. "This is your fault."

With great effort, Henry forced himself to meet Mason's glare. "We never should have sold him," he said, and meant it.

"We never should have dug him up," Mason growled. "And now he's making these leeches rich. They even got his gun."

"It's not his," Henry said, genuinely taking offense. To lay such an obviously false weapon on the body was wrong. He'd never felt comfortable with the sale and now he knew why. This was a great man. Yes, he was a villain, but what did that matter? To treat the Hanged Man as a nothing more than a prop in some sideshow museum was disgraceful, unthinkable.

"It's a travesty, all of it," Henry said. "We should definitely—"

Mason grabbed Henry by the collar. "What? Dig up another corpse? Find us another dead man worth more than the box he's buried in? What?"

Henry searched for an answer, and found one, pulsing softly against his chest. It had been there all along, of course. When he spoke, his voice was calm and clear.

"Let's rob the place."

12

"The gate closes at ten," Mason said. "Then we take it all."

Henry nodded, as did Hugh. Charlie did not. After searching half the carnival, they'd found him lingering behind a tent belonging to a contortionist named Baby Sue. An illustration painted on the side of the tent suggested she was capable of twisting her body into any number of amazing and unusual shapes.

"Um, okay," said Charlie. "But I don't want to skip out on Miss Sue. She promised us a special show."

Mason scowled. Since deciding to rob the carnival, his drunken stupor had been replaced by a headache that cut through the haze like a dagger. The pain brought the night into focus, but it also made the man very angry.

"You think she'll twist her bits for you after you steal from her boss?"

Charlie hesitated. "She might if I paid her."

Mason rubbed his temples with both hands. "Screw this up and I'll gut you, Charlie."

Charlie looked to Hugh, who quietly shook his head. Based on the brothers' expressions, Henry suspected Mason had never seriously threatened either man, but he was now, of that there was no doubt.

Mason turned to Hugh. "That little one-armed freak, she was still collecting when we came back tonight, right?"

"Had a lockbox and big, dumb-lookin' rube by her side."

"Find 'em. That's where the cash'll be."

"What am I supposed to do?" Henry asked.

Mason pointed in the direction of the Hanged Man's tent. "You're gonna walk back in there and light the dead man on fire."

Henry shuddered. "What?"

Mason forced a smile. "Said it wasn't right what they done to him, didn't ya?"

Had he said that? Henry couldn't remember.

"Here's your chance to set things right. Ought to make for quite a distraction, eh?"

It would. Mason's plan was simple enough. Henry would cause a ruckus, draw as many of the circus folk to him as possible, while Mason, Hugh, and Charlie collected the cash. The weakest part of the plan—as far as Henry was concerned—was how he would make his escape.

"And I'm supposed to just slip away after starting a fire in front of a tent full of people?"

"Once the fire gets rolling, ain't nobody gonna stick around to point fingers," Mason said. "You'll be fine."

Henry had his doubts, but said nothing more.

Hugh and Charlie found the one-armed girl floating above the crowd, riding the shoulders of an enormous brute whose smile was almost as big as her own. The front gate was closed, the cash box tucked under the brute's arm. As the odd couple strolled the midway, they collected the evening's receipts from the shows that charged additional admission. Their last stop was the Hanged Man's tent, where they received a hefty pouch from Garibaldi.

Mason watched the giant and his rider exchange a few words with their boss and then disappear behind a tent.

"All right, crowd's starting to thin out. Let's make this fast. Hit 'em while there's still some cover."

Mason led the way between a pair of tents to the sparsely lit area just beyond the midway. A young couple strolled past and beyond them, slipping behind a row of wagons, their target.

"Five minutes," Mason said, eyeing Henry. "Then I want to see smoke."

Henry nodded. He watched the three men draw their weapons and cautiously move into the shadows, before turning back toward the main thoroughfare. The crowd was thinner, with most headed for the exit. Henry made his way to the Hanged Man's tent, where the line was only a few people deep at the entrance.

Henry took his place at the end of the queue, paid his dime, and passed through the flap, which was soon closed behind him. There were fewer people inside than earlier, but Henry kept his place rather than cut ahead.

He was in no hurry.

Why should he be? He was in control now. It had been his idea to rob the circus, after all. Certainly, his and Mason's visions of what they were stealing differed slightly, but when all the shouting was done, Henry was convinced Mason would see it his way.

The Hanged Man would make sure of that.

The idea of resurrection first occurred to Henry in a dream. He didn't realize it at the time, but that was only because he didn't understand. He did now. It was no coincidence that he skipped ahead in his reading to the passage detailing the returning of life to the nonliving. He was drawn there as clearly as he'd been to the

Hanged Man's grave. The fact that the words were easier to decipher, much more so than any other passages, served only to confirm his course of action. It was obvious. He was meant to bring the Hanged Man back to this world, to give him back his life.

And Henry would be his master.

That was how it worked. The book was very clear that a body returned to this world would be indebted to the living, specifically the one who did the deed. That would be Henry. The Hanged Man would be under his control and together they would . . . what?

Henry hadn't worked that part out yet. In fact, as he stepped closer to the body, he found his determination slipping, ever so slightly. He'd felt that way all day—confident but confused. Had he really found a spell that would bring the dead man back to life? Was that really what he was supposed to do? And then he heard his answer.

(*always*)

Henry laid a hand over his chest, felt the square shape beneath his jacket beat in time with his heart, and knew it was true. He'd been meant to read those words today, just as he was meant to use them, here and now.

The resurrection curse was a lengthy one requiring elaborate preparation, hours of chanting, and numerous organic and inorganic items, some of which were completely foreign to Henry. Fortunately, there was a shortcut. When the living body had been prepared for death—such as when the living chose to curse themselves prior to death in order to preserve their remains, as the Hanged Man had obviously done—resurrection required only three things: the curse words, a belief in them, and blood.

Henry was in possession of all three. He would speak the words, believe them, and, since he was unlikely to put his knife to another man, he would bleed. It would hurt only a little.

The tent was nearly empty. Henry kept his head down, his eyes otherwise occupied, not wanting to see the dead man before he was ready. He made the last turn in the line and moved to the center of the display.

An old woman stood in front of him, staring up at the body. She murmured something under her breath, made the sign of the cross, and then moved away. Henry stepped into the vacant space and slowly let his gaze rise to meet the Hanged Man's.

Garibaldi's hand fell on Henry's shoulder at the exact moment he locked stares with the dead man.

"Can't keep your eyes off him, eh?"

Henry didn't respond—he couldn't. Every one of his senses was focused on the propped-up corpse. The world around him passed into a fog and all he knew was the depth of the black-eyed stare. There was only himself and the Hanged Man, standing before him, standing beside him. When he finally did feel Garibaldi's touch, it wasn't the carnival master's hand he imagined on his shoulder.

"Tried to stare him down myself once we got his eyes propped open," Garibaldi said. "Had to put a bit of face paint on him, too, make him look more the part of the deceased. Didn't figure he'd mind."

Henry saw the carnival boss, saw him lying on the ground bleeding, the knife that had stuck him held firmly in Henry's hand. He saw this clearly and then it was gone.

Garibaldi stood at his side, his hand on Henry's shoulder. Henry blinked, surprised to be staring into the eyes of a living man.

Garibaldi smiled and shook his head. "Intense feller, ain't ya?"

The knife was in Henry's pocket. He'd plucked it from his saddle pouch without thinking just prior to returning to the carnival. Its purpose now known, Henry chose not to use it. He spoke quickly before his mind could be changed.

"You're being robbed," he said, returning his gaze to the Hanged Man. "My acquaintances are, as we speak, trying to decide the best way to separate that large feeb from his diminutive charge and, more importantly, the small treasure chest he carries."

Garibaldi looked at Henry, searching for some sign that his words were for amusement. He found none.

"I daresay someone might get shot."

Garibaldi pointed a finger at Henry. "Stay here," he said, and ran for the exit.

"No place I'd rather be."

Two men who had been watching over the display trailed after their boss as he ran out of the tent. With no one to stop him, Henry stepped over the rope and approached the Hanged Man's body. Up close, he could easily make out the ashen makeup applied to the dead man's face.

"They've tried to make you a clown."

"Looks more like a scarecrow," said a young voice behind Henry.

Henry didn't have to turn to know it was the boy he'd stood behind in line.

"Does he frighten you?" Henry asked.

"Course not."

"He will," Henry said, drawing the revolver from the dead man's belt. A moment later, he was alone.

Henry closed his eyes. Upon opening them, his gaze once again fell on the Hanged Man, and this time he met the dead man's stare without succumbing to it. *Let him look at me awhile,* he thought.

Henry studied the pistol in his hand. It was the same weapon that had come out of the ground with the dead man, albeit with a fresh coat of paint. He checked the cylinder and was surprised to find it loaded.

"Nice of them to arm you," he said, and slipped the gun into the holster on the right side of the dead man's body.

A gun was fired somewhere outside the tent, startling Henry, and for a moment he was free. There was no book, no body, no resurrection—all he had to do was turn and run.

(*stay*)

Henry closed his eyes and let the warm words fill his body. He would be a captive, but the words would keep him safe. At that moment, Henry thought it a fair trade.

Several more gunshots rang out, but Henry didn't flinch. Carefully, he retrieved the black book from his inside coat pocket, opened it to a page covered with rough notes and scribbles, and began to read.

Sixty-seven miles to the south, a rogue swell struck the *Año Nuevo* broadside, tilting the vessel hard to starboard.

Andre rode the wave from the edge of his bed as it tilted the room past twenty degrees, enough to send his suitcase sliding across the floor. The world hung at odds with gravity for a moment longer, then rolled back to right and the otherwise calm waters of the Oregon coast.

Andre received no such reprieve.

"No, no, no," he said, although there was no one in the room to hear him. His world had been dealt an even more powerful blow moments before the wave struck. He would later decide the two events were connected, but for now he knew only that the worst had occurred. His connection to the book had been severed. It had a new master.

And he was using it.

Mason ducked as a bullet blistered the corner of the flatbed wagon, filling the air with splinters. Second and third shots whizzed past overhead, and then he popped up long enough to return fire, before another volley answered his own.

"Where's my fire!" he screamed at no one in particular.

Mason ejected the spent cartridges from his pistol and quickly reloaded. At his feet, a bag lay torn open, its cache of coins and a few government notes spilled onto the dirt. There was no lockbox. At the first sign of trouble, the brute had tossed the box and the tiny, one-armed woman on top of a trailer, out of sight and out of reach. That left the take from the Hanged Man's tent and little else. Charlie had snatched the money bag from the brute's belt, but it had cost him.

"How is he?"

Hugh shook his head. "Shoulder's busted. Some ribs, too."

"I'm fine!" Charlie said and then sucked in a gulp of air. "Hurts like a bitch, though."

"Good," Mason said. "Pain means you ain't dyin'."

Mason scanned the area around them. They were at the south end of the camp, farthest from the entrance, and on the opposite side of the big top from the Hanged Man's tent. Garibaldi and half-dozen carnival folks had them pinned down on two sides. From here, they could cut back to the midway or take their chances on the steep western slope behind the camp, which in the dark would likely be suicide.

A few stragglers remained on the midway, apparently not alarmed at the sound of gunshots, or the flames that should have been lighting up the night sky.

"Where's my g'damn fire!"

Henry held the knife firmly against his thumb, waiting for the blood to come. It didn't. It wouldn't, until he broke the skin. This was proving more of a problem than he'd anticipated.

"Come on," he whispered to himself. "Just a little slice. Won't hurt a bit."

Henry didn't believe it.

He believed what he read. The words on the page had flowed into his eyes, through his mind, and out of his mouth. They were resurrection, life, and redemption (*vengeance*), for himself and the dead man to whom they were directed. They were true.

The condensed version of the spell was only a dozen lines long and Henry had spoken them clearly and correctly, he was sure. There was only one line left.

But first there was blood.

"Don't think about it, do it."

Henry closed his eyes and pressed the knife against his flesh. Still no blood. There wouldn't be until he pulled the blade across his skin and he knew it. For all the strength given him by the book, it had somehow failed him on this one thing. He was afraid of the pain.

(*coward*)

Henry opened his eyes. "I'm not a coward."

The knife slipped easily across Henry's thumb, cutting deeper than he'd intended. It was cold and painless. He stared at the red, inch-long line crossing his fingerprint as it swelled and overflowed with blood. And then the pain came.

"Ouch."

Henry waited for the fear to return, but the stinging in his thumb had the opposite effect. His head was clear, his path laid bare before him. He would share his blood with the dead man and . . .

"Make him my own."

Henry raised his now-dripping left thumb to the Hanged Man's forehead. He pressed it there, letting the blood flow onto the face of the dead man. A single drop rolled across the bridge of the nose, cutting a crimson line through the pale makeup before slipping into the right eye. Henry watched as his blood spread across the yellowed white, tinting it orange and then red.

Henry drew back and admired his handiwork. Was it enough? The book was vague on the amount of blood needed for resurrection, as well as where to apply it. It referred only to "wetting the flesh." He glanced at the cut on his thumb, where fluid continued to seep, and thought it best not to be stingy.

Henry traced the faint scar across the Hanged Man's neck with his thumb, leaving a fresh trail of blood. He half expected the scar to open and swallow the red line, but it did not. Henry considered touching each of the bullet scars on the dead man's chest, but held back. Had they always been scars? When would he have had time to heal before dying?

"That's enough," he said, cutting off the questions. Henry backed away a few steps and waited.

A fresh volley of gunfire erupted outside the tent, followed by men yelling and then more shooting. Henry barely heard it. The shooting was someplace else, somewhere that couldn't touch him, not now, not ever again.

"Rise, my friend."

Nothing happened.

Henry blinked. His thumb hurt. What had he done wrong? A moment of panic faded away almost immediately and Henry smiled.

"Not done yet," he said, pulling the black book from his pocket. Somewhere in the back of his mind, Henry was surprised that he'd lost track of the book, even though it now pulsed in his hands. It had left him, but only for a moment.

Henry started to open the book, but caught site of his bloody thumb and stopped. He didn't know why, but getting his blood on the pages would be bad. He slipped the book under his arm and then tore a strip of cloth off the sheet that hung beside the Hanged

Man listing his crimes. Henry wrapped the fabric around his injury, seeing the word *murder* roll about his thumb and then disappear beneath the next wrapping. When it was done, he took the book in his left hand and let it fall open, finding the point where he'd left off immediately. Henry read:

"Blood given, bloed reduco, vita captus, mortuus haud magis. Thou art risen, élévation et come forth. Sto in nex umbra and wag vir niks. I call to thee . . ."

Henry stopped reading. He stared at the text, not sure what to say. He'd read over the spell several times, had practiced the foreign words until sure he was speaking them correctly, but somehow he'd missed this before.

I call to thee, (nom).

He'd read it before as it was written, but now understood he was not supposed to say the word but rather to insert a name—the name of the dead man.

What name?

Hugh and Charlie had argued this topic repeatedly before concluding the man didn't have a name. He might have at some point, but it had been long forgotten, if it had ever been known. His name was the Hanged Man.

Henry wasn't so sure. That name was his, but was it the man's true name? Would it speak to whatever power was to bring him back to the land of the living? Henry stumbled over the question in his head several times before coming to the obvious answer. There wasn't another name to use.

Henry looked at the Hanged Man's face. Thin streaks of blood ran down either side of the nose, turning to black tears in the ashen makeup. Without thinking, Henry reached up and drew down the eyelids. The right one refused to close completely. It would have to do.

Henry looked to the book, but he already knew the words to speak. He never got the chance to say them.

Mason's gun pressed against Henry's temple made sure of it.

"Where's my fire, Henry?"

Henry's eyes flicked to his right. Mason was only a few feet away, his face bloodied in much the same way as the Hanged Man's. Henry was so engrossed in his task, he'd missed the man's approach entirely.

Mason sniffed the air. "I don't smell smoke. I should smell smoke," he said, and pressed his gun harder against Henry's temple. "Where's my g'damm fire, Henry!"

Henry opened his mouth but said nothing. He wasn't afraid. He wouldn't make an excuse, he wouldn't lie. He didn't have to.

"I'm lighting it right now," he said.

Henry turned back the corpse, closed his eyes, and spoke:

I call to thee, Hanged Man, forever sent, never to return; I call to thee, return to me."

The last half of the sentence was a translation from the Latin and French hodgepodge that was scribbled in the book. Henry didn't think about it, he just did it. He knew the words. At that moment, he could have spoken the entire text of the spell in English, or any language, in fact. He knew it.

Henry opened his eyes.

The Hanged Man's were still mostly closed.

Mason looked from Henry to the Hanged Man and back to Henry. His gun never moved.

"What? You trying to start a fire with magic? You an idiot? Use a g'damn match!"

"No," Henry said, his voice wavering. "I spoke it all, all of it.

Every word. He's supposed to . . ." Henry reached for the Hanged Man.

Mason grabbed his collar and threw him down. "Never should have brought you. Just a stupid kid."

"Shoot him."

Henry turned on his side to see Charlie drop to the ground at his brother's feet. Both men were wounded, Charlie obviously worse than Hugh.

"Put a gun in his paw and throw him out front," Hugh said. "Give 'em something else to shoot at 'sides us."

"No," Henry said. "Wait! He's coming, he's coming back."

"Who?"

Henry pointed at the corpse behind Mason. Mason didn't turn around.

"Is that what you're doing?" Mason laughed. "Trying to raise the dead?"

Hugh and Charlie exchanged glances as Mason moved back to the tent entrance. He slipped open the flap as little as possible and scanned the grounds. Satisfied, he dumped the spent cartridges from his pistol and began to reload.

Henry registered that Mason's weapon had been empty, but he didn't care. His attention was back on the dead man. What had he done wrong? He made a mistake in the reading, he must have.

"I can fix this," Henry said, flipping open the book. He scanned the pages, his finger darting over the words, his mouth repeating them silently. The words in his head matched those on the page. Where was his mistake?

"What have you got left?" Mason asked Hugh.

Hugh glanced at his pistol. "Two and I'm out."

Charlie handed his weapon to his brother. "Full six, but that's all I got."

Mason looked around the tent, finally spying the gun in the Hanged Man's holster.

"That loaded?"

Henry didn't look up from the book.

Not waiting for an answer, Mason strode toward the body, but was struck high in the left shoulder by a bullet fired from outside the tent. He spun on the spot and went down in front of the dead man on display.

Hugh dropped low and returned fire, emptying his pistol blindly into the side of the tent. He switched to Charlie's, fired once more, and then dragged his brother behind a pedestal in the center of the room on which a Native headdress was displayed.

Shots rang out on all sides of the tent. Most of the bullets passed through one wall and exited the opposite. A single shot grazed the Hanged Man's right thigh. None of the men in the tent noticed as blood began to ooze from the wound.

Finally, a voice called out, "Hold yer fire, dammit!"

The shooting stopped.

Mason rolled over on his hip, sat up, and scanned the tent, front to back. There was no place to hide that didn't back up against canvas, a poor proposition for defensive purposes. One of the torches beside the Hanged Man had fallen and was within reach. Mason picked it up, weighing his options in either hand. Fire back or fire?

"Give it up, son," called out the circus master. "Got nowhere to go. Give up now, you live. That's my one and only offer."

Mason looked at Hugh and Charlie. Both brothers had had enough. They wouldn't be of help. Henry was only a few feet away, his face buried in that damn book. He was useless. That left Mason and the dead man. Mason smiled.

"Always heard you were good in a fight," he said to the corpse and then tossed the torch into the coffin. A moment later, the Hanged Man's pant leg caught fire.

Henry flipped another page, then nearly screamed in pain as his leg began to burn. Only it wasn't his leg.

Henry leaped to his feet. He grabbed the torch and threw it across the tent, where it struck canvas and fell to the ground still burning. Without hesitation he swatted at the flames with his bare hands. There was pain, much of it focused in his bloodied thumb, but the fire was out quickly. The pain in his leg subsided.

"Thanks," said a voice beside him. "Hate to see my investment go up in smoke on the first night."

Henry turned to see Mason, Hugh, and Charlie under guard. Garibaldi, the brute at his side, had his weapon trained on Henry.

Henry took a step back. This was where it would end. His new life would come to a crashing halt before it had begun. It wasn't fair. It wasn't supposed to happen this way.

And then a hand from above fell on Henry's shoulder and changed everything.

13

The Hanged Man thought it odd that none of the weapons were aimed at him.

Three men were down, injured, and held at gunpoint by three others, two with pistols, another with a shotgun. One man was not *armed* at all but rather held a revolver with his foot while balancing on the other. Of the gunmen, the Hanged Man knew he would be the most formidable.

Closer to the Hanged Man, a large idiot carrying no weapon but his size backed up an older man whose colorful vest and pristine gold-plated Volcanic pistol suggested he was the boss.

The last man, the man close enough to reach out and touch, was Henry Macke. The Hanged Man already knew all he needed to about him.

As for the rest, he didn't need to know any more. They were all about to die.

John Garibaldi followed the hand on Henry's shoulder back to its owner. The Hanged Man's glassy-eyed glare returned his own, as it had every other time he'd looked at the dead man, but then something different happened. He blinked.

Before Garibaldi had a chance to explore this development, the Hanged Man drew the gun on his hip and shot the circus master in the chest. His second shot took a chunk of scalp and a little skull off the brute. The armless freak managed to turn his weapon toward the Hanged Man before a bullet exploded his shooting leg at the kneecap. The other two men were struck in the back as they attempted to flee, the last already outside the tent when he tumbled face-first into the sod.

"Holy Christ," Mason managed, getting to his knees. "You actually brought the bastard back." He grinned at Henry, thinking his situation had improved. When he looked to the Hanged Man, Mason discovered otherwise.

The Hanged Man fired again, striking Mason in the cheek, tearing off the man's ear in the process.

"No," Henry said, weakly. "Not him."

The Hanged Man tilted his head toward Henry. Henry looked into the living dead man's eyes—one bloodred, one putrid yellow—and understood his world would never be the same.

The Hanged Man pointed his weapon at Hugh and pulled the trigger. Nothing happened. He pulled back the hammer and depressed the trigger again. Nothing. Finally, he took a closer look at his weapon. There was paint on his hand, rubbed off from the handle.

"Not my gun," he said, his voice deep and ragged.

Hugh shot Henry a look and then scooped up his brother and stumbled out of the tent. A single shot was fired outside the tent, but no more.

Henry raised a hand to the Hanged Man and tried to back away but was thrown aside by something massive.

The brute, blood pouring from beneath the loose flap of skin clinging to his scalp, advanced on the Hanged Man, screaming at the top of his lungs. He smashed into the coffin and the man, sending both toppling into a support beam that snapped, bringing the back third of the tent down on top of them.

Henry rolled away from the melee and onto his feet. He couldn't see the two monsters but could hear the brute wailing nonsensically before abruptly stopping. There was a guttural grunt and then nothing more.

Henry stood still, unable to move. This was his doing. By all rights he owned this monster. That's how it worked, that's what he'd read in the book. It had *promised*.

Something shifted beneath the canvas. There was a sharp tear and then a rip as a knife plunged through the canvas, cutting an arcing line from left to right. The flap fell away and he stepped through, hands and chest bloodied, though it was not his own.

The Hanged Man held up the small knife Henry had used to draw blood from his thumb. He flipped it at the younger man's feet, where it stuck in the ground.

Henry flinched but otherwise didn't move.

"I made you," he managed.

The Hanged Man stared at Henry, showing no emotion. His eyes fell upon the small black book gripped tightly against the young man's chest.

The book vibrated in Henry's hand. It wasn't the comforting heartbeat that had brought Henry to this place but rather a call to its master.

"No," Henry said. "I'm the master."

The Hanged Man grinned and was immediately struck in the gut by the first bullet ever fired from John Garibaldi's vintage Volcanic pistol. The second hit the man in his thigh, the third grazed his shin.

There were two more shots in the gun, but the carnival boss

couldn't hold the weapon aloft long enough to fire again. The pistol dropped at his side into a pool of blood. He looked up at Henry.

"Run, you idiot," he choked out.

Henry stared at the injured man, momentarily unsure whether he should help him or take his advice. And then he heard the words that made his decision easy:

"You got something belongs to me, Henry Macke."

Henry ran.

The screams and gunfire continued long after Henry stumbled through the carnival exit and into the woods above Tillamook. He ran as far his legs would carry him and then collapsed beneath a giant fir tree, striking his forehead sharply against the trunk as he went down. Henry blinked back stars, fighting to stay conscious long enough to put the tree between himself and the circus. Satisfied, he listened.

Nothing.

Henry tried to judge the distance he'd covered. Was it far enough? Was he safe? He shook his head.

"I'm the master."

Upon exiting the tent, he'd been met by a crowd of armed circus folk, including the skinny man, who took one look at Henry and knew.

"What did you do?"

The answer came from a bullet that passed through the skinny man's left lung before coming to rest in the arm of the green-skinned acrobat standing behind him. All eyes turned from Henry to the tall, shirtless man emerging from the ruined tent. In his right hand was the carnival boss's gold-plated pistol, which he fired, striking the apeman in the neck. He dropped the weapon and re-placed it with one of the three other pistols tucked behind his belt.

Shots rang out as the carnival folk fired back. Henry saw at least two bullets hit their mark, but neither slowed the Hanged Man as he emptied the second pistol, every shot tasting flesh. Henry broke through the crowd before the villain drew again.

The last thing Henry saw as he left the circus grounds was the Hanged Man, his made-up mug glowing brightly in the carnival lights, strolling down the midway, shooting anyone who crossed his path. Fifty yards stood between them, but the man still found Henry in the crowd and paused to show him the bloody grin on his face.

The image stayed with Henry until he passed out thirty min-utes later under a fir tree.

Henry awoke to the warmth of a fire and a dull headache. He put a hand to his pain, finding a large bump in the center of his fore-head. He remembered hitting it against the tree. He must have passed out.

Who built the fire?

Henry sat upright to see the Hanged Man squatting on the other side of a small fire, trimming the overgrown fingernails on his left hand. No longer half naked, he now wore a clean white shirt and plain black jacket that seemed to fit him quite well. A wide-brimmed hat sat atop his head, hiding the evidence of his previous death. Minus the makeup and blood, he looked almost normal. Henry knew that was a lie.

Henry moved slowly at first, backing away from the dead man as a wave of nausea threatened to keep him from moving at all. It passed and with it any pretense of staying put. Henry scrambled to his feet and bolted into the darkness. He didn't get far before he heard its call:

(*come back*)

The feeling wasn't so much pain as loss. He felt it in his heart. Henry stumbled to a stop, putting a hand into his coat pocket for reassurance, but finding none.

It was gone.

Henry spun on the spot. The Hanged Man remained by the fire only now he was staring directly at Henry. He raised the black book in his hand and grinned.

Henry walked back to the fire and stopped just short of the flames. The Hanged Man turned his attention to the book as he flipped through its pages.

"That's mine," Henry said, surprised by the fearlessness in his voice.

The Hanged Man didn't respond but stopped flipping pages. He raised the book into the light of the fire, illuminating an otherwise unremarkable page that featured a bloody thumbprint on the upper left-hand corner.

"So it is."

A sliver of pain pulsated within Henry's cut thumb.

The Hanged Man snapped the book closed and tossed it across the flames to Henry. The moment the book fell into his hands, Henry felt better. It was his. He was the master. How could he have ever doubted it? He let the book fall open in his hand, sure it would land on the page he wanted. It did.

"Earth and dust, sang et os, I call to thee ut lord quod bass!"

The Hanged Man listened intently as Henry continued, flawlessly mingling English, French, Latin, and African phrases in perfect cadence and pitch. When he was done, the Hanged Man stared at Henry a beat, then returned to trimming his nails.

Henry blinked. "I brought you back. You have to do what I say."

The Hanged Man cut across a long nail and then tossed the clipping into the fire.

"You have to," Henry repeated. "You're under my control."

The Hanged Man stood. As a corpse, his size had been a burden, but reanimated the man's lanky six-and-a-half-foot frame was steady and fast. He stepped across the fire and grabbed Henry by the neck, forcing him back against a tree. Henry struggled, but found no slack.

"No man controls me."

Henry stared into the dead man's eyes. The right had mostly cleared, so it now matched the yellowed orb on the left. A single, crooked red line cut across the pupil that appeared to pulse with blood. Henry wondered if it was his own.

"But the book," Henry managed and then began to choke. The Hanged Man tightened his grip, closing off Henry's air supply. He held firm for a moment, then loosed his hold, as if distracted by an unexpected thought. Abruptly, he released Henry, who fell to the ground gasping for air.

The Hanged Man plucked the book from Henry's grasp and turned to the fire. He could not feel the heat on his legs, his hands, or anywhere else on his body. He thought he might come to miss it, but the lack of pain in his gut-shot belly seemed a fair trade. He would not be the same man. Perhaps he wouldn't be a man at all. Either way, the Hanged Man didn't care. The hate in his heart burned as brightly as ever.

"But I brought you back," Henry said weakly.

The Hanged Man nodded.

"Then why?"

The Hanged Man held the book before the flames, unsure whether he wanted to let it go, or even if he could. He doubted it would burn, regardless. It wasn't his anymore. That didn't mean he couldn't still be its master.

"Wrong name," he said, and dropped the book at Henry's feet.

Henry snatched it up in both hands, feeling warmth greater than anything emanating from the fire. He would never let it go again, no matter the hand that tried to steal it.

The Hanged Man was counting on it.

Henry gathered himself, unsure of his next move. He could run, but to where? The Hanged Man had caught up to him easily enough. It was the book. The Hanged Man could feel it and was perhaps even connected to it. It would call to him, as it did to Henry. There would be no escape. Not yet.

"What do you want with me?"

The Hanged Man turned and walked away toward a pair of horses tied to a tree at the edge of the firelight. He dug into a knapsack thrown over one of the saddles and pulled out a pistol. He returned to Henry and knelt beside him, holding out the weapon butt-first.

The red paint on the handle had mostly worn off, but Henry would have recognized it with or without the false decoration.

"That's the gun we found buried with you."

The gun spun so fast in the Hanged Man's grip, Henry wondered if the barrel had always been pointed at him.

"Liar."

"I'm not lying! That's all we found. That gun and the book."

The Hanged Man pulled back the hammer, locking it into position. He liked the way the trigger felt under his finger. It was a modest-size weapon, sturdy, and one that was oddly familiar. He wanted very much to pull the trigger. The fact that he could not was troubling.

"The old man!"

The Hanged Man cocked an eyebrow.

"The marshal, uh, Kleberger, I think. He took it, he must have."

"Kleberg," the Hanged Man said. He knew that name.

"Yeah, him. I saw him bury you years ago—with your gun, the real one—but he must have come back and swapped it out for that one."

The Hanged Man lowered the weapon. An ancient memory, the first he'd fully recalled since regaining consciousness, began to unspool in his mind.

In it his hate found a purpose.

The Hanged Man is dead—or nearly so. Death will come soon despite the whisper in his pocket telling him otherwise. It never lies, but he can barely hear it, now, calling to him, singing a sweet lullaby.

The marshal is there, floating above him, the black hole in his hand aimed at the Hanged Man's heart.

"Look familiar?"

Suddenly the weapon spits fire, again and again.

There is no pain, but the whisper goes quiet. The Hanged Man is alone. He wants to scream, wants to tear into the man's flesh, but he can't. The last thing he sees is the red-handled revolver as the barrel is pressed to his forehead. Kleberg leans close, a smile growing across his lips as he speaks. . . .

"This I might keep," the Hanged Man said, repeating the echo of the last words to filter through his living head.

"Keep what?"

The Hanged Man grabbed Henry around the collar, although this time with less deadly intent.

"Where is he?"

"The marshal? I don't know! He left—no, they chased him off. 'Cause of all the graves he dug up."

The Hanged Man opened his hand and Henry scuttled backward, putting some distance between himself and the unpredictable outlaw.

"That's when I remembered where you were buried. He left . . . and I remembered everything."

The Hanged Man eyed Henry. "Once he was gone?"

Henry nodded.

The Hanged Man remembered the grave—*his grave*—and the final moment of his previous life. There wasn't much of it left at the time, but enough to survive had the marshal not shot him eleven times with his own weapon. He had it still. He must.

"Somebody in Astoria probably knows where he went," Henry said, getting to his feet. "Try the general store."

The Hanged Man motioned for him to come closer. Henry's feet were moving before he could stop them.

"I told you everything I know," he said, gripping the book tightly to his chest. "I don't know what else you expect me to do."

The Hanged Man leaned over Henry, tapping the book lightly with the pistol.

"Keep readin'."

14

The mayor's garden party was in full swing by the time the Wyldes arrived. The guest list had swelled to nearly a hundred, most arriving with guests of their own. Not that the mayor objected. A happy guest was a happy voter.

The garden portion of the party was on an acre of gently sloping, extensively landscaped grounds, dotted with trees and bushes. A large fountain sat in the middle of a courtyard that stretched from the mayor's residence to a raised stone stage in the center of the grounds. Carefully pruned hedges on either side of the stage resembled the city's two new bridges. Most impressive was the rose garden, a curling line of three dozen large bushes, each either a different color or style. All but a few were in full bloom, adding a heady floral fragrance to the air and offering a welcome respite from the boggy stench that hung over much of the city.

Joseph could smell the roses a block from the estate, but now that he was among them the aroma was overwhelming. He and Kate had been to the mayor's home on a handful of occasions, but this was a first for the kids, both of whom were drawn instantly to the flowers.

"Holy crow," Kick said. "Look at all the colors."

"Agatha preens over every bush," said the mayor. "I must say I hardly ever see her in the spring as she spends more time out-of-doors than in."

The marshal sniffed loudly. "Smells like a perfume shop."

The mayor nodded. "Wonderful, isn't it?"

The marshal raised an eyebrow but kept his tongue in check. "Maybe you oughta have another festival for your flowers."

"Oh, don't let Agatha hear you say that. She's already after me to make the rose our city's official flower. Thankfully, she can't decide on which one." The mayor bent down between the twins. "In fact, I'm sure she could use some help. Why don't the two of you inspect each one, and see if you can't pick out the flower that best represents our fine city."

"Okay," said Kick and ran straight to the nearest rose, from which he breathed deeply.

Maddie hesitated just long enough to get a subtle nod from Kate before following her brother into the garden.

"Now," the mayor said, turning back to the adults. "Let's introduce you to a few of our special guests."

The mayor's special guests included an explorer just back from the Yukon Territory, a professor of history from Willamette University, a geologist, a volcanologist, the owner of the largest local brewery, three bankers and two bankers' wives, a pair of Chicago business-men who had invested in the festival, and numerous local and na-tional politicians, including senators from California, Missouri, and Ohio.

It was an eclectic bunch and it took Joseph only a few hand-shakes to realize none of them was the star attraction. The very special guest, the guest the mayor took pains to introduce to every-one in attendance, was the marshal, who, according to the mayor, had single-handedly cornered and killed the Hanged Man, saving the West and every man, woman, and child living in it.

For his part, the marshal tried several times to revise the mayor's story, before realizing it was a lost cause. He found the less he protested, the sooner the mayor moved on to the next introduction. Given the number of people standing around eagerly waiting for the mayor's attention, a nod and a shake seemed the best course of action.

It wasn't that the marshal objected to being branded a Hero of the West, something he felt he'd earned after thirty years' serving his country. What bothered him was that his career could be distilled to one event—the killing of one man. That his life had meaning only because he put an end to the vile and despicable acts of the Hanged Man diminished everything else he'd accomplished. The idea that he would be forever linked to the man was repulsive.

He also suspected it was true.

Kate could see the meet and greet wearing on her father and was glad when the mayor promised the next introduction would be the last. By the time they got to the three men lingering just far enough from the crowd to make mingling a bother, Kate was more than ready to join them.

"Gentlemen, you're not trying to hide from me, are you?"

"We're trying, Jim," said the oldest of the three, a well-dressed man with a wide, curled mustache. "But you aren't making it very easy."

The mayor laughed, boisterously as ever. "This is my very old friend Oliver Olsen. Mr. Olsen is a longtime writer for the *Sacramento Bee* and is not to be trusted."

"Ah-ah," Mr. Olsen said, wagging a finger at the mayor. "Telegraph lines run both ways, remember? I can have you calling for tax on California olives in tomorrow's edition."

The mayor rolled his eyes. "See what I mean?"

"Pay him no mind, madam," Mr. Olsen said, taking Kate's hand. "Your mayor is not but a rogue with good taste in men's fashions. Now, unless I am misinformed, you would be Mrs. Wylde, yes?"

"I am. It's a pleasure to meet you, Mr. Olsen."

"Call me Ollie, please," he said, bowing formally. He then offered a hand to Joseph. "And that would make you Mr. Wylde."

"It would."

"Well met," Ollie said, smiling broadly. Despite his practiced manners, there was a jovial quality to his voice that made most people feel at ease. Kate and Joseph were no exception.

"I'm pleased to say Jim has spoken very kindly of you both in our correspondence."

Joseph wondered what kind of correspondence might include such a mention, but thought it best not to ask in present company.

"I'm glad to hear it," he said instead.

Ollie took Joseph's response and the slight pause that preceded it exactly for what they were and smiled.

"Mr. Olsen and I often share opinions on matters of a political nature . . . and such," said the mayor, perhaps a bit off his game given the stresses of so many guests.

Several uncomfortable seconds later, Ollie clapped his hands and redirected the attention to the well-fed man standing to his left.

"And please allow me to introduce my new acquaintance, Dr. John Gillman, director of your recently opened medical school on the hill."

"Hello," said the doctor.

Kate brightened. "Oh, the son of one of our neighbors—Andrew Kinsey—will be coming to study with you this fall. He's very excited."

"Good. Then he will study very hard."

Kate smiled politely, but was glad when Ollie gestured to the slender, clean-shaven man on his right.

"And this fine young man is Mr. Samuel Edmonds of Monterey, California."

Edmonds tipped his hat. "Hello, sirs, madam."

"Mr. Edmonds and I have shared a most interesting journey from California, isn't that right, Mr. Edmonds?"

"Oh, um, yes, it was very pleasant."

"You traveled together?" asked Kate.

"Met along the way," said Ollie. "And what a fortuitous meeting it was, given our common destination. You see, Mr. Edmonds will be, in my humble opinion, the most important man at the festival."

It was at this moment that Joseph realized the mayor had yet to introduce the marshal. His newspaper friend had knocked him off his game, had done so easily, which Joseph thought was not an altogether bad thing.

"So," said Kate, "what is it that will make you so popular, Mr. Edmonds?"

"He's a weatherman," said Ollie.

Joseph cocked an eyebrow. "A what?"

"Technically, I'm a meteorologist," the younger man said. "I collect data on atmospheric conditions and then forecast probabilities based on observed weather phenomena."

Ollie chuckled. "What he means to say is that he can predict the future!"

"Oh, no," said Edmonds. "Just the weather—sometimes—it's not an exact science, not yet."

"How fascinating," said Kate. "Can you really tell us what's going to happen tomorrow?"

"It'll be sunny, I think."

"You think?" said the doctor, unimpressed.

"I've only been in Oregon for a few days and haven't had a chance to collect readings for an accurate forecast."

"Yes, yes," Ollie said, "but tell them the good news—Jim, you're going to love this."

Edmonds hesitated, then blurted out with more enthusiasm and volume than he intended, "It's going to rain!"

A brief silence was followed by clapping as numerous people who had drifted closer to follow the mayor's conversation broke out in applause. The mayor practically beamed.

"You're certain?" he asked.

"I would say there's a sixty percent chance that Portland should experience an extended period of precipitation beginning no later than Thursday."

"First night of the festival," said Ollie. "Very fortuitous."

"Cutting it a little close, but I'll take it," said the mayor, patting Mr. Edmonds on the back.

"How exactly do you arrive at your prognostications?" Joseph asked.

"It's very interesting, actually. By studying recent local conditions and coordinating them with observations from other locations, it's possible to build a model of the weather on paper, on a map, but with weather instead of rivers and mountains."

"And then what?" said the doctor. "You divine the results by mixing a few raindrops and snowflakes in a lab?"

"Actually I don't have much use for a laboratory. The weather is outside, so I spend most of my time in the field, measuring the temperature, wind, humidity, even pressure. Given enough information, I can forecast what the weather will be like up to five days in advance with at least fifty percent accuracy."

"Only half the time?" the doctor said, grinning. "I believe I can match those odds for predicting sun or rain."

Ollie put a hand on the weatherman's shoulder. "My dear Dr. Gillman, I believe it's more complicated than that. Isn't that right, Mr. Edmonds?"

"Well, there are different kinds of rain," said Edmonds, only a little deflated. "As are there many kinds of clouds, snow, hail, sleet, and wind. It's very exciting, especially in a place like Oregon, where you have plenty of local weather to follow."

"Pardon my skepticism," said the doctor. "I'm afraid my tolerance for the new sciences is rather low."

"Actually, the study of meteorology is very old. And most of the devices I use to take measurements have been in use for centuries. In fact, I've got a barometer in my personal collection that's almost one hundred years old. It's quite beautiful—and it still works!"

Joseph was not at all surprised to hear there were fluctuating pressures in the air. He'd known for years—could feel them, in fact—and was known to predict the odd thunderstorm or heavy rain well before it arrived. He generally kept such information to himself, however, and was curious to see if his heightened senses were in tune with the young man's scientific equipment.

"I'd be very curious to see that, Mr. Edmonds."

"It'd be my pleasure, Mr. Wylde. I believe I'm to have a booth at the festival, isn't that right, Mr. Mayor?"

"Yes, definitely."

Ollie leaned closer to Kate. "I told you he would be a man of considerable interest."

Kate nodded. It was then that she noticed her father standing just outside the circle. He'd drifted slightly, having received no formal introduction.

Ollie picked up on her discomfort and its direction almost immediately.

"Jim, it appears you've been holding out on me. Is this who I think it is?"

The mayor, briefly caught off guard, recovered quickly.

"Just saving the best for last. Gentlemen, forgive my tardiness, this is Marshal James Kleberg, formerly of Astoria, but now a proud resident of Portland."

The doctor raised an eyebrow. "Of the U.S. Marshals?"

"For a time," said the marshal. "Retired."

"Retired, but not forgotten," said the mayor. "Gentlemen, you are standing in the presence of greatness. Marshal Kleberg is the man who brought the vile Hanged Man to justice."

"Who?" asked Edmonds.

The mayor scoffed. "The Hanged Man! Surely you've heard of the most despicable, murdering scoundrel ever to prey upon the good people of the West. The Dead Man? The Man with the Red Gun?"

"No, I'm sorry."

"You'll have to pardon my young friend, here, Marshal. He's originally from New York," said Ollie. "If there's not a James or a Hickok in the headline, chances are they've never heard the story."

"That's all right."

"But yours is quite a tale, if I recall, one worth repeating. It involved a fairly bloody shootout, did it not?"

"It did," said the marshal. He waited a beat for the mayor to jump in, but when the man didn't, the marshal continued. "Wasn't just me, though. Took two or three dozen men to corral the son of a bitch. I just got to put the last bullet in him."

An image popped into the marshal's head—his hand before him, the Hanged Man's gun in its grip, firing, again and again.

"Ah, but that's not the first time you encountered the man, correct?" asked Ollie.

The marshal caught up to Ollie's words a little late.

"What? Oh . . . that's right. I chased him up and down creation for years 'fore I put him down." The marshal's eyes drifted to Joseph. "Me and a few other good men."

"Of course," said Ollie. "But I was referring to the hanging, the first one. The day the cretin got his name."

The marshal blinked. This fellow knew some things. Fortunately, the marshal remembered.

"Yeah, I was there when they tried to hang him."

Those gathered around the mayor's group, who up to that point had been casually eavesdropping, gave up the ruse and seemed to lean in en masse as the marshal continued.

"Couldn't quite kill the bastard, but they did make him famous."

Ollie nodded. "This was in sixty-eight, yes?"

"Sounds about right."

The marshal was surprised to find his memories of the botched hanging clearer than those of the Hanged Man's eventual demise, especially considering they were nearly a decade older.

"I missed the actual hanging. Some townsfolk took matters into their own hands and decided to string him up before I could process him upstate. He weren't nobody at the time, just another delinquent with courage enough to steal from folks that ain't got much." The marshal paused, letting his story sink in. The truth of the Hanged Man made the bastard seem less important somehow. The marshal didn't know why but that made him feel better.

A question came from the crowd: "What did he steal?"

"Twenty-seven dollars and a horse wasn't worth half that," said the marshal, smiling just a little. "Don't suppose it was his first crime, but definitely the first time he got caught. Put him in a foul mood."

"Which he would never relinquish," said Ollie.

The marshal's expression darkened. "No, but there weren't no sign of the man he would become, neither. I'd a known, would have strung him up myself."

More questions came from the crowd, faster than the marshal could answer.

"Is it true he cut himself down from the hanging tree, even after he was dead?"

"Was he buried first?"

"Did he rise from the grave?"

"Did he always wear the noose?"

The scowl he'd worn for much of the previous week returned, but only until the marshal caught the eye of his grandson. Kick had silently drifted back to his mother's side along with his sister and was now watching his grandfather, eyes wide and ears open. He was just starting to look like his father had the first time the marshal met the man who would ultimately marry his daughter. It was a hard to frown at a face like that.

"Weren't nothing supernatural about it," he said. "Fools that strung him up didn't know a damn thing about tying a noose. Unraveled ten seconds after the drop. Surprised the hell out of 'em, which was just long enough for the man—who *weren't* dead—to bolt into the bushes."

"But then why did they call him the Hanged Man?"

"He called himself that," said the marshal. "Had a bit of scar 'round his neck, which was enough for most folks."

"And it was after this that he truly made a name for himself," said Ollie.

"He started killin' folks, if that's what you mean."

"It is. But I can't say I ever learned the man's Christian name."

"He kept it a secret," said the marshal. "Wouldn't tell me when I arrested him that first time. Nobody in town knew it. After the hanging it didn't matter."

"But you learned his name eventually, of course," said the mayor. "That's how you cornered him in Astoria, yes?"

The marshal tried to remember. Did he know the Hanged Man's name? Was he supposed to? *How could you forget?*

As the silence stretched out, Joseph wondered if his decision to let the marshal find his way through the past alone was a mistake. He wasn't the only one.

"Marshal, your silence speaks louder than words," said Ollie.

"It does?" mumbled the mayor, echoing the sentiments of many in the crowd, the marshal included.

"Of course the marshal knows who he was, but by choosing not to say, he's buried the man, name and all, making him all the less relevant. We shouldn't remember the monster and his deeds, but rather his unfortunate victims." Ollie bowed to the marshal. "A very noble sentiment, Marshal, and for that you have my respect."

"And mine," quickly added the mayor.

There were murmurs of agreement from the crowd.

"Well," said the marshal, eyeing Joseph. "I suppose not all things are worth remembering, anyway."

"Hear, hear!"

Joseph felt Kate's hand take his own and squeeze lightly.

"Jim, I daresay my prediction as to who will be the star of the festival may be in doubt," said Ollie. He put a hand on Edmonds's shoulder and added, "No offense, young man, but a hero of the West is hard to beat."

"I agree," said Edmonds. "And you know I think I did read something about this Hanged Man fellow when I was younger. I remember a story about a very bloody shootout and something about a magic gun."

"Magic gun?" said the doctor. "What nonsense is this?"

"Yes, yes, the Bloody Pistol," said Ollie. "Whatever happened to that, Marshal?"

"I have it," said the marshal, regretting the words even as he said them.

The mayor beamed. "You have it? In your possession?"

The marshal nodded. He didn't bother to look at his daughter. He knew what he would see on her face and it would still be there waiting for him later.

"You must bring it to the festival," said the mayor. "For a practical demonstration."

"What was the myth?" asked Ollie. "That it could be fired without reloading?"

The marshal's hand started to itch. "Something like that. Never tested it," he lied.

"I didn't know you kept his gun," Joseph said, unable to save his question for later.

"Couldn't leave it behind. Too dangerous. Some fool might pick it up and start calling himself the Hanged Man all over again."

"You could have destroyed it."

Joseph's words made the marshal flinch. He could have destroyed it, could have dismantled the weapon and thrown the pieces into the Columbia River, but he hadn't. He wouldn't. It was his gun now. No one was going to take it away from him, no matter how hard and long he stared at the marshal with his one eye.

"I kept it safe."

"What of the body?" Ollie asked.

The marshal answered right away: "Burned it."

He was lying. Joseph heard it in the old man's voice, although he didn't understand. What the marshal believed was a lie was true as far as Joseph knew. Could that explain the marshal's nocturnal diggings the week before? Had he been searching for the gun or for something else?

"Oh," Ollie began, softening his tone ever so slightly. "I only ask because our journey north brought us through Astoria, where it seems there's been a rash of grave disturbances over the past few weeks."

Joseph felt Kate's grip once again tighten, but sensed no change in the marshal's demeanor. The mayor's unfortunate question would put an end to that.

"Were any bodies stolen?"

"Just one," said Edmonds.

The marshal stepped forward. "What did you say?"

"One body went missing, the day before we made port, I believe. Apparently, there was a second incident in a grave apart from the others."

The marshal took another step toward the weatherman. "Whose name was on the stone?"

"I don't know," said Edmonds, shrinking back. "I didn't ask."

"There wasn't a stone," said Ollie. "No marker at all, just a hole and an empty box."

"But I didn't find—" the marshal began and then stopped.

"Gentlemen, please," Kate said, pulling both children to her side. "Can we find a topic more suited to all ages?"

"Cry your pardon, Mrs. Wylde," said Ollie.

Kate received similar apologies from the other men, but hardly noticed as she turned to face her father.

"Dad?"

"I'm fine," he said, and strode into the garden without another word.

15

"Do you know what it is?"

"No idea," Ollie said, staring up at the tall, slender object hidden beneath several layers of drapery. "Jim likes his secrets, you know."

Joseph did.

Five minutes earlier, one of the mayor's aides had directed Joseph and Kate to the study, where they'd found the newspaper man leaning against the remains of a large wooden crate. The contents of the box stood before them, a mystery wrapped in cloth.

"He'd better start spilling his secrets soon," Kate said. "It's getting late."

Ollie smiled, shifting his attention from the tower to his new company. Joseph wasn't surprised. The man had been angling to get him alone for much of the afternoon.

"Mr. Wylde, would you mind if I asked you a question?"

"Only if you agree to call me Joseph."

"Of course, Joseph. Pardon my inquisitive nature, but your father-in-law's amazing tale has awakened the journalist in me."

"I didn't realize that was something you put to bed," Kate said.

"No, I suppose it's not."

"It's all right," Joseph said. "Ask me your question."

"Thank you. I'm wondering if you recall another story from some years ago, one involving the Hanged Man and an attempted jailbreak."

Joseph smiled.

Ollie raised an eyebrow. "Ah . . . you know the story?"

"I do."

"Because you were there."

Joseph felt Kate close the gap between them.

"I was the one he tried to break out, if that's what you mean."

"Then it's true you were partners with the Hanged Man."

Joseph hesitated, but only for a moment. "For a time."

"A very short time," Kate added.

Joseph took Kate's hand. "I was young, and angry at the world. When I met the man our interests were much the same."

"Pardon my skepticism, but I find it hard to believe a respected citizen such as you would have associated with such a violent man."

"I'm embarrassed to say I did. Granted, this was well before he started killing with such relish. The man was a criminal, but not the monster most folks remember. Something happened after we . . . parted ways."

"But he still called himself the Hanged Man, correct?"

Joseph nodded. "Before a job he would twist a piece of rope around his neck to scratch up the skin, make the scars look fresh."

"The theatrics of fear," Ollie said, mentally checking the facts in his head. "Now, you were in jail for . . ."

"Robbing Tom Sherman's livery . . . unsuccessfully."

"And it was the marshal who arrested you?"

"No, but he's the one who kept me in jail," Joseph said. "Three weeks, waiting for my partner to show his face. I wasn't particularly happy about it, not at first, at least."

"Oh? What changed your mind?"

Joseph nodded to his wife, who answered for him.

"He met me."

She is the most beautiful thing he has ever seen and when she looks at him—sees him—Joseph knows his world will never be the same. He tries very hard to imagine her in it.

"Hello," Kate says, hopeful the young man won't reply. She didn't mean to say anything. She doesn't know why she did.

"Hello," he says, barely. No word has ever been so difficult to get out. She blinks, uncomfortably. She's afraid of him.

Kate glances across the jailhouse to where her father stands, back to her, speaking with a pair of local men, deputies, perhaps. He hasn't seen her. When the smell of fresh biscuits finds its way to him he will turn. She turns first.

"My name is Kate," she says, approaching the man behind bars. He's handsome, she's decided. Smells a bit like horse manure, but so do half the men (and a few of the women) she's already met in town.

"Wylde," he says, grateful.

"I'm sorry?"

"Wylde—Joseph Wylde—that's my name."

"Oh."

She's going to walk away . . . and she smells so good, like buttered biscuits. He should say something, anything, before . . .

"I only tried to steal a horse."

Kate stares at Joseph Wylde. He has nice eyes.

"Why?"

Joseph shrugs. "I needed a horse."

"You shouldn't steal from people, Joseph. It's wrong."

"It is, you're right," he says, desperate to hear her say his name again. He will never steal again.

"I take it you were unsuccessful."

Joseph leans against the bars. "What gave you that idea?"

Kate starts to laugh, but quickly covers her mouth.

Too late. Joseph has seen her smile.

And she sees his.

"Katie!"

Kate and Joseph both jump at the sound of the marshal's voice. He's already halfway across the room, the grimace on his face clearly visible. Joseph steels himself.

"Better go. The marshal doesn't like me much."

Marshal Kleberg stops directly in front of Joseph, his face red. He's never seen the lawman so mad.

"Is that true, Daddy?"

Joseph glances at Kate, his jaw slipping open.

Kate shrugs.

"Talk to my daughter again, glance in her direction, and I'll have your ass in the stockade. Got that?"

Joseph eyes the marshal, nods. Her father. This will be difficult.

The marshal turns to his daughter, taking her by the arm.

"I appreciate you bringin' me lunch, Katie, but come on in, next time. Don't be lingerin' up here."

Next time.

Joseph holds his gaze on the marshal just long enough for him to glance back and be satisfied. Then he finds hers.

And she smiles.

"Hand to God, one smile and my days as a criminal were over."

Kate offered Joseph a refresher, followed by a soft kiss on the cheek.

"You were never much of a criminal, dear."

Joseph didn't quite believe that, but said nothing. He was happy for it to be mostly true.

"I see," Ollie said. "Love conquers all. But there's still the matter of your escape."

"Wasn't much to it. The Hanged Man showed up early one morning and started shooting."

"Even though he knew the marshal would be expecting it? You meant that much to him?"

Joseph shrugged. "I never saw him be generous with anyone else, but there were times when he spoke to me as would a friend. Can't say the feeling was mutual. He was a hard man to like."

Kate shook her head. "He was a killer, Joseph. I don't believe he cared for anything or anyone."

"Oh? Why do you think he was so mad that I chose you over him?"

"You refused his help?" Ollie asked.

"Worse. I stood against him. Backed up the marshal."

"I imagine he didn't like that."

"He did not," Joseph said, squeezing his wife's hand.

"But he escaped."

Joseph nodded. "Not sure how. Last I saw of him he was a bloody mess. Took a bullet myself, though it wasn't serious."

Kate smiled. "I patched him up."

"That you did."

Ollie let the information settle. He knew more about the story than Joseph was aware, but nothing the man had said contradicted the facts. There was more to know, however, and Ollie found it never hurt to ask.

"You said this was before he became overtly violent, before his villainy became legend. Did you ever meet the man again?"

Ollie saw Kate react first, tugging on her husband's hand, whispering in his ear. Joseph shook his head.

"Best we can figure, he vanished into the Cascades after the shootout. Assumed he was dead, but about a year later he reappeared, as I'm sure you know."

"Sacramento. I remember."

Joseph nodded. "The claims office. The attack was so vicious I didn't think it was him. I rode with the man for a year, but didn't figure him for a remorseless killer. I was wrong."

"Perhaps," Ollie said. "Or perhaps not. The pendulum swung for the Hanged Man as it did for you, only in opposing directions. You were transformed into a man of moral conviction, he a monster. There's a lovely symmetry to it . . . journalistically speaking, of course."

"Of course."

Ollie let the moment linger, not wanting to seem too eager. There was another question, one he'd wanted to ask for quite some time.

"If it's not too personal, do you mind me asking how you lost the use of your eye?"

Joseph blinked. The memory was close. It always was.

A kerosene-soaked rag, amber vapors rising before his eyes, burning even before the match is lit, before his world turns to red . . . and then to black.

Joseph blinked again and the mayor's study returned. Kate stood at his side, holding his hand, Ollie before him, waiting.

"Another time," Joseph said, pushing the memory aside.

Ollie smiled. "My apologies. I don't mean to pry."

"What's that, Ollie?" the mayor said, sweeping into the room alone. "Sticking your nose in where it doesn't belong, again."

"As always, Jim."

The mayor grunted. "Sorry for my tardiness, but as mayor it is my duty to tend to any and all admirers."

"Modest to the last, Jim. And you've given us plenty of time to become suitably curious. What have you got under wraps here, Mr. Mayor?"

The mayor moved directly to the tall object at the center of the room and began untying a rope that held the cover taut.

"Gentlemen and lady, I give you the real star of the festival."

The rope undone, the mayor tugged on the sheet, which fell away, revealing a nearly nine-foot-tall totem pole carved out of a large section of an ancient cedar.

"Oh, my," said Ollie.

"It's a totem pole," said Kate.

Joseph had already formed a mental picture of the object simply from the sound of the sheet falling around it, but Kate's clue brought it into focus. That picture changed, however, after he laid a hand on the surface of the pole.

"This isn't wood. It's stone."

"Correct," said the mayor. "The splits and cracks are actually cut into the rock. Whoever carved this wanted it to have the appearance of old, weather-beaten wood."

"I've never heard of such a thing," said Kate.

Joseph slowly followed the procession of figures with his hand. At the base was a man, his arms raised above head to support the weight of whale, bear, wolf, beaver, and raven. A seventh creature sat perched above them all, and even though Joseph's outstretched fingers could reach only the claws of the mythical bird, that was enough to give it away.

"Thunderbird. Very traditional, although it's unusual for two birds to be stacked one on top of the other."

Joseph laid his hand flat on the raven's broad beak. It was surprisingly smooth, with only the slightest grain evident between the faux wood details. Embedded throughout, however, were flecks of a different kind of rock that were sharper and a fraction of a degree warmer than the rest of the sculpture.

"There's firestone in this."

"Yes, quite a lot, actually."

"Which would make it worth a small fortune," said Ollie.

"So I've been told," the mayor said. He dug into his desk, producing several small glasses and a bottle of something suitably stronger than the punch served out on the lawn.

Kate looked at the mayor. "You've already had it examined, then?"

"Indeed. I've had numerous experts poking and prodding at it for weeks, but thus far none have offered me anything that speaks to its origin or activation." The mayor poured several of the glasses full. "Whiskey?"

"Why not," said Ollie, taking one of the glasses.

"No, thank you," said Joseph. "What did you mean by 'activation'?"

The mayor took a drink. "It's a storm totem."

Joseph pulled his hand off the stone.

"Frankly," continued the mayor, "I'm a bit suspicious of its authenticity at this point. I realize we're under water up to our kneecaps, but it's not exactly falling from above, is it?"

"Forgive my ignorance," said Ollie. "But what exactly is a storm totem?"

"It's a rainmaker," said Joseph.

"That's what the fellow who sold it to me claimed, that explorer, Wilhelm Horace Smith. You may recall his visit a few weeks back. That was the last day it rained in Portland." The mayor took another drink.

Joseph turned back to the pole. His touch had revealed unfamiliar flourishes in the carving, but that in itself was not unusual. There were countless artistic styles to be found in the totem poles of the Northwest tribes, many of which Joseph had encountered in his travels. In that regard, the artificial weathering and the use of stone were more curious than the carvings themselves.

Joseph opened his senses wider, letting the pole's aroma fill his nostrils. He picked up hints of the sea, beach, forest, and even the firestone, which to Joseph smelled faintly of crushed pepper.

"Where did Smith find it?" Joseph asked, still studying the totem.

"He removed it from an island north of Seattle. He claimed that Lewis and Clark found a similar heathen sculpture in December of '05, which accounted for the exceedingly wet winter they experienced at Fort Clatsop. I think he may have been telling tales, on that count."

Joseph moved closer to the pole. There was something else tickling his heightened senses. It was faint, not a smell but rather a sound, not unlike breathing.

Joseph held his own breath to confirm what he heard, but Ollie leaned in next to him.

"Find anything interesting?"

The smell of the whiskey blunted Joseph's senses, which didn't improve when Ollie dipped a finger into his glass and then rubbed it against the stone.

"Just a smudge," he said, smiling.

Joseph nodded and then turned to the mayor.

"It's fascinating, Mr. Mayor, but what exactly is it you want us to do?"

The mayor drained his glass in one gulp. "I want you to make it rain, Mr. Wylde."

Kate laughed, but caught herself when no one else joined in. "Oh, you're serious?"

"Absolutely. My people couldn't make heads or tails of the thing, told me the legend was just that—a story invented by the heathens or, more likely, a savvy explorer with a very large artifact on his hands. But then I remembered my friends, the Wyldes, and all your interesting experiences and resources and . . . connections."

Joseph couldn't remember telling the mayor the details of his family tree, but the man obviously knew Joseph's maternal grandmother had been Nez Percé. It was not a fact he'd hidden, or advertised, but it had helped him establish a friendly relationship with several of the area's local tribes.

"We do have an extensive collection of tribal lore at the store," Joseph said. "Much of it unpublished oral traditions that might have some information about such things."

"Excellent. I knew you were the right person to ask."

"I don't know about that," Joseph said, turning back to the totem pole. "We don't have much experience drawing water from a stone."

"Rainmaker or otherwise, it's going to make an excellent centerpiece for the festival," said the mayor. "Although it would be better if it rained."

"Perhaps," said Ollie, "you should pit this pole against your weatherman, eh, Jim? Modern science versus Native magic?"

The mayor laughed, but was soon turning the idea over in his head.

Joseph turned to Kate, whom he correctly guessed was smiling. She would enjoy a job that didn't involve confrontations with criminals. She would not, however, allow the thing inside her house.

"Can you have it delivered to the store?"

"First thing Monday morning. Now, shall we return to the party? I hate to be away for too long."

Ollie followed the mayor out of the room. Kate turned to leave, but stopped when Joseph didn't follow.

"Coming?"

Joseph hesitated for a moment longer, then returned to Kate's side.

"Just listening," he said as the two walked out of the room.

A moment later, a drop of water fell from the ceiling and hit the ground near where Joseph had been just listening. Second and third drops would follow, but no more. The tiny pool that formed on the floor smelled faintly of whiskey.

16

———◆———

"Nineteen?"

Andre turned the number over in his head. *Nineteen.* He'd expected it to be bad, but that many wounded was far worse than
he'd imagined. The first accounts they'd heard after coming ashore
in Newport described a wild shootout, although who was doing
the shooting was not clear. By the time Naira procured horses and
provisions for the journey north, the shootout had become a "massacre" and the perpetrators a "gang of outlaws." The day-and-a-half
ride to Tillamook brought more accounts, many describing a single
villain killing without remorse. Just outside town, they met a man
clutching a small wooden cross to his breast who claimed Death
had descended on the traveling circus to pass judgment on the
wicked.

Now that they had arrived at the scene, the worst of the stories
appeared to be true. The midway was in disarray. Many of the
booths and platforms had been knocked over or destroyed, some
had burned. A handful of carnival workers pushed at the debris
with brooms and shovels, none seeming to grasp whether they were
packing up or shutting down for good. A tiny man scrubbed the
floorboards of a stage, trying to remove a deep red stain.

Andre and Naira stood before the smoldering remains of a larger tent at the end of the midway. A sign trampled underfoot was too scorched to read save for a caricature of a man hanging from a tree. The burned-out husk of a coffin sat in the center of the wreckage.

Andre pulled the hat from his head, squinting into the sun, and asked a question he had no desire to hear answered.

"How many dead, Sheriff?"

Sheriff Matt Taylor, who throughout his tour of the carnage with Andre had been otherwise subdued, finally perked up.

"Just the one."

Andre glanced at Naira. This was not the answer either of them had expected.

"And he died of a knife wound," the sheriff continued. "Rest is still kicking, far as I know. Some of 'em are an awful bloody mess, but they're alive."

Could Andre's theory be wrong? Might it not be him?

"Show me."

Andre walked among the wounded, letting the emotions collected inside the big top flow into him. Fear filled the space, only it wasn't the fear of death or sickness but something more primal, more intense. Andre had an idea what to name it, but held out hope his fears would not be realized.

The sheriff stopped alongside the bed of a young man with an oblong face. There were scars along his neck and chest, but only his shoulder was bandaged.

"Kid's one of the lucky ones," said the sheriff. "Caught it in the shoulder. Them other marks is, ah, well, he was like that 'fore he got shot." The sheriff glanced about the tent and then leaned closer to Andre. "Lot of 'em was shot ain't exactly normal folk, you catch my meanin'."

Andre did. "Carnivals tend to employ a rather colorful cast of characters."

The sheriff grunted. "Maybe that's why so many of 'em survived. What's another scar when you already look like that, huh?"

Andre gave the sheriff a look that most men would rightly have interpreted as an invitation to shut up. The sheriff missed this completely.

"Hell, some of 'em might even end up better-lookin' minus a little meat."

Naira touched the sheriff's arm.

"These people deserve your care and comfort, wouldn't you agree?"

The sheriff stared at Naira, seemingly unaware he'd been asked a question. Finally, he nodded. He did care. Of course he did.

Andre put a large hand on the sheriff's shoulder. "Who did this?"

"Ah . . . robbers," he managed. "Five or six, maybe as many as ten. Don't know for sure. We caught three of them, but they ain't said much." The sheriff paused before adding, "Well, they ain't said much useful."

"What does that mean?"

"They're trying to blame somebody else for what they done. Said they was set up by some fella out of Astoria. Something to do with a dead man and a fancy pistol. I don't know, maybe they was tricked, but they did the robbin' even if the other fella did most of the damage."

Andre raised an eyebrow. "I thought you said there might be as many as ten."

"Oh, well, that's just an estimate, based on the amount of shootin' and such. Most of the, um, employees seem to think there was just one man doing most of it."

"One man?"

"Yup," said the sheriff, not bothering to mask his skepticism.

"Shot up the place all by hisself, started a couple fires, even won a few lead souvenirs on the midway."

"They shot him?"

"Half-dozen times, or so say the eyewitnesses. Didn't slow him down, though. No, sir. They tell me he just kept right on shootin'." The sheriff gestured for Andre to come closer. "What it tells me is that carnival folk can't shoot worth a lick."

Andre straightened up. He could make the sheriff understand, make him see the people around him, feel their suffering. Naira had such an easy time leading the man in the direction they wanted to go that it was obvious his was a simple mind. But what good would come from it?

Andre looked at the young man in the bed before him. He opened his eyes, smiled weakly, and then closed them again.

"Take me to the carnival boss," Andre said.

The sheriff led them to a cot near the back of the tent. A handful of people were already standing around it, including a tiny one-armed woman sitting on a stool, an average-looking man with two small bumps on either side of his forehead, and twin Asian men who shared a single pair of legs. Seated upright in the bed with a wide bandage triple wrapped around his bare chest was John Garibaldi. Several spots of blood dotted the dressing, but otherwise he appeared in good condition for someone with a bullet in his chest.

The assembled carnival folk regarded the sheriff with obvious disdain, but when their eyes fell to Andre they found their spirits raised for the first time that day.

"Mr. Garibaldi, this is, um, this is . . ." The sheriff knew the man's name, tried to spit it out, but found he couldn't get his tongue around the word. He stared at Andre for help.

Andre nodded. "Thank you, Sheriff, I can handle it from here."

Sheriff Taylor looked from Andre to Naira and then realized he was needed elsewhere. He must be. He left without another word.

Andre turned back to the injured man to find him grinning. Garibaldi nodded to his own people, who left without protest. Only the one-armed woman, who Andre saw was legless as well, remained at her boss's side. She smiled broadly at Andre, a gesture he gladly returned.

"Careful, Mary," said Garibaldi. "There might be a hoodoo curse behind that smile. He'll have you clucking like a chicken in no time."

Andre shook his head, but kept the smile. "Hello, John."

"Andre, my friend, nice of you to come all this way just to catch the show. I'm afraid we're between performances at the moment."

Andre nodded. "You seem in good spirits for a man so recently shot."

Garibaldi rolled up the wrapping on his chest, revealing a small, circular wound with what appeared to be a bullet still lodged at its center.

"Half shot," he said. "Bullet never got through the heart bone. Damn thing's stuck there, if you believe that. They tried pulling it out, but it's worked its way in good. I think the doctor's just afraid to give a good yank, figures I'll spring a leak."

"I might be able to do something," Andre offered.

Garibaldi shook his head. "Thanks, but I'll be fine."

Andre wasn't so sure. John had brushed away the offer a little too easily. He knew what Andre could do, had seen his hands in action during a smallpox outbreak in Eureka five years earlier. Something had him spooked, something unnatural.

"Besides," Garibaldi said, "I finally get to fit in with my freaks."

The small woman gasped. "John!"

"I'm one of you now. Don't pretend you don't call yourselves freaks when I'm not around. I hear things, Mary. I'm the boss, remember?"

"We don't use that word. Not in polite company."

Garibaldi rolled his eyes. "My apologies if I have offended your finer sensibilities, Andre," he said and carefully slipped the bandage back into place.

"That is an unusual wound," Andre said. "Remarkable that the bullet penetrated no further."

"Not really. Gun was only loaded with half powder, probably less."

"How do you know?" Naira asked.

"I loaded it," Garibaldi said. He paused, as if just realizing what he'd said was true, and then chuckled to himself. "Don't know why, actually. It was a prop. As it turns out, I was lucky to be one of the first ones shot, 'fore he picked up another pistol."

The carnival master's grin faltered.

Andre waited for his friend to take another breath before asking his question. "Who shot you, John?"

Garibaldi looked away from Andre. His eyes flitted from bed to bed, each time hurting a little more by what he saw.

"There were four of 'em," he said. "Three idiots and some kid who didn't know what he was doing. And they had a body for sale."

Andre felt the truth hit him before he understood it, but both came quickly. The fear would come next.

"John . . ."

"Yeah, I bought the damn thing. Thought I was doing 'em a favor."

"You put him on display."

"I put *it* on display," said Garibaldi. "There was no *him*, it was just a body."

"It was evil, John, how could you not see that?"

"We don't all see as clearly as you, Andre. Sometimes we have to walk in the shadows to get where we're going."

"Is that true? And did you make back your dime before your god reached down and slapped you in the face?"

Garibaldi stared at Andre. For a moment, neither man gave an inch. Finally, the carnival man lowered his gaze. Mary reached out with her tiny hand to find her boss's. She gripped it tightly.

Andre bent his tall frame to kneel at the edge of the carnival man's bed.

"This was not your doing, John, I know that. And I trust you will take care of these souls."

"Whatever they need," Garibaldi said without hesitation. "We're a family."

"I know," said Andre.

"What about the book?" Naira asked.

"What?"

"Was there a book, small and black?" Andre asked. "One of the men might have carried it with him."

Garibaldi thought for a moment and then nodded. "One of the shooters tried to sell me a notebook, said it was full of spells. Looked like a bunch of scribbles. I offered two bits, but the kid wouldn't part with it. Got pretty angry about it."

"What happened to him?"

"I don't know. He was there when it happened, when whatever it was woke up. I told him to run and he did."

Andre knew the young man would never be able to run far enough or fast enough, but at least he'd run. That was something.

The carnival boss took a deep breath and slowly let it out. He glanced at the small woman by his side before turning back to Andre.

"You'll want to talk to them, I expect."

"Who?"

"The idiots," Garibaldi said. "Though I don't know how much help they'll be."

Andre suspected they might be more useful than his friend, but never got the chance to say. Something had Naira spooked.

"What is it?"

Naira shook her head. "Trouble."

Garibaldi sat up a little straighter despite the pain. "Where? I don't—" he said, and then his words were cut off by the sound of a single gunshot echoing across the camp.

The body of the brute lay in the dirt, face up to the sun. A small black hole in the dead man's forehead and the pistol in the sheriff's still-shaking hand told much of the tale.

"He attacked me," he said, as Andre and Naira arrived. "I told him to stop, but he just kept comin'."

Andre slipped through the crowd gathered around the body and knelt beside it. Several recent injuries, including a scalp laceration and numerous stab wounds to the chest, were still caked with dried blood. There was no fluid, dried or otherwise, on the forehead.

Andre looked at the sheriff. "He attacked you?"

"Came barrelin' outta the tent chasing some girl. Saw me and changed his mind . . . I told him to stop."

An older woman wearing a long black dress stepped forward, her arm around a younger, similarly dressed woman who hid her face at the sight of the body.

"It's true," said the older woman. "We were to prepare him."

"For burial," Andre said.

The woman nodded. "The medical man tried his best. He was surely dead."

"Seemed awful lively to me," said the sheriff.

Andre laid a hand on the dead man's chest, finding no life to it. "He is gone now, Sheriff."

The sheriff said nothing but did finally holster his pistol.

The silence stretched out, broken only by the sobs of a few carnival folk. In time, Andre nodded to Naira, who gently took the hand of the young woman in black, waiting for her to raise her head before she spoke.

"Tell us what happened, dear."

The woman wiped away a tear but answered right away. "Big Tom weren't much for cleanliness, but I came to wash him. He deserved that. I only touched his coat and he grabbed me around the wrist and pulled me down. He tried . . . he tried to bite me."

Andre felt the hair on the back of his neck stand up. She was speaking the truth and it was worse than he'd imagined.

"How was he killed?" he asked, slowly rising to his feet. "The first time."

"Tom died saving my life," Garibaldi said, leaning on another man for support. "Stabbed . . . by the bastard that shot me."

The crowd parted, allowing their boss room to stand beside the fallen man. Mary, the one-armed girl, pushed in beside him on a small rolling cart. At the sight of her friend she silently began to cry.

Garibaldi looked to Andre. There was hate in his eyes.

"Find him, Andre. And kill him when you do."

"I will find him, John."

Garibaldi nodded. "Talk to Mason. He might be able to help."

"Who is he?" Naira asked.

"One of the idiots."

The Tillamook County Jail was small and out of the way, perfect for a population that rarely had a use for it. Two twelve-foot-square cells were more than enough to hold the occasional card cheat or inebriant incapable of stumbling home. Should an actual criminal be in residence, the jail was equipped with two sets of wrist-to-ankle shackles. After the carnival shootout, the jail's population had soared to three, none of whom was deemed to be in any condition to cause trouble. The shackles remained on the wall.

"This one's got a fractured scapula, four broken ribs, and a bullet lodged in his lower back that's going to have to come out eventually," said the doctor, pointing over his shoulder at a bloodied and bandaged young man curled up on the cot at the back of the first cell. A second man, a relation by the looks of him, sat nearby, leaning against the bars. "The other one's got a load of buckshot in his thigh, which I'd call very fortunate, all things considered."

Andre looked at the two men. Hugh raised his head long enough for Andre to read the truth on his face. The man was just as broken as his brother. Neither would follow the path that had brought them to this place. Their days on the wrong side of the law were over.

Andre motioned to the adjacent cell. "What about him?"

The doctor ran a hand through the few hairs remaining on his head. It had taken him nearly two days to get to the men in jail, and despite a mighty headache and almost no sleep, he'd treated them fairly and honestly. This one, however, had pushed his limits.

"Mr. Mason has a broken shoulder," he said. "And a broken arm, just above the elbow. He also took a round in the face that punched through the cheek and tore off most of that ear."

"Will he survive?"

"Oh, yes. Won't be much to look at, but he'll live."

Andre took a step toward the cell, but the doctor held him back.

"This one's a bit feisty. Deputy had to hold him down while I attended his wounds. Didn't give him anything for the pain, either. Not trying to be cruel, but I've got more-deserving folks up on the hill."

Andre nodded.

The doctor picked up his coat and bag. "When the deputy returns, please inform him that I've gone back to the carnival."

"Of course. Thank you."

The doctor nodded. He paused, giving Andre and Naira a final consideration, and then walked out the front door, leaving them alone with the injured outlaws.

Mason didn't wait for a proper introduction.

"You come to collect me, big boy, is that it?"

Andre turned to see Mason standing, his right hand gripping one of the bars to keep himself from falling. Blood oozed from beneath the bandage wrapped around his head. His speech was slurred, almost wet as he spoke.

"You one of the government's pet slaves, boy?"

Mason made a guttural slurping sound and tried to smile. He couldn't hold it without a great deal of pain, however, and returned to his grimace.

Andre stepped forward and closed his much larger hand over Mason's, pinching it firmly against the bar. Mason hissed in pain. He tilted his head down to the man, showing the criminal exactly how big he was.

"Mr. Mason, it would be wise to adopt an air of respect in my presence, honest or otherwise," Andre said in a voice half an octave deeper than that he'd used when talking to the doctor. It wasn't a trick or a push, but the effect was just as powerful. Mason tried to slip deeper into his cell but his hand wasn't going anywhere.

"I have some questions for you," Andre said, tightening his grip on the outlaw's hand. "If you answer them to my satisfaction, I will see that the good doctor finds he has enough medicine to soothe the pains of *all* the wounded."

Mason felt a fresh wave of pain sting what remained of his left cheek. He bit into the right, trying to balance the misery, but managed only to make the wound flare up even more. He did his best to ignore it.

"What do you want?" he asked.

"There were four of you—"

Mason's eyes lit up. "Is he dead?"

"Who?"

"That traitorous son of a bitch, Henry! Tell me them freaks shot him."

"They did not," Andre said. "He escaped, as did his accomplice."

Andre felt Mason's heart rate spike as the man tried to pull away again, forgetting he had nowhere to go.

"Tell me about Henry," Andre said. "Do you know his last name?"

Mason stopped squirming. "Why would I know that?"

"Macke," Hugh said from the other cell. "His name was Henry Macke."

"That coulda been it," Mason said. "And this was his doing, it was his plan from the beginning."

Mason thought he was lying, but Andre suspected it might be closer to the truth than the man knew.

"Tell me about it," he said.

Mason described the aborted holdup in Astoria, Henry's plan to go after the gun, and their excavation in the cemetery. Andre was keen to hear more about the other graves that had been disturbed, but Mason had nothing to offer.

"Somebody else dug 'em up," Hugh said. "I don't know who it was. Henry knew, I think."

Andre thought he might know as well.

"Did you find the gun?" Naira asked.

Mason scowled at the woman. "Think we'd be having this conversation if I had?"

Andre tightened his grip. He could break the man's hand, giving Mason even more of a reason to want the doctor's relief, but he didn't. He was not a violent man. Instead he released his grip, freeing the outlaw.

Mason stumbled back into the cell and sat down roughly on the cot. The shock of it nearly made him pass out, but he managed to keep his attention focused on the giant man standing before him. Mason incorrectly believed this would make the man respect him.

"Mr. Mason, I have no desire to punish you. The county constabulary will no doubt see to that. I am, however, eager to know what you know. Please believe me when I say I will have this information with your cooperation or without."

Mason flexed the muscles in his hand, surprised to find them still functional. "Gun was gone, already stolen," he said. "Didn't want to come away empty-handed so we took the only thing in the ground of any value."

"Selling the dead man was your idea?"

Mason hesitated. "Well, it was, but I don't know . . . maybe it wasn't. Mighta been Henry made me do it. He coulda used one of them tricks on me."

"Tricks?"

"From that damn book," Mason snarled, circling in on his own answer for how everything had gone so wrong. "Oh, he kept it close to him, didn't he? Right from the start . . . he weren't after no gun, it was that book he wanted all along. Used us to dig him a hole, didn't he?"

"You said Henry did most of the digging," Naira said.

Mason shot her a look. "You wasn't there."

Naira grinned, eager to put the man in his place. Andre held her back with another question. "Did you ever see him read it?"

Mason shrugged. "Once or twice."

"He read it all the time," Hugh said. "When we was riding, eating, even when we was sleeping. I don't know if he was actually awake or not. Couple times I walked right past him and he didn't flinch, but he had that book open in the moonlight and his lips were moving."

"Did he understand it?"

Hugh shook his head. "I don't know, but he could definitely read it."

"Reading and understanding are two very different things," Andre said, more for his own benefit than that of the prisoners. "Either way, your friend is in a great deal of danger."

"He ain't a friend of mine," Mason spit out. "Got that? Him and his partner is gonna pay for what they did to me."

Naira moved closer to the cell. "The dead man was in on it, then?"

"Weren't no dead man," Mason said.

Andre wasn't surprised by Mason's disbelief. In fact, he found it one of the few redeeming qualities of the man. Mason would rather have been conned by a young store clerk than be party to the resurrection of the darkest soul the West had ever known.

"He musta worked it out with the fella before we got there," he said. "Made him up to look like the dude, or something. It was just a con."

"A con," Andre repeated before turning to Hugh. "Is that what it was?"

"I don't know," Hugh said. "We dug up a dead man in Astoria, rode with him for a few days, and sold him to the circus. If it were the same man what stepped out of that coffin Friday night, I can't say. I hope not."

Andre opened his mouth to agree with the man, but an abrupt choking sound from behind caught the words in his throat. By the time he'd spun around it was over.

Mason stood with his face pressed against the bars, his throat firmly in the grip of Naira's left hand. With her right she held up a six-inch surgeon's blade.

"I believe the doctor left this behind," she said. "Mr. Mason was kind enough to bring it to my attention."

Andre took the knife from Naira. There was a streak of dried blood on the blade, which no doubt belonged to a victim of the recent attacks, possibly one of the men in the jail. Andre took another look at the man curled up on the cot and then wrapped the knife in a handkerchief and dropped it into his coat pocket.

"Gentlemen, I'll see to it that you are given something for your pain."

And with that the conversation was over.

"I have seen enough suffering for one day," Andre said as he and Naira descended the front steps of the jailhouse. He hoped a preemptive strike would settle the matter before Naira could question his reasoning.

She said nothing.

Andre unloosed the reins of his horse from a hitching post in front of the jail. "They deserve to be punished, but for their crimes, not their companions."

Naira smoothly climbed onto her horse and still said nothing.

With considerably more effort, Andre pulled himself onto the saddle atop his own horse, which shifted under the added weight. Andre settled in and then stared at his friend.

Naira held his gaze, blinked her very large eyes once, and smiled.

Andre sighed. "You are content to let me argue with myself?"

"You're winning."

"Am I?"

Naira raised an eyebrow in mock surprise. "You're not sure?"

Andre had already lost. He knew it. Fortunately, he was a stubborn man.

"I have made my decision, Naira. We will pay the doctor a visit before heading north," he said, then directed his horse into the street.

Naira prodded her steed to follow. "Our destination remains Astoria?"

"Yes," Andre said.

"Are we following the book or the man?"

Andre couldn't feel the book—not as he had before. It had chosen its new master and in doing so had closed itself off to him save for a vague sense that its pages once again had eyes upon them. It was a relief in many ways, but the lack of contact would make it much more difficult to track. Unfortunately, Andre suspected that tracking the man—and his body count—would not be a problem.

"He is not a man," Andre said. "Though what he is I cannot say for certain."

Andre knew the spell Henry would have used. *Malédiction du résurrection*—the curse of resurrection. Performed correctly, it would produce a being known as *zombia,* a powerful creature, but also a slave. Bound to its creator, it would follow his or her command while exhibiting no free will of its own. The curse was a simple one, especially if the shortened version was used, as Andre suspected. It was, in fact, a hard spell to get wrong.

But Henry had.

According to John, Henry had run away from his creation, a sure sign he was not the one in control. What the young man didn't know—but likely had since discovered—was that running would get him only so far. The creature might not follow his commands, but it would follow him. It was bound to Henry as Henry was to it. In such a relationship, strength usually won out, and Andre had no illusions as to who was stronger.

"I believe wherever the Hanged Man goes, so too will the book . . . and so too will Henry."

"Astoria."

"He will return to the end of his old life before he begins a new one."

Andre felt a cold shiver try to fight its way to the surface of his being. He pushed it down, willing it to retreat.

"You're convinced it's him?"

Andre leaned back in the saddle. "I would very much like to believe that Henry Macke had a partner who helped him set up Mason . . . very much, indeed."

"But he didn't."

"No," Andre said. "But I imagine he has a partner now."

17

Kate leans over the unconscious body of her husband, tilting the bundle in her arms just enough to reveal a tiny pair of eyes.

"That's your daddy, Samuel. He loves you very much."

The baby coos and kicks sharply. Kate can't help but smile.

"Oh . . . you're just not going to give that up, are you?"

The boy, only days old, looks at his mother and sees her—of this Kate is sure. She has never known anything so alive.

Joseph moans softly, stirs, but does not wake. Kate touches his arm lightly.

It's been ten days since the warning came, a week since Joseph rode into the mountains to face his past alone. He returned only last night, bloodied and delirious, his words unsettling and few. Joseph fought the Hanged Man—shot him, he said—but flames had taken Joseph's sight. He left to protect his children and now would never see them.

"I'm so sorry, my love."

Joseph quiets at the sound of Kate's voice. Before the tears come again, she turns her gaze to the window. Fresh drops of rain spot the glass, too small to make a sound. She can't see the men her father left behind, but knows they are there: three men with guns, standing guard against a monster she doubts will ever come.

"Never should have let you go."

A reply comes not from her man but his daughter, whose cry starts softly, then rises to a wail.

"I think your sister is awake," she says to the child in her arms.

Kate descends the steps to the first floor slowly, the pains of childbirth not yet relieved. She finds baby Madeline in the bassinette by the fire, eyes open, cheeks ruddy and moist. At the touch of her mother the cries subside, but stop completely only once the twins are side by side. Kate wonders if this is how it will always be.

Abruptly, both children begin to cry. Even before she turns, Kate knows she is not alone.

He stands before her, grinning, eyes wide open with the Devil's intent. The Hanged Man has come, evading the marshal's posse and slipping past the protection he left behind. No, not past, but through; the bloody knife in the bastard's hand tells the truth.

"Hello, Mrs. Wylde," he says, scraping the blade against his pant leg before returning it to its sheath.

Kate stands between the killer and her children. "What do you want?"

The Hanged Man draws the coat back from his hip, revealing the red-handled revolver that has become legend. Kate feels a chill in the air despite her proximity to the fire.

"I would speak to your man. We have business to discuss of a personal nature."

"You've come to kill him."

The Hanged Man moves forward, forcing Kate against the bassinette.

"I only wish to talk," he lies.

"I don't believe you."

His hand is around her throat before Kate can think to scream.

"No," he says, turning his attention to the twins. "If there is to be any killing today, I'm hopin' it won't be your husband who dies."

Kate feels the scream rise through her body but doesn't make a sound.

"Kick, be careful."

Kate stood at the base of a ten-foot ladder, holding it as securely as possible. Above her, Kick leaned out from the top rung, straining to reach the highest level of a floor-to-ceiling bookshelf that ran the length of the storeroom.

Kate cringed. "What did I just say, Kick?"

Kick ignored his mother, letting his fingers dance along a series of leather-bound journals until they came to a volume with gold-stenciled letters that read, *Darcy: Victoria & Beyond.* He slipped a finger under the spine and pulled it out, letting it fall into his sister's waiting hands below. Two seconds later he was on the floor.

Kate could only shake her head.

"All right," she said. "Let's see it."

Maddie handed the slightly oversize journal to her mother. It was dusty and worn but otherwise in reasonable condition. The spine creaked as Kate opened the book to the title page.

"'The Explorations of Captain James L. Darcy: A Journey of the North Coast of America from Victoria Strait to the Yukon Territory,'" Maddie read aloud.

Kate flipped through the journal, revealing dozens of maps, sketches, handwritten notes, and a smattering of typeset pages. Most of the drawings were of plants, animals, and waterfalls, with which the author seemed particularly fascinated. There were also sketches of the Native peoples, their villages, canoes, and quite a few totem poles. Kate came to an image of a tall, slender pole decorated with animals. She stared at the picture for a moment, then spun on the spot and looked up.

Situated in the back of the storeroom between two freestanding bookshelves was the storm totem. The mayor's men had delivered it late Sunday night rather than on Monday, hoping to keep local curiosity to a minimum. The trip had been largely successful save for bottoming out on a dry patch along Stark Street. The flooded alley behind the store provided good cover to offload the large sculpture directly into the Wyldes' storeroom.

Tucked into the cramped space between shelves, the totem looked bigger than Kate remembered, even though at barely nine feet it would be considered small for a totem with so many figures carved into it.

"The bear is different," Kick said, his eyes darting from the drawing to the storm totem. "So is the wolf. And this one doesn't have a man, or whatever that is," he added, pointing to the figure at the base of the pole.

"It's a man, but you're right, it is different. Similar, but different." Kate handed the book to her daughter. "Add it to the collection."

Maddie promptly deposited the new addition on a table already crowded with more than thirty tomes, including more leather-bound volumes, a few cloth-covered books, and several collections that were little more than loose pages held between backer boards and straps of leather.

"I think we've got enough to get started," Kate said.

The kids went to work, each selecting a book from the stack. Kate turned back to the storm totem, which in the low-hanging storeroom lights also appeared more sinister than it had in the mayor's study. She made a mental note to ask Joseph to open the storeroom skylight before the sun went down.

Kate ran a hand along a series of interwoven lines connecting the killer-whale carving to the bear above it. It was actually a sea bear, a mythical beast found on many Northwest totems. The lines grew from the bear to the wolf, then to the beaver, to the raven, and finally to the thunderbird on top. It was a curious feature though not unprecedented. None of the animal designs was unique, but the fact that they were carved in stone remained unprecedented in Kate's experience.

"So unusual," she said under her breath, although what she felt was something very familiar. Native totems were symbolic of many things, but all had one thing in common—they told a story. The storm totem was no different. There was a story here, one that was not entirely clear to Kate, but familiar nonetheless.

Returning to the table, Kate picked through a few of the loose collections before finding the one she wanted. She untied the binding, revealing a stack of papers, most of which were handwritten transcriptions of oral traditions. This particular collection she knew well, having been present when Joseph had written down many of the legends. There were nineteen similar volumes, each a collection of the history and mythology of a single Northwest tribe. Over the past six years, Joseph had, with the help of several like-minded locals, compiled the volumes with hopes of publishing them in a single book celebrating the customs and culture of the tribes. Kate thought it a lovely idea. Thus far, none of the publishers Joseph had contacted shared her assessment.

The current collection was culled from the Nuu-Chah-Nulth tribe, a loosely connected community spread across Vancouver Island. There was a single story in particular that Kate was interested in, one told to them by an elderly man they'd encountered sitting alone on a rocky beach.

Halfway through the stack, Kate stopped turning pages. A small sketch of a bird—not entirely dissimilar to the raven found on the storm totem—sat in the lower-right corner of the page. Above it were the words: THE WHITE RAVEN.

Kate smiled. There was no such bird, at least none that she'd ever seen. The classic Oregon raven was as black as any other and twice the size. Most kept to the coast, although Kate had seen a few mingling with the local crows, content to spend their days cawing at the boats that traveled up and down the Willamette River.

The raven of the Native story was twice the size of a man and the color of sunlight. Kate had initially pictured it as a golden creature but was overruled. Apparently, her blind husband could *see* the true color of light and deemed it white. The old man had agreed, pointing to a pile of sun-bleached oyster shells for comparison. Kate kept one of the shells, which upon closer inspection had a polished, rainbowlike sheen on one side. She tried to revise her argument, but Joseph had already transcribed the story, naming the titular bird "the white raven."

According to the legend, the great bird rose from the sea with a foamy flourish and alighted on a large chunk of driftwood at the top of the tide line. There it found a young maiden waiting for her brother to return from a fishing trip. The raven claimed the brother's boat had capsized and all hands had been lost. The woman was devastated but refused to cry, saying her sibling loved the sea and would often speak of slipping beneath the waves when it was his time to pass on. The maiden's noble sadness moved the white raven to shed an enormous tear, which broke on the sandy flotsam, releasing the fishermen from their watery prison. The albino bird then imparted the secret of the tides to the woman and flew away.

Or something like that. The old man was a little unclear about the ending. It was possible the bird had snatched up the maiden and flown away with her, leaving her brother to curse the skies. Joseph and Kate decided the happy ending was more fitting.

Joseph had included the alternate ending in a footnote, along with a sketch of the old man and another interpretation of the magical bird.

This was what Kate had remembered.

The second drawing looked nothing like the raven on the storm totem but was nearly identical to the bird perched on top of it. Joseph had heard only the words of the storyteller and had sketched a perfect match. Kate had long ago learned to trust her husband's visual instincts, despite his obvious limitations. He could see things others could not, things unseen, even things found only in the mind of another man, such as the thunderbird that topped the storm totem.

It was a thunderbird, not a raven, which meant that either the old man had described something else or they had misinterpreted his meaning when he spoke of the great bird. It was possible this was another mythical creature. Numerous winged beings appeared in Native myths (the cannibal bird, Hokhokw, was one of Kate's favorites), many of which were commonly found on tribal totems. Could this be something other than a thunderbird?

Kate slid the ladder along the bookshelf until it was within a few feet of the totem. She climbed two rungs, tested its steadiness, then stepped up two more. With considerable mental effort, she ascended one more rung, putting her almost face-to-face with the winged creature on top of the totem.

"What are you," she whispered. "Thunderbird or other bird?"

A single multicolored fleck sparkled in the creature's eye as Kate tilted her head. It was the firestone peeking through the stone, but it still sent a shiver through Kate's body. She leaned in closer and abruptly the ladder shifted. Kate froze. Before she could gather herself to retreat, a hand grasped her ankle.

"I've got you," Joseph said.

Kate carefully made her way down the ladder and once on solid ground kissed her husband on the cheek.

"One of the kids should hold the ladder when you're on it. Safer that way, right, Kick?"

Kate shot her son a look before he could respond.

Joseph turned to the desk. "Find anything interesting?" he asked, flipping through a book on top of the nearest stack.

"Nothing concrete," Kate said. "Some familiar designs, but nothing approaching the overall aesthetic."

"The third animal is a sea bear, not a grizzly bear," Maddie said.

Kate smiled. "She's right. And I'm not sure that's a thunderbird on top. It actually looks a lot like a sketch you did for one of the Nuu-Chah-Nulth stories."

Joseph ran a finger over the drawing Kate had pulled out. In his mind, he saw the great bird, wings outstretched, sunlight glistening from beneath its wings. When he finally got to finish his hands-on inspection of the totem, he would find that his vision and reality were very similar.

"William is going to come by later today," he said.

"Billy Red Fish?"

Joseph chuckled. "He hates it when you call him that."

"I know," Kate said, grinning. "What did he have to say about our storm totem?"

"He's run across a few in his travels. None made of stone, however. He was very curious."

"Good. We could certainly use some firsthand experience."

Kick snapped his second book closed and tossed it back onto the table. "Where's Gran'pa?"

"Practicing," Joseph said.

Kick's eyes widened. "Shooting?"

"Yes."

Kate raised an eyebrow. "Where?"

"Bonner's field," Joseph said and then answered the question Kate wanted to ask: "He needed the distance for his rifle. That's all he took with him."

Kate wasn't convinced. "How come you didn't go with him?"

"I offered, but he said he could use the time alone."

Kate grabbed her husband's wrist and walked him back to the storeroom entrance.

"You let him go off with his gun alone?"

"It was a rifle and he knows how to handle it."

"That's not the point. In his state of mind, I don't know what he's going to do. He could hurt himself, or somebody else."

"I don't think he would do that."

"Are you sure?"

Joseph didn't answer. Instead he closed his uncovered eye, which had the effect of focusing all his attention on his wife. Only Kate understood the gesture.

"Don't stay mad at him."

"Why shouldn't I? He brought that thing into my house—into *our* house."

"I don't think he did it on purpose. In fact, I'm not entirely sure he even knew what it was when he brought it with him."

Kate shook her head. "He knew. He knew enough to hide it from me."

"He didn't hide it very well. Blabbed to the mayor the first chance he got. I'm sure everyone in Portland knows by now."

Joseph put a hand on his wife's waist.

"Don't try to talk me out of being angry," Kate said, stepping out of Joseph's grasp. "If he's going to stay with us, he's going to have to leave some things behind. God knows what else he's got stashed away."

Joseph recalled the discovery of the carved box in the marshal's attic. He remembered who had found it and decided his wife didn't need to know that piece of information.

"It's just a gun," he said.

"No, it's not." Kate glanced over at the kids, neither of whom seemed to be paying any attention but both of whom were no doubt following every word. She leaned in closer to her husband. "It's much more than that and you know it."

Joseph nodded. "And that's why he's agreed to destroy it. We'll break it apart and toss the pieces into the river."

Kate frowned. "After the festival."

"He promised a demonstration. You don't want him to disappoint the mayor, do you?"

"A little disappointment might do Jim Gates some good."

Joseph once again placed a hand on his wife's hip. This time she didn't retreat.

"He needs this."

"Needs what? To fire off some old pistol just because the mayor asked him to?"

"In a way," Joseph said. "He's kept it for more than a decade, kept it safe. I think he believed he was protecting us."

"From what?"

"I don't know, but I'm starting to think he wanted to get rid of it back in Astoria. We all assumed he was trying to dig something up. What if he was looking for a place to bury something instead?"

The idea that her father might have been trying to do something noble definitely had its appeal. And Kate could almost put the pieces together, though they didn't quite fit. It wasn't much, but it made her feel the tiniest bit better.

And then Kick opened his mouth.

"Gran'pa didn't even find it."

"What?" Kate said.

Joseph tried to wave off his son, but it was too late.

"I found the rose box in the attic. He didn't even know it was there."

Kate looked at Joseph and then back at Kick. "You found the gun?"

"Um, yeah," Kick said, realizing his admission was not going to put his mother in a better mood. "But Gran'pa said I couldn't have it."

"Your grandfather wouldn't let you keep the gun."

"No, the box! I only wanted the box and Pa said I should ask Gran'pa first."

Kate slowly turned back to her husband. Joseph felt her eyes fall to him, her smile widen. She wasn't happy, far from it, but when she wanted him to hear her loud and clear, big, broad expressions worked best, especially when he was in trouble.

"I didn't know what was in the box," Joseph said.

"I find that hard to believe."

"It was heavy. I knew it wasn't empty, but I didn't, I couldn't, um . . ."

"Yes?"

Before Joseph could dig the hole any deeper, a bell rang at the front of the store.

"Customers," he said and made his escape.

18

Kate joined her husband a few minutes later as he was studying a series of Oregon elevation charts with the mayor's celebrity weatherman.

"Good morning, Mr. Edmonds," she said, laying a hand on Joseph's shoulder as she drew up behind him. "Planning a trip?"

"What?" Edmonds said, glancing up from the map. "Oh, hello, Mrs. Wylde. A pleasure to see you again."

Kate nodded politely and peered over her husband's shoulder. "And are we still expecting rain by festival time?"

Edmonds beamed. "Oh, yes. In fact, I've raised my expectation to seventy percent!"

"Sounds like a sure thing," Kate said.

"Close to it. Of course, if I can update my maps with accurate elevations, I might be able to adjust my calculation another ten percent one way or the other."

Kate was pleased to see the man in his element. Without the mayor and his extended guest list looking over his shoulder, Edmonds seemed much more at ease. He'd swapped his coat and tie for an explorer's jacket of sorts, lined with a multitude of pockets from which various instruments and measuring devices protruded.

The look fit Kate's vision of the science heroes found in Jules Verne's early works: studious, prepared, and dashing.

"How very interesting," she said.

It wasn't the tone of her voice but rather Kate's breathing that caught Joseph's attention. She *was* interested in Edmonds's predictions—too interested. This was his punishment, and the fact that he knew Kate was teasing him didn't make him feel any less jealous.

Joseph tapped the map laid out on the counter. "Mr. Edmonds says the height of our mountains actually dictates how much rain we get."

"Which mountains?"

"All of them," said Edmonds. "The local hills would play only a minor roll, of course, but I have no doubt this coastal range has a tremendous effect on local weather patterns and precipitation totals."

"What about Mount Hood?" asked Kate. "That's a big mountain."

"Yes, but I'm guessing most of your weather comes off the Pacific Ocean. Tell me, which way does the wind blow through town?"

"That depends on where you are and when you're there," Joseph said. "In the summer it can come from almost any direction."

"But it most commonly blows west to east, correct?"

Joseph hesitated. He could have given Edmonds a detailed accounting of the seasonal wind patterns, having cataloged them just as accurately as he had the city streets. He could have offered up a remarkably accurate profile of the big windstorm that had struck Portland the preceding November. He also could have listed the most blustery points on the map, as well as the calmest. He chose to keep it simple.

"That's right."

Edmonds nodded triumphantly. "Classic West Coast weather

pattern. And that's why it's going to rain on Thursday—a big blow, if my calculations are accurate."

"Because of the wind," Kate confirmed.

"Because of the ocean."

"I thought it was the mountains," Joseph said.

"Oh, yes, them too," said the weatherman and returned his gaze to the elevation chart without further explanation.

Kate glanced at Joseph and saw an equally amused if only slightly less confused expression on his face. She wasn't ready for her husband to smile just yet and sidled up to Edmonds, close enough for both men to notice.

"So, mountains can affect the weather," she said. "They can actually make it rain?"

"Well, in some instances higher elevations can draw higher rainfalls. In fact, I've read about a volcano in the Sandwich Islands that receives ten times the rainfall on its western slope compared to the eastern. The west side draws all the moisture from the clouds."

"Fascinating," Kate said. She was about to rest a hand on his shoulder when a question occurred to her that seemed more vital than her husband's temporary discomfort. "Mr. Edmonds, do you have any devices in your collection that can make it rain?"

Edmonds looked up from his writing. "Has the mayor put you up to this? He's convinced I know the secret for coaxing water from blue sky. I made the mistake of mentioning a theory I'd heard of sending certain chemicals aloft via helium-filled balloons to seed the clouds with moisture. He's been rather persistent."

"He is at that," Kate said. "But I was thinking more along the lines of an earthbound device, a rainmaker of sorts."

Edmonds smiled. "Mrs. Wylde, I believe you may have confused science with fiction. Measuring I can do, but I can no more make it rain than I could turn day to night."

"Something from another culture, perhaps? Not so much scientific as religious?"

"Are you referring to mysticism?"

Kate nodded.

"I'm sorry, I don't subscribe to such things. I realize there are wonders in this world that man has yet to fully comprehend, but to assign them magical powers as a way to explain their existence seems rather shortsighted to me."

Mr. Edmonds spent the rest of the morning going over every Northwest chart and map Joseph could dig up for him. He was thrilled to have so many available. When Kate produced a diary detailing nearly twenty years of local weather as recorded by a longtime resident, Edmonds actually giggled with delight.

The store was unusually busy for a Monday morning, although not so much in sales. Most visitors seemed content to wander the aisles searching for items they never seemed to find. It wasn't until Joseph overheard one of the patrons mention a midnight delivery that he understood the influx of lookie-loos.

"I guess the mayor shared his secret with a few more folks," Joseph said to Kate the next time she reappeared from the storeroom. "They're looking for a show."

Kate shook her head. "Nothing to see here."

"No luck?"

"The information just isn't there. We couldn't find a single reference to a storm totem or anything remotely close to such a thing."

"What about the white raven?"

Kate shook her head. "There's the sketch you did and a few others that share similar carving styles, but that's it. The kids went through every book, some more than once."

Joseph had suspected their search might not bear fruit. He remembered most of what had gone into his own writings and doubted the published books would include anything better. They were mostly full of speculation and outright lies anyway.

"What about a ceremony?"

Kate nodded. "There were a few references to so-called rain dances, but not from any northern tribes. I would imagine there's little need to summon what falls freely from the sky on most days."

"Except when it doesn't," Joseph said.

"Yes, and didn't the mayor say the rain stopped *after* this thing was brought to town? Maybe the fellow who sold it to him got it wrong. It's not a rainmaker."

"It's a rain*taker*," Joseph finished. "That would certainly add a twist to things."

"Indeed. But who's to say? Hopefully Billy will have some insight."

"To be honest, my friend, I'm stumped."

William Axtell, known in some circles as Billy Red Fish due to an incident involving a cracker barrel full of sockeye salmon, had spent the better part of an hour silently studying the storm totem from top to bottom. Joseph had always known him to be thorough and let him take his time.

Joseph put a hand on Billy's shoulder. "I was hoping for something more."

"I'm sorry, Joseph. I've not seen anything like it."

Billy had seen a lot. At the age of fourteen, he'd run away from a reservation in the Yakima Valley, ultimately ending up in Portland, where he found work at a short-lived cannery. A chance encounter with a desperate captain led to a job aboard a merchant vessel making regular runs up and down the coast from San Diego to Vancouver. An unmatched ability to pick up any of the dozen or so Native languages spoken along the coastal route soon made him the ship's unofficial Indian liaison. His discovery that the locals had jewelry to trade, much of it featuring large orange crystals, made him very popular with the crew.

In the summer of 1885, at the age of twenty-four, Billy returned to Portland hoping to track down the family he'd left behind. He found his way to Joseph, who helped him navigate the government's impenetrable record-keeping system until they located a sister transplanted to a reservation in Kansas. Billy made several attempts to contact her, finally receiving a terse, single-line telegram that read in full: FAMILY IS ALL DEAD.

Billy remained in Portland, helping Joseph and Kate at the bookstore before taking a position at the Columbia Indian Affairs Board as a translator and tribal liaison. Local efforts to improve relations with the Native community kept him busy, but he made it clear that he would always be available should his friends need assistance. This was the first time Joseph had asked.

Billy put a hand on the face of the bear, running his fingers across the bridge of the nose and inside the creature's open mouth.

"The beasts are like that of Haida and Tlingit, but the lines are Salish—but not the color."

"What color?" said Maddie.

"Exactly," said Billy. "Where is the color? There is no black, no red, no green . . . very unusual. I would expect to see all three if this was from the Northern Island."

"Maybe it faded," Kick said.

Billy looked closely at the color remaining on the human figure. He scratched at it briefly, then stepped back and looked directly at Joseph.

"We are meant to believe that."

Joseph nodded. "Who carved it?"

Billy shrugged.

Joseph laughed out loud. "That's it? You don't have any idea, not even a guess?"

"A guess is not the truth."

"I'll settle for a half-truth, then."

Billy returned his gaze to the totem. "The use of stone is unusual, but not unprecedented. There is a story I've heard, not along the great river, but farther north, beyond the Northern Island, that speaks of a tribe that worked in stone, and not just for jewelry."

"Stone like this?" Joseph said touching the pole. "Firestone?"

"Stone that breathes, they called it. I do not know why. That tribe is gone, disappeared long ago. The stone is all that is left—small pieces, carvings, figures, other trinkets. I have seen a few pieces, not much, and certainly nothing this big."

"And the tribe just disappeared?"

"I met a man once who claimed to be a descendant of the stone makers. He turned out to be an Irishman of ill repute, so I am inclined to doubt his assertion."

Joseph had heard the register close up and the front door lock moments earlier, so he wasn't surprised when Kate slipped the key into his vest pocket after entering the storeroom without detection.

"Well, what's the verdict?" she asked.

If Billy was surprised by Kate's silent appearance he didn't show it. Joseph was impressed.

"Billy thinks it might have been carved by a mysterious lost tribe."

"Oh, the mayor will like that," Kate said.

"Will he?" Billy said. "I understand he's hoping to make it rain."

"A downpour would suit him just fine."

"Then perhaps he should have this removed from the city limits."

Joseph shook his head. "It's keeping the rain away, isn't it?"

Billy nodded. "You asked for a guess earlier, and my best as to its function would be just that. It calls to the sun, not the clouds."

"Do you believe that?" Kate asked. "That it's magically sucking all the moisture out of the air?"

Billy shrugged. "It is just a guess."

Kate sighed. "Well, the mayor definitely won't like that."

"How do we stop it?" Joseph asked.

"Good question," Billy said.

Joseph hesitated for a moment before suggesting, "You have no idea."

"None," Billy said. "My solution would be to ship it east to the badlands. No one will notice if it is not raining in the desert."

It was obvious to Maddie what needed to be done, but she waited until her parents and Billy had left the storeroom before turning to Kick.

"What if we got it wet," he said, beating her to the punch.

"Yes, because of the lines," she said. "They flow around the figures, in and out of the shapes, encircling the entire pole, but they aren't just lines, they're channels—channels where water could flow."

Kick stared at his sister. "I just want to get it wet."

"Look here," Maddie said, pointing to a line that wrapped around the sea bear. "See how it has a curved lip on the front of the line? Water will stay in that channel, I'm sure of it. In fact, I bet there's a reservoir on top where the water flows down from."

Kick was on the ladder before Maddie had finished her sentence. He climbed to the top and then leaned over the totem pole.

"There's a well on top the bird's head, like a small bowl, and there's a hole in the bottom of it."

"That's it. If we pour a small amount of water in there, I'm sure it'll run through the entire channel system carved into the stone."

Kick slid down the ladder and hit the ground with a thump next to his sister.

"And then what?"

Maddie thought about it for a moment. She, like her mother, was more in line with the weather expert's thinking that science always trumped magic, eventually. That said, she really liked the idea of making it rain.

"I don't know," she said, finally. "Maybe it'll rain."

Kick didn't wait for further instructions. He grabbed a small pail in the corner of the storeroom and exited through the back door. Ten seconds later he returned with a bucketful of floodwater drawn from the submerged alley. He was on the ladder before Maddie could slow him down.

"Just a little," she said. "Don't pour the whole bucket."

"Okay."

Kick reached the top of the ladder and began to lean out over the totem pole. He lost his grip and slipped slightly, spilling some of the water.

"Hey!" Maddie shrieked as water splashed over her shoulder.

"Sorry," Kick said before steadying himself. Once again he leaned over the pole, this time tilting the bucket directly above the bird's head. The water poured into the small bowl but didn't fill it up immediately, despite what appeared to be a rather shallow well. Kick kept pouring, but the water simply disappeared down the hole in the base of the well.

"Kick, don't use all of it."

"I know, just enough to fill it up," Kick said. And with that the bucket was empty. Kick watched the last of the water swirl around the small indentation and then drain away. "Oh, I guess I used all of it."

Maddie sighed.

Kick climbed down the ladder and stood next to his sister, who had eyes only for the totem.

"Anything?" he asked.

"I don't know. I think I can hear watering dripping, but . . ." Maddie slid to the right and then pointed at the beaver. "There!"

A thin line of water could be seen racing around the beaver. It followed a line around the head, circled the stomach, and then crisscrossed the tail, filling numerous lines, before disappearing into the pole.

"Over here," Kick said, pointing to another line of water racing around a series of rings that wrapped completely around the pole. "And there, too."

And there were more. Channels all over the storm totem were filling with moving water. Soon every line on the pole seemed to hold liquid—all of it moving.

"Where's it going?" Maddie asked.

Kick walked around the pole, studying the humanlike figure at its base. He expected to see water spilling from the base, but there was none. Upon closer inspection, he found something even more remarkable.

"Maddie," he said, kneeling down next to the base of the pole. "I think the water is flowing up."

"That's impossible," Maddie said, bending to get a better look.

Kick was right. The water flowing around the legs of the stubby figure was definitely flowing up. In fact, lines all over the totem seemed to be carrying water up, not down. Maddie stared at a stream of water flowing at a forty-five-degree angle over the curve of the killer whale's back.

"Something is pumping the water," she said.

Kick leaned closer to the pole. "I hear something. Sounds like breathing."

"That's it! There must be a steam engine inside that's pushing the water around the pole."

Kick stood up, never taking his eyes off the storm totem. "But doesn't a steam engine need heat?"

Maddie frowned. "It could be the water. As it flows from the top, it could be pushing water at the bottom back up."

"Maybe," Kick said. He stared at the pole for a moment longer, then went to the back door and peered out into the alley. "It's not raining. Not even a cloud."

Maddie wasn't surprised, but neither was she disappointed. The lack of precipitation didn't diminish the remarkable find that she and Kick had just made.

Kick was disappointed. He returned to the totem and was about to stick a finger into one of the channels when a drop of water struck his arm.

"I think it's leaking."

"What?"

Kick showed Maddie the spot on his sleeve where a droplet of water had struck.

Maddie glanced back at the totem. "Where? I don't see any—" was all she got out before a large droplet hit her on the cheek.

"Told you," Kick said.

Maddie wiped the water from her cheek and was about to do the same to the smirk on her brother's face when another drop of water hit her. And then another. And another. She and Kick looked up at the same time.

A cloud had condensed inside the storeroom, filling the space from a few feet above the totem all the way to the ceiling. The tops of the bookshelves disappeared into the fog, which seemed to pulse and billow slightly.

Kick moved closer to his sister. "Maddie, what do we do?"

"I don't know," Maddie said, wiping off a few more drops that had hit home.

And then they got very wet.

19

Walter Peterson grimaced as he tossed another shovelful of dirt into A. P. Bott's open grave. A week's worth of digging—or, more accurately, filling—had turned his spine into a twisted rack of stiffness and ache. Each night was a little worse, and tonight, having already reburied three of the dearly departed, Walter found himself rethinking his position on cemetery security.

"Shoot on sight," he mumbled to himself. "That'd put an end to it, right quick."

In the wake of the marshal's misadventure, a series of disturbances had plagued the cemetery as rumor spread that there were riches buried among the permanent residents. There was no treasure. Walter put up a sign on the front gate proclaiming this fact, but his troubles had continued. One upturned grave had become two, then three, then six.

"And I'm the only one has to fill the holes? Ain't right."

Walter raised another shovelful of dirt, but a horse whinny stopped him cold. He drew a pistol from his coat, raising it to the darkness.

"Who's there?"

No answer came.

"Cemetery's closed. And there ain't no g'damn treasure!"

Walter grabbed the oil lamp at his feet and made a full sweep of the yard, revealing nothing. Sensing a presence behind him, he spun quickly—too quickly—and toppled into the open grave. The coffin broke his fall and the lantern with it.

Opening his eyes, Walter found little to focus on. The hole was barely five feet deep, but dirt piled around the edges made it impossible to see beyond them without the lantern. Exposed, he frantically searched the soil for his weapon, finding only a shard of broken glass.

"Damn this night!"

After wrapping a snot rag around his throbbing palm, Walter made several one-handed attempts to escape, failing each time. A final try left him on his back, a chunk of metal digging into his spine. At least he'd found the gun.

"If anyone's out there, I could use some help," he said, trying not to sound afraid and nearly succeeding.

Walter waited for a response, but none came. He was alone. He'd be stuck in the hole until someone came looking for him tomorrow or possibly the next day. Surely they'd miss him by then.

That's when he saw the light.

Henry walked to within ten feet of the open grave and stopped. He'd seen the caretaker digging, but, like the light, the man was now gone. Or hiding.

Henry took a step toward the hole.

"Don't come any closer," a voice said from inside the grave. "I've got a gun."

Henry stopped. "Walter?"

"Who's that?"

"It's Henry Macke."

"Henry?"

Henry strode to the edge of the hole. The caretaker was indeed standing in the middle of the open grave, holding a pistol in one hand, a bloody rag in the other.

"What are you doing down there?"

Walter stared at the man for a beat, then looked around at his surroundings as if seeing them for the first time.

"I fell."

Henry glanced over his shoulder and then offered a hand. Walter took it gladly.

"Now, go," Henry said, once the caretaker was out of the hole. "Get out of here."

Walter brushed some of the dirt from his jacket and stared at Henry. The man was scared, more scared than the caretaker had been a few minutes earlier.

"There's no treasure here, Henry."

Henry looked over his shoulder and then snatched the pistol jutting out of Walter's pocket. He pointed it at the man's face.

"Just go, Walter!"

Walter took several steps back, mindful of the open grave.

"What have you gotten yourself into, Henry?"

A voice from the darkness explained everything:

"Kill him."

Walter spun to find himself face-to-chest with the Hanged Man. Terror filled his heart. It was tactile, heavy, and it rooted him to the ground. He would never move but rather die on the spot, scared to death.

And then his heart beat again, and again, and a dozen times more in a second.

The Hanged Man drew his revolver, but Walter was already running, darting between headstones, leaping over an open grave, and generally trying to wish himself a smaller target. He didn't hear the gunshot but felt the bullet strike his left forearm just below the elbow. It hurt like hell, but Walter never stopped running.

The Hanged Man watched the caretaker disappear through the front gate of the cemetery, stumble to the ground, and then continue down the hill and out of sight. He could have shot him again, several times, in fact, but that wasn't the way it was supposed to be. One shot—that was all he'd ever needed. Things were different now.

He didn't like it.

"I couldn't shoot him," Henry said. "I know the man."

The Hanged Man holstered his weapon and stared at Henry.

"Good reason to kill him."

Henry met the Hanged Man's gaze. "You didn't."

Henry was as surprised by his words as the Hanged Man. The surge of confidence that had prompted them was already gone, but Henry knew where to find more.

The Hanged Man walked around the grave to stand before Henry. Whenever the dead man was close, Henry felt ill. The putrid stench that clung to his body got inside a man, made his guts feel twisted and his heart pound faster. Henry tried to keep his distance, but the Hanged Man rarely let him out of his sight.

The Hanged Man eyed the gun in Henry's hand. Henry tightened his grip. It would be a useless gesture, but the thought of it—

The weapon was out of his hand and pressed to the bottom of his chin before Henry could react. The speed was shocking, unnatural even.

As the dead man leaned in, Henry felt his breath on his cheek. Only it wasn't breathing but merely the stale air that moved out of his mouth when he spoke. Dead men didn't breathe.

"Do what I tell you."

Henry nodded.

The Hanged Man withdrew the weapon and tucked it behind his belt.

"Bring the shovel."

The Hanged Man's grave was easier to dig the second time, although Henry wasn't sure what value there was in the chore. The grave would be empty, assuming one of the other bodies hadn't been put in the Hanged Man's place by mistake. Henry told the dead man as much, but he insisted on seeing for himself. Why? Was there some power to be found within?

(*you have power*)

Henry touched the small bulge in his coat pocked, pressing it against his chest. There was warmth there, quieter than before, but still there.

He was too close.

The Hanged Man stood ten feet from the hole, watching the cemetery. He hadn't moved from the spot in the last half hour, and although Henry wasn't sure, it appeared the dead man was listening. To what, Henry was afraid to ask.

They weren't alone, of course. Like the preceding nights, there were eyes glowing in the forest beyond the lantern light. Most were those of small rodents, although Henry had also seen a deer and what he thought was a wolf. They came and watched—silently, for the most part. The night before, Henry had heard squealing, although it hadn't lasted long. The noises that had followed sounded like tiny mouths feeding. Henry had not slept well.

The ride from Tillamook had been difficult. The Hanged Man pushed the horses hard, leading them from beach to bluff and into the hills in some places. If he was following a trail, Henry couldn't see it. Throughout the ride, the dead man barely said a word, which was fine with Henry. The silence kept him from screaming—that and the thought of reading.

It was well after dark when they'd stopped the first night. Henry was exhausted, but that didn't keep him from slipping the book from his pocket as he curled up, his back to the Hanged Man. Henry waited until the fire died back and then let the notebook flutter open in his hand. A warm feeling spread across his face. He'd barely read a sentence before he remembered.

He wants me to read it.

A slight breeze caught the pages lifting one over another until they all rolled over and the book snapped closed. The air was warm but left Henry cold just the same. He wouldn't read another word that night.

Henry stopped digging long enough to check on the horses, both of whom were tied to small trees at the edge of the cemetery. Henry's had actually drifted as far into the light as it could, enough to bend the young fir practically horizontal. It stared intently at the woods—*watching the eyes,* Henry thought. The other horse's head drooped toward the ground, its eyes surrounded by yellow puss. Henry knew very little about equine matters, but even he could see the animal wouldn't last another day under its current rider.

"I can hear them."

Henry nearly jumped, the voice was so close. The Hanged Man stood at the edge of the open grave, close enough for Henry to touch. He hadn't heard the dead man approach, but now understood why there was bile building up in the back of his throat.

"Hear who?"

The Hanged Man grinned and walked away.

Henry spit into the dirt and resumed digging.

The dead man's horse died twenty minutes later, slumping to the ground in a heap, its last breath a long, slow gurgle. Henry's horse broke its tether and strode to the opposite side of the grave, well away from the dead animal. It stared at Henry, afraid to leave the light, but suggesting that perhaps together they could make it. Henry knew better.

Henry struck wood a few minutes later. The coffin was half filled with dirt but otherwise unoccupied. Henry removed enough of the soil to reach inside the box but not so much as to make room for another body.

The fear that Henry had felt inside the coffin returned. He was alone again, in the dark, only this time there was no book to discover. The Hanged Man would take it and force him into the box. That had been his plan all along. Before he knew what he was doing, Henry pulled the book from his coat pocket, flipped to a random page, and began reading aloud.

"*I am the judgment of him and his hand is mine, intertwined.*'"

Henry felt a surge of power pass through him—real power, not just confidence or warmth. He stared at the words he'd read, realizing he'd once again translated the text from multiple languages. He scanned the rest of the page, seeing all the words in English, instantly understanding them, and then . . . and then not. The words lost their meaning just as quickly and his understanding was gone. He was not alone.

Henry slipped the book back into this pocket and turned to face the dead man, totally unprepared for the *other* dead man, whose body landed on top of Henry, knocking him to the ground.

"Bury him."

Henry sat up, shoving the corpse into the opposite corner of the grave. This dead man wore a frayed black suit, which appeared to be the only thing holding the body together. The flesh about the neck and face was brittle and papery, revealing more skull than skin. Despite the decrepit state, Henry thought there was something familiar about the man, perhaps even *familial*. He looked away, not wanting to see more.

"Bury him," Henry said. "In your grave."

The Hanged Man nodded.

"Hurry up, Henry. He's a biter."

Henry hesitated at the odd instruction before deciding he didn't care. He grabbed the dead man's feet, promptly snapping them off at the ankles. He tossed both into the open coffin and then began to stuff the rest of the corpse inside, breaking more than a few bones in the process. When the rib cage caught on the splintered lid, Henry used both hands to crush the dead man's chest, flattening it. It was then that the jaw fell open.

And closed.

Henry scrambled back as the jaw snapped open and closed twice more. It wasn't fast, but powerful . . . and hungry. One of the dead man's arms reached out, clawing at Henry's leg. Henry swatted it away, breaking off several fingers. Undeterred, the remaining digits reached out again. Henry grabbed the hand, yanking the entire arm free of its socket. It ceased moving.

The jaw continued to snap at Henry.

"Finish it," said the Hanged Man.

Henry tentatively crawled forward again. He tried pushing the shoulders into the box, but the skull continued to snap at him. Finally, he shoved the loose arm into its mouth, giving the not-so-dead man something to chew on. He quickly jammed the rest of the corpse into the box, pushing the top of the skull in last, cracking the dead man's arm.

Had Walter been in attendance, he would have appreciated the ease with which Henry got himself out of the grave. For his part, Henry suspected any slower and he'd never have made it.

"What was that?"

"An actor."

Henry shook his head.

The Hanged Man stared at Henry, his intentions obvious before he gave voice to them.

"I would kill again."

Henry slowly put it together. "You think if you put a body in the ground in place of your own you'll be able to kill again? You think God won't notice?"

The Hanged Man didn't answer but rather picked up the shovel and began refilling the hole. Henry saw something move in the box just before being covered with dirt.

"But why was it . . . alive?"

"Not alive. And not alone."

Henry didn't understand. And then he did. There were at least a hundred stones covering the gently sloping field atop the mountain. Many of the graves had been freshly dug (or dug up) and at least a few remained open. Henry found just such a plot thirty feet from where he stood. He could make out the mounds of dirt piled on either side of the marker and the dark hole in front of it. Something was in the hole, something moving—hands, digging at the soil, searching for a handhold, trying to find a way out. A pair of glowing eyes peered over the top edge of the hole.

Henry stumbled backward. "What did you do?"

The Hanged Man didn't answer; he didn't have one. He'd done nothing to disturb the eternal slumber of the local inhabitants, nothing intentional. It was possible he didn't have a say in the matter. His presence alone might be enough to wake the dead. Either way, he didn't know. Nor did he care.

The Hanged Man added one last shovelful of dirt and surveyed his work.

Henry stared at the hole. "It's only half full."

The Hanged Man tossed the shovel at Henry's feet and walked away.

Henry stole a glance over his shoulder. The dead man was still struggling to escape the grave, but a second corpse, a woman in a tattered, light-colored dress, stumbled past on the right, arms dangling at her side, one leg dragging behind. Her head lolled forward, unable to stay upright. Henry watched the dead woman long enough to confirm that she was moving toward him.

Henry ran to his horse and pulled himself into the saddle. He half expected the Hanged Man to drag him down—or worse, to join him—but instead the dead man brought his own horse around. It was not dead, after all.

Except it was.

It was like him, or more accurately like the creatures in the forest, because that's what they all were—dead. No living creature would have been drawn to the Hanged Man, but wherever he went the dead would rise and follow him, watch over him, protect him. Rodents, wolves, horses, people. They would rise from the ground, given new life as Henry had given the Hanged Man. His existence was a disease and it would spread wherever he trod. Henry knew this to be true because he had made it happen.

The living dead steed raised its head and spit out a red-and-black bundle of snot, which dangled from its nose briefly and then slipped to the ground. Its eyes glowed in the lantern light but there was no life in them.

Henry's horse sidled away from its companion, sensing the creature was an abomination. Henry wished he could do the same.

The Hanged Man directed his horse through the cemetery. Henry followed.

The front door to the marshal's house was locked, but the Hanged Man pushed it open without breaking stride.

Henry followed, bringing the lantern around to reveal a foyer devoid of furniture, wall hangings, or anything that might suggest a state of occupancy. The same was true for the front room, hall, and kitchen, save for a few mismatched plates stacked in an open cupboard alongside a single, cracked cup. The house was empty, abandoned.

"Not much left," Henry said. "I guess the marshal ain't coming back."

The Hanged Man paused at the bottom of the stairwell, waiting for Henry and his light.

"He weren't supposed to leave."

The second floor was just as sparse, with only the back bedroom featuring more than a layer of dust. A short dresser, bureau, and bed frame made it seem lavish compared to the other rooms. The Hanged Man scanned the walls and was about to leave when something caught his eye. He held out his hand.

Henry handed over the lantern and watched the Hanged Man raise it above his head, illuminating a large brown stain on the ceiling. He studied it for a moment, then passed the light back to Henry and walked out of the room. Henry took one last look himself but saw nothing out of the ordinary.

Unlike the rest of the house, the attic was flush with boxes and furniture. The Hanged Man pushed his way through the clutter, opening several of the cartons, more out of frustration than a desire to find what lay within. None of them would have what he was looking for and he knew it.

"He probably took it with him," Henry said, immediately sorry he'd opened his mouth.

The Hanged Man said nothing.

Henry turned to the nearest box and began flipping through a collection of papers. Many were legal documents—remnants of Kleberg's law enforcement days, no doubt. Mixed in with the pages were maps and a few random photographs. A formal portrait caught Henry's eye. It showed a man with a patch over his left eye, a handsome woman, and two children, a boy and a girl, neither of whom appeared to be more than ten. The woman must be the marshal's daughter, Henry thought. He had never been formally introduced, but he'd seen her around town with her husband.

An ancient memory surfaced that suggested this man and the Hanged Man knew each other. Henry had no idea where it had come from, but it felt true.

"I found something," he said.

The Hanged Man took the photo from Henry. He held it under the lamp briefly before turning toward a small window. The moon had risen, but Henry couldn't imagine it offered more light than the lantern.

The Hanged Man studied the photo intently. His lips barely moved, but Henry thought he heard him say, "He lives." The Hanged Man then flipped the photo over and read the inscription loud enough for Henry to be sure what he heard.

"'*The Wyldes of Portland, 1885.*'"

The Hanged Man stared for a moment longer, then crumpled the photo into a ball and let it fall to the floor, which is where he found the marshal's words carved into the wood.

WHERE IS HE?

"He was supposed to keep watch," Henry said. He was familiar with the concept of watching over the dead man. Hadn't that always been his job?

"You only came to me after he left," the Hanged Man said, reading Henry's eyes if not his mind.

Henry shook his head but found the words were true. The memories of that day hadn't always been with him. They had returned less than a week earlier. And hadn't Asa told him of Kleberg's departure around the same time? He'd gone to live with his family. That's why the house was so empty. That's why—

Henry felt his chest suddenly tighten as the Hanged Man put a hand on his shoulder.

"The day I died, did you see the dark giant?" he asked.

Henry searched for meaning in the words but found none.

"I didn't see anyone but the marshal and you." There wasn't anyone else . . . *was there?*

The dead man opened his right hand.

"I can feel it," he said, closing his eyes. "The grip in my hand, the weight of it, the heat . . . they took it from me."

"No, I only saw the marshal."

The Hanged Man opened his eyes, half expecting the red-handled gun to materialize in his hand. It did not.

"Joseph," he said, his eyes finding Henry but for a moment seeing someone else.

A terrible wave of nausea enveloped Henry's senses and for a moment he knew nothing but the dead man's hate. And then it was gone.

"Stay here," the Hanged Man said. "We ride for Portland before dawn."

Henry never said a word as the Hanged Man disappeared down the stairs, leaving him alone in the attic. A minute later he saw him through the small window as he rode down the hill on a dead horse.

He was not alone.

Six men and two women in various states of decomposition slowly lurched after him. They appeared dazed, unable to control

their movements, only their direction. These were not the same beings as the Hanged Man but rather mindless, animated corpses
one step removed from death. Henry feared them just the same.

One of the dead men rolled his head across his shoulders until
he appeared to meet Henry's gaze. The man's body jerked to the
right, and soon he was staggering toward the house. Henry stepped
back from the window and the dead man's stride faltered. His head
bobbled from side to side and then spun back in the direction of his
companions. His body soon followed.

Unable to look away, Henry watched the group lurch toward
town. Their spastic gait was both sickening and oddly hypnotic.
When one of the dead shuffled through the gate of the nearest
neighbor and then pitched forward onto the front steps, Henry
finally turned his back on the scene. He made his way to the first
floor, found a spot of moonlight beneath a window, and pulled the
black book from his pocket.

All was quiet as he began to read.

Early Tuesday morning, Marvin Daniels was shot in the back, just
below the neck, as he walked from his home on Seventh Street to
his job at the Astoria Cannery. Miraculously, the bullet struck no
major organs or arteries, leaving Marvin bloodied but alive. He
never saw his assailant.

The first person to arrive on the scene offered no assistance but
rather only the observation that the victim would survive his wound.
This, Marvin thought, seemed to displease the man who never descended from his horse.

Gunplay would normally have caused quite a stir in Astoria,
which, other than one infamous shootout eleven years prior, rarely
saw scenes of violence.

This day would prove very different.

20

───◆───

"I want to see it."

Kate sat down on the edge of the bed next to her father. He eyed her suspiciously.

"Sure 'bout that?"

Kate took a deep breath and slowly let it go. "Yes."

The marshal held his gaze for a few seconds longer before unwrapping the cloth-bound object in his hands. *Don't let her touch it*, he thought but did not say upon revealing the Hanged Man's red-handled pistol.

Kate had hoped seeing the pistol would blunt the power it held in her memories. It was, as Joseph reminded her, just a gun. But, of course, it wasn't. It was part of the man who had nearly destroyed her family. It had bruised the skin of her newborn daughter and brought her husband to within a whisper of death. It was an evil thing. Had it not been for the suspicion that the gun would make her sick should she touch it, Kate would have flung the thing out the window.

"How could you bring this into our house?"

The marshal tightened his grip on the handle.

"I'm sorry."

Kate studied her father's face. He was a stubborn man, but she'd never known him to lie, not to her.

"I believe you," she said, softening, though only slightly. "But I have to understand why you brought this from Astoria. Why did you even kept it?"

The marshal didn't have an answer, not a good one, even though he'd asked himself the same question numerous times. He gave the best he had.

"I couldn't leave it there. Not where somebody might find it, might use it."

"That's what you were doing in the cemetery. You were looking for a place to bury it."

The marshal thought that might have been it. Or had he been looking for something else . . . or someone?

"I couldn't find, I couldn't . . ."

"That's fine, Dad. I'm sorry I wasn't there."

"What would y'ave done? Take away my shovel?"

Kate laughed. "No, but I should have visited more. I know you like your privacy, but isn't it better having family close-by?"

"Course it is, Katie."

Kate leaned on her father's shoulder. The warmth of the gesture reminded him of why he'd spent so many years away from his family. He was protecting them. It's what he'd always done. That his daughter would never understand made no difference.

"As for that," Kate said, motioning to the gun, "Joseph told me what you plan to do after the festival. Thank you."

The marshal blinked. He'd spoken to Joseph after the mayor's party, when Kate was still too mad even to look at him. They'd come to a decision, an agreement, but what had it been?

"Throw it in the river," he said under his breath. Had he really agreed to that?

Kate kissed her father's cheek and then folded the cloth back into place, careful not to touch the revolver. She didn't notice the marshal's fingers were white from gripping the handle tightly.

"Bury it deep," she said, motioning to the closet. "I don't want the kids to find it. They know better, but they're curious."

The marshal nodded. "I'll hide it good."

Kate smiled and stepped into the hall.

"Katie?"

Kate leaned back into the room. "Yes?"

"Close the door. Don't want anyone to see my hidin' spot."

Kate nodded and shut the door. She stood in the hall for a moment longer, listening, but there was nothing to hear.

By Tuesday afternoon, downtown preparations for the festival were in full swing. Banners had been hung across Third Street at a dozen intersections, each painted with a different scene celebrating the city's love of all things wet. Most of the local storefronts were showcasing rain-themed displays in their front windows, many featuring running water and elaborate dioramas. The block-long scene laid out in the picture windows of Meier & Frank Clothiers told the story of Lewis and Clark's heroic journey down the Columbia River to the Pacific Ocean.

New to this year's festivities were the copper umbrella-shaped lanterns that hung from every lamp post and telegraph pole in the business district. Each of the firestone-powered lanterns would burn continuously without oil or electrified power for the entire weeklong festival, regardless of the weather or time of day. After a baker's dozen were stolen on the first day, organizers had the lights raised so as not to invite the criminal element. Only three had gone missing since.

The heart of the festival activity could be found at Foundling Square, where finishing touches were being put on the grand stage, as well as the numerous demonstration and entertainment booths that surrounded it. Each booth was constructed along a raised boardwalk and firmly anchored to the local terra firma. The main platform stood a good six feet above the waterline to ensure that no matter how much it rained, the stars of the festival could keep their feet dry, more or less.

Elsewhere in the downtown area, sidewalks and scaffolds were repaired and, in some cases, widened to accommodate increased foot traffic. A fleet of ten passenger barges was now anchored along Third Street, one at each of the major intersections. The usually deserted First Street blocks were filled with boatmen, testing their skills against the Chinese ferrymen who would dominate the races over the weekend. While betting on the official festival regatta was frowned upon, money flowed freely closer to the river.

Perhaps no project was more important—or secretive—than the Park Street water-evacuation effort. Seven steam- and ore-powered pumps worked night and day to remove water from the flooded streets in the northernmost part of downtown. What was not widely known was that rather than be diverted downriver, the water was pumped directly into the primary festival blocks to ensure the area remained flooded. The festival organizers did not want a repeat of last year's "puddle festival," which had resulted in terrible congestion, a muddy and disgusted citizenry, and hundreds of lost shoes.

Mayor Gates had signed off on the project despite warnings from advisers that intentionally prolonging a flood might hurt his reelection efforts. He was convinced that another secret project would make or break the festival, one about which he'd just received some very good news.

The mayor ducked his head as he passed beneath a string of navigational charts showing the relative depths and dangers beneath the waves at the mouth of the Columbia River. He ducked again under a low-hanging dictionary and once more below a still-dripping line of *Portland Post* periodicals.

A web of laundry lines crisscrossed most of the available head space in the Wyldes' storeroom, only it wasn't clothes or sheets but rather the store's overstock that was hung out to dry. Nearly everything in the storeroom was wet. Even the floor, which had remained dry throughout the downtown flood, was now covered by an inch of water. Only a small area at the base of the storm totem was dry, kept so by a circular barricade of sandbags.

The mayor ducked once more and popped up next to the totem, which itself was bone dry. He placed a hand on the snout of the sea-bear carving.

"So it works," he said.

"Very well," Joseph said from the top of a nearby ladder. He finished tying off another line and then climbed down to join the mayor. "We'll be drying out our inventory for weeks."

Joseph had directed the comment at Kick, who was on bucket duty at the back of the storeroom. Kick emptied another pail of water into the ally and then couldn't resist pointing a finger at his sister, who was hand drying some of the less-waterlogged volumes.

"It was Maddie's idea."

Maddie eyed her brother. "I told you not to use so much!"

Kick made a series of hand gestures directed at his sister, finishing with a wide arcing windmill of his left arm.

Maddie stared at her brother in disbelief. What he'd just said— what he'd called her—went beyond the pale. She made a simple, almost muted gesture that ended with a synchronized wiggle of both pinkies.

Kick shook his head, but the damage was done. She'd understood exactly what he'd said and she was going to make him sorry for it.

Joseph took in as much of the conversation as he could, which was enough to know that Kick was in trouble. The boy needed to learn when to keep his mouth shut when Wylde women were involved.

Oblivious to the family pantomime, the mayor continued to examine the totem up close. While circling the pole, he accidently bumped the levy built up around its base, splashing a small amount of water into the danger zone.

"Careful," Joseph said. "It doesn't take much to get it raining again."

The mayor glanced about the room. "Terribly sorry about the inconvenience, Joseph. I'm sure we can find a little extra in the festival budget to cover your losses." The mayor nodded to his assistant, who was waiting at the entrance to the storeroom.

Avery perked up. "Just give us a number, Mr. Wylde. I'll take care of everything."

Joseph smiled. "That's very generous, thank you."

"It's the least I can do," said the mayor. "Now, tell me, will this thing work as well out of doors as it has in-?"

Joseph dried has hands on a towel tucked into his belt. "I don't know. I'm not entirely sure how it works at all."

"Well, as you said, it seems to work quite well."

"True, but this is a small space. As wet as it is in here, the same amount of water outside would be barely measurable. Hardly even a sprinkle, I'm afraid."

The mayor soured. "I see."

Joseph didn't like lying to the mayor, but he felt the truth might lead to bigger problems. He had no idea what the totem would do if it got wet outside, and that scared him. Once the sky opened up and started to pour down on the thing, would it ever stop? He'd managed to slow the downpour only after throwing a tarp over the top of it, and even then it hadn't stopped drizzling until all the channels carved into the totem had run dry. It was hours before the humidity in the room had returned to normal.

"It's possible that its job was to make it rain only in a very small area," Joseph said, trying out a theory he hoped would appeal to the mayor. "It would be good for a ceremony, some kind of Native ritual, but I doubt it would do much for the crops."

The mayor perked. "Put on a show, eh?"

"Something like that. Any chief or shaman who could make it rain on command, especially indoors, would be seen as powerful, even godlike."

The mayor had been in politics long enough to recognize when someone was appealing to his ego.

"You're suggesting that if I were to bring the rain indoors, say for the opening-night ball, I'd be seen as a god?"

Joseph laughed. "Well, perhaps deification is too much to hope for, but I suspect a great many voters would be impressed."

"And very, very wet. I love it. I'll send the men around to pick it up this evening."

"Tell them to bring plenty of canvas and rope to wrap it up. You don't want this thing getting wet before the show."

The mayor pointed to his assistant, who immediately wrote another note in his ledger. The mayor then stepped carefully around the storm totem to stand next to Joseph.

"It's going to be a fabulous festival—and it's going to rain, I can feel it in my bones!"

Joseph didn't disagree. "Your weatherman certainly thinks so, all local evidence to the contrary."

"Yes, he's quite certain. Speaking of recent events, what do you make of the violence on the coast?"

Joseph sensed both kids stop what they were doing at the mayor's question. No doubt they'd been listening all along, but this piqued their interest.

"Sorry?"

The mayor's eyes lit up. "You've not seen this morning's paper?"

"I've been a little busy," Joseph said, motioning to the mess around him.

"Tillamook, several nights ago," said the mayor. "A group of men shot up a circus, burned part of it to the ground."

"A circus?"

The mayor nodded, a little too enthusiastically. "Horrible, horrible spectacle, dozens injured. We dispatched a group from the medical college to assist with the wounded, of course. Least we could do."

"What of the assailants?"

"Three were captured, one a man wanted by the Oregon Mining Company named Mason, I believe."

Joseph shook his head.

"A minor outlaw, I'm told, and not a very good one at that. Barely survived the robbery." Perhaps picking up that young ears might be listening, the mayor leaned in and whispered, "In truth, he may have been shot by his own man, and—this is where it gets interesting—it was the Hanged Man."

Joseph blinked. "That's not possible."

The mayor smiled. "Well, of course not, but this was a very clever ruse. There was a body on display, the Hanged Man's corpse—"

"They burned it."

"Yes, yes, but not everyone knows that. Anyway, at some point the dead man was to rise from the grave—part of the show, of course—and terrify the locals. The carnival folk then would pretend to put the dead man down and the next day their ticket sales would go through the roof. Brilliant bit of marketing; very theatrical."

Joseph thought it rather ghoulish but bit his tongue. "What happened?"

"It was a setup—an inside job. Mr. Mason used the chaos of the show to stage a robbery, only the criminal corpse wanted a bigger piece of the pie—all of it, apparently. Shot his partners and everyone else, by most accounts."

The twins had drifted closer to the conversation, no longer pretending to hide their interest. Joseph searched for something to tone down the decidedly downbeat story.

"But only one man died?"

"Yes," the mayor said. "Twice."

"What?"

"Apparently, the corpse rose up and attacked someone before they could put it in the ground. Ghastly."

"He must not have been dead."

"My inclination as well, but then I heard the news out of Astoria this morning. You know about the grave disturbances of recent weeks, of course?"

Joseph nodded, not sure if the mayor was being polite or had simply forgotten who had been first to break sacred ground. The kids certainly remembered.

"Well, it may not have been robbers trying to break in," the mayor said. "It may have been the dead trying to get out."

Maddie gasped, unable to stop herself. She was pleased to find her brother's hand so close to her own.

The memory of a dark dream crept onto the stage in Joseph's mind. He couldn't see it, yet, but he could feel it, waiting, breathing life into itself. Only the truth would keep it at bay.

"Tell me everything."

"That's ridiculous," Kate said.

Joseph had just finished retelling the mayor's story to Kate and her father. All three were seated around the Wyldes' kitchen table, empty save for cups of coffee and the late edition of the *Portlandian*. Perched on the first and third steps of the stairwell just off the kitchen were Maddie and Kick.

"I know it's hard to believe," Joseph said. "And I'm sure there's some exaggeration, but you read the story."

"About a shootout," Kate said, sliding the newspaper across the table to her husband. A single column below the fold followed the headline, CARNIVAL SHOOTING CLAIMS ONE, before continuing eight pages later. "There isn't a single word about walking corpses. And there's no mention of *him*."

Joseph was surprised to find that the newspaper had failed to include what seemed a fairly significant part of the story. It was a ruse—it had to be—but it was also sensational, which was fertile ground for selling papers.

"I don't know why he's not mentioned," Joseph said, running his fingers across the paper. "It does say there were others involved who avoided capture."

"Men, Joseph, *live* men with guns." Kate didn't intend to look at her father as she said this, but she did. He was staring straight ahead, not paying attention to the conversation.

"Do you think the mayor is lying?"

Kate stood up from the table and walked to a window on the side of the kitchen. Much of the city was already dark, but Mount Hood remained clearly visible in the distance, bathed in pink light.

"I think Jim Gates likes a good story."

"True," Joseph said. "But something happened in Tillamook— more so than what it says in the paper—and that something is very likely related to the violence in Astoria."

"Maybe so, but isn't it most likely another con? Who needs the circus when you've got a gang dressed up like long-dead relatives to scare the locals? Did anyone bother to check if any of the banks had been robbed?"

"I don't know. This just happened, so the news is . . ."

"Unreliable," Kate finished.

There was more, which Joseph would have shared had the marshal not spoken up.

"Where'd they get the body?"

"What's that, Dad?"

"The body," said the marshal, continuing to stare straight ahead. "Said it was at a circus?"

"He wasn't dead," said Joseph. "It was a trick, an actor dressed up like the Hanged Man, to sell tickets."

The marshal turned to Joseph. "You sure?"

It was the first time since they'd returned to Portland that the old man had really looked at him, and Joseph was surprised by the weight of the marshal's gaze.

"I don't know all the details," Joseph said. "But it makes sense. Even if they did use an actual corpse and then made a switch between shows, it certainly wasn't the real thing. You made sure of that."

"Did I?"

Kate returned to the table and took a seat next to her father. "Years ago, Dad."

The marshal looked at his daughter. In her eyes he saw the good faith he very much wanted to feel, but couldn't because . . .

"I don't remember," he said. *And you never will.*

"There was a fire," Joseph said, picking his words carefully, for both the marshal and the young ears seated on the steps behind him. "There wouldn't be anything left to put on display, especially not after so many years."

"I don't remember a fire," said the marshal.

"We know, Dad," Kate said, putting a hand on her father's elbow. "It's been a long time."

"No," said the marshal, a little agitated. "No, what I mean is I remember there *weren't* no fire."

In an instant, the marshal saw a dead man and a grave. He saw himself with a shovel. He saw a gun. And then it was gone, as if it had been plucked directly from his mind . . . stolen.

"I buried him," he said, immediately doubting his own words. The marshal blinked and looked away, once more staring at nothing.

The weight of his gaze lifted, Joseph heard the marshal's breathing even out and his heartbeat slow. The spark was gone.

"Marshal?"

The marshal didn't respond.

"Dad?"

The marshal looked at his daughter. "What?"

"Are you all right?"

The old man frowned. "Course I am," he said, then glanced at Joseph. "Gonna finish your story?"

Kate sat back in her chair. A dozen questions bounced around in her head, all of them difficult. She knew which one Joseph wanted to ask.

"Dad, why were you digging on the hill?"

The marshal raised an eyebrow. "I ain't been digging."

"Not here, in Astoria, two weeks ago."

The marshal pushed back on the wall in his head, but it didn't budge. He didn't remember. He couldn't. Rather than repeat what he'd surely said a dozen times already, the marshal pushed his chair back from the table and stood up.

"I'm tired. Think I'll have a rest 'fore supper."

The twins parted to give their grandfather room to climb the stairs. Once they heard his bedroom door close and lock, both turned back to their parents.

"Are we eatin' supper again?"

"No, Kick," Kate said. "Your grandfather . . . he forgot."

"He couldn't remember at his house, either," Maddie said. "About the digging, I mean."

Kick nodded. "But he said it was a good idea at the time."

"He was making fun," Maddie added.

"About crackin' open a coffin?"

"No, about it being a good idea."

"Oh," Kick said. "Then why was he diggin' 'em up?"

Kate was surprised not by how much the kids knew but that they had information she did not.

"I'm not sure he knows what he was doing," she said. "Sometimes when people get old they become forgetful, do funny things."

"Like diggin' in graveyards," said Kick.

"Yes, like that."

"You talked to him about this," Joseph asked. "And he made a joke?"

Both kids nodded.

Joseph turned to Kate. He didn't say a word but knew they were thinking the same thing—*if he can joke about it, he can get past it*. It was something.

Maddie broke the silence. "Why would someone pretend to be the Hanged Man? I thought everyone was glad he was dead."

"It was part of a show, honey. Like a play that's supposed to give people a scare and then they can laugh about it."

"But the mayor said he shot people."

"That wasn't part of the show," Joseph said. "But the same theory applies. This villain, whoever he was, wanted to get folks running for cover while his partners committed a crime. Fear is a powerful motivator, especially when it's armed."

Maddie thought this over but let Kick ask the next question.

"If this fella's a fake, how come you're scared?"

Joseph blinked. *Was it that obvious?*

Later that evening, outside under the stars that had become so common that spring, Joseph told Kate the rest.

"I think I know why your father was digging in the cemetery."

Kate tensed up just a little. "You don't think he was trying to bury the gun?"

"He was looking for the Hanged Man."

Kate stared at her husband and then turned away to face the city lit up beneath the house. The night air was cooler than it had been in weeks, the warm wind replaced by a brisk but not unpleasant breeze. The weatherman was right: it would rain soon. At least one thing was returning to normal.

"They burned the body, Joseph. You know they did."

"Do I? I didn't see the fire. I wasn't exactly lucid, as you recall. And you heard your father. The marshal may have actually remembered something tonight."

"You're basing this on Dad's memory?"

"Not entirely. Do you remember Walter Peterson?"

Kate shook her head.

"We met him last October at your father's place in Astoria. He was walking up the hill on his way to work."

"The caretaker, sure. What about him?"

"He was one of those attacked last night."

Kate rolled her eyes. "By a walking dead man, I suppose."

"By the Hanged Man, or whoever's pretending to be him," he

added quickly. "This man shot Walter while he was trying to flee, shot him in the cemetery."

Kate folded her arms over her chest. "You got this from the mayor?"

"I contacted Deputy Barker in Astoria this afternoon. He relayed the information."

"Why didn't you mention this earlier?"

"I wanted to hear what the marshal had to say before I spoke to anyone else."

Kate understood without being told. "You're going to Astoria."

Joseph held on to his answer for a beat, giving Kate time to accept it.

"I think it's best we have a firsthand account, don't you?"

Kate frowned. "I don't know what you think you're going to find."

"Answers, hopefully. From those responsible. They've already got two men in custody."

"Who?"

"Locals. One of them is the deputy's brother."

"That's surprising."

"Yes," Joseph said, nodding. "Especially since he died over a year ago."

21

The zombie lunged against the bars, arms outstretched in a futile effort to grasp a prize just out of reach. Only the left arm came close; the right swung freely, no longer anatomically sound. Had the creature been alive, the pain would have been excruciating. The zombie felt nothing. The only pain it knew—the only *thing*—was hunger.

Joseph approached the jail cell, close enough for the creature's bony fingers to brush against his jacket.

"Careful," said Deputy Collins. "Thing's stronger than it looks."

All three deputies—the tall and lanky Collins, an older veteran named Kendle, and Barker, a quiet, dark-haired man whom Joseph had first talked to—stood well back from the cell. They had no desire to be close to their prisoner but were eager to know exactly what it was they'd captured.

Deputy Collins took a tentative step forward. The creature rolled its head in the deputy's direction but seemed to regard the skinny man as not worth the effort.

"We wrenched this one's shoulder pretty good, but it don't seem to mind."

Joseph noted what appeared to be a broken collarbone pushing up against the dead man's jacket at the left shoulder. There were also several small holes in the fabric, two in the chest and one in the right side of the abdomen. Given the dirty but otherwise reasonable condition of the suit, Joseph guessed these were bullet holes.

"You shot him?"

Collins nodded. "Three times."

"For all the good it did," mumbled Kendle.

Joseph studied the zombie's face. It was pale and sunken, the skin stretched taut against the skull. The lips had pulled back, making every dry lick of the tongue clearly visible inside a mouth missing half its teeth. The eyes, impossibly black, stared lifelessly ahead between brittle lids that would never blink again. A shock of black hair fell across the left side of the creature's forehead, off-setting its starboard droop.

Joseph waited for the zombie's attention to drift elsewhere and then snatched its outstretched arm at the wrist. No pulse. Curious, he reached forward with his other hand, stopping a few inches from the creature's mouth. The zombie snapped at his fingers but couldn't push far enough through the bars to gain satisfaction. It did, however, break free of Joseph's grip, and would have grabbed him around the collar had he not backed away.

"Told you it was strong," said Collins.

The zombie issued a low moan that lingered in the back of the sherriff's office. A weaker, thinner wail came from the floor of a neighboring cell, where a second male corpse lay mostly still on the floor. Only its jaw moved, slowly opening and closing.

"That one you can get close to," Collins said. "Ain't moved since we dumped it in there this morning. Just keeps flappin' its gums, what's left of 'em, anyway."

"How many others were there?"

"Four we know of," said Kendle. "All dead, we think. They ain't movin' at least."

Joseph returned his attention to the standing corpse as it slammed against the bars with surprising speed.

"They're fast when they wanna be," said Collins. "Pretty slow most other times, but they'll fool ya."

"Is he alive?"

The question came from the third deputy, the one named Barker. Of the three, only his face registered anything other than sickening curiosity.

"Your brother?" Joseph said, pointing to the livelier of the two zombies.

The deputy nodded. "James. Died last June. Thought he did."

Joseph heard the sadness in the deputy's words and told him what he hoped very much to be true.

"I don't believe this creature is a relation, Deputy, not anymore."

Deputy Barker took a step toward the cell. The zombie regarded him with modest interest before returning its attention to Joseph.

"That's not James?"

"I don't think so," Joseph said. "There's no heartbeat, no breath intake, no recognition in its eyes. By any scientific measure this creature is dead."

"Can it see me?"

"I suppose it can. But I doubt very much it knows you."

"That is correct, Mr. Wylde."

Joseph recognized the newcomer's presence all at once, his senses all but telling him the man had materialized in the jailhouse out of thin air. It was a sensation he was not entirely unfamiliar with, given Kate's abilities, but Joseph had never encountered another so skilled at camouflage. He turned to face the man, bringing his impressive size and African features into focus.

The deputies were equally surprised, each reaching for his pistol as they turned.

"Whoa, mister," Collins said, his weapon in hand. "Who the hell might you be?"

Andre smiled, disarming the deputy instantly.

"My name is Andre Labeau, gentlemen. I believe I am expected."

Collins lowered his gun. "You the fella up from Tillamook?"

"I am," Andre said, moving forward to take a closer look at the creature behind bars. "And it does appear you could use my help."

"Boy, we sure could, Mr. Labeau," Collins said, holstering his weapon. The other deputies offered appreciative nods, although Barker held on to his weapon. "I figure with you and Mr. Wylde here, we ought to be okay."

Andre turned his attention to Joseph, but not for the first time. He'd been studying him since making his presence known, Joseph was sure of it. There was energy about the big man unlike anything he'd ever encountered, and yet he seemed familiar. For Joseph, such a man would be hard to forget.

"Have we met, Mr. Labeau?"

"I do not believe so," Andre said, extending his hand. "I do know your father-in-law."

Joseph shook Andre's hand and was shocked by the strength of the man's heart: it beat loud enough that he should have heard it thumping from across the room.

Andre smiled. "I am very pleased to meet you, Mr. Wylde."

"And I you, Mr. Labeau."

Andre held Joseph's gaze for a moment longer and then turned back to the prisoner.

"And you are correct. This creature is not the deputy's brother, but rather a soulless biological reanimation. I can tell you it knows nothing of itself or its family. It knows only an insatiable hunger."

"That we noticed," said Collins. "This one tried to bite the sheriff and me both."

Andre furrowed his brow. "Did it draw blood?"

The deputy lifted up his boot to show off a jagged tear near the toe. "Ruined my boots, but never laid a tooth on me. Took a chunk out of the sheriff, though."

Joseph noticed Andre's attention flit briefly to a place where there was no one to receive it—only there was.

"Where can we find him, Deputy?" Naira asked.

Joseph had not felt the young woman's presence at all—and could *still not,* save for her disembodied voice. He was stunned.

"The sheriff? He went to the doc's to get patched up," Collins said. "Think he was gonna check on some other folks was hurt after that."

Andre shook his head. "We need to see him as soon as possible."

"Why?" Joseph asked, still reeling from the young Native woman's appearance. She was Indian, he was sure of that. "What's going to happen to him?"

"If he has been bitten by the infected—" was all Andre managed before the gunshot rang out.

A single bullet fired from Deputy Barker's gun pierced the chest of the zombie he'd once called brother. The creature stumbled backward but did not fall. A moment later, it lurched forward, reaching through the bars toward the deputy.

"Dammit!" yelped Collins, trying to make himself heard over the ringing in his ears. "What the hell are you doing, Barker?"

"I can't look it no more. I can't." The deputy brought his gun up again, but Andre stayed his hand.

"You need to destroy the brain. Or what remains of it. That is the only thing that will return this body to rest."

Deputy Barker raised his pistol three inches and fired again, striking the creature squarely in the forehead. The zombie flinched once and then crumpled to the ground. The deputy moved to the neighboring cell and dispatched the second zombie without hesitation. When he spoke again, the sadness was gone from his voice.

"You said you needed the sheriff?"

"Yes," said Andre. "Right away."

"You think he'll get sick," Joseph said.

"He ain't sick," Collins said. "Just a scratch. He'll be fine."

"No," Andre said. "He will not."

Sheriff Al Buellton had been shot twice while on the job, once thirteen years earlier and again five years later. In both instances, he'd come close to dying but managed to pull through. He felt he knew what constituted life-threatening; and no matter how he looked at it, the small gouge on his left calf hardly seemed a mortal wound.

"You're telling me I'm going to turn into one of them," Buellton said, making no effort to mask his disbelief. "I'm gonna die, come back to life, and then start bitin' folks."

Andre nodded. "Yes, within the week."

The sheriff chuckled to himself. "I'll turn into one o' them freaks we got locked up in back, just like that," he said, snapping his fingers.

"Not like that," Andre said. "First, you will feel a tingle in your leg, a minor itch. Best to ignore it, but by tonight that itch will be a fire raging up and down your leg, and you will scratch—just enough to tamp down the worst of it. You will continue to tell yourself this, even after fingernails scrape against bone. Assuming you do not bleed out, you will start to feel better, much better. Warmth will fill your belly, and for a while you will know nothing else. This is because your guts have begun to rot. Soon the pain will come, but not death, not yet. If you are right enough in the head to put a bullet in it, consider yourself lucky. If not, then you will come to know the hunger for human flesh before you die. I am told it is unpleasant."

Andre's words had the desired effect on the deputies as all three began checking themselves for wounds they may have missed.

Joseph felt their power, although he was too busy trying to focus on the man's young companion to look for bite marks.

"That's a pretty good story," the sheriff said.

"But you do not believe it," Andre said.

"Well, sir, I find myself wanting to hear the rest of it."

Andre was surprised. He'd imbued a hint of his will in the telling, enough to make most men, even those he didn't maintain eye contact with, fall in line. The deputy's reactions were proof of that. He expected Joseph to be immune, but the sheriff had resisted, as well, which Andre found curious.

"Where would you like me to begin?"

"Tillamook," said Joseph.

"That sounds about right," the sheriff concurred.

"I see. You think I had something to do with that?"

"I think when my deputy tells me I gotta meet some important fella just up from the scene of a massacre, right after we have our own troubles . . . well, I think maybe I need to know more about this man."

"Perhaps you need to hear from a different voice," Naira began. Andre cut her off with a look. They would play the sheriff straight. Naira didn't like it, but she kept her words (and gaze) to herself.

"I am tracking a man," Andre said. "Two men, actually, but only one is dangerous." It was a lie, but Andre had no intention of explaining how a book he'd lost twenty years ago made Henry much more dangerous than the Hanged Man. "Both were in Tillamook last Friday night and I am certain they came here directly after."

"We did have us a pair of unexpected visitors last night. Caused a ruckus up at the boneyard 'fore this other ruckus happened. I'm thinkin' they may be connected."

"A safe assumption," Andre said. "Did anyone witness this, um, ruckus?"

"Caretaker," said Collins. "Recognized one of 'em as a local went missing last week."

"Henry Macke," Andre said without hesitation.

"Yup," said the sheriff. "Now, you mind telling me who he was riding with, 'cause I'm having a hard time reconciling that part of the story."

Andre considered his words carefully before asking, "How long have you been in Astoria, Sheriff?"

"Long enough."

"And you find it difficult to believe the man you seek may in fact be the Hanged Man of legend."

Joseph had thus far avoided bringing up the dead man's name. He'd been afraid to after seeing the creatures behind bars, afraid what the truth might bring. He was not the only one.

"We killed that son of a bitch years ago," said the sheriff. "Got us a sign up on Main Street to commemorate it. And I seem to recall his body being burned."

"It was not," Andre said. "As I believe Mr. Wylde's father-in-law will confirm."

The look on the sheriff's face changed. Gone was the defiance, replaced by a dawning realization that some of the things he'd been led to believe might not be true.

"He's gone," the sheriff said.

Andre looked at Joseph. "Gone where?"

"To Portland. He lives with us now."

Andre connected that piece of information to those he already knew.

"He left recently?"

Joseph nodded. "Last week. There was an incident in the local cemetery. He took a shovel to a few of the plots. Said he was trying to find something, but when I asked him what, he couldn't remember."

Or was made to forget, Andre thought. But if that was the case, how had Henry found the Hanged Man? Had Kleberg told him? Could he have? And how had the man left town so easily? Such a departure meant Andre's own magic had failed . . . or been broken.

"I need to see the burial site," Andre said.

The sheriff shared a look with his deputies. "Which one?"

"All of them."

Andre put his ear to the ground and listened. Even through six feet of earth, it didn't take long for the sound to reach his ears.

"I can hear them."

"Hear who?" asked the sheriff, sure he wouldn't like the answer. He and his deputies stood behind Andre, well back from the grave at which he was kneeling. Joseph stood beside the headstone, his gaze seemingly elsewhere, or so thought the sheriff. It was difficult to tell what the one-eyed man was looking at in the day's waning light.

"Bodies of the dead," Andre said, standing up. "They are awake."

Deputies Collins and Kendle drew their weapons and began scanning the cemetery.

"Like them others in town?"

"Yes, but you may lower your weapons, gentlemen. These poor creatures remain firmly planted in the ground."

Joseph placed a hand on the grave marker. He could feel them through the stone, clawing at wood and dirt, moaning, hungry. The image fixed in his head all too clearly.

"They're in pain," Joseph said, almost under his breath. Andre heard him.

"What they feel does not matter. They are an abomination and they must be put down."

Collins holstered his weapon. "I miss something? If they ain't come up outta the ground, what's there to put down?"

Andre looked at Naira, who was just returning from a quick survey of the graveyard.

"One hundred and one markers," she said. "Six open graves, six empty coffins. Twenty-three recently disturbed with no signs of escape, and one . . . escape in progress."

Naira led the group to a grave on the far side of the cemetery where the head and arms of a woman protruded from freshly dug ground. As the group approached, the zombie twisted around, revealing a dirty young face that might once have been beautiful. The creature bared its teeth and began clawing against the dirt.

"My god, that's Gretchen Vail," said Barker. "She died only a few weeks ago."

"She's stronger," Joseph said. "The muscles have yet to deteriorate."

"Yes," Andre agreed. "It also appears this grave was one of those disturbed, suggesting the coffin may have been compromised."

The sheriff drew his pistol and shot the zombie in the top of the head. Its jaws snapped shut once more and then it slumped facefirst into the dirt.

"That leaves ninety-four that will have to be checked and destroyed if necessary," Andre said. "You understand what needs to be done?"

The sheriff nodded unenthusiastically. "You want us to dig up every g'damn grave so we can put a bullet in the head of anything we find moving."

"Yes. I am sorry, but if this is not stopped here and now, it will find a way to spread."

"Like plague?" Joseph asked.

"In a manner," said Andre. "A plague born of man a long time ago in a place very far from here. Born of words, foul deeds, and dark intentions. Spread through contact with the infected."

"I get that," said the sheriff. "All the biting and such. But if these dead folks is trying to dig themselves *outta* their graves, how'd they come in contact with anyone in the first place?"

This was a question Andre had only just answered for himself. He'd heard of such things—of such evil—but to stand in its presence was chilling, even for a man who rarely felt the cold.

"A carrier," he said. "One who is . . . diseased, but not like them. This creature has control of his faculties, his actions, his mind. Merely his presence is enough to transform the dead into what we have seen here."

"You're talking about the Hanged Man," Joseph said.

"I am. Dead for eleven years, but not destroyed. He was buried in a plot just beyond the borders of this cemetery, beneath the cold, unmarked earth. There was no funeral pyre, Joseph. That was merely a bit of theater created to bring satisfaction to the masses."

"It was a lie."

"Not a lie," Andre said. "A different kind of truth. Simply burying the man would not have been enough for many who suffered his reign of violence. The Hanged Man had to be destroyed completely and visibly. Fire is very visible."

Collins snorted. "I'd say turning a man to ash is more than just visible."

Andre sighed. Explaining the presence of the undead was hard enough with the proof clawing its way up through the ground. Digging into the depths of the Hanged Man's black heart and the dark power that kept it beating was complicated and would raise more questions than Andre was prepared to answer.

"Fire is not always a destructive force," he said. "Sometimes it can be a cleansing agent, a rebirth for those who are prepared."

"Resurrection."

"Yes. And while burning the Hanged Man would have destroyed his physical form, he ultimately would have found a way to return stronger than before. To truly arrest such power one has to take away that which makes it strong."

"Belief," Joseph said.

Andre nodded.

The sheriff furrowed his brow, but it was Collins who asked the obvious.

"Belief in what?"

"Faith, magic, and his own abilities," Andre said, which was accurate, albeit simplified. "If you kill the man—"

"He stops believing," Joseph finished.

"Yes, but in the case of the Hanged Man, it also meant the fear of those he terrorized. His strength came not only from within but also from those who believed he might do them harm. His death would allay such fears, but only time would erase them."

Joseph thought of a long walk in the dark and a baby crying. He doubted such memories would ever leave him.

"Why keep it a secret?" Deputy Barker asked.

"Burying his body in an unmarked grave left no altar for his power."

The sheriff narrowed his eyes. "*You* buried him?"

"No. But I attended the funeral."

"The marshal," Joseph said.

Andre nodded. "Other than myself, he was the only man who should know the location of the Hanged Man's grave. It was never meant to be disturbed."

"But someone did disturb it," said Joseph. "Someone dug him up and turned him into one of these creatures."

"No, the Hanged Man has become something much worse. He

knows who he is and has set upon a path to regain his power. Those who stand in his way are in grave danger."

There was no name attached to the threat, but Joseph heard one just the same.

The sheriff stared at the corpse half buried in the soil. The body had long since stopped moving, but it still made his skin crawl. It was several seconds before he realized he was scratching his leg above the knee.

"Is there a cure?"

"If the process is arrested in time, yes," said Andre. "I carry medicines with me that will arrest the effects."

The sheriff shook his head, almost smiling. "How much will that cost me?"

"Not a penny, Sheriff. It is an herbal concoction, one for which I will gladly share the recipe should you require more after our departure."

"And that's it?"

"No," Andre said, once more searching for the words that required the least amount of explanation. "I would also prescribe a passage be read nightly for seven days."

"A prayer?"

Andre smiled. "If you like."

The sheriff ran a hand through what little hair remained on his head. "'Fraid I ain't much good at talking to God."

"This is a different kind of prayer," Andre said, failing to mention it was also for a different kind of god.

Over the next hour, the sheriff and his deputies dispatched the inhabitants of fourteen of the twenty-three recently disturbed graves. The rest remained deep enough or weak enough not to require immediate attention. The sheriff hadn't decided whether it would be better to enlist a few dozen townsfolk for the remaining cleanup or to try to keep the task quiet so as to protect the psyche of the community. Realizing the job would fall to them alone without help, the deputies assured the sheriff the town could take it.

Joseph went to the marshal's house, not surprised to find the lock on the front door smashed. There was no obvious damage inside, but a stench in the air left little doubt as to who had been there. He soon found the crumpled photograph in the attic, and although Joseph couldn't see the family smiling up at him, the handwritten title on the back told him everything he needed to know.

Andre and Naira were waiting for him when he came downstairs.

"He was here."

"Looking for Marshal Kleberg," Andre said. "Perhaps more."

Joseph didn't have to guess. "The gun."

Andre nodded. "You know of its power."

"I know the myth."

"It is more than a myth, Mr. Wylde. The weapon is cursed; it makes him a killer."

"Then I guess it's a good thing the marshal took it with him."

"He has it?"

"He's going to put on a public demonstration in a day or two as part of the Portland Rain Festival."

For the first time since meeting Andre Labeau, Joseph felt a shift in the man's demeanor. He was afraid. Naira felt it, too.

"He'll hear it," she said. "It will call to him."

Joseph thought he, too, might recognize the sound of the gun, but still found the choice of words unusual.

"He must not have it," Andre said. "The marshal knows this."

"That's why he stayed, isn't it?" Joseph said. "To watch over the body, make sure nobody found it or the gun. He thought he was protecting us . . . but he forgot. He dug up all those graves looking for the Hanged Man."

"It's unfortunate he didn't find him," Naira said.

Joseph nodded. There was more to it, but how much he wasn't sure.

"You said he'll try to regain his power. How so?"

"There are ways he can be made more powerful, more alive. The closer he comes to living, the more dangerous he becomes." Andre hesitated for a moment. "He will come for your father-in-law, Mr. Wylde, and for his weapon."

Joseph didn't need to be told. He knew the truth of it—all of it.

"Won't just be the marshal, Mr. Labeau. If the man is clear about who he was, the one person on this earth he'll want to kill above all others is me."

Early the next morning, Andre and Naira paid visits to three homes where they found five people in need of special attention. Andre gave each the same elixir and prayer, along with a mental push to ensure that all followed through with the treatment. A known sixth victim proved more elusive. It was almost noon before the pair rode east en route to Portland.

Joseph was already gone, having hitched a ride on an empty ore vessel heading upriver. The last thing he did before leaving town was to send a message to Kate. The telegraph operator asked several times for clarification, but each time Joseph assured him the words he'd read back were correct.

KATE—HANGED MAN ALIVE.
WANTS GUN. DO NOT LET MARSHAL USE—HIDE IT.
STAY OFF STREETS. AVOID CEMETERY.
WILL RETURN SOON. BE SAFE—JOSEPH.

22

―――・―――

The first day of the Rain Festival arrived without a cloud in the sky. The front page of the *Portlandian* happily predicted a wet opening, but most who got the early edition doubted they'd need more than a hat to keep the sun out of their eyes.

Despite the clear skies, the buzz downtown was one of anticipation—at least as far as the weather was concerned. The sidewalks and plank ways were crowded with the usual Thursday-morning merchants and businessmen, as well as locals eager to get a glimpse of the festival attractions before the out-of-town throngs arrived. The official kickoff wouldn't begin until evening, but many of the festival booths were already open along the boardwalk surrounding the main stage.

Rain-related merchandise dominated the wares offered by most vendors, from simple rain gauges and mercury-based barometers to silk umbrellas with telescoping handles and the latest styles of vulcanized Wellington boots. Seattle Storm Catchers, purveyors of ornamental weather vanes and lighting rods, had already sold three of its six-foot Franklin attractors. John Dale's Waterworks of San Francisco proudly displayed the latest in fountain technology, including a steam-powered copper salmon that could shoot bursts of water thirty feet into the air, which it did regularly, to the delight of every child in sight.

There also were numerous historical attractions, including a corner booth documenting the city's most famous floods. A not entirely accurate depth-measuring pole planted in the waterlogged street marked the relative heights of various surges. The current waterline topped out at almost eighteen feet, which was below the twenty-one feet of the week before and well off the more than twenty-nine feet of 1877. That the pole itself was submerged in only three feet of water remained a point of confusion, despite a sign explaining the height was in relation to the river, not to the road.

Tucked into the narrow space between the Oregon Ice Works and the Tualatin River Crawfish Society was a long booth papered with charts and a simple hand-painted sign that read: ATMOSPHERIC PROBABILITIES.

Samuel Edmonds sat near the front of the booth, behind a table displaying numerous weather-data-gathering instruments including a hundred-year-old barometer that had once belonged to Thomas Jefferson. Edmonds had spent the morning gathering additional data that he was currently using to formulate a final set of predictions for the day. His concentration thus distracted, he failed to notice the first visitors to his booth until an orange-tinted "Lightning" jar half full of water was set in front of his face.

"Look what I got, Mr. Edmonds!" Kick proclaimed and slid the canning jar toward the meteorologist. A piece of string tied around the top of the jar held on a small tag on which WORLD'S LARGEST RAINDROP was scribbled. It took him several seconds to grasp the meaning, long enough for Kate to catch up to her son.

"Good morning, Mr. Edmonds."

Edmonds looked up to see Kate standing behind her son. Maddie stood on the other side of her mother, looking at one of the weather maps Edmonds had drawn up for the festival.

"Oh, Mrs. Wylde, good morning."

"Ready for the big day?"

Edmonds tried to smile but it came out as more of a cringe. "I certainly hope so."

"So, what do you think?" asked Kick.

Edmonds glanced from Kate to her son. "About what?"

Kick picked up the glass jar and shook it. "This!"

Edmonds caught Kate's uneasy smile, which helped him find his own. He took the jar from Kick and made a show of studying its contents. By all outward appearances it looked to be roughly a half quart of dirty water that, according to the back side of the tag, had cost Kick (or his mother) a nickel.

"Very interesting," he said, handing the jar back to Kick. "Where'd you get it?"

"From that booth back there," Kick said, pointing over his shoulder. "They also had the biggest hailstone and the biggest snowflake, 'cept that one was melted."

"I told him it was a waste of money," Maddie said. "It's not real."

"Says you," Kick said and held the jar up to the light. He shook it, kicking up a cloud of tiny particles. "Look, you can see cloud dust floating around inside the drop."

"That's not dust," Maddie said. "That's rust falling off the lid!"

Kick frowned and shook his head. "You're just mad because I found it first."

Maddie crossed her arms. "You don't even know what cloud dust is."

"Do too. It's the stuff that makes rain clouds dirty. That's why they're gray. When it rains, the water washes all the dust out and then they're all clean and white." Kick turned to Edmonds. "That's what happens, isn't it?"

"That's a very interesting theory."

"See?" Kick said, turning back to his sister. "He likes my theory."

Maddie shook her head. "He didn't say it was accurate."

Kick shrugged. "Interesting is better than accurate."

Maddie rolled her eyes around to Edmonds. "Is that true?"

The meteorologist obviously wasn't prepared for conversational combat this early in the morning, which was why Kate tossed him a lifeline.

"So, Mr. Edmonds, should we still expect rain this evening?"

It took a few moments, but Edmonds finally responded, "Oh, yes, definitely."

"Definitely? As in a one-hundred-percent probability?"

"I think so," said Edmonds, happy to be back on surer footing. "In fact, I'm a little concerned about how much it might rain."

"Really?"

Edmonds nodded. "The latest reports I received from our westernmost relay stations suggest a dramatic increase in cloud cover over the northern Pacific. The waves at Cape Disappointment are already breaking ten feet above normal, which means there's a storm on its way, a big one. Couple that with a significant drop in local pressure just this morning and we've got the makings of a real downpour."

"That should be good for the festival."

Edmonds glanced at the neighboring booths and then leaned over the table. When he spoke, his voice was barely above a whisper. "I'm not so sure. An inordinate amount of rain could seriously overtax the local waterways, causing floodwaters to rise, possibly much more than anticipated, and overflow the current barriers, spreading into new sections of town."

Kate understood the man's concern, but she, like every other longtime resident, had been through high waters on numerous occasions. Getting one's feet (and ankles and calves and knees) wet simply wasn't that scary. It was a way of life.

"I'm sure we'll be fine, Mr. Edmonds. This city has been through a great many floods in its short existence." Kate motioned to the raised walkways and flood barriers built up around them. "As you can see, we know how to handle a little unwanted water."

"But what if it's not a little? What if it's a lot of water all at once? What if the flood level rises three feet in an hour? Every business in the downtown area that is currently protected will be under water. The current scaffold-sidewalk system could collapse. If the storm comes on as suddenly as I suspect it will, there could be several thousand people caught downtown in rising floodwaters."

"Six," Kate said. "The mayor's office is hoping for at least six thousand people at tonight's opening ceremonies, more if it rains."

Edmonds sat back in his chair as the enormity of what he was predicting struck him. If his predictions were right—and he had no reason to believe they weren't—it was going get ugly.

"I should speak to the mayor."

"Maybe you should," Kate said, knowing the young man's pronouncement of excessive rain would be greeted by cheers at city hall. "While you're at it, why not pass along your information to the fire department. They've got one of their water cannons on the other side of the stage. If there's any rescuing that needs to be done, they've got the biggest boats capable of navigating the city streets."

"Good idea," Edmonds said and began gathering up his latest maps and calculations. He took a long look at his collection of weather paraphernalia, unsure whether to pack it up or trust that no one else would find it of any value.

"Would you like us to watch over your equipment while you're gone, Mr. Edmonds?"

"That would be wonderful. I won't be long." Edmonds snatched one last chart and then took off down the boardwalk. He got to the corner before turning around and coming straight back.

"Do you happen to know the current location of the mayor?"

"I do," said Kate.

"Seems a mite agitated, doesn't he?" said Ollie.

Kate turned toward the conversation across the room. While certainly there was no argument, both the mayor's and his weatherman's voices had been raised at times.

"I hadn't noticed," Kate said, turning her attention back to the main attraction in the room: the placement of the storm totem atop a small stage in the center of the Corbett Hotel's two-story ballroom. A bank of floor-to-ceiling windows faced the main square, making the large room ideal for additional festival activities and for refuge should the weather prove inclement. Kate couldn't help but wonder if the mayor had informed the hotel's owners of his plans to bring the weather indoors. She suspected that fact might have been excluded from the arrangements.

"I'd say he seems very excited," Ollie said. "And it's been my observation that Mr. Edmonds is quite unflappable on most matters. The only time I recall him raising his voice was with regards to the weather."

Kate was not surprised.

A few minutes later, the mayor escorted Edmonds to the door and then rejoined Kate and Ollie.

"Everything all right?" Ollie asked.

"Better than all right, my friend. Mr. Edmonds claims it's going to rain buckets tonight. An epic flood, by his estimation."

"Oh, dear. And you're happy about this, Jim?"

The mayor beamed. "Delighted."

Ollie raised an eyebrow but said nothing more.

"It seems our Rain Festival is going to live up to its name and then some. Good thing, too. I was loath to spend the weekend explaining away the sunshine."

"It can be a nuisance," Kate said without a hint of irony.

"Yes," said the mayor. "It's unnatural. We've had so much this year it's a wonder the land doesn't burst into flames."

Ollie chuckled. "Let's hope it doesn't come to that."

"Quite," said the mayor.

Kate turned to the storm totem.

"What do you think of your star attraction?" she asked.

The mayor studied the totem pole, looking at it from the left and then the right. Several times he glanced out the front windows as if judging the view from the downtown square. Finally, he nodded to himself. He'd made his decision, which he announced to all:

"Take it outside."

A few of the festival workers groaned, having spent the morning getting the totem in the perfect position. Kate shared a glance with Ollie.

"Outside? Are you sure? Joseph said it would work better inside."

"Mayor's prerogative, my dear. The weatherman says it's going to rain, but what if it's only a sprinkle? No reason not to up the odds."

"But if a storm comes in, it might make things worse," Kate said, letting some of the unease she felt slip into her voice. "It could get pretty wet."

"Mrs. Wylde, you sound positively Californian!"

Kate could have slapped him. Instead, she smiled and decided to hold her comments for the first reporter to ask her whose idea it had been to drown the voting public.

"All right, gentlemen. If you'll excuse me, I have a store to open for business."

"Pleasure to see you again, madam," said Ollie, tipping his hat.

Kate nodded and headed for the exit, the mayor slipping along beside her.

"Now, when can I expect your man tonight?"

"Tonight?"

"I'll need him by my side, of course. He's my expert in all things heathen."

"Of course. I believe he's due back late this afternoon."

"Perfect. Send him along no later than six o'clock. And be sure he brings that father of yours."

Kate reached the main entrance to the hall and stopped.

"I thought the marshal was part of tomorrow evening's grand entertainment."

"He is, but I'd like him at the opening ceremony, as well. I thought we might offer a preview of upcoming events. It's never too early to stir up some excitement."

"I suppose not," Kate said, wondering how much the mayor's decision was based on recent events. Along with a festival preview, the latest edition of the *Portlandian* had a lengthy follow-up story about the violence in Tillamook, along with a report of the attacks in Astoria. The Hanged Man's name had appeared in both articles, suggesting a link between the two incidents. The story made clear that it was not the infamous villain himself but rather an unknown agent hoping to take advantage of the dead man's reputation. There was, however, substantial information about the Hanged Man, including the circumstances of his demise at the hands of Marshal James Kleberg. The paper was kind enough to point out that the marshal would be appearing at the festival.

Kate smiled. "I'll let him know about tonight."

"Actually, I'd speak to him prior to the show, if I may. We have details to discuss."

Six blocks south, the marshal arrived at the store and found the front door locked. He was late, but apparently he was not the only one. Kate had offered him a key, but he'd turned her down, afraid he'd lose it. No matter; he would wait.

The marshal walked to the edge of the wooden sidewalk. A makeshift rail had been added since his visit a few days earlier, which he tested before leaning against it with his full weight. The intersection at Third Street was more crowded than it had any right to be, given that there was still no actual street. The floodwaters had receded, although not enough to discourage local water traffic. Numerous small boats and rafts were tied up along Alder on both sides of the road, three deep in some places.

Despite the continued sunny weather, the marshal had chosen his favorite riding coat for the day. It wasn't a particularly effective defense against the elements, hot or cold, but it was long—long enough to cover the weapon holstered on his hip.

The Hanged Man's gun was heavy but not uncomfortably so. It belonged there. It felt right. Kate would surely balk at his wearing it in public, but the marshal needed to get used to the gun if he was going to be shooting in front of an audience.

And perhaps his daughter didn't need to know.

When the show was over, the festival done, he would pack it away. He would dismantle it. He would destroy it. He'd promised. No matter how good it felt on his hip . . . or in his hands.

The marshal considered sliding his right hand inside his coat to feel the butt of the gun, but it was already there. It felt good.

Thus distracted, he missed the scruffy young man's arrival and subsequent attempt to gain entrance to the bookstore. Failing, the man saw the marshal and approached him.

"Hey, you work here?"

The marshal slowly withdrew his hand from beneath his coat and turned to his questioner.

"Excuse me?"

"The bookstore—you the owner?"

"Not me," he stuttered. "Family owns it, my daughter and her husband. I'm just here for special negotiations."

"Oh," said the courier, not fully understanding, or caring. "I got this telegram needs signin' for, and this was the address they gave me. Addressed to . . . Kate Wylde."

"That's my daughter."

"You can sign for it then," the young man said, passing over a register and a pen. "Right on the dotted line."

The marshal hesitated but then went ahead and made his mark. The courier glanced at the signature, then handed over a folded sheet of paper.

"Good day, sir. Enjoy the festival."

The marshal watched the man slip between a pair of pedestrians and then dart over a scaffold walkway to the other side of the street. Once the man was out of sight, he unfolded the telegram and read the words printed on it.

And then he read them again.

He was still staring at the message several minutes later, when Kate arrived.

"Sorry I'm late, Dad. I ran into the mayor."

Kate unlocked the front door and pushed it open, but the marshal had yet to join her. He remained standing at the sidewalk's edge, his attention elsewhere.

Kate took a step toward him. "Did someone send you a telegram?"

The marshal looked at the paper in his hand and said, "From home."

"Astoria? Is it from Joseph?"

"Well-wishers," the marshal said quickly. "News of my festival appearance has reached the ears of my neighbors. Seems I'm a celebrity."

The marshal tucked the telegram into a pocket and walked past Kate into the store.

"The preparations went well, then?"

"Yes, fine," Kate said, following him inside. "Rain or shine it should be quite a show tonight, which apparently you are to be a part of."

"Tonight?"

"It was news to me, as well. The mayor plans to speak to you about it."

The marshal stepped behind one of the half-height bookcases. He wasn't looking for a book but rather cover as he slipped a hand into his jacket. He saw no reason to alert his daughter to what lay under his coat. She might try to take it away. The marshal could not have that.

"What about Joseph?" he asked.

"The mayor wants to see him, too. He has big plans for you both."

The marshal said nothing. For a moment, all he heard was the sound of skin tightening around polished wood and metal locking into place. There was no mistaking what it was.

"Marshal?"

The marshal looked at Kate, letting go of the pistol beneath his coat, unsure even why he'd been gripping it so tightly.

"What is it, Katie?"

Kate glanced down, catching a glimpse of something shiny beneath her father's coat.

The marshal saw the recognition in her eyes and moved swiftly to the front door.

"Takin' a walk," he said and left before she could stop him.

By the late afternoon, a slow-moving avalanche of billowing white plumes began rolling over the western hills. The long reign of the sun was nearly over in Portland and every citizen knew it. It would be a few hours before the sky truly opened up, but the rain would come. There was no stopping it now.

The approaching storm was good news for the festival, which was officially open for business. The crowds around the plaza continued to swell as out-of-towners poured into the city. Every berth along the downtown waterfront was occupied by steamer, ferry, or other river-borne transport. Travelers streamed from the boats, delighted to find their time on the water would continue as they transferred from riverboat to water taxi for their first journey around town.

The roads leading into Portland were likewise congested, notably from the south and west. For those catching their first glimpse of the city from atop the western slope, the view was particularly spectacular. All of the city could be seen, as could ten miles of the Willamette River, most of the surrounding valley, and, for a few hours more, the three great mountains, Hood, Adams, and St. Helens.

Henry Macke had never seen such a thing. His only previous trip to the city had been when he was too young to remember, and since then he'd rarely traveled outside county limits. Portland, spread out across a vast landscape with enormous volcanoes reaching into the sky beyond, was truly a remarkable sight to see.

"I didn't know they made cities so big."

The Hanged Man brought his steed in line with the younger man's, much to the displeasure of Henry's horse.

"You should see one burn."

Henry grimaced at the Hanged Man's voice. Neither had spoken for two hours, which was almost enough time for Henry to forget that his riding partner was a monster. Almost.

Henry glanced over his shoulder at the approaching clouds.

"Looks like rain. Hard to start a fire if everything's wet."

The Hanged Man eyed Henry.

"You'd be surprised."

Henry felt his stomach churn and twist. His horse must have sensed its rider's discomfort and trotted forward without command. Henry didn't correct the animal.

The path cut down the hillside a short distance to a wider road already clogged with traffic. Henry was surprised there were so many travelers. On this road, as well as several others visible from the hill, he could see hundreds of riders, carts, and pedestrians all moving toward the center of the city.

Henry waved to a man on horseback as he passed by.

"Where's everyone going?"

"Festival," said the rider, not slowing down. Sensing Henry's confusion, he stopped and drew his horse back to Henry. "You know, the Rain Festival?"

Henry shook his head.

"They do it every year. Big party downtown—lots of folks, drinkin' in the rain. It's great fun."

"Getting wet is fun?"

"Sure, why not?"

It was then that the Hanged Man came down the hill. He didn't join Henry but stopped ten feet behind. It was close enough for the rider and his mount to take notice.

"Everyone's invited," he said, immediately wishing he hadn't. His horse bucked and whinnied. "Whoa, now! Settle down." The rider pulled his horse around and let the animal carry him back into the flow of traffic. He glanced back at Henry and the dark figure but didn't say another word.

Henry didn't look around. He didn't have to. He turned his horse and climbed back up the hill until he was once more at the Hanged Man's side.

"There's some kind of festival. Looks like a big crowd. I don't see how we can make a play for the old man with so many people around."

The Hanged Man ignored Henry and instead turned his head to the south.

Henry followed the dead man's gaze to a hillside cemetery on the edge of town. The knot in his gut grew tighter.

"I don't know," he said. "We'll have to wait until dark with so many people about. And then what? More digging?"

The Hanged Man closed his eyes and breathed in the air—or at least appeared to. Whatever it was, it seemed to please him. Henry doubted he'd feel the same but asked the question anyway.

"What is it?"

"Death," said the Hanged Man, pointing at a large building on the hill just beyond the cemetery. The dead man then pulled his beast to the right and directed it off through the hillside brush. He crossed the road shortly after, eliciting a wide berth from the other travelers.

Henry felt his own horse lean in the opposite direction—a course he was very tempted to follow. It would be so simple. Ride down the road, blend in with the crowd, and disappear.

(*find you*)

He'd go to the authorities, then. Tell someone who'd believe enough of the story to take up arms against the dead man. He wouldn't last against so many men. He couldn't.

(*he would*)

Henry sighed. He'd already lost the argument a hundred times since leaving Tillamook. Nothing was going to change. There was only one voice that mattered now, and it told Henry to follow his master. It told him everything would be all right.

The pain in his belly subsided and Henry hoped, as always, that it wouldn't return. He turned his horse against its will and directed it to follow the path laid down by the Hanged Man. The cemetery loomed directly ahead. Henry began to prepare himself for the digging that would surely come soon.

It never occurred to him there might be something worse.

23

At five minutes to seven, the first report of thunder rumbled overhead, earning a cheer from the assembled masses. The crowd at Foundling Square had swelled to nearly four thousand, less than what festival organizers had hoped for but still the largest turnout ever for opening night. Many stood on the large raised platform built over the center of the festival square, with the rest lining the boardwalks, rooftops, and boat docks surrounding the plaza. A few had brought waders so they could stand in the water, which was now below the knees of most patrons.

Mayor Gates climbed onto a raised stage at one end of the platform to respectable applause. A seven-piece band played a slightly off-key version of "Hail to the Chief" until the mayor finished glad-handing those closest to him.

"Welcome to the Portlandtown!" he said, his voice projected throughout the plaza by a two-foot-long megaphone. "I officially declare the Rain Festival of 1887 open for business!"

Another cheer went up from the crowd. Right on cue, the first drops of rain began to fall. A murmur turned to clapping as more people felt drops hit their faces.

The mayor beamed. "Let it rain! Let it rain!" he cried, to more cheering and hooting.

The rain soon found its rhythm, settling into a light but steady sprinkle that was cool and quite pleasant. A few umbrellas popped open—out-of-towners, no doubt—but most in the crowd simply smiled and drank it in.

Joseph climbed onto the platform at its southern end, oblivious to the rain and the mayor's overzealous encouragement. He'd already been to the bookstore, finding it locked up for the night, and was about to head home when Mr. Williamson asked if he was going to join his family at the festival. The smoke-shop owner had met Kate on her way barely an hour earlier. He said she'd been in fine spirits.

Joseph pushed through the crowd, searching for anything that might reveal his family's position. In particular, he listened for a high-pitched whistle Kick had used to torment his sister for the better part of a year when the twins were eight. He'd eventually found better ways to bother Maddie, but whenever it rained, Kick now whistled. Joseph had no idea why but found it useful for keeping track of his son, especially in bad weather.

Nearly to the stage, he finally heard it.

"Kate!"

Joseph wrapped both arms around his wife, the strength of his embrace enough to alert her that something was wrong.

"What is it?"

"Why are you here? Didn't you get my message?"

Kate shook her head but then understood.

"The marshal got a telegram."

Joseph held his tongue.

"I knew he was hiding something," Kate said, shaking her head. "He didn't show me. Said it was well-wishers."

"Doesn't matter," Joseph said, still holding back the name he didn't want to speak aloud. "I have to tell you something."

"That my father lied to me? That I know."

"No, Kate, listen: he's alive. The Hanged Man is alive."

The words caught Kate by surprise. She smiled, thinking them a joke. They must be, she thought, though they weren't particularly funny. She was about to say so when her husband's name echoed across the square.

"Joseph Wylde, there you are!" said the mayor through his megaphone. "Get him up here!"

"No, I can't," Joseph managed before being hastily ushered onstage. He lost Kate in the crowd but soon discovered he was not the only man Jim Gates had called out.

"About time," the marshal whispered. "Thought you were gonna make me go through this alone."

Before Joseph could respond, the mayor put an arm around his shoulder and led him forward.

"Folks, I want to share a mystery with you," the mayor said, letting his words linger in the rain. "Many of you know Mr. Wylde as one our finest booksellers, but I'm here to tell you he's more than that—he's a man of intrigue. Why, just this past week he solved a puzzle that had scientists from around the country stumped. Show them, Joseph."

The mayor passed a length of rope to Joseph.

"Go on. Give it a good tug."

It dawned on Joseph that the large object positioned on the stage behind him, an object he'd ignored, was in fact the storm totem under wraps. The mayor had brought it outside against his instructions and now wanted him to unveil it in the middle of a rainstorm. Joseph was dumbfounded.

The mayor frowned and turned back to the crowd. "It appears our hero needs a little persuasion, folks. Give him a hand!"

The applause exploded in Joseph's ears, effectively blurring his concentration. He quickly tried to regain focus, reaching out to steady himself on the totem, but his hand found the marshal. He knew at once what lay beneath the man's coat.

"You brought it with you?" he said, clearly seeing the pistol strapped to the marshal's hip. "Loaded?"

The marshal sneered at Joseph and snatched the rope from his hand. A quick jerk released the covering, revealing the storm totem in all its glory.

The crowd gasped and then grew quiet as the mayor raised his hands.

"Ladies and gentlemen, I give you the infamous Storm Totem of the Yukon," he exclaimed over oohs and aahs. "Discovered in the northernmost reaches of the Arctic and delivered at great cost in both lives and treasure. Not a single soul who took part in its passage escaped unscathed. The very vessel that transported it upriver sank barely a day after unloading its cargo. It is cursed . . . but also contains great power."

Joseph felt the crowd move closer en masse.

"They say it's a rainmaker, a storm bringer, a hundred-year flood."

"It works!" yelled a voice in the crowd.

The mayor beamed. "Yes! But the ancient heathens who carved this totem knew more than just how make it rain. This is a conduit directly to the clouds. It is the storm itself to be called upon by its master."

The mayor went to the edge of the stage, where he was handed a bucket. Had Joseph known what he was about to do, he would have pushed him from the stage.

"Tonight, I am the master of the storm and I call upon thee . . . make it rain!"

The mayor swung the bucket around, splashing its contents over the storm totem and several people standing behind the stage. The water quickly found its course, flowing through the channels carved in and around the figures. The movement was erratic at first, but soon the various pockets of liquid caught up to one another and flowed as one.

Joseph felt the vibration through the stage but the hum soon grew loud enough for both Mayor Gates and the marshal to take notice. The water rushing around the totem's channels grew faster. The rain falling around it grew stronger.

"We have to cover it," Joseph said, but no one heard him.

Lightning flashed, followed half a second later by a sharp *boom* that startled many in the crowd. Despite an average rainfall of almost fifty inches a year, electrical storms were rare in the Northwest, especially west of the Cascades. The cheer that went up after the initial surprise wore off was more muted than previously.

"Well, how about that?" the mayor managed before his words were swallowed by a near-simultaneous flash and ear-piercing *crack* directly overhead.

Many in the audience ducked and a few screamed. The mood of the crowd turned almost as quickly as the weather. The sprinkle became a heavy downpour. Everyone not already under cover was soaked to the bone in seconds. Those few dry souls had to make room as the rest of the festival crowd bolted for cover. The booths filled quickly, as did the businesses open around the plaza. With nowhere to go, many simply took to the streets in search of higher ground.

Another lightning strike exploded directly overhead, louder than anything Joseph had ever heard. In that moment, he saw the storm totem and the water rushing through its channels with unnatural speed. There was heat coming off it, heat born of the firestone gears that turned inside the thing, pulling water from the air and turning it to steam. It was drinking, now, and was very thirsty. Joseph doubted it would ever be quenched.

"It's making the storm worse!" Joseph screamed over the downpour as he grabbed one end of the fallen curtain and then pointed to the other, at the marshal's feet. "Help me, Marshal!"

The marshal blinked, breaking the trance that had held him. He snatched up the sheet and helped throw it over the top of the totem, and Joseph hastily tied it off. Steam escaped from between the folds, hot enough to burn.

Joseph pointed toward the hotel. "Get inside. Find Kate, if you can."

The marshal nodded and left the stage. Joseph turned to the mayor, whom he found staring in disbelief at the chaos around him.

"Mayor, I think it's time to get out of the rain."

Fifteen minutes later, Joseph stood at the back of the Corbett Hotel ballroom, listening. His best guess was that about two hundred people had found their way inside, filling the hall, though not quite to capacity. Most were drenched and still buzzing about the storm, although the panic had faded. These were Portlandians: no one was going to let the weather ruin their evening.

"I still don't see them."

Managing the voices of a few hundred was easier than a few thousand, but Joseph had to concentrate to do it. He'd scanned the room several times before finally settling in on a slow, careful pass through which he heard small fragments of nearly every conversation in the room.

Finally, he heard it—whistling.

"There they are," he said pointing toward one of the entrances.

"Where?" said the marshal, straining to see above the crowd. "Oh, I got 'em. Katie! Over here."

A few seconds later, Maddie latched on to one of her father's legs. Kate took his arm.

"What a madhouse," she said.

"Are you okay?"

"The crowd pulled us away from the stage. I knew you'd be here, but we couldn't get through. So we found some cover and waited for the people to thin out."

"I saw lightning hit a boat!" Kick said. "We were under the platform and I could see through an alley straight down the river and then *boom*! It went right down the smokestack."

"Sounds amazing."

"It was!"

Joseph felt Kate squeeze his hand. She was more concerned about the sudden storm than she would ever admit, but there was more. Much more.

"We're safe in here," he said.

"Are we?" she asked, letting her gaze slip to the marshal.

The marshal didn't notice. His eyes were on the mayor as he stepped onto a small stage at the center of the hall.

"Guess the show ain't over."

The mayor raised his arms, but when the crowd didn't quiet down right away, he snatched the megaphone from one of his assistants.

"Hello, folks."

The words bounced around the room, effectively halting all conversation. Satisfied, the mayor lowered the megaphone.

"Everyone can hear me?" No one suggested otherwise, so the mayor continued. "Good. First, let me say how glad I am to see so many of you made it in out of the rain. Quite an auspicious beginning. Never let it be said that Portlandians don't deliver as advertised."

There were hoots and a smattering of applause. "Mayor Rainmaker!" exclaimed a man in the back, and the applause grew louder.

"Thank you, thank you. You'll be happy to know the hotel staff has fresh towels on the way so we can all dry off. Even better, I'm told they're about to open the bar."

That earned the mayor his biggest ovation yet. It also made him irrelevant.

"Now, folks, don't all rush over at once. I'm sure there's plenty for everyone."

Sensing he'd already lost them, the mayor threw up his hands and motioned to the band reassembled behind him, which immediately broke into a rather soggy rendition of a local favorite, "Portlandtown Rain."

"Is that it?" Kick asked. "What about Gran'pa's show?"

"Guess I won't be doin' no shootin' tonight."

Joseph felt Kate stiffen beside him. He deftly stepped between his wife and her father, drawing the twins to him.

"Why don't you kids go see if they've got any root beer."

"Okay," Kick said, snatching the coin his father offered. He was gone a second later.

Maddie hesitated for a moment before following her brother.

Joseph let them disappear into the crowd and then turned to see his father-in-law staring at him. He didn't have to ask.

"You gonna try takin' it from me, now?"

Joseph frowned. "I'm not going to take it. But you can't shoot it."

"Why not?"

"Yes, why not?" Kate asked, finding she was almost as angry at Joseph as she was at her father. "What did you mean before you rushed onstage to play celebrity detective with the mayor?"

The words stung, but Joseph let it go. "Exactly what I said. The Hanged Man is alive . . . or something close to it."

Kate shook her head. "That's not possible."

"It's true, Kate. What I saw in Astoria . . . I can't explain it, but I met a man who will when he gets here."

"What man?"

"His name is Andre Labeau."

The marshal knew that name, didn't he? Why did he know it? Abruptly, an answer popped into his head that must have been there all along.

"He can't be trusted."

Joseph shook his head. "No, Marshal, I think—"

The marshal shoved a finger into Joseph's face. "You don't know what I think!"

It was at that moment that Ollie chose to appear behind the marshal.

"Hello, Wyldes! I must say, you Portlandians do know how to kick off a party."

The marshal backed away from Joseph, turning his attention to the newspaperman.

"You ain't even wet."

Ollie revealed an umbrella tucked under his arm. "I was told there was a chance it might rain."

Kate forced a smile onto her face and calm into her voice. "Where is your friend Mr. Edmonds? I haven't seen him since before the rain started."

"Last I saw of our intrepid weatherman, he was headed for a rooftop to take measurements of the storm. Very committed, that boy."

"Or stupid," mumbled the marshal, looking toward the bar. "Gonna get me a drink."

"Dad, wait," Kate began, but the marshal ignored her. The moment passed and then she turned to Ollie. "I'm sorry; he's upset about the rain. He won't get to shoot."

Ollie smiled, needing nothing more. "Quite all right. Perhaps I'll keep him company."

Joseph nodded and Ollie left to find the bar.

Kate looked at Joseph, waiting until his full attention was hers before she said, "Tell me everything."

"Are they still arguing?" Maddie asked.

Kick climbed onto a chair and then onto his tiptoes to see over the crowd. Maddie stood in front of the chair, a bottle of sarsaparilla in each hand.

"Nope. Gran'pa just walked away."

Maddie frowned. "I still think something's wrong."

Kick watched a little longer and then hopped down. Maddie offered a bottle of soda, which he took and brought immediately to his lips.

"How can you tell?" he said, after swallowing. "Gran'pa is always kind of grumpy."

"I can tell."

Kick took another long swig, draining the bottle. He tilted it upside down, just to be sure. That's when he noticed Maddie's bottle was still nearly full.

"Just because you're a girl doesn't mean you're smarter than me."

"You're right, that's not why I'm smarter than you," Maddie said, taking a sip.

Kick blinked. "Wait, what?"

While her brother worked it out, Maddie slipped her thumb over the top of the bottle in her hand and began to shake it lightly.

"Hey!" Kick exclaimed, finally putting it together. "That's not what I said."

"Sorry," Maddie said, raising the sarsaparilla to Kick's face. "Peace offering."

Kick smiled and snatched the bottle before his sister could change her mind. He was instantly sorry he had. He saw it coming—a sudsy splash of cold soda to his face—but couldn't stop himself from grabbing the bottle. He wanted that soda.

"Great," he said, setting both bottles on the chair. "Now I'm wet and sticky."

"Told you I was smarter."

Maddie gave her brother a wide-eyed grin and then feinted to her right—which he was expecting—and then darted to her left before Kick could change course. She ran along the front windows, behind a group of dripping-wet recent arrivals, and then slipped through a door at the south end of the ballroom—that was what Maddie had intended to do, at least.

Kick was faster than his sister and by the time they reached the end of the hall, he'd made up the ground between them. He slid in front of the door just as Maddie reached it and she tumbled into him, unable to stop. Kick wrapped his arms around his sister, managing to stay upright despite her momentum and minuscule height advantage.

Maddie didn't need a special bond to tell her what was going to happen next. The look on Kick's face said everything she needed to know.

"No, Kick, Mom wants us to stay inside!"

Kick wasn't listening. He pulled his sister away from the side exit to one of the front entrances that opened onto the plaza.

"Kick! No, stop it! I don't want to get wet again. We'll catch cold."

"It's just water, Maddie."

Kick got the door open and then backed out dragging his sister along with him. He stayed upright for a few steps and then slipping on the wet boardwalk, losing his grip on Maddie and his balance. Kick took one more floundering step back and fell off the walkway into the flooded street. By some miracle, he managed to keep his head above water.

Maddie stopped under the hotel entry's overhang, just out of the rain.

"Are you okay?" she asked, stifling a laugh.

Kick got his feet under him. The water was much higher than it had been an hour earlier and was still rising. If it had been moving, he would have had difficulty standing, but the water was oddly calm. It was still raining, though not as dramatically as it had earlier. Kick took a deep breath and stared at his sister.

Maddie tilted her head at her brother, then stepped out into the rain. She stood at the edge of the boardwalk, closed her eyes, and spun around in the downpour, letting it soak through her dress once again. She stopped and opened her eyes, looking directly at Kick.

"Satisfied?"

Kick shrugged. "I s'pose," he said and held out his hand to her.

Maddie reached out to take it but stopped short.

Kick gave his sister an exasperated look. "Heck, Maddie, I'm not that mean."

Maddie shook her head. She wasn't looking at her brother but at something behind him, over his right shoulder.

Kick turned and saw a man, perhaps thirty feet away, struggling to get through the floodwaters. He stumbled, fell to one knee, then jerked himself upright again. It was nearly dark and the nearest streetlamp had failed to come on, making it difficult to see clearly, but it appeared he was clothed only in a thin white gown that floated on the water's surface at the man's thigh.

"Hey, mister," Kick called out.

The figure stopped, tilted his head toward Kick, and stumbled forward again. After a few steps, the man lost his footing and tumbled face-first into the water.

"Help me up, Maddie!"

Maddie pulled Kick back onto the boardwalk and together they ran to the nearest crossing. This particular bridge had been built with double-width boards, making it more stable than most. Kick bounded up the plank, with Maddie hot on his heels. When they reached the man, he was on his knees with his garment pulled over his head, struggling to free himself.

"Hang on, mister," Kick said, kneeling to help untangle the man from his clothes. That's when he saw the Y-shaped scar on his chest. It was massive and sewn together with large looping stitches—fresh stitches.

Kick scooted back, nearly slipping off the back of the bridge. Maddie held him steady.

"What is it?"

Kick pointed just as the man's gown slipped back into place. Maddie never saw the scar—she didn't need to. What she saw was much worse.

The man had no eyes. Where there should have been life there were only black, bottomless sockets oozing dark fluid and rainwater. The same mixture poured forth from the creature's mouth, which hung open much wider than should have been possible. Deep gashes split the cheeks from the corner of the mouth nearly to the ears on both sides. Loose stitches stretched across the gap but no longer held it closed.

"Kick, what's wrong with him?"

The zombie flinched at Maddie's voice and then stumbled forward, catching itself on the scaffolding. It leaned its head toward the twins and, swinging it from side to side, bit at the air, searching for something on which to feed.

Kick pulled his knees back and then kicked forward as hard as he could. He caught the creature squarely in the chest, knocking it backward into the water, where it disappeared beneath the surface.

Maddie stared at the water. "You kicked him."

"He was trying to bite me!"

Maddie shook her head. Something wasn't right. She didn't fault her brother's reaction but rather her own. Why hadn't she fought back? Why had she hesitated?

"I didn't know he was going to," she said softly. "Did you?"

Kick heard what his sister had said but didn't respond. Maddie opened her mouth, but Kick quickly silenced her with a hand gesture. He pointed at the water.

The zombie had resurfaced. It was sitting up, head and shoulders above the water, but turned away from the kids. Very slowly, it began to turn.

Kick made a single gesture, which Maddie correctly interpreted as *listening*. Silently, he got to his feet, positioning his sister in front of him. He motioned for her to move. She didn't. Her hands told the story.

There are more.

Two figures, one in a long gown, the other stripped down to a pair of ragged leather pants, stood on the boardwalk near the end of the crossing, swaying back and forth. A third, draped in what could only be a ragged bedsheet, stumbled forward in the water along the walkway's edge. When the bridge stopped its progress it let out a low, sustained moan and was soon joined by the two standing on the boardwalk.

The zombie in the center of the street repeated the plaintiff cry, drawing the attention of the others. Maddie saw what she was sure were eyes catching a flicker of light from somewhere in the darkness. These creatures could see.

As proof, the two on the boardwalk quickly focused their attention to the twins. The shirtless zombie managed a few tentative steps out onto the crossing before tumbling over the edge and into the water. The second creature ventured out more slowly, having learned from its companion. It didn't get far, however.

"Hey, you fellas all right there?"

A man dressed in a long coat and a wide-brimmed hat approached the edge of the crossing. His attention shifted from the zombie on the bridge to those in the water. He appeared not to notice the twins.

"Bad night to be stuck in the mud. Come on, give me your hand," he said, reaching out to the creature nearest to him.

"No!" Maddie screamed much too late.

The zombie was fast. It grabbed the man's wrist and pulled him into the water with one swift jerk. The man bobbed up, tried to get to his feet, but was knocked down as the creature standing on the bridge fell on top of him. The man struggled but stayed under this time, unable to rise with the weight of the creature on top of him. He wouldn't drown, however. He wouldn't have the chance. Both zombies opened their mouths wide and then dived beneath the surface. The man soon stopped struggling.

Kick and Maddie stood at the center of the crossing, neither able to move. The connection that had kept them so close, had always allowed them to act as one, was gone. Physically they were only inches apart, but it might as well have been miles. They had gotten so used to following each other's lead, they were lost without it.

Kick wanted to run, but his sister wasn't moving.

Maddie wanted to run, but her brother wouldn't budge.

The shirtless zombie, unable to find a way through the scaffolding to join in the feast, turned its attention back to its original target. A fifth creature, this one with long, black hair and a slender, feminine figure, had also spied the twins. It stepped onto the bridge and slowly began to close the gap. The blind zombie was on its feet and walking—not toward the twins but rather the opposite end of the crossing. It was moving to cut them off.

Maddie held her hand behind her back but relayed no message. Kick reached out and took it. That was all they needed to reconnect, to understand, to be one again.

And that's when hands grabbed each around the waist and pulled them backward into the water.

24

By the time Joseph and Kate reached the bar, the marshal was already partaking in a second round.

"Whiskey?" he said, raising an eyebrow to Joseph.

"No, Marshal."

The marshal shrugged. "Suit yourself."

Kate watched her father empty his glass and then motion to the bartender for another.

"Dad, we need to talk."

The marshal waited for his glass to be filled. "'Bout what?"

"I think you know, Marshal," Joseph said.

The marshal lifted the whiskey to his lips but didn't drink. Instead, he pulled a folded slip of paper from his pocket and set it on the bar.

"Got your message. Can't say I put much stock in it."

"It's true, Dad."

The marshal looked at his daughter. "Bunch of ghosts, is what it is, Katie."

Kate felt Joseph's touch and pulled back her anger. If what he'd told her was true, the weapon beneath her father's coat was made to bring out the worst in a man. He might not be able to help himself.

Kate reached out to her father, only to have him pull away, the look of suspicion in his eyes one she'd never seen before.

"Dad?"

The marshal glared at his daughter, not sure who she was until the first tear slipped down her cheek. That was for him.

"Oh, Katie, I'm sorry."

Her embrace was warm and full and the marshal worried only for a moment that his daughter might be trying to steal it.

"Let's go home," she said. "We can talk this through there."

The marshal nodded and then turned back the bar to finish his drink. Upon seeing the telegram, he lowered the glass. "Think I'm done for the night," he said, pocketing the paper.

Kate smiled and hooked her father's arm. "Joseph?"

As soon as Kate and her father had come together, Joseph let his senses go, reaching into the conversations about the hall in search of a familiar young voice or two. This time, it took barely a minute to determine the twins weren't in the room.

"They're not here."

"No doubt getting into trouble," Kate said, losing her smile. "They're quite accomplished in that regard."

"They were supposed to find us."

"It's a big hotel. They might have gone exploring, upstairs, or . . ."

Joseph followed Kate's gaze past the front door and out into the night. The worst of the thunder and lightning had passed, but the rain continued. He pushed his senses harder, subtracting the celebration around him until all that remained was the muffled patter of raindrops on rooftops, sidewalks, and flooded streets. The downpour actually helped to define the landscape, give it dimension. Joseph could see the street more clearly in the storm than most people would be able to in the light of day. He moved between the drops, listening for any signs of life. Finally, he found one—his daughter.

She was screaming.

Maddie hit the water but, to her surprise, didn't go under. Whoever had pulled her from the bridge had also kept her from submerging. She got to her feet and then felt the hand loosen its grip on her waist. Maddie spun on her attacker to find the weatherman standing before her.

"Mr. Edmonds?"

Before Edmonds could answer, the female zombie stumbled off the bridge and into the water behind the kids.

"Come on," Edmonds said, motioning for the kids to follow.

They did.

Joseph pushed through the crowd toward the front entrance, with Kate right behind him. They were almost in the clear when a woman's scream shut down all conversation in the room and froze Joseph in his tracks. He found the woman ten feet to his right, scuttling backward into the crowd. In the silence, Joseph heard the wet scraping very clearly.

"Oh my god," Kate whispered.

It was the twisted foot of the thing dragging across the floor that made the noise. The zombie lurched forward into the light of the hall, dripping wet and naked save for a swatch of leather hung across its waist. Only it wasn't leather, it was skin. The creature's stomach had been cut wide open and sewn back together, only to have the lower flap come undone. A single section of intestine that dangled from the left side of the opening swung back and forth with each stagger. The belly cavity was otherwise empty, having already spilled most of its loosely packed contents in the street.

Try as he might, Joseph couldn't fix the horrific image in his head. It made no sense, even after what he'd seen in Astoria. It couldn't be as he imagined it.

"Joseph, is he alive?"

Joseph listened but heard no heartbeat or gathering of breath. Like the others, it was already dead.

The zombie stumbled forward, tilting the crowd back on their heels. The hotel manager stepped in front of the creature and raised his hands.

"Sir, please, can I help you?"

The zombie tilted its head as if confused by his inquiry.

The manager, finally able to see the extent of the man's condition, swallowed hard. "You're hurt, sir. You need a doctor."

The creature snapped its mouth closed with a wet smack. The people standing nearest to it recoiled.

It was then that a second zombie thumped against one of the large sidewalk windows, followed by a third and then a fourth. All three wore long, white gowns that did little to hide the fact that they were just as grotesque as the first. The windowpane cracked as the creatures began slowly pounding on it.

The manager cringed at the damage inflicted on his hotel and wondered briefly if he could add it to the city's tab. The thought would be his last.

The naked zombie fell on the man, driving his body to the floor. The manager's head struck the floor with enough force to render him unconscious, sparing him the worst of his assailant's attack. Those standing close enough to see the zombie sink its teeth into the soft tissue of manager's throat received no such kindness.

Two men attempted to wrestle the creature off the manager but were themselves attacked by a trio of half-naked nightmares. One of the men slipped free; the other stumbled over the first zombie and fell to the floor. All three creatures set upon him at once.

It took the sound of shattering glass to finally break the spell of confusion that had kept the shocked citizenry frozen in the presence of such horror. Screaming filled the hall, and the tentative retreat that had begun moments earlier became a stampede to find an exit. The front entrance was not an option. Six more zombies had already navigated the double doors and more were climbing through broken windows on both sides of the entrance. The exit on the south side of the hall was quickly cut off. A few people made it to the doorway on the far side but quickly turned back as a tall, armless man stumbled through the opening. There were two doors at the back of the room, but because of the festival stage only one was accessible. The small staff door quickly became clogged with bodies trying to force their way through.

Despite the chaos around him, Joseph held his ground at the leading edge of the otherwise retreating crowd. He'd finally reconciled his mind's view to reality and was now refocusing his attention on what stood between him and the front door. All extraneous noise and nuance fell away, leaving only the ever-increasing army of the dead staggering into the hall. Joseph tracked fifteen in the room, six more trying to get in. He gauged their movement, speed, and aggressiveness, searching for strengths and weaknesses. There were plenty of both.

Kate, having pushed aside her fears in favor of survival, leaned close to her husband.

"What do we do?" she asked.

"Get outside."

"How do we do that?"

"They're clumsy," Joseph said. "Get them off-balance and they'll fall. They're strong, though. Watch that they don't grab you."

"Can't grab what they don't see."

Kate slid from behind Joseph, moving in such a way as to seem part of the background. The closest zombies adjusted their approach to take on two targets rather than one. Kate stopped.

"They can see me."

"So it would seem. We do it the hard way, then. Stay close."

Joseph had nearly worked out a path through the horde when the first shot rang out. A zombie at the lead of the pack staggered but didn't fall. Two more bullets hit the creature's chest, one passing through completely to strike a second zombie. Neither went down.

A pair of police officers moved through the crowd until they were less than ten feet from their targets. It took only a few seconds to empty their weapons, each bullet finding flesh but doing little damage.

The zombies closed in.

"Shoot them in the head," Joseph yelled.

One officer glanced Joseph's way as the other attempted to re-load his pistol. He was fast, but not fast enough. The zombie was on top of him before he could raise the weapon.

Joseph stepped forward, kicking the creature in the leg, crushing its knee, and sending it sprawling to the ground. A second zombie lunged but caught only air as Joseph slipped under its outstretched arms.

The officer finished his reload and fired point-blank into the nearest target. Three shots to the heart did nothing. A fourth shot struck the creature square in the forehead and it crumpled to the ground. The shot had not come from the policeman's weapon.

Joseph knew immediately who had fired the shot. He recognized the sound of the gun, just as he had known he would. It was the Hanged Man's red-handled pistol, wielded by the marshal from atop the bar.

"Get down!" the marshal barked, and nearly all who heard him did as ordered.

The marshal fired again, striking another zombie in the head. It hiccupped, blinked, and fell to the floor a lifeless corpse. The marshal repeated the action again and again with similar results. His sixth shot took the ear off a short zombie but didn't knock it down. The marshal didn't bother to reload. He didn't have to. The seventh shot hit the creature in the eye, bringing it down instantly.

"Hit 'em in the head, men!" cried the marshal. "That'll take 'em down."

The marshal engaged once more and was soon joined by both police officers and several other armed locals. Unfortunately, none of the other shooters was the marshal's equal in accuracy or judgment. Two zombies went down, along with three members of the crowd, struck by stray bullets. The chaotic scene worsened as the crowd scrambled to avoid being shot, attacked, or both.

Joseph did his best to make sure neither he nor Kate was in the line of fire and then refocused on an exit strategy. The situation had not improved. More zombies continued to pour into the hall. Many were shot, but in doing so ended up as obstacles to a quick escape. Joseph plotted what he believed was the best course and then found Kate's hand.

"Ready?"

"As I'll ever be."

Joseph took a deep breath and lifted his voice above the chaos. "Marshal, we need a path!"

The marshal was already attempting to do just that, but all the damn people were making it difficult. He steadied his aim and fired.

Two zombies directly in front of Joseph and Kate fell on the spot. That was enough. They ran, Joseph first, jumping over bodies and scooting around the outstretched arms of a livelier corpse. Kate had to spin around the same creature as it reoriented its attack to her. That brought her face-to-face with a dead woman who briefly mirrored Kate's surprise in her expression before opening her mouth wide. The creature never got the chance to bite, as Joseph grabbed a handful of its long, black hair and yanked it away from his wife.

Kate's eyes widened. "Behind you!"

Joseph was already moving, taking the legs out from under both zombies that had come at them. He grabbed Kate's hand and led her to the front entrance. A single zombie stood on the other side of the door.

"Get down!" Joseph yelled.

Joseph opened the door and hit the deck along with Kate. The zombie stood, confused, for a moment, never getting the chance to enter the hall before a bullet blew what remained of its brain out through the back of its skull. It fell to the floor in a heap.

Joseph hesitated, waiting for his senses to sound the all clear. There was chaos all around them, except directly in front. It was the best they were going to get.

"Let's go," he said, and together they ran out into the storm.

Edmonds pushed Kick over the edge of the platform, which was now barely three feet above the floodwaters. Maddie helped her brother to his feet and then offered a hand to the weatherman. Once they were all safely atop the deserted stage, Edmonds gathered both kids before him.

"Are you hurt?"

"No, but one of them tried to bite me," Kick said.

"They attacked a man," Maddie said. "I think they might have killed him."

"I saw."

"I don't understand," Maddie said. "Why are they hurting people?"

Edmonds shook his head.

"Who are they?"

Edmonds looked over his shoulder. A single zombie struggled through the water near the other side of the street. A little farther down, a pair of creatures bobbed in the water. It was too dark to see what they were after, but Edmonds had an idea.

"I don't know," he said. "I was on a rooftop collecting data when I saw the first. I thought he was just a drunk, lost in the storm. But he wasn't moving right. And then I saw more."

"More?"

Edmonds nodded. "Dozens."

Maddie found her brother's hand and held it tightly.

"They look sick," Kick said.

"Worse than that," Maddie said. "One of them didn't have any eyes."

"And his face was all cut up and stitched back together, and his chest, too."

"His chest? How so?"

Kick drew a large Y across his torso.

Edmonds cringed. He'd seen such a pattern before. Before deciding on meteorology, he'd briefly considered a career in medicine. It had taken half of one Human Anatomy class to change his mind. The image that had stuck with him was that of a woman laid out on a large slab and the Y-shaped incision the instructor made in her torso to begin the examination. The fact that she was already dead had not made it any easier to watch.

What Kick's observation implied about the strange folks currently wandering the streets of Portland terrified Edmonds. He decided not to share this information with the kids.

"Where are your parents?"

Kick pointed across the plaza. "They were in the hotel with everybody else."

"I heard gunshots," added Maddie.

Edmonds nodded. He'd seen the creatures flock to the front of the hotel and force their way inside. Several festival booths currently blocked his view of the main entrance, but he could still see numerous zombies milling about the sidewalk.

When the lights in the main hall went out, the collective scream from the people trapped inside was loud enough to be heard above the rain.

"If they've got guns, they can protect themselves," Edmonds said, hoping it was true.

"Do you have a gun?"

"No, but I think we're safe up here. They don't seem to climb very well."

"I don't think they have to," Kick said, pointing across the platform.

One of the creatures stumbled off a ramp at the far corner of the stage. It picked itself up and angled toward Edmonds and the twins as two more zombies made it across to the platform.

"Maybe if you talk to them," Kick said. "You're an adult. Maybe they'll listen."

Edmonds doubted his age would improve his chances at communication but figured it was worth a shot.

"Gentlemen, do you need help?"

One of the creatures moaned. All three stumbled forward more quickly.

"If you're in need of medical assistance, I'm sure we can locate a proper physician."

The zombies closed to thirty feet. Kick recognized the female figure with the long, black hair.

"We should leave now," Maddie said, pulling on Mr. Edmonds's arm.

"I agree."

The trio turned back to the street to see two more of the creatures wading toward them through the floodwaters.

"What do we do?"

"Jump," Edmonds said. "The water will slow them down."

"It'll slow us down, too," Maddie said.

"We can swim," Kick said. "And they can't see us if we stay under water."

Edmonds glanced over his shoulder. The zombies were almost on top of them.

"Get to the other side of the street if you can," he said. "Go!"

Both kids jumped from the stage. Out of the corner of her eye, Maddie saw Edmonds turn to face their attackers and then she hit the water. She popped up almost immediately, but Mr. Edmonds was gone. From her low vantage point she could see the heads and shoulders of the creatures above the edge of the stage, but not the weatherman.

And then something grabbed her shoulder.

"Maddie, come on," Kick said, pulling his sister back toward the stage.

"But Mr. Edmonds said the other side of the street . . ."

"There are too many of them!"

Kick disappeared beneath the water and then popped up a few seconds later on the other side of the scaffolding under the stage.

"Swim under, Maddie. Take my hand."

Maddie took a deep breath and ducked below the surface. She found her brother's hand in the dark and let it guide her between the wooden slats that crisscrossed under the platform. When she came up, there was barely a foot of clearance between the bottom of the stage and the rising water.

"I don't think they can get to us," Kick said.

"Are you sure?"

Kick pointed to a zombie bumping up against the scaffolding a few yards away. It reached a hand between the slats but progressed no farther.

"They can't think it through. They're not very smart. What happened to Mr. Edmonds?"

Maddie shook her head.

Kick wiped the water from his face. His mind raced through the possibilities, but he forced it to stop before his superior visualization skills kicked in.

"Maybe he got past them."

"Maybe," Maddie said, then made a quick survey of their surroundings. The stage was built on very slight hill, which meant the water was already touching the bottom of the platform on the other size of the plaza. They'd actually climbed under at the highest point on the street, but if the waters continued to rise at their current pace, their heads would be under water soon.

"The water is still rising," she said. "We can't stay here or we'll run out of room to breathe."

"We need to find Mom and Dad," Kick said. "They're already looking for us."

"Are you sure?"

"Aren't you?"

She was. There was no doubt in her mind, and that was a problem.

"They won't find us if we stay hidden."

Kick nodded. "And they won't stop looking, which means they'll be out there with them."

Maddie glanced back at the street. There were three zombies at the edge of the structure now, struggling to push through the slats but gaining no ground. One had managed to force its head through an opening but was stuck, its face partially submerged in the water. There was movement beyond the barrier, but in the dark it was difficult to see. Maddie tried to listen, searching for something tangible between the raindrops. What she heard was the low moan of hundreds of wooden slats slowly breaking.

"Oh, no," Maddie said.

Kick looked at his sister and knew. A moment later, the platform creaked loudly and shifted above their heads, sinking two inches as the support structure began to collapse.

"This way," Kick said, pushing his sister in the opposite direction of the water flow.

The platform dropped another few inches, forcing the twins beneath the surface. Kick popped up to get his bearings and one last breath. Maddie was up a second later.

"Take a deep breath," Kick said.

"Got it," Maddie said, then took her brother's hand.

The platform dropped onto the water just as the kids ducked under the surface. Maddie opened her eyes but could see nothing but black. She closed them again and pushed forward until her free hand found the wooden structure still holding the back side of the platform in place. It was leaning toward them but hadn't yet collapsed. It would soon.

Maddie felt her brother tug on her hand, leading her toward an opening just large enough to navigate. She got both hands on the wood and pulled herself through, only to have her dress catch on the structure. Maddie suddenly became keenly aware of the burning sensation in her chest. How long had she been under? Thirty seconds? A minute? She wouldn't last much longer. She felt her brother's hands around her ankles, trying to free her. And then she sensed something else—a body, dropped into the water directly in front of her. Hands were reaching out, trying to find her. She felt her dress tear, she was loose, but it was too late. It had her.

Maddie broke the surface, gasping for air and struggling against the hands that had pulled her to safety.

"Maddie! It's okay, I got you."

Maddie opened her eyes to find she was in her father's grasp. The panic in her chest finally eased and she hugged him.

"Maddie, give me your hand!"

It was her mother, reaching from the partially sunken platform. For a moment, Maddie refused to let go, fearful of what might take hold of her beneath the surface. Then she remembered her brother.

"Kick!" she said, taking her mother's hand. "He's still down there."

But Joseph was already under the water. He was up seconds later, Kick limp in his arms. He brought him to the edge of the stage and handed him over to Kate.

"Behind you!" Maddie screamed.

The zombie closed on Joseph and would have grabbed him around the neck had he not disappeared under the surface. The creature dunked its head briefly into the water but refused to stay submerged. The water had risen almost to shoulder level and it was having trouble staying upright. Finally, it noticed Kate, who at the edge of the platform seemed an easier target. Before it could make a move, the zombie was sucked into the black.

Kate never took her eyes off her son. He'd been unconscious when Joseph handed him over, and now a trickle of blood was running down his forehead. Kate found a small gash in his scalp, and when she touched it, Kick immediately began coughing up water.

Satisfied that her brother was alive, Maddie turned back to the water. It was an agonizing ten seconds before her father burst through the surface.

"Dad!"

Joseph pulled himself onto the stage and into his daughter's arms. She would not let him go this time.

Joseph looked to his son. "How is he?"

"Hit his head," Kate said. "Swallowed quite a bit of water, too, but I think he'll be all right."

Joseph put a hand on his son's face. "You're not a fish, you know?"

Kick blinked several times and smiled weakly.

Joseph pressed his face to Kate's. A tear rolled from her cheek to his, momentarily warming Joseph's skin before disappearing among the raindrops.

"We'll be all right."

Kate let go of the breath she'd been holding. "Will we?"

Joseph reached out with his senses. The chaos of the hotel had spilled out into the plaza, and though masked by the rain, it was all too clear to Joseph. Locals ran in all directions, and there were at least twenty of the creatures in the immediate vicinity. It was difficult to track the exact number because they made the same noises, offering little to distinguish one from another. They moved in the same lurching manner, made the same disturbing guttural growls, and attacked with the same relentless horror. Twenty at least, most likely more.

"We've got the stage to ourselves," Joseph said. "But I don't know for how long."

"Did you see Mr. Edmonds?" Maddie asked. "He helped us."

Joseph shook his head. There had been a group of zombies on the platform when he and Kate had arrived, but all had tumbled over the edge. If the weatherman had been among them, Joseph hoped he'd escaped . . . or drowned quickly.

"Maybe he got away," Maddie said hopefully.

"If so, he had the right idea," Kate said. "We can't stay here."

Joseph didn't argue. "Most of them are still around the hotel. We need to get out of the plaza and head toward higher ground."

"They're slower in the water," Kick said with some effort.

"So are we," Kate said. "And I don't think you're in any shape to swim."

"Water's rising too fast," Joseph added. "Most of the sidewalks will be swamped soon, so if we don't go now we'll all be swimming."

Right on cue, the platform shifted and abruptly sank six inches, dropping it below the flood line. Water rushed over the stage, forcing the family to their feet. Kick tried to stand but immediately wished he hadn't. He swayed forward and then back, teetering on the edge of the platform before losing his balance altogether.

"Kick!"

Maddie reached out to her brother, just missing his outstretched fingers as he fell into the water.

Kick had just enough time to register that he was once again under the cold darkness before his father brought him back to the surface. He spit out the water halfway down his throat and fought to stay conscious.

"I got you, son."

Kick focused on his father's face. In the low light of the plaza it was all he could see clearly, but it was enough to keep him in the moment.

"I'm okay," he said between coughs and tightened his grip around his father's arm.

Joseph turned to Kate and Maddie.

"Let's go. Everyone in the water."

Kate bundled up the lower portion of her dress and stepped off the platform. She turned back to help Maddie, who hopped in without prompting.

"Stay close," Joseph said and turned toward the opposite side of the street.

It was only thirty feet to the boardwalk, but with the water at chest height even Joseph found the crossing difficult.

The family pushed through the floodwaters and would have

reached the boardwalk without incident had a section of the nearest wooden crossing not broken free.

"Kate, take Kick!"

Joseph passed off his son and then spun in time to meet the flotsam with outstretched hands. It was heavy, but he held his ground, slowly turning the large chunk of scaffolding away from his family. With his attention stretched thin, Joseph missed the zombie clinging to the opposite side of the wreckage.

"Dad, look out!"

Joseph sensed the creature a moment before its fingers closed around his wrist. It was strong. Joseph jerked back his hand, pulling the determined zombie partially over the broken bridge, which was now slowly dragging him away from his family. A second hand thrust forward, striking Joseph in the face and then latching on to his collar. Joseph gave up trying to slow the wreckage and instead braced his feet against the structure and pushed. His body arched upward, but the creature wouldn't let go.

The scaffold jolted to a stop as it struck a large chunk of sidewalk jutting out into the flooded street. The zombie's grip slacked momentarily, giving Joseph an opening. He grabbed the creature's right hand and broke three of the fingers at the knuckles. The zombie reacted by pulling Joseph even closer with the opposite hand, its mouth ratcheting open and closed as it did.

For a moment, the light from a lantern hanging on a nearby telegraph pole illuminated the creature's face. This was not one of the pale, sickly beings that had attacked the hall but rather someone Joseph recognized. It was a man from the party, one who'd been attacked in front of Joseph. There were numerous gashes in his neck and face and what were surely teeth marks in his cheek. The front of the man's shirt was soaked in blood and rainwater. He had been murdered by the creatures and now he was one of them. It was madness.

Joseph struggled to break free but found no leverage. Sensing victory, the zombie gathered itself and was abruptly shot in the forehead. The creature's face contorted, its body slackened, and then it fell forward onto the broken bridge. The zombie flinched once and then was silent.

Joseph pushed away from the wreckage and found the marshal standing above him, holding the Hanged Man's red-handled pistol.

"Damn lucky there's still one light workin' in this town," the marshal said, gesturing to the lantern. "Not sure I make that shot in the dark, not without clippin' your ear."

Joseph pulled himself onto the boardwalk just as Kate and the twins caught up. He took his son from Kate and turned to the marshal.

"You take that shot every time, Marshal. Light or no light."

The marshal nodded.

Kick coughed and dropped his head onto his father's shoulder. "Can we go home now?"

His son was heavier out of the water, but Joseph barely noticed. Nor did he feel the exhaustion that would likely overwhelm him should he stand still for too long. He sensed only the fear of his family and an absolute need to protect them, regardless of the cost. He tightened his grip on Kick and reached out to Kate and Maddie.

"Stay close."

It was a beautiful sound.

It called to him. It sang to him. It begged him to come closer. The Hanged Man had heard it many times before but never so clearly.

Find me, it whispered, *use me*.

He would, soon.

Henry had heard the distant gunshot as well but sensed nothing special about it. Sporadic gunfire had echoed across the city continually since they'd reached the flooded downtown streets. Most of the action had elicited little response from the Hanged Man, but this most recent report had stopped him in his tracks. More disturbing, it brought a sickening grin to the dead man's face.

The Hanged Man stepped off the sidewalk into a flooded alley. What little light there was on the street dissipated quickly in the alley and soon the dead man was swallowed up by the darkness.

Henry stood his ground, once more putting his will to the test. He felt his heart beat against the small shape in his breast pocket and wondered—not for the first time—if he didn't feel it beating back.

The beat grew louder.

Henry stepped off the boardwalk and waded into the darkness.

25

Six blocks from the plaza, Kate and Maddie turned down an alley that cut between Stark and Washington Streets. A few moments later, Joseph made the turn, nearly slipping as he stepped off the boardwalk and into the flooded alleyway.

"Kate, wait."

Joseph caught up to his wife and daughter halfway down the narrow backstreet. The water was only ankle deep, but rising. Two hours earlier, the alley had been bone dry.

Kate raised the firestone lamp they'd liberated from a telegraph pole, bathing the alley behind them in amber light. "Where's Dad?"

Joseph glanced over his shoulder. "He's coming," he said, shifting his son's weight onto his hip. "How's your head, Kick?"

Kick thought for a moment. "Better. I can walk now."

"No, I got you."

Kate touched her husband's arm. "Joseph, let him down for a moment."

Joseph lifted his head to protest, but all at once he felt the strain of the evening catch up to him. He let Kick slide out of his arms and into the shallow water without a word. The boy landed on his feet but never let go, clinging to his father's side. Joseph was glad for it.

A single gunshot echoed from around the corner. Soon after, the marshal joined the family in the alley.

"I think we're clear of 'em. Last one was across the street and headed in the other direction. Haven't seen any others for two blocks."

"That doesn't mean we're safe," Kate added.

Joseph listened. The events of the evening had taken their toll, dulling his perception, but he could still pull details from a block away, mostly splashing feet in the floodwaters. There was nothing to suggest any of them belonged to the shambling creatures that had attacked them.

"Marshal's right. I think we've time enough to catch our breath."

"I'll keep watch," the marshal said and strode back to the alley opening. The adrenaline rush that had propelled him since he'd first drawn his weapon remained. He felt good, energized. Every time he pulled the trigger, he felt more alive. Halfway down Stark Street, the marshal spotted a pair of young men running in the opposite direction of the plaza. They were no threat. He tracked them, just the same.

Kate watched her father for a moment longer, then turned to Joseph.

"In the dark, in this weather, we're an hour from home, at least. Maybe we should make for the store."

Joseph nodded.

"We can barricade the doors," Kate added. "Shutter the front windows. I don't think anyone could get in. If they don't know we're there . . ."

"They won't try."

"Yes. Then we can make a plan."

Joseph looked up. "A plan?"

Kate didn't explain—she didn't have to. Joseph understood his wife's intentions because he was thinking the same thing.

"You want to go back."

Kate smiled. "Of course not, but if the kids are safe, don't you think we should?"

He did.

"You're going to leave us?"

Kate touched her daughter's cheek. "Honey, you'll be safe. One of us will stay. And your grandpa—"

"But we could come," Kick said, only slightly groggy.

"People need our help," Maddie added. "We can help."

Kate looked at Joseph. He was just as surprised.

"No," Joseph said. "No, it's too dangerous. And you're hurt."

"I'm lots better," Kick protested. "Besides, Maddie can hold me up."

"Sure I can!"

Kick let go of his father's waist and slipped an arm around his sister's shoulders. Together they stood, side by side in the rising floodwaters, ready to walk back into the most horrifying night of their lives to help their neighbors. Joseph had never been prouder . . . or more terrified.

"No, we stay together—all of us," he said. "Marshal? Come on, we're going."

The marshal trotted back to the family.

"All clear behind us."

"Good," Kate said, "because we need to backtrack to get to the store."

The marshal nodded. Move toward danger? He liked that idea just fine.

Joseph opened his arms to his son. "Kick, let's go."

"I can walk."

"No protesting, Kick. Come here before I . . ." Joseph's words trailed off. Somewhere in the deep recesses of his perception an alarm was sounding, one he hadn't heard for a very long time.

The Hanged Man stopped. It was close, now, very close. He could feel the vibrations and hear the soft hum of metal and wood. And more—the old man was with it still.

And he wasn't alone.

The Hanged Man drew the useless revolver from his belt, a gun that would do no lasting harm as long as he was forced to pull the trigger, and stepped into the alley opening.

Kate couldn't hear the alarm in her husband's head, but she could read his face. Something was wrong.

"Joseph, what is it?"

Joseph recognized the figure that had materialized before him but refused to accept it. It didn't matter. In his mind's eye he saw only the truth. Joseph knew the man too well and would not be fooled by an impostor. It took only the dead man's voice to make him believe.

"Marshal! You've got something of mine."

The family turned as one to see the Hanged Man standing at the far end of the alley. He was more than a hundred feet away, but the dread that swirled around him like a cloud closed the distance in an instant. Kate drew back, sliding Maddie behind her as Joseph did the same with their son. The marshal slipped forward between the two, never taking his eyes off the demon before him.

"He wants it," he whispered.

―――――

The Hanged Man could hardly believe his good fortune. Not only had he tracked down his weapon and the man who'd used it to murder him, but here, too, was his old partner, alive and well, and with the family that had cost them both so dearly. He would pay for his crimes.

They all would.

The Hanged Man swings again, landing a roundhouse right to the left side of Joseph's already bloodied face. The bandages around the young man's head have come undone, revealing a mask of seared skin and two sunken yellow slits where bright eyes should be. Both cheeks are swollen, nose likely broken. The Hanged Man's fists are hard. He hits Joseph again, sending his old partner to his knees.

"Stop it!"

For a moment, the baby boy pressed to his mother's bosom ceases crying, startled by her scream. The baby girl never stops. Her wailing has been constant since the Hanged Man took her in his arms. Held firm against his shoulder, she is the only reason Joseph has not felt the full force of the Hanged Man's unnatural strength.

She is also the reason Joseph has not fought back.

"Surprised you made it," the Hanged Man says. "Long way to suffer the dark."

The Hanged Man looks at the child in his hand. He feels nothing.

"For so very little . . ."

Joseph raises his head, defiant.

"My life for theirs."

The Hanged Man stares at Joseph, searching for the man he once knew. A stranger glares back at him.

"Made your choice then?"

"I made it a long time ago."

The Hanged Man frowns. "Won't be a rifle in the trees, not this time. We end it like men."

The Hanged Man draws a pistol from his belt—not his, but a smaller revolver, one he's never used. He flips it to Joseph, thinking nothing of the man catching what he should not see.

"Recognize it? You carried that pistol once, drew it beside me."

Joseph turns the weapon over in his hands, testing its weight.

"Feels light."

"One round each. All we'll need."

Joseph nods slowly, then fixes his attention on the Hanged Man.

"Let her go."

The Hanged Man glances at the child in his arms. It would be so easy. He could set Joseph free, though his friend would not understand. He must be made to.

"Cross me again and I will kill them . . . beginning with this one, I promise."

"I believe you."

The Hanged Man hesitates before holding the child out at arm's length.

The woman comes forward, snatching the child away quickly. Brought together at their mother's breast, both infants cease their wails almost immediately. She turns to escape, but the Hanged Man's hand is already on her shoulder.

"No, my dear," he says, drawing the woman back. "You stand with me."

"I made a promise to our boy, Marshal," called the Hanged Man, raising his voice above the storm. "I'll have my gun back."

The marshal felt the pistol grow warm in his hand. Soon it was red hot. He didn't care. It could blister his fingers until they bled. He would never let go.

"Have it, then!"

The marshal raised and fired the Hanged Man's weapon. It felt good. He cocked the hammer and pulled the trigger five more times in rapid succession, each shot finding its intended target.

The Hanged Man never raised his gun.

The last bullet snapped the dead man's head backward and then he went down, flat on his back in the water.

Henry was ten feet from the Hanged Man when the last bullet dropped the dead man into the shallow water. From his position at the edge of the alley, he couldn't see who'd done the shooting and had no desire to step into view lest he become a target as well. What he wanted to do was run, in the opposite direction, as fast as he could.

(*not yet*)

Henry did as he was told.

The marshal cocked the hammer but did not depress the trigger. He waited, arm raised, site aligned on the dead man. Slowly, his hand began to shake. His breath became ragged. His vision blurred. The fire that had burned so brightly in his heart and in his mind since unleashing the weapon was doused, leaving him cold and exhausted and standing ankle deep in a flooded alleyway drenched in orange light.

A hand touched his shoulder. "Marshal?"

The marshal caught Joseph's eye, felt it stare right through him, and knew his son-in-law was blind and had been for more than a decade. And still the man could see him, clearly, as he always did.

"I'm sorry," the marshal said, lowering the dead man's weapon.

Joseph opened his mouth to speak, but no words came out.

He was still alive.

There was no heart to begin beating, no breath to start breathing, but Joseph sensed the Hanged Man return to life moments before the dead man rose from the water.

"Oh my god," Kate whispered. "Joseph . . ."

"I see him."

The marshal swung his gaze forward again to see the Hanged Man striding toward them. He wanted desperately to raise the red-handled pistol and fire again, but suddenly it felt so heavy in his hand the marshal couldn't begin to lift it. He stumbled forward, laboring to raise the pistol above his waist.

"Damn you!"

Kate reached for her father. "Dad, no!"

"Kate!"

Joseph made several decisions at once, the first being that they would not escape the way they had come before the Hanged Man opened fire. That left two options: stand and fight or hope that the door immediately to his left was as poorly secured as the back-alley entrance to the bookstore.

Joseph raised his foot and kicked the door, popping it open on the first try. Water poured through the opening and down a flight of stairs into the basement of the building.

"Kate, come on!" Joseph said, snatching up Kick.

Kate saw Maddie disappear through the open doorway, quickly followed by Joseph and Kick. She turned back to her father and grabbed his free hand.

"Dad, let's go!"

The marshal pulled away from his daughter. "Leave me, Katie!" For a moment, the pistol was light enough for the marshal to raise it to chest height and take aim.

"You will not touch my family, you son of a—"

A gunshot rang out in the alley, although it was not the marshal who had fired his weapon. To his surprise, neither was it the Hanged Man. There was, however, no mystery as to the intended target.

"No!" Kate screamed as her father stumbled backward, gripping his right shoulder. She steadied him before he could fall into the water.

The Hanged Man halted. He didn't raise his gun to finish the job but rather turned on the spot and yelled into the darkness behind him.

"They're mine!"

When the dead man turned back, the world exploded in fire as the lantern struck his chest and shattered.

By the time the alley came back into focus it was empty.

Kate touched only the edge of the last step as she and the marshal pitched forward into the darkness. She let go of her father just before they both hit the floor with a wet thump.

The water was already several inches deep, with more continuing to pour in through the open doorway. Kate sat up and reached for her father, finding nothing. The room was dark, but the marshal had to be close. She blinked hard, trying to will her pupils wider.

She heard movement.

"Marshal?"

"I got him," Joseph whispered.

Kate got to her feet. "Where are the kids?"

Joseph led Kate and her father past a series of shelves stocked with boxes and equipment. After several more twists and turns they came to a second stairwell, which climbed to a landing and a door. There was no one there. And then there was.

"Mom?"

Kate closed her eyes and put her arms around Maddie. Kick

said nothing but found room in his mother's embrace alongside his sister. When she finally opened her eyes, Kate was surprised by how well she could see in the dark. The pain on her father's face was easy to see.

"How bad is it?"

The marshal coughed. "Stings is all."

Joseph pressed lightly on the front of the marshal's shoulder and the old man hissed.

"Bullet's lodged in the muscle near his clavicle. Needs to come out, but I think he's okay for the moment."

"I'm fine," the marshal said, gritting his teeth as he stood up. "I can walk. Where are we?"

"Jenner Hardware and Electric," Joseph said. "Basement, by the looks of it."

"There's a front entrance on Washington Street," Kate said. "We can cut back to Third and then the store is just—"

"No," the marshal said. "You can't hide from him. He's not like the others. He'll find me . . . he'll find you."

"He won't find me," Kate said. "If he's not like the others, he'll have the same blind spots as anyone else. I can hide in plain sight and he won't see me."

"Or us," added Maddie. Kick nodded.

"Then we'll split up," Joseph said. "I'll lead him away."

The marshal shook his head. "Bastard doesn't want you, he wants . . ."

The marshal reached to his belt and closed his hand on nothing.

"Oh, no . . ."

It was gone. The bullet had been a distraction, but now the pain in his shoulder was nothing compared to the empty feeling in his hand. How could he have lost it?

"Marshal?"

"I dropped it!"

"Dropped what?"

"The pistol! When I fell it must have slipped, somewhere in the water, by the door, I couldn't . . . I have to go back!"

"Leave it," Kate said.

The marshal didn't understand. "We can't let him have it."

"It didn't even slow him down, Dad. What good is it?"

Joseph knew.

"It's not what it does to him, but what he can do with it."

Kate stared at her husband and saw he believed this to be true.

"I never reloaded, not once," said the marshal. "If he . . . if he has it—"

"Marshal!" called the dead man's voice from inside the basement.

Joseph pulled the kids behind him. He motioned for Kate to do the same, but she held her ground. It was the marshal who moved first.

"Don't wait for me," he said, and tried to move past his son-in-law. Joseph cut him off.

"I'll go," he whispered. "I'm better in the dark."

The marshal shook his head. "My fault. I go."

"You're shot."

The marshal didn't care. He would take another bullet if he had to. It was his mistake, thus it was his mistake to fix. *It* was his.

"I don't care," he said, then realized Joseph was no longer paying attention to him. "Don't turn your back on me, Joseph. You can't take this on by yourself."

When Joseph turned back, the marshal could see the man's fear, even in the dark.

"Your daughter already did."

The Hanged Man listened for the telltale hum of the red-handled revolver, but it was gone. He'd lost it after the woman had thrown the lantern in his face, but now that his head was clear he should have been able to pick it up again. The marshal couldn't have put enough distance between them to quiet its call. Something had changed.

He peered down a row of shelves filled with boxes. Nothing. They were close, he was sure of it, but without the pistol's voice to guide him, the Hanged Man moved more cautiously.

He wasn't afraid—they couldn't kill him, no one could—but the dead man was beginning to sense he might not be as indestructible as he'd once believed. The wounds he'd suffered at the carnival, while causing little damage, had refused to heal. He had no doubt the marshal's assault would prove equally insignificant, but one of the bullets had struck his hip and now he could feel the bones grinding together unnaturally. If such a wound did not heal, would it ultimately render him lame? He couldn't die, but could he be broken? That might be worse.

The Hanged Man didn't know. Perhaps Henry could find an answer in the book. If not, there was always . . .

No.

Not yet. Not without his weapon. Not without blood.

Something splashed behind him and he spun to see Henry kneeling in the water at the foot of the stairs.

"Dammit," Henry said. He started to stand but was grabbed around the neck and hoisted completely off his feet by the Hanged Man.

"Stay out of my way."

Henry managed to choke out a sound that might have been agreement and then was dropped onto the wet floor.

The Hanged Man turned away from the young man, half expecting to be shot in the back. The bullet never came.

"I'm waiting, Marshal."

The Hanged Man listened. He heard water falling, and the fool breathing behind him, but there was nothing else, no hum, no call. He peered down another aisle and then moved on. Only he didn't move. Something wasn't right. He couldn't see it, he couldn't hear it, but something in this particular aisle felt wrong, something right in front of his face.

The Hanged Man's eyes fell on Kate. He didn't see her, but it required every ounce of concentration Kate could muster not to scream. The basement storeroom offered little in the way of camouflage save for shadow and boxes, which meant even a shallow breath might give her away. The dead man's eyes crossed Kate's and she was sure he had her.

But the eyes moved on, and soon so did the man, down the center aisle, deeper into the basement.

Toward her family.

Kate moved forward silently. At the end of the aisle, she waited as long as she dared and then peered around the corner. The Hanged Man was gone. Looking the other way, she saw the door ajar, water still flowing down the stairs, but nothing else.

He has a partner, Kate thought. She'd heard the Hanged Man speaking to someone moments earlier, but whoever it had been was gone.

Or hiding.

Staying low, Kate slipped around the corner and began searching the water for the Hanged Man's pistol. It was too dark to see beneath the surface, which meant feeling her way along the floor until she found the thing that until recently she'd wanted desperately to be lost. The irony was not lost on Kate.

Something moved in the dark beside her.

Kate froze, searching the darkness for trouble. There was nothing to be found. She listened for a moment longer, then returned to the search. It had to be close. Both hands slipped across the basement floor and then her fingers touched metal—she'd found it.

Kate lifted the dead man's gun from the water. It was heavy, enough so that it required both hands to hold it comfortably by the handle. And it did feel comfortable. Kate wondered why she'd been reluctant to hold it in the marshal's presence.

Somewhere, in the distance, she thought she heard a faint hum.

The Hanged Man smiled.

Kate stood up, her attention still consumed by the weapon in her hand, which was why she failed to notice Henry until he was standing right beside her.

"Don't move, lady."

Kate moved.

Henry didn't have time to react as Kate spun and knocked the weapon from his hand. Had his finger been on the trigger, Kate would have been shot. Instead, she was able to level the Hanged Man's gun at Henry's head before he could recover. It never occurred to Henry that a wet pistol would never fire.

Kate knew this gun would.

"Where's your friend?"

"I don't know," Henry said, but his eyes betrayed him.

Kate slipped behind Henry in one fluid motion, never letting the red-handled pistol drop from its target.

The Hanged Man stepped from the shadows twenty feet away. His gun was drawn, but it remained at his side.

"Come any closer and he dies," Kate said, hearing the words in her head only after they'd been spoken. Had she really said them?

The thought of taking man's life made her heartsick. She wouldn't do it—she couldn't!

Could she?

"Go ahead," said the Hanged Man. "Be doin' me a favor."

Kate put a hand on Henry's shoulder, steadying her grip even though she could barely hold the weapon with one hand. Slowly, she pulled back the hammer.

"Stop."

The Hanged Man stopped. He didn't want to, but his body refused to move forward. It believed her. He could not kill the man, nor because of his actions allow Henry to be killed. They were bound, in life and death. He so desperately wanted to kill someone.

For his part, Henry was not concerned about being shot. He knew it wouldn't happen. The Hanged Man couldn't kill him and the woman wouldn't. He knew this. The dead man may have suggested otherwise, but Henry was protected. He was safe. It told him so.

"He just wants the gun," Henry said, speaking the words aloud as quickly as they poured into his head. "Just drop it and run before he kills us both."

The pistol grew warm in Kate's hand. She slid the barrel around Henry's head until it found a new target.

"No!" Kate screamed, not recognizing the anger in her voice. "You can't have it, it's mine!"

The Hanged Man smiled and found himself once again able to move forward.

Kate wanted badly to pull the trigger, regardless of whether or not it would do any good. *Do it,* a voice inside her said.

(*yes do it*)

Kate hesitated. Why was she suddenly so eager to kill? That

wasn't like her. The doubt lingered only for a moment longer and then was gone. Emotion flooded back into Kate's conscious mind so quickly that it nearly staggered her. Her aim faltered ever so slightly and that was all it took.

Henry was faster this time. He grabbed the barrel of the red-handled gun and twisted upward while spinning to face the woman. Kate nearly lost her grip but managed to hook a finger around the trigger guard and refused to let go. Henry grabbed Kate's wrist, which had the unintended result of tilting the gun in the direction of his face. He lost concentration, momentarily retreating, only to find that Kate had grabbed his coat.

Henry struggled to free himself, but Kate held strong, her hand digging into an inside coat pocket, causing it to tear slightly. She felt the momentary sensation of something very warm touching her fingers.

Henry felt it, too.

Henry and Kate locked eyes. A flicker of understanding passed between them and then vanished. All that remained was fear.

The Hanged Man considered shooting them both, knowing neither would die, but at least the woman might be hobbled. Such an action might also create an opening for her to shoot Henry, and that stayed the dead man's hand. It would be safer to steal back his weapon as they struggled. He could see it, still held above their heads, its dark brilliance flashing in the dim light. He would have it.

The Hanged Man was still ten feet from the prize when he raised a hand to take it. He never saw Joseph slip behind a tall wooden cage holding various lengths of pipe. When it began to move, the motion registered, but the Hanged Man did not react. It was no concern of his. The flimsy structure broke apart before crashing on top of the dead man, burying him beneath a thousand pounds of plumbing.

Kate barely registered the calamity as she struggled against the young man. She felt her grip on Henry's jacket weaken as the fabric tore further. To her surprise, Henry let go of the gun and her wrist to save his coat. Finally free, Kate fell backward onto the steps, hitting her head on the railing.

The room threatened to darken completely, but with considerable effort Kate stayed in the moment. She blinked her eyes and saw the red-handled pistol in her hand. Before her, she saw Henry pull a small book from his pocket and hold it tightly to his chest. Behind him, the Hanged Man had disappeared beneath an avalanche of metal pipes. And she heard yelling. It sounded like her name. Someone was yelling her name. Beyond the rubble she saw Joseph. He was calling her name and telling her to run.

And then Maddie touched her mother's arm.

"Mom?"

They ran.

26

The rain felt good on Kate's face. Any lingering doubts about what to do with the pistol still gripped tightly in both hands were washed away by the cold, cleansing waters of the Oregon sky. She knew what to do.

Drown it.

Kate jumped a gap that had opened between two sections of boardwalk and then started across the scaffold bridge connecting the two sides of Second Street. That the bridge remained intact was a miracle, considering that the floodwaters would soon be approaching historic levels. There was nothing but water half a block closer to the river, but Kate would be clear of that momentarily.

Joseph led the marshal around the corner in time to see Kate reach the other side of Second Street just as the twins were starting over the bridge. Joseph stopped at the broken section of boardwalk and searched for a way around. Before he could find one, the marshal made a clumsy attempt to step over the gap. He succeeded, but fell to his knees on the other side in obvious pain. Joseph made the leap and then helped his father-in-law to his feet.

"Kate!"

Kate stopped and waved. "Are you all right?"

"Yes, we're fine. Where are you going?"

"To the pier," Kate replied as the twins caught up to her. She held up the Hanged Man's red-handled revolver and shouted, "To the river!"

"She means to throw it in," Joseph said under his breath.

It took the marshal a beat longer to grasp her meaning, but once he did, the strength in his legs suddenly returned.

"He'll catch her," he said. "He'll take it!"

The marshal ran across the bridge before Joseph could offer a hand.

The Number 19 riverboat dock was one of only two empty berths on the west side of the Willamette River. An hour earlier it had been occupied by the sternwheeler *Lurline,* but rising waters had snapped the lines, setting the boat adrift until it smashed into the nearby Morrison Street Bridge. The vessel remained lodged against the span, slowly crushing itself against a steel-and-wood structure already stressed by the water cresting its roadway. The bridge survived the night; the steamer did not.

Kate reached the upper section of the pier, an area normally reserved for top-level boarding, to find it barely five feet above the waterline. A single lamp bathed the dock in orange light, revealing a platform much longer than it was wide. Kate stepped to the edge and peered into the rushing darkness below.

Maddie and Kick followed their mother to the end of the pier. Kick, still a little wobbly, leaned on his sister and tried not to fall over. Maddie made sure he didn't.

Kate raised the red-handled pistol in her hand. It was still unnaturally warm, but it no longer spoke to her. The compulsion to hold on to it—to use it—had passed. She was in control now, and all she had to do was let go.

"Katie, don't you do it!"

Kate turned and saw her father approaching with Joseph right behind. She didn't wait for him to reach her to give her reply.

"I have to, Dad. It's the only way."

"No, Katie, you can't," he pleaded. "Give it to me."

Kate shook her head.

Joseph reached out to stop the marshal but the old man shrugged him off.

"No!" the marshal said, stopping halfway between his daughter and her husband. "I kept it safe all them years, I did that!"

"At what cost, Dad? Eleven years of your life? Was it all for this?"

The marshal tried to recall the past decade of his life and was surprised by how little he remembered and, worse, how little he cared.

"Whatever it was, I paid it. It's mine to do with as I please."

The marshal closed the space between himself and his daughter. He stopped close enough to reach out and take the pistol from her hand, but didn't. He wouldn't have to. His daughter would give it to him.

"If anyone is goin' chuck it in the river, should be me," the marshal said and held out his hand.

Joseph heard the deception in the marshal's voice but didn't believe it. His father-in-law wouldn't either, in the end. He would remember.

"Give it to him, Kate."

Kate stared at her husband for a moment, and then set the red-handled revolver in her father's open palm without another word.

The marshal expected to feel something at the return of the gun, just not the dread that washed over him like a cold fire. It bit into his flesh, clawed at his heart, and filtered every thought in his head through fear. Was this what he desired?

No.

The dread was born not of the marshal but of the thing in his hand. No matter how much he wanted it, the thing did not want him. It never had.

"It wants me," said the dead man.

The Hanged Man swung his massive right fist, striking Joseph just as he began to turn, connecting solidly with his patch-covered eye.

"Joseph!"

Joseph stumbled backward, spinning as he did to face his attacker. In an instant, he filled the blind spot in his vision, sketching a picture of the twisted creature before him. One of the Hanged Man's ankles had crumpled, causing him to teeter on the side of his foot. A portion of his head was crushed, the remains of an ear dangling by a thin flap of skin beneath it. There were other broken bones, many loudly scraping together, which caused Joseph to wonder how such a monster could have approached unnoticed. The world went black before he found an answer.

"Joseph," Kate cried again and dropped to her knees beside her husband.

The Hanged Man drew the false weapon that had been buried with him for more than a decade and pointed it at the marshal.

"That's my gun," said the marshal, pleased to see his old Colt Navy, despite the circumstances.

"Have it, then," said the dead man, never taking his finger from the trigger.

The marshal felt a powerful compulsion to reach for his old side-arm but caught himself in time. He forced a smile, the first that was truly his own in days.

"Throw it in the river, Dad!"

The marshal shot a glance over his shoulder at the water and then looked at the weapon in his hand. Could he?

The Hanged Man thought the old man could and adjusted his aim in the direction of his daughter to make sure he didn't.

"Give me the gun, Marshal, or watch your family die."

Henry stood along the pedestrian walkway at the western edge of the Morrison Street Bridge. He saw the confrontation taking place on the pier but had no desire to be a part of it. The fact that he was as far away from the Hanged Man as he was suggested their bond was weaker, no doubt due to the dead man's current state of duress and damage. Should the Hanged Man survive the encounter—and Henry held no illusions that he wouldn't—Henry would go to him.

Until then he would watch. And read.

In his nightmare, *Joseph stands on the hill above the marshal's house halfway between the graves of Agatha and Althea Flynn. A gust of salt-tinged air stings the blisters about his eyes, but the pain barely registers. Joseph has fixed his attention—all of it—on a shadow in the dark, a figure defined by the heel of a boot kicking the soil level against the grade.*

Forty-one feet away, the Hanged Man turns to face Joseph.

"I am here, Joseph. Do you see?"

Joseph opens his senses further, straining to fill the blind spots in his sight. Kate . . . she is so quiet, so still, only the twin murmurs coming from her breast give her away. And then she is there—a whisper of lilac carried on the breeze. He can see Kate standing before the villain, babes in her arms, one last punishment for Joseph's betrayal.

"Do you see what has come between us?"

The Hanged Man is a foot taller than Kate, but from Joseph's slightly downward angle along the slope he is effectively shielded behind her. Joseph imagines his wife staring straight ahead, eyes wide open, tears on her cheek, and hopes she can see him as he mouths the words hold still.

"You're a coward," he says.

The Hanged Man laughs. "No, my friend, this is your doing, your choice."

The words fill Joseph's mind not with anger but information. No longer does he stumble through the endless night—he can see the man. He can see the red-handled pistol on the Hanged Man's hip, hear it as it slips from its holster. He can see the bastard shift slightly to the left, clearing Kate's shoulder. It's not much of a target, but Joseph is a good shot. Today he will have to be great. He reaches for his weapon, but her voice gives him pause.

"Joseph?"

"Trust me, Kate—"

He can't see his hand raise the pistol before him—but he can.

"You're not alone."

"No, Joseph," the Hanged Man says, drawing his revolver to his chest. "All men die alone."

"He ain't alone," says the marshal, stepping from behind a fir tree at the edge of the cemetery. A Winchester rifle rests against his shoulder, its muzzle aimed at the Hanged Man's head. "Unlike yourself."

The Hanged Man glances at the lawman . . . and elsewhere.

"Sure about that, Marshal?"

"I am," he says. "Your partners gave you up a long time ago."

Joseph imagines the grin on the Hanged Man's face faltering ever so slightly.

"Turns out they were more afraid of the noose than a Hanged Man."

The marshal nods to another man that has approached through the cemetery on his right. Five men with rifles rise up behind him as four others approach from the road below. There are more. Joseph stops counting at twenty, but their numbers rise until even the Hanged Man seems resigned to his fate. He mumbles to himself, though Joseph does not hear the words.

"Ain't gonna be a hangin' this time," says the marshal.

The Hanged Man looks to the marshal and then—of this Joseph is certain—turns to destroy everything.

Kate is gone.

She will not repeat the feat for years, but for a moment Joseph is sure his wife has vanished. He is not the only one who has lost her.

Infuriated, the Hanged Man stutters and raises his weapon to take aim of the only true target left to him.

In the seconds before the marshal and his men open fire, Joseph is shot by the Hanged Man, though not before discharging his own weapon. It is the third time he has shot at a man—the same man, in fact—and although his bullet fails to hit flesh, it still finds its target traveling in the opposite direction. The projectiles graze each other, altering their trajectories enough so the bullet that knocks Joseph to the ground misses his heart by two and half inches. Kate will not let him rise for three days, but he will live. The Hanged Man will not.

But in this nightmare, he does.

Wake up, Joseph.

"You don't belong in this world," Joseph said, finding the stage much as he left it. The dead man now aimed a weapon in his direction, but its handle was thankfully not red. "We chased you off a long time ago."

"Resilient," said the Hanged Man. "I always liked that about you."

Joseph got to his feet with Kate's help. White flashes of light cut across his mind's eye, bleeding in from the real world. The Hanged Man's blow had done some damage. No matter. Joseph adjusted the patch over his scarred left eye, blocking out the worst of the phantom light.

"What about yourself?" Joseph asked. "You can barely stand up."

Kate felt her husband pull away from her. "Joseph, no."

"It's all right, Kate. Look at him. It won't take much to knock him down."

The Hanged Man didn't entirely disagree with his old partner's assessment, but he felt Joseph was missing the obvious. To prove it, he fired the marshal's old pistol, striking Joseph's thigh. He'd been aiming for the gut.

Maddie screamed.

Joseph grasped his leg but with Kate's help did not fall.

The Hanged Man adjusted his aim, centering the barrel on Joseph's head, then held out a hand to the marshal.

"Give it to me."

The marshal looked at the dead man's hand and then at the red-handled pistol in his own. He could still hear its call—not to the marshal but to its master. It wanted so badly to return and he had only to let it go.

It was Joseph's voice that called to him.

"Throw it in the river, Marshal. Let it go."

The Hanged Man caught Joseph's eye, the one he pretended could see, and realized the blind man saw much more than he let on.

The marshal saw the dead man flinch and knew his weakness.

"You're not the master," he whispered.

The marshal remembered a message he'd received earlier in the day, a warning not to let the Hanged Man have his gun. It was wrong. In fact, at that moment he was sure of it.

The marshal held out the pistol, handle first.

"Take it."

"Dad, no!"

The Hanged Man dropped the marshal's useless pistol and took what had always been his. His fingers wrapped around the blood-stained wood and the Hanged Man was complete. For one fleeting moment, he knew nothing but joy—and then it was gone, replaced by dread. Something was wrong, something he'd missed, something close and coming closer. He heard the heavy footfalls just before the giant announced his arrival with a primal scream, but it was already too late.

The Hanged Man spun on the spot and was met squarely in the chest by Andre Labeau at a dead run. The jolt knocked the pistol from the villain's hand and sent him to the ground under 270 pounds of Louisiana muscle. There was no air to knock out of him, but Andre enjoyed the sound of the dead man's ribs snapping just the same.

The marshal scrambled out of the way as Andre rose and began to pummel the Hanged Man with both fists. It took the dead man a moment to get his bearings and by then his jaw was cracked. He managed to get his right arm free and quickly grabbed his attacker around the throat.

"You!"

The Hanged Man dug his nails deep into the soft flesh of the shaman's throat and would have torn away the man's jugular had the flying girl not appeared above his head. He let go in time to block several whirling swipes from a long wooden pole. The last slipped past his defenses, catching the dead man beneath the chin, snapping his head backward.

Andre rolled off, gasping and holding his throat. The Hanged Man was strong, much more so than he'd anticipated. His was a powerful curse and it would take more than muscle to defeat it.

The Hanged Man used the rail to drag himself upright. He was cornered and hurt, but in a straight-on fight he would ultimately gain the advantage, flying girl or not. If he could find his gun—

"Looking for this?"

The marshal stood ten feet to his right, waving the red-handled pistol above his head.

The Hanged Man's fury refocused on his old nemesis and he

lurched toward him, but not in time. The marshal spun around and then lofted the gun into the air.

He saw it clearly—polished iron reflected in amber light, arcing overhead just out of reach. The Hanged Man turned and pushed off his good foot, launching his body over the railing, never once losing sight of his treasure. In the instant before he hit the river, the dead man's outstretched fingers touched metal. Then he crashed into a writhing mass of floating debris and was violently sucked beneath the surface.

Andre stepped to the edge of the railing and looked into the river. Debris clogged the fast-moving water, making it difficult to see the surface clearly. There was no sign of the Hanged Man.

The marshal joined the large man at the rail.

"I wish you had not done that."

"Me too," the marshal, said rubbing his shoulder. "I liked that gun."

Andre turned to the marshal.

"Hated to bury it with the bastard all them years ago. Finally get it back and I gotta throw it in the river? Damn shame."

The marshal held the red-handled pistol out to Andre.

"Take it. I don't want it anymore."

Andre stared at the gun, surprised to have it offered so easily. There was power in it, great power, but it had gone quiet. He knew it would not stay that way.

"Keep it. For a time."

The marshal held the weapon at arm's length for a beat before reluctantly sliding it back into his holster.

Naira pulled Andre's hand away from his neck to inspect his injury. Three crescent-shaped gashes marked the left side of his throat, a fourth cut deeper on the right.

"Leave it," he said. "There are other, more pressing wounds in need of attention."

Naira narrowed her eyes, staring deeply into her partner's. Andre never faltered. He would be fine.

Kate approached the newcomers, Kick and Maddie at her side. She was not sure what to make of the pair but recognized them as allies.

"Thank you."

Andre nodded. Naira tilted her head and smiled.

Kick returned the gesture, earning a laugh from the big man. Maddie slipped a little closer to her mother.

Kate stared at the pair for a moment longer before finally asking, "You would be Andre Labeau, yes?"

"He's a hoodoo man," said the marshal.

Andre raised an eyebrow. "You remember?"

The marshal shrugged.

"Good," Andre said, then turned to Kate and Joseph. "Mrs. Wylde, I am pleased to make your acquaintance. This agile young woman is Naira. We traveled a great distance to be here tonight. And as I'm sure your husband has suggested, we have much to discuss."

"Took your time getting here, Mr. Labeau," Joseph said. "But I'm glad you did."

"As am I. Tell me, Mr. Wylde, is the weather here always this pleasant?"

Joseph grinned, raising his face to the falling rain.

"Welcome to Portlandtown."

27

The citizens of Portland came together in the light of day to put down the zombie horde that had invaded their community. It took only a few hours to organize a citywide hunt, although it would be weeks before the last of the afflicted were captured and destroyed. A list circulating among the searchers carried the names of those still missing, many of whom had been washed away by the storm, never to be recovered. They were deemed the lucky ones.

Forty-seven bodies were recovered on the first day, most floating in the floodwaters that had already begun to recede from the record heights of the night before. Twenty-three of the dead were confirmed to be locals or visitors in town for the festival. Some of the victims had been murdered twice—once at the hands of a monster and later by those of a neighbor. Nearly all the waking dead put down in the days to come would bear familiar faces.

The rest of the deceased were ultimately identified as medical-college cadavers. Dr. Gillman relayed the tale of two students who had been in a basement storage room when remains procured for research began to reanimate. Remarkably, the young doctors were not attacked but rather bore witness to the evacuation of thirty-one corpses, on foot, to the front gate of the facility, where a pair of men on horseback waited. The dead surrounded the larger of the two and when he pointed down the hill they shambled off en masse. Dr. Gillman was dubious of the account, despite the horrors of the night before.

One item that remained unaccounted for was the storm totem. Most assumed it had been carried off by the floodwaters, never to be seen again. A few of the more superstitious locals suspected the totem had been taken by the souls of the damned, angered by the city's celebration of unnatural phenomena. The following year would see Portland's first ever Rose Festival.

In fact, the totem had not left the city limits. Before the sun was even up, it had been wrapped in several layers of lacquered canvas, bound, and transported to a small, city-owned structure three blocks west of Wylde's, Booksellers and Navigation. The interior of the building remained dry, but an extra layer of sandbags was added around the exterior just in case.

Andre Labeau spent much of Friday explaining what had happened to city officials and anyone else who would listen. The shock of the attack made his job easier, although there was some resistance to Andre's methods of recovery. A few of the more-learned Portlandians found the notion of using potions and prayers to heal their wounds too fantastic to follow. In such cases, Andre appealed to their intellects, using a more strongly worded argument, and the doubters soon fell in line, some even becoming evangelicals for the cause. Andre was happy for the help.

Mayor Gates was glad to have an expert on hand, especially one so well regarded by the western papers. After only a ten-minute conversation, he appointed Andre head of the Emergency Commission to Restore Metropolitan Wellness, a post he invented on the spot. The title wasn't Andre's first, but he was pleased to have it come without the slightest mental push on his part. The mayor's first suggestion was that Andre liaise with one of the city's favorite sons, a man of special talents, according to him. His name was Joseph Wylde.

Andre thought that a fine idea.

"I read about you," Joseph said.

Andre raised an eyebrow. "Oh?"

"You visited the Nez Percé a few years back. Made quite an impression on the chief, according to the local paper. Convinced him to accept government terms for relocation."

Andre took a sip from the cup in his hand. It was coffee, good coffee, which was exactly what he needed after a day of talking. He suspected there would be more conversation this evening and downed another sip.

"Do not believe everything you read, Mr. Wylde."

Joseph smiled.

The two men sat opposite each other at the Wyldes' kitchen table, evidence of the previous night's encounter with the Hanged Man clearly visible on both. The welts on Andre's neck had subsided, but the cuts had only just begun to heal. As for Joseph, the area around his left eye was purple, but the ringing in his head had faded and his leg felt much better, despite the hole in it. He suspected Andre had something to do with that.

"Thank you," he said.

Andre nodded. He found himself staring into the man's good eye, wondering exactly how *good* it might be.

"What'd you do to my shoulder?" the marshal asked. He was seated on Joseph's left, his arm in a sling, which he raised and lowered without showing any discomfort. "Doc said it was the cleanest wound he'd ever seen."

"I simply applied a few natural remedies."

"Uh-huh. Just so long as you ain't put no curse on me."

Andre took another sip from his cup.

"My head feels better, too," Kick said.

The twins shared a chair at one end of the table. Maddie had been listening intently, but Kick kept stealing glances at the young native woman perched on a stool between himself and the giant. It was to her that he'd offered his observation.

"I'm glad," she said.

Naira enjoyed the boy's attention, innocent as it was, but had thus far pretended not to notice. His mother was watching and she would undoubtedly be more cautious with her appraisals than her son was.

Kate refilled Andre's cup and then returned the kettle to the stove.

"How did you find us?" she asked, slipping around the table to stand next to her husband. "I can't imagine it was easy, given the storm."

Andre glanced from Kate to Joseph. Joseph already knew the answer.

"The Hanged Man."

Andre nodded. "He makes very little effort to disguise his trail."

The marshal slid forward in his chair. "It was really him, then?"

"I have no reason to doubt it," Andre said. "Unlike the others, his is the body *and* mind of a man slain eleven years ago, though he is no longer a man."

The marshal raised an eyebrow. "No soul?"

"I wouldn't presume to know the path of the soul, but I do know the creature is not alive. The body may be perambulatory, but the heart does not beat, the lungs gather no air, the blood does not flow."

"But he could think," Joseph said. "And reason."

"Yes, although how clearly I cannot say. He would not feel

physical pain, which is how he continued to give chase despite his wounds."

"He could barely stand by the time we got to the pier," Kate said. "I don't imagine he would have lasted much longer even if the river hadn't swallowed him up."

Kate caught an exchange between their guests. It wasn't much, but a decade of watching the twins had made her aware of even the subtlest of communications.

"But you don't think he's dead, do you? That's why you're after him. If he could be destroyed like the rest, you wouldn't need to chase him down. He has help."

"There is a young man who helps him," said Naira.

Kate leaned forward. "Helps him how?"

Andre smiled.

Kate felt her cheek twitch. It wanted to return the big man's expression, but she wouldn't let it, yet.

"What are you really after, Mr. Labeau?"

Andre had intended to share everything (or nearly so), but was surprised by how quickly the conversation found its way to the truth.

"There is a book," he began.

Joseph shared a glance with his wife. "Books we know."

"This is not a volume you will find in your collection, Mr. Wylde. There exists but one copy, which is already one too many."

"Books aren't dangerous," Maddie said.

"Unless you throw 'em," Kick added, eyeing his father.

Joseph grinned. "Larger volumes, maybe, although there are those who say certain ideas can be dangerous—in the mind of someone with evil intent."

"Were this merely a collection of bad intentions, I would not have traveled so far to retrieve it. No, I am afraid words can be dangerous. Spoken aloud they can control, deceive, and destroy, as long as there is someone to believe them."

In his mind, Joseph saw the Hanged Man crouched by a fire. It was an old memory, one seen with two eyes. The man, wounded but very much alive, read a passage from a small black book and the flames flared, first amber and then black. He held a handkerchief over the fire and watched the flames slither into the fabric and disappear. What came next had stolen Joseph's sight and changed his path forever.

"You're talking about magic."

Andre nodded.

"We've got a dozen books on the subject down at the store," Kate said. "I don't think anyone has ever hurt themselves reading one."

"My apologies, Mrs. Wylde, I am not making myself clear. This is not a book of tricks or stagecraft, but power—dark power. The power to make men do as you wish, to twist the heart and bend the will, to raise the dead."

"It's a book of curses," Joseph said. "That's what gave him his power."

"It did," Andre said. "Once, it nearly made him invincible."

"Not near enough," said the marshal.

"True, Marshal. Eleven years ago you broke his link to the book and thus his source of power. He was truly dead."

"But now?"

"The book brought him back to this world, although he does not possess it. It now belongs to young Henry Macke. Fool though he is, Henry could not stop himself from reading it."

"Why?"

"It told him to."

Kate flinched at an echo in her head—two voices, speaking in the dark.

"Who would write such a thing?" she asked.

Andre hesitated, which was more than enough for Joseph to see the truth.

"Doesn't matter," he said before Andre could answer. "Not if you mean to destroy it."

Andre stared at Joseph, seeing in the man's face more than his words revealed. Andre nodded, once more wondering exactly how much Joseph truly saw.

"That is not so easily done."

"That was the mayor's aide," Joseph said, returning to the living room. He rubbed the key in his hand, noting the number on its head, and then tucked it into his shirt pocket. "He's checking up on us. Wants to make sure we're on the team."

Kate looked up from the couch. "We're a team now, are we?"

Joseph smiled. "Apparently. He also mentioned that they found Mr. Edmonds."

"Alive?" Maddie asked.

"Barely. But they think he'll pull through . . . with a little help."

Andre nodded. "I'll check in on him as soon as I can."

Joseph stoked the fire, adding another log before returning to his place on the couch between Kate and the twins. There was just enough seating in the living room for everyone, although Andre barely fit in the chair he'd chosen. He was used to it.

"Tell me about the book," Joseph said. "You buried it with the Hanged Man, correct?"

"Yes. With no master, it was safer in the ground, soon to be forgotten."

"Why not burn it?" Kate asked. "Burn it and the body together. Wasn't that the story everyone was told?"

"I believe there was some miscommunication about his funeral arrangements."

Andre tacked a smile onto the end of his attempt at humor, but Kate didn't laugh. It did, however, elicit a grunt of recognition from the marshal.

"You made me bury him. Tricked me into it with one of them curses."

"I was there," said Andre. "And I helped you to do what needed to be done. But it was not a curse."

"The hell it weren't! You put a hex on me so I'd forget—but I didn't. Oh, no. I remembered just enough to keep an eye on the dead bastard all these years, for all the good it did."

Joseph leaned forward. "Marshal, I don't think accusing Mr. Labeau of cursing you is going to help."

"No," said the marshal, standing up. "I want to hear him say the words. I want to know. God knows I ain't gonna think it up on my own."

Andre felt the block in the old man's mind slipping. Yes, part of it had been put in place by his hand, though not the worst of it. He lowered his voice and did what he could to push the barrier out of the way.

"I only did what you asked me to do, Marshal."

The marshal shuddered as the memory tumbled into place and all at once he knew it was true. All of it was true.

"You sure I ain't gonna remember this?" the marshal asks. The star on his jacket glistens in the afternoon sun.

Andre tamps down the last shovelful of dirt on the dead man's grave and nods. "Only what you need to, Marshal Kleberg."

"Good," the marshal says. "Just as soon forget as much as possible."

"You will never truly forget, but the memory will remain hidden, safe. It will grow old with you and die with you."

The marshal chuckles. "Shouldn't take long."

"Do not be so sure. I see a long life ahead. Quiet, happy, and full of respect from those you love."

"And whiskey, I hope."

The big man smiles. The marshal knows he has a name, but he can't quite place it.

"Always loved the view from up here," he says, appraising the town and river below. "Kids want me to move to Portland, but think I'll stay put awhile."

"A fine idea, Marshal."

The marshal glances back, but he is alone. He has been all day. He spies the shovel on the ground and picks it up.

"Don't want to forget this," he says and walks down the hill.

"You made me forget," the marshal said, plopping back down in his chair. "'Cause I didn't want to remember."

"Yes," Andre said.

"All this time, thought I was losin' my mind. Hell, I been getting it back."

Andre glanced at Naira, who quickly redirected his gaze toward Kate, but too late.

"It's true, then?" Kate said. "You put a curse on my dad?"

"It was not a curse. And your father accepted the charge freely—it was his choice to stay and watch over the dead man."

"How did he have a choice if you made him forget?"

"It's all right, Katie."

"No, Dad, it's not."

"Yes, it is. I wanted this—I asked for it—for you, for the family.

It was my decision. Just didn't work out quite how I expected." The marshal looked at Andre. "Thought I wasn't supposed to remember nothin'."

"You were not."

"Well, I did. Remembered just enough to think I'd forgotten something really important. Damn near drove myself crazy."

"For that I am sorry," Andre said. "But I believe it was a crack in your memory that you yourself created years ago. It was only a matter of time before it failed completely."

The marshal stared at Andre. He knew. Course he did.

"A crack? What does that mean? " Joseph asked.

The marshal frowned and pulled the gun from his coat. He held it briefly before laying it on the small table between them. The handle glowed crimson in the firelight.

Kate's breath caught in her throat but she managed not to make a sound.

"He means I went and dug this damn thing up a couple months after buryin' it. Couldn't never forget it, I s'pose."

"It has a voice that is loud and clear," said Andre. "Few men could resist its call."

"Take it." The marshal sighed. "I don't want it no more."

For a moment no one said a word, then Kate found her voice.

"I still don't understand. You buried these things, these evil things, and then what? Made my dad watch over them, even though he didn't know it? Why wouldn't you just destroy them?"

"It is not so easy to unmake a thing, especially one that holds as much power as the Hanged Man's weapon. I understand the desire to melt it down or simply throw it in the river, but the curse that is bound within would not be broken, but rather set free. It would only make matters worse."

"Worse?"

"Yes," Andre continued. "But to bury a thing beneath time

and earth—to render it forgotten—that is a powerful weapon, indeed."

"The marshal remembered," said Joseph. "He dug it up."

"But he kept it hidden for more than a decade. If he had not gone back for it, I believe someone else would have."

"Someone did."

Andre said nothing. He didn't have to.

"Henry Macke," said the marshal. "How'd he know about it?"

Andre shifted in his chair. "That was my mistake. I believe he was on the hill the day we buried the Hanged Man, hiding amongst the trees. I was so focused on the task at hand, I missed his presence."

Maddie jumped in. "So why didn't he dig it up right away?"

"He would have been just a boy," Kate said. "Younger than you are now by a few years, I think."

"True," Andre said. "And it is my belief that because he heard my words he was bound by the same charge laid upon the marshal. Young Mr. Macke forgot what he saw. He likely would have remained ignorant had the marshal not left Astoria. But the charge fell to him in the marshal's absence and his memory resurfaced, unclouded, it seems."

"He knew right where to dig," Naira added.

"Why would he dig up a dead body?" Kick asked, glancing at his grandfather. He was pleased to receive an approving nod from the old man.

"I do not know," Andre said. "There were others involved, criminals who may have influenced Henry's decision. They may have been after the gun. Not finding it, they took the body, hoping to sell it."

"But kept the book," said Joseph.

Andre nodded. "Henry kept it. Mostly to himself, I have no doubt. He used it to lift the Hanged Man from his slumber."

"Weren't no slumber," said the marshal. "I put a dozen slugs in the bastard with his own gun. You were there. Man was dead."

"Very much so. But he had prepared himself, using words from the book to preserve his body. He no doubt had a different plan in mind should he be cut down, but eleven years on it finally came to fruition."

Kate folded her arms over her chest. "You believe he planned to come back from the dead?"

Andre shrugged. "He took precautions."

"You know a lot about what's in this book," Kate said, choosing her words carefully. "I take it that means you've read it."

"I have read it," Andre said. "Once, as I wrote it."

Andre's explanation of how the book came to be was careful, considered, and perfectly rational. His personal penance for losing it had been harsh, and his efforts to recover and ultimately render the book inert were thorough and fairly accomplished. He had done everything he could to atone for an error of youthful indulgence and it was not his fault that so much evil had come from something born of his hands.

And yet Joseph was certain Andre didn't believe a word of it. The man blamed himself and always would.

"But you never used a single curse?" Joseph asked. "Not even to see if they worked?"

"I believed they would. To use them would be wrong. It was my intention to stop others from using such words and for that I needed only to know them."

"Very noble," Kate said.

"And very foolish," Andre added.

Kate stared at the man currently overflowing her mother's favorite chair. He wasn't holding anything back now. His story was fantastic, but it was honest. He believed it, and despite her better judgment, Kate found she did as well.

"Then I guess you'll just have to bury it again," she said. "If you can convince Mr. Macke to return it, that is. What about the gun?"

"We destroy it," Andre said.

Kate laughed. "You just told us we couldn't."

"Eleven years ago that was the prudent course of action. Today circumstances are different."

"You still think he's out there," Joseph said.

"Evil such as the Hanged Man is not so easily washed away."

"Alive, dead, drowned . . . whatever he is, best to bust it up," the marshal said, finding it easier not to look at the weapon. "S'pose I didn't need to clean it."

"Fine," Kate said, starting to rise. "I'll get a hammer and we can smash it to bits right now."

Joseph caught his wife's arm before she could step away.

"Mr. Labeau, correct me if I'm wrong, but the Hanged Man and this weapon are connected, yes? That's how he found us. He can sense when it's nearby?"

Andre nodded. "It speaks to him. Or, more accurately, the curse placed on it does, and he must heed its call."

"Then it could be used against him."

Kate stared at her husband. He'd been waiting for this moment, waiting for her to accept Andre's words so he could offer his own. If it came down to it, he would chase after the man. He'd done it before.

"You're going to keep it?"

"Just until we're sure he's dead."

Kate shook her head. "He's gone, Joseph."

"If he is, then I'll take the hammer to it myself . . . I promise."

Kate looked from her husband to the faces of her children, rapt and eager. Memories that had danced around in the back of her mind all day slipped forward to remind her of what happened to men who challenged the Hanged Man—to men and their families.

"It can't stay here, Joseph."

Joseph reached out to his wife and was glad when her hand closed around his.

"It'll be gone by morning."

The marshal grunted. "You gonna bury it in the yard?"

"No," Joseph said. "I have another place in mind."

The front door was boarded, but the key was for an entrance on the side of the three-story building, which opened without protest. Joseph entered first, followed closely by Andre and Naira. Kate came last, pulling the door closed behind her.

"Make sure your feet are dry," Joseph said, wiping his boots with one of several rags strewn on the floor. "We need to keep as much of the water outside as possible."

The air inside was warm and uncomfortably dry compared to the humidity of the flooded streets. It felt as though something had sucked the moisture from the room, which Joseph suspected was not far from the truth.

"Interesting," Naira said, running her hand along the spines of several books hanging from a clothesline. A dozen more lines criss-crossed the room, holding hundreds of books. "I've never seen books displayed in such a fashion."

"We had some water damage in our storeroom."

Kate laughed sharply. "Some?"

"A lot," Joseph added. "The mayor was generous enough to donate this space so we could salvage our overstock."

"They do seem dry," Naira said, flipping through one of the tomes. "Mostly."

Joseph ducked under a line and through a doorway into a much larger space. A row of tall, covered windows along the front wall let in just enough light to reveal the room and its contents. Elaborate, ceiling-high pillars stood half constructed along each of the main walls, a long, unfinished countertop shoved against one of them. The floor, cut stone rather than wood, echoed underfoot despite a layer of dust and debris. Numerous oversize crates sat stacked in the back corner, well away from a long, canvas-wrapped pillar laid lengthwise in the center of the room. An arrangement of lumber remnants kept the storm totem three feet above ground level at all times.

Andre was drawn to the mystery, finding it too curious to ignore.

"The totem you spoke of," he said, placing a hand on the canvas. "Still warm to the touch."

"Yes," Joseph said, loosening the restraining boards on one side of a crate nearly as tall as himself. "It has some very curious properties. I would be interested in your assessment when you have the time."

"Certainly."

"Just don't get it wet," Kate added. "Please."

Joseph slid the crate face away to reveal a large bank safe stored within. He studied the steel box only briefly before placing one hand on the dial at its center, the other, fingertips only, on the door. Slowly, he twisted the dial to the left, stopping after a three-quarters turn.

"This building was going to be a bank," he said, turned the dial back to the right. "But the financiers backed out before it was finished. They did, however, leave behind this very nice safe, which according to the manufacturer is nigh impregnable." Joseph slowed to a stop and then rotated the dial to the left once more, freezing after only a few clicks. He turned the handle and the enormous door swung open easily.

Andre raised an eyebrow. "Unless you have the combination."

"Right," Joseph said, then held out his hand. "If you please."

Andre opened the pouch at his side, drawing forth the Hanged Man's pistol wrapped in cloth, which he passed forward. Joseph set the gun on the center shelf of the otherwise empty safe and shut the door, spinning the dial around twice. He pulled on the handle, but the door didn't budge. Satisfied, he took a step back and let his focus settle. Six inches of steel now surrounded the dead man's weapon on all sides, but Joseph could still see the revolver clearly through the door.

"Do you think me a fool, Mr. Labeau?"

"I do not."

"You see, Kate? Not a fool."

Kate shook her head. "I never said you were a fool, Joseph, merely foolish."

"Is there a difference?"

Kate glanced at both Joseph and Andre before giving her answer.

"We'll see."

Both men were silent for a time. Joseph felt Andre's heart thumping beside him and took comfort in the slow, steady rhythm. He could not discern the man's partner until the sneaky young woman revealed herself at his side.

"You now believe the Hanged Man lives."

"I do."

Naira looked to Andre, who was slower with his response.

"Henry Macke is still in possession of the book. With it he can keep the dead man in this world."

"Does he have a choice?" Kate asked.

Andre looked up, ready with his answer, but instead found another he hoped would prove true.

"Every man, even a cursed one, has a choice."

EPILOGUE

———◆———

Four miles south of the Morrison Street Bridge, a stand of birch trees rose from the Willamette, splitting the river in two. Surging floodwaters had swallowed much of the island, leaving behind a mass of floating wreckage to strangle the trees. In the shallows of the eastern fork, the river slowed to a crawl as more debris found its way to shore. It was here that a young man came to wait at the water's edge.

Henry wasn't familiar with local currents or flood plains, but he knew exactly where the body would wash up, battered and unconscious—a dead man to all but Henry's eyes. He still couldn't bring himself to think of the Hanged Man as alive, but the true death would not come so easily—not while his corporeal presence haunted this world.

Henry grabbed the Hanged Man's collar and dragged him as far as he could up the sand-and-gravel embankment before rolling him onto his back. His skin was pale and shriveled. The frame that had once been menacing was now crooked, the shoulders uneven, legs bent backward and likely broken. He wouldn't walk without help.

374 · ROB DEBORDE

(*help him*)

Henry frowned.

"Did you get it?" he asked, already knowing the answer.

The Hanged Man stared into the sky, not saying a word.

Henry checked the holster on the dead man's hip. Empty.

"No, I thought not."

Henry twisted the left leg forward sharply, tilting the foot upright as he reset the ankle. The sound of bone scraping against bone brought the taste of bile to his tongue.

"Going to have to fix you up myself," Henry said, drawing the belt from the Hanged Man's waist. Carefully, he looped it under the left arm and over the chest, pulling the leather strap taunt behind the dead man's neck.

"I have words that will mend broken bones, possibly dead ones."

Henry yanked the belt, jerking the shoulder back into place with a sickening crunch. He then tested the arm, pulling it forward and twisting it until satisfied. It wasn't perfect, but it would do. *For how long?*

Henry dropped the arm and stared at the broken body, clearly seeing the trials that lay ahead.

"Damn fool, they beat you!"

The words were so bold—so true—that it took Henry a moment to realize he'd spoken them aloud. But he had. And there were more. He would have to listen.

"Ain't the man you used to be, are you? The Scourge of the West? Not you, not anymore. The sooner you figure that out, the better off we'll be."

That was a lie. The body was more vulnerable, but the man was every bit as dangerous as he had been in life, perhaps more so. Henry knew this. Perhaps the Hanged Man did not.

"You're no good to me all busted up. Keep fighting and you'll break something that can't be healed, not with words or a strap of leather." Henry hesitated, considering his words carefully despite the lack of an audience to hear them. "Still, there might be ways to make you strong again, more resilient."

(*alive*)

Henry shuddered. "Possibly. It's complicated."

(*you can't read them*)

Henry shook his head. "No, I can read the words, I just don't understand all of 'em." Henry dug the book from his pocket and began flipping through the pages. "Everything else makes sense, but this passage . . . it's only a few pages, but I can't unwind it. I know the answer must be here, it has to be, but—"

"She doesn't want you to understand."

Henry looked up from the book. The Hanged Man remained on his back, neither alive nor dead but definitely unconscious. He had not spoken the words, though Henry was sure he'd heard them aloud—a voice so close, it could have been his own.

Henry turned his gaze to the sky. The air was cool, but the clouds had departed, allowing the sun to shine unmolested. A crow circled overhead, content to observe from afar. It let loose a single *caw*, then turned southeast and disappeared beyond the trees.

This was the direction they would travel. Henry was sure of it, although he couldn't say why.

(*home*)

"Time to get on your feet again," he said, flipping pages until he came to a passage he knew quite well. "Got a long ride ahead of us. I'll be damned if I'm going to drag you around by the collar."

Henry ran his hand across the pages, feeling the ink beneath his fingertips. Warmth coursed through his body, igniting a cold fire in his heart that reminded Henry of who he now was.

"Listen up, partner," he said and started to read.